Tim Wilson was born and brought up in Peterborough on the edge of the Fens. He was a student on the University of East Anglia MA Course in Creative Writing under Malcom Bradbury and Angela Carter. He and his wife Mary-Anne live in Peterborough with two cats.

*Also by Tim Wilson*

Purgatory
Close To You
Freezing Point
I Spy . . .
Cruel To Be Kind

# A Singing Grave

Tim Wilson

HEADLINE

First published in hardback in 1998 by
HEADLINE BOOK PUBLISHING

First published in paperback in 1999 by
HEADLINE BOOK PUBLISHING

10 9 8 7 6 5 4 3 2 1

ISBN 0 7472 5655 1

Printed and bound in Great Britain by
Clays Ltd, St Ives plc

HEADLINE BOOK PUBLISHING
A division of Hodder Headline PLC
338 Euston Road
London NW1 3BH

For Roy and Maria

# ONE

'Dad?'

The dream flung her violently on the shore of waking. Her arms groped and her hair was in her mouth as she called out. In the dream there had been a kiss, and there had been her mother's emaciated cheek, and the cry had been the old wail of loss.

But the waking cry was puzzlement and fear, a reaching into the night, which was full of strange sound.

'Dad?'

Light streamed up from the hallway and through the transom above her bedroom door. It was an assault to sleep-hooded eyes.

Rebecca's mind floundered in the transition from the distress of the dream to this. Noise and strangeness . . . Should she fear it? Was it, like the dream, an illusion and lie?

Trembling, she jumped out of bed. Downstairs in the house, a human voice rose, wild and deep, the vocalization of a forbidden thrill. A reverberation shook the walls: she felt it fleetingly in the handle of the bedroom door as she flung it open.

Skimming down the stairs, it was as if she had no weight. Only the pressure of her bare heels, smooth against the weave of the stair carpet, anchored her to the world.

'Dad?'

The air abraded her face as she leapt the last four stairs, landed on the cool quarry tiles of the hall, then burst like a sprinter into the sitting room. Thus she had run when she was a child, full of night terrors; but now she was nineteen and it was an adult fear that enveloped her, acrid and cold.

The voice was so vast. She could feel it in her belly, a grip of sound. For several moments she stood frozen, trying to

1

make sense of the room. Her brain was still half caught up in sleep, where magic is the locum of logic: she could only stare and blink and wait for comprehension. Like an amnesiac Rebecca, quivering in her nightdress, groped for recognition, while the great voice rose and climbed on crystal steps of anguish.

Her eye fell on a little row of green lights that rose and fell with the sound, a luminous graph. Her waking brain asserted itself at last: that was the equalizer display on the amplifier of a hi-fi. Her father's stereo was playing at full volume to a room that, her waking brain now confirmed, was empty.

Rebecca crossed the room, knelt down at the hi-fi in the corner and switched off the music. The case of a CD lay on the floor nearby. She picked it up and looked at the cover. The music – and though her waking brain had not told her this, some deeper aspect of self had known and followed its soarings like a blind hand along a railing – was Mahler. The *Kindertotenlieder*.

Songs on the Death of Children.

She stood up and looked around. The silence that replaced the music seemed to swim with meaning. She saw things – a whisky tumbler on the side-table, a sheaf of music paper tossed down by the side of the armchair, the hands of the mantelshelf clock showing half-past two, the butts of two Café Noir cigars in an ashtray. Also, the selection of well-sharpened pencils, of various hardness and colour, with which her father worked. He was meticulous about them – faddy even. But now they were scattered on the carpet like a game of spillikins.

'Dad? Dad, where are you?'

Not in the house, though she roamed it swiftly, and searched with a thoroughness weirdly appropriate for a weird time, turning on every light and peering into the boxroom and behind the bathroom door. His bedroom – and how quickly she had begun to think of it as his, Dad's room, not Mum and Dad's – was dark, the bed untouched. Everything was untouched: and though she was tensed and ready for the gaping window, the intruder's footstep, she felt in her blood that this was something else.

Rebecca ran downstairs again, with the same unearthly glide. If it were so, she thought randomly, if the worst were

2

true then she would never forgive him: understand, but never forgive.

'Dad!'

She opened the back door to the conservatory, and shouted it into the darkness. She was hating him for the fear that was pushing, a relentless captor, between her shoulder blades.

'Dad! Where are you?'

The security light above the back door revealed the whole of the rear garden. Though there was no breeze in the cool night, the cherry tree in the centre of the lawn moved its branches in a faint self-communing way, as if it were breathing.

He had seemed fine today, she told herself. Or had he? Was it only hindsight that discerned a quiescence, an inwardness about him that triggered alarm like a shout in the far distance?

Or *should* have triggered alarm.

And then this evening, when he had elected to work after sharing a bite of supper with her . . . Of course, it was quite normal for him to work in the evenings – but in that very dismissal she caught herself in an evasion. For nothing was normal, in truth, since they had left her mother in the hospital for the last time five months ago. And what of her feeling of relief – admitted now, if not at the time when he had retired to the sitting room with the sheaf of music paper; guilty relief that for a while at least she *could* pretend that things were normal, and not have to share the leaden burden of his grief?

She hurried into the utility room, dragged on a pair of jeans still clammy-damp and unironed, and stuffed her bare feet into tennis shoes. Going through the connecting door into the garage, her haste brought her shin crashing against the rear bumper of her father's Volvo: painful confirmation. Hopeful, though – that he had not driven from the house? God only knew. Also, taking courage, Rebecca had to stoop and peer into the driver's side of the car. She knew that people who did that had the engine running and a pipe leading from the exhaust through the window but still she had to be sure, to peer into the dark and empty interior with thumping heart before pulling up the garage door.

There was darkness at the front of the house, where sandy turf ran down to the low brick wall fronting the minor road to the village. At first, after the halogen glare of the rear, it seemed impenetrable. Dithering at the gate, Rebecca wondered if she should fetch a torch. But soon her eyes took in clear starlight, and she could make out the contours of the dunes and even, beyond them, a glimmer of moving sea.

A fine night. A fine night for walking and thinking, especially by the seashore; and that was something her father often did. Rebecca held this reassurance a moment, turned it over, found it base coin.

Because not like this. This was something different. The house, lit and booming with inconsolable song, made it different. Her mother, dead from cancer (dead from pain, rather – pain, Rebecca thought, killed her) made it different. The hour made it different. Her father's state of mind made it different.

And what *was* his state of mind? Conjuring some composite inquisitor – doctor, lawyer, policeman – she imagined being asked the question. And answering that she didn't know.

Grief, yes. But grief was immense and elemental, like the sea. And she didn't know what currents her father was subject to, nor where they were taking him.

Rebecca cupped her hands to her mouth.

'Da-aad!'

She knew the cry would carry far. On this flat and bare coast you could walk on the beach and eavesdrop on the conversation of strollers two hundred yards ahead. She waited for a hallooed reply, but it was a false waiting and her fingers were already fumbling with the latch on the gate.

Rebecca crossed the road, no more than a sand-blown lane, and began to climb up the dunes on the other side. Though she could smell sea, the tide was so far out that the sound of waves was no more discrete than the sound of her own blood pumping round her body. The night was irrational, but reason was all she could bring to bear, and reason said that this was where her father took his walks, over the dunes and along the beach southwards towards Ingelow.

She was sweating and her ankles were laced with scratches from the sharp marram grass when she stood at the highest point of the dunes. Starlight was enough to show her the ribbed tracings of the tide on the sand, and here and there a sparkle of salt crust where the dry weather had followed high tide, but if there were footprints she could not see them. The white tumbling rim of the sea was way off, almost coterminous with the horizon line – that retiring Lincolnshire sea, subject of a thousand holidaymakers' jokes. It looked normal and innocent, as of course had her mother's suitcase when they had brought it home from the hospital full of clothes she would never wear again.

'Da-aad . . .!'

Songs on the Death of Children. The melody that her father had left to thunder through the house remained in Rebecca's mind, pure and sweet and decadent at the same time.

Her mother had been buried beside Thomas, the child they had lost years ago, before they adopted Rebecca. It was right – as right as such a tremendously wrong thing could be.

Rebecca scrambled down the sea side of the sandhills and across the duckboards at their foot. She hit the beach running.

Soon, as she ran southward along the empty beach, she had no breath for shouting. Her father's name kept coming from her dry throat, but it was for herself, an incantation. Ahead of her a bow of lights, the seaside resort of Ingelow, twinkled remotely. She would reach its hut-lined sands eventually, if she kept running onward like this; and if she did, what then? Go up into the town, perhaps: walk into the police station and say she had lost her father. No: could not find her father.

Then for a moment she allowed herself to entertain the thought that her father had despaired and walked into the sea. She let it in; and in the emotion that flared up she found outrage. How could he? How could he do it to her? So she was confronted with her own selfishness, alone on a deserted shore in the small hours, and it was bleak. She found herself hating him anew for forcing her into such a recognition.

Eventually, she simply could not run any more. Rebecca knelt down on the damp sand, hands on twanging thigh muscles, and hung her head as she panted for breath. She found herself mentally repeating a mantra from the ancient days of her first childhood, before the adoption – the primeval time of clutching the banisters or hiding under the blankets while the smoky adult laughter turned to shouting and crying. *God I promise God I promise I will be a good girl just make it all right . . .*

Strange it should come back now, and not five months ago when her mother was dying. Perhaps she had felt then that God simply did not negotiate on such matters: perhaps the primitive promise was in order now because she had not been good, because she had tended her own garden of grief while her father's grew wild.

Her burning lungs cooled, and she raised her head. She saw a light far out at sea where none had been before: a ship, demonstrating the curvature of the earth. Also a new light in the darkness – she was tired and distressed enough to grasp at the symbolism, if not to believe in it. She got to her feet.

Turning, she saw that she had come further from Salters Cottage than she had thought. Ahead of her the blank seashore broke into a feature. Her eyes made out the hummocky crest of a low bank. Though she could hardly believe she had come so far, it must be the outfall of Tetby Haven, where a creek meandered from inland through gluey silt to the sea. Scrub clothed its banks – not high.

Certainly not as high as that upright silhouette she could see standing on the bank.

She could run, oh yes she could run.

'Dad . . .!'

The silhouette turned about – became recognizably her father as she scrambled up the bank.

'Dad – Dad, what the hell are you . . .?'

He stood on the crest of the bank, in shirtsleeves and corduroys, regarding her. Rebecca's arms went up to hit, to swipe and slap at him for her fear and relief. But by the time she reached him, they could only hold and hug.

'What's wrong, what are you doing . . .? I was so worried . . .' The Dad-smell in her nostrils as she embraced him – cotton, his cologne, a hint of tobacco.

'I'm sorry, Rebecca. I wasn't thinking, I suppose. Well . . .' He gave an odd little chuckle. 'I suppose I was thinking. Too much.'

She drew back to arm's-length, and was impatient with the tears that stood in her eyes.

'About Mum?'

He nodded, looking down. 'About a lot of things. And then I had to come out, I just . . . God, is that blood on your ankle?'

She shrugged, suddenly angry again. 'For Christ's sake, I thought . . . when I came downstairs, I thought . . .'

He winced. 'Ah. No, no. I wasn't thinking, you see, and . . .' He fell silent, his hand on her shoulder, and his gaze turned in the direction of the sea.

Not seeing, though.

She said, 'It's my fault.' She felt his eyes on her, seeing this time. 'I'm not helping enough,' she said. 'I should be there for you more, or—'

'Helping?'

'Well, you must need to talk. Losing Mum. You can't be expected to cope with the grief of it.'

'What about your grief? So you're supposed to carry mine as well as your own, is that it?'

'It's different for me. I miss her like crazy. But it seems – more natural somehow. Losing her. I mean, you and Mum – I suppose deep down I always felt I hadn't got any right to you. It was more like this tremendous gift and I couldn't really complain if it was taken back in the end.'

He shook his head. 'No,' he said, squeezing her shoulder. 'No, sweetheart. You had every right to expect to have a mum for the rest of your days. But I know, I do know what you mean. It's pretty well exactly what I've felt. Anna was . . . my luck. Like you say, a gift that was never deserved.' His voice was oddly clipped and precise as he added, 'I always felt it would have to be paid back some time.'

'Well. I still say you should have been able to talk to me about it. But I've just been – I don't know, trying to get on with life. I thought it was the best way but—'

'It's the only way. Oh, love. It's a long time since you've done this.'

'What?'

' "All my fault." That was how you were when you first came to us. If ever anything went slightly wrong, you thought it must be because of you. I remember once when the washing machine broke down and Anna threw a bit of a wobbly – and then we saw this look on your face . . . It took us a long time to clear your mind of that way of thinking.'

She remembered, though she didn't like to.

'Come home now, Dad.'

'Yes. Yes, I will.' He did not move: just turned his face to the sea again. 'I've worried you sick. I won't do anything like this again.'

'It doesn't matter. As long as you're all right.'

'Oh, yes. I'm not just saying it. I had to come out here, you see, to settle something in my mind.' With a conscious effort, he turned round and pointed down the bank to the creek. Only the faintest glimmer showed the low brackish water at the bottom. 'This is where it happened, you see. This is where they found him.'

For a moment Rebecca, her mind lingering with her mother, did not follow him.

'Oh,' she said, 'that little boy who was killed.' Her body was cooling after the heat of exertion, and perhaps that made her shiver.

'Twelve years ago now,' her father said, digging his hands into his pockets.

'Has that journalist guy been pestering you again? It's too bad, it really is, at a time like this—'

'I met him.'

'What?'

He nodded. 'Last week. You know, when I was in London for the Wolfe prize-giving. Obviously he must have found out that I was going to be there – easy enough information to come by. He approached me afterwards, face to face. He asked me if I would meet him for a drink and a talk. So I did.'

'But . . .' Now she was lost. For something like a year now her father had politely refused to talk to Adam Dowling, a journalist who wanted to interview him. He had nothing to say – that had been the line, and she had repeated it herself once or twice on the phone when Dowling had made calls to their home. 'What, was this to get him off your back?'

'In a way. The fact is . . . after Anna died, I thought about a lot of things. When something like that happens, it's as if your mental map changes. You have to reorientate yourself, you have to – review everything. And maybe you see more clearly. Maybe there's that to be said for unhappiness. So.' He sighed. 'I'm going to have to do it. With Anna gone . . . well, there's no more excuse. I just wish for your sake, Rebecca, that it didn't have to be this way. Because it's going to mean changes, I

8

think. It's not a simple matter. There'll be repercussions. I have to tell you that before I do it.'

Still he did not look at her; kept his eyes fixed on the black creek that wound its sluggish way out to the sea. As ominous as his words, and seeming to reflect them, was the way his face – how? – had physically darkened. And then she realized that the stain of dawn was on the sky behind him, making of him a dark cameo.

'So, we talked. All about that case. The murder of that little boy.' At last her father turned to Rebecca, and his haggardness shocked her. 'And now I know that . . . I made a mistake. And I've got to try and put it right.'

# TWO

It was the smell of these places, Adam Dowling thought, as the prison officer opened the glass door to the visiting hall, that was most eloquent of their soul-destroying effect. They could redecorate them, as they had done with Whateley – the institutional green-and-cream he remembered from his first visits had been replaced by pastel shades – and they could abolish slopping-out and introduce resident counsellors and set up every kind of educational workshop, but they could never get rid of this smell. It was like putting your face in a warm dustbin full of old clothes and potato peelings.

The smell was so pervasive that it reached even here into the visiting hall, which was separate from the main block of the prison. The hall was a pleasant single-storey building of new brick with broad windows, and reminded him of a suburban community centre, right down to the moulded plastic chairs and hessian screens and the tea-urn and trolley in the corner. A pity it was attached, via a glassed-in corridor, to the monstrosity that was HM Prison Whateley proper. Whateley was not one of those huge mill-like Victorian prisons – it had been built, Adam knew from his researches, in the early twenties, partly with prisoners' labour – but its dingy brick, narrow barred windows and numberless pepper-pot chimneys were no less foul in their effect. When he had presented his Visiting Order at the gate-lodge, and joined the shuffling queue of visitors, mostly women and quite a few tired and fractious children, being ushered through door after door by the fat-necked officer who seemed to take pleasure in walking as slowly as possible, Adam had experienced his usual feeling of deep, molten indignation.

His St George feeling, as Angela called it – with an irony he sometimes suspected was not entirely unmalicious. Not that he cared, because it was true: he did feel, whenever he came here, that he was fighting dragons. The dragons of injustice, error and prejudice.

And if he were honest with himself, Adam had to admit that as well as the indignation there was excitement. That smell disgusted him, and it also set his adrenalin flowing.

Especially today. Because today he was entering the dragon's lair, he felt, bearing the sharpest of swords.

As he waited, seated at the little melamine table with the empty chair opposite him, he glanced around at the other visitors – with no great curiosity, for he had come to recognize most of them in the year or so that he had been coming here. These wives and relatives were visiting Category A prisoners, men who would spend a long stretch in here and could expect little sympathy either inside or outside; and they themselves had something of the grim, patient, mistrustful look of the convict. A few of them were chatting to each other, but none gave Adam any kind of acknowledgement or greeting.

Since they found out who it was he was visiting, they never did.

His gaze drifted to the big window on the left-hand side. There was an area of well-tended lawn and then a fenced area of asphalt that was very much like a school playground, with lines for games marked out in yellow paint, and a basketball hoop. Beyond that the end was just visible of another new and spruce-looking building, of red brick with a white fascia. It might have been any small office block but for the twenty-foot wire fence that surrounded it and the adjoining tower, something like a pylon, that Adam knew housed a security camera.

That was the special unit. It was where they segregated prisoners on Rule 43 – prisoners kept apart from the rest for their own safety.

The man Adam had come to see had steadfastly refused to invoke Rule 43, against all the urging of those who were concerned for his welfare, for the past twelve years.

That was partly why Adam was here. The man he was visiting claimed to be innocent of the crime for which he had been convicted. Not that there was anything unusual in that – take any prisoner and he would be likely to tell you he had been stitched up one way or another – but the important

11

difference was that Adam Dowling, and a small but growing number of other people, believed him.

The man's steadfast refusal to take Rule 43 proved nothing in itself. But it added weight to his claims. It spoke of a tremendous inner belief. For this man, to have taken Rule 43 would have been to have given in. To ask the prison authorities for protection would have been to admit that they had some right to hold him here, to supervise his life. And he had never accepted that.

It was the same with parole. After seven years a lifer was at least theoretically eligible to apply. But a request for parole was itself tainted with confession. You asked them to think about letting you out because you had learnt your lesson and would be a good boy in future. But if you refused to admit you had ever been a bad boy, then the whole question of parole was irrelevant. It was a paradox of the system – a Catch-22, Adam had called it in his first notes on the case, before erasing the journalistic phrase. Too many things were called a Catch-22 nowadays, he thought. Style mattered to him.

A door squeaked at the far end of the hall. Adam turned his head.

As always, when the men came filing in he thought of school. Like schoolboys, the men were wearing clothes that they would not have chosen to wear – the Sunday-best grey uniform, stiffly ironed – and like schoolboys some had made little adjustments of rebellion, with an eccentrically knotted tie or a discreet badge. Their air of constricted maleness, its subdued strut, was pure school – in Adam prompting a shuddering reminiscence of his own private school and its pathetic, ritualized machismo. And most suggestive of school was the way they walked. They trod an invisible path. These men were only allowed to walk in certain places at certain times and that fact was ingrained in their movements. It never ceased to strike Adam, because one never saw it in adult people anywhere else. Far more than the uniform, it marked them as unfree.

The men made their way to their various tables, some with a quickening of step, some almost with reluctance. One man – elderly, leathery, strange – began as always to kiss his wife in the rigid tight-lipped way of old movies.

The prisoner Adam had come to see was the last to enter. This too was usual: he had learnt to avoid having anyone behind him.

Adam equipped himself with a smile of welcome. And then he felt his own smile fading, with as much physical discomfort as if it were being peeled from his face.

'My God,' Adam said. Involuntarily he edged his own chair back a little as the prisoner, with a nod of greeting, sat down opposite him at the table.

'Hello,' the prisoner said. He made himself comfortable in the chair and folded his hands calmly on the table. They were large hands with small nails, and very white. 'How are you?'

'Me, I . . .' Adam shrugged, and in nervous perplexity reached for his packet of cigarettes. He offered them across the table, and got a solemn shake of the head in return. 'No, of course, you don't. I'm sorry, I was forgetting . . . What the hell happened?'

'You mean this?' The prisoner put a hand up briefly to his right cheek. 'Oh, there's a new bloke on the wing. He was transferred from Parkhurst. Always a troublemaker, apparently. I suppose he thought he had to prove himself.'

Adam lit a cigarette. He was adaptable, swift; now that the first flinching shock was past he studied the scar, running like a crimson handprint from the prisoner's cheekbones down to the collar of his shirt. It looked like a burn or a scald. It looked unbearably painful.

'A hard nut,' he said.

The prisoner shrugged. 'Armed robbery,' he said. 'That's what he's in for. I heard about it. A security guard got most of his hand shot off. But that still makes that man better than me, apparently. Oh, well.'

'It looks terrible,' Adam said. 'How did he do that to you?'

'Hot water with sugar in it. He threw it at me after tea, last Tuesday. An old trick, apparently. Jail napalm, they call it.'

Adam noticed again that fastidious detachment he maintained whenever he used prison terms. He had never heard this man, who had been incarcerated for twelve years, use prison slang without audible quotation marks. The message was clear: these things are nothing to do with me. A dissociative stance.

13

'It must have been bloody agony.'

'The doctor was very good. It looks worse than it is. It'll heal up soon enough.'

'What about the other chap? Will they discipline him?'

The prisoner shrugged again. 'What are they going to do?' The faintest of smiles touched his lips. 'Lock him up?'

Not for the first time Adam found himself marvelling at the composure of this man, who woke each day to a renewal of what most people would find, if not hell, then a passable purgatory. When he spoke of these things, in that soft, guttural, precise voice with an accent that Adam would have found unplaceable but knew to be Lincolnshire, it was easy to forget that he was not telling of someone else's experiences. This was how he lived.

An uneasy thought came to Adam, coinciding with the prisoner's next words.

'The Welfare Officer had a bit of a fit over it. Said I should go on Rule 43 and be damned to it. Said she was going to strongly recommend it at the next Board meeting.'

'And how do you feel about that?' Adam said. He could hardly blame the man if he did go for segregation after this latest incident; but just at this critical moment, it might look bad.

'Like I say.' The prisoner frowned slightly, as if Adam were being dim. 'Like I've always said. I'm not a nonce, as they call it. So I won't go in the nonces' place.'

Adam nodded, trying not to show his relief. At the same time he wondered about that scar. He doubted it would heal that quickly. What effect would it have, if events took the rapid turn he was now expecting? On the one hand, it might elicit respect, sympathy – the guy had guts. On the other hand, there was no denying it gave his face a rather sinister look.

He felt these things shouldn't be important – the St George part of him felt it, anyhow; the realistic side of Adam, which usually predominated, acknowledged that they were. For his part, he had never been able to decide whether Howard Gandy's looks worked for him or against him. Certainly, he did not look ordinary, and the newspapers had made the most of that, twelve years ago. The camera was an accomplished liar: lenses placed close and low had produced images of a towering, slab-faced brute, disdaining the covering of a blanket as he was hustled into the court to shouts of execration. *Portrait of a Monster*.

Yet really, Adam thought, it was only his size that was exceptional – and six foot six was hardly unheard of in the vitamin-rich modern West. The addition of bulk, perhaps, struck an odd note. Men usually achieved that height at the expense of width. This man was just uniformly big – big feet, big arms, big joints, big earlobes. And though he gave an impression of massive, quiet strength, and though Adam knew he had taken up weightlifting and gym training in prison, there was no tapering about him, no muscle definition. He might have been carved from soft soap. His skin was fair and unlined and – unfortunate, this – his torso, in its smooth roundness, its lack of narrowness at the waist, was suggestive of nothing so much as the body of an infant boy, hugely magnified.

His face too was large, and not at all angular. Again perhaps unfortunately, it was like a child's drawing of a man's face: round, the features small, dark blobs of eyes, lips a pink enigmatic curve. He had short brown receding hair that was curly, or crinkly – period hair, Adam would have called it. A broad smile – which was rare in this man – showed a couple of missing teeth, though the rest were strong and white, and the losses seemed unlikely to be due to decay. He was forty years old, but he might have been thirty or fifty. He smelt strongly of aftershave, applied liberally in the manner of an adolescent: since Adam had been coming to see him the only request he had made, as far as gifts from outside were concerned, was for bottles of this cheap pungent cologne. Perhaps, Adam thought, it was another dissociative gesture, warding off that frowsty prison smell.

'Well,' Adam said, 'I admire your guts. It can't be easy. Have you had any more aggro from this character?'

'This and that. There'll be more, no doubt.'

Adam nodded. The assault had, at least, been frontal. He knew that the usual inflictions on prisoners of this sort were covert: the meal laced with human excrement, the broken glass in the shower. And it was not only the other prisoners who used the nonce to exercise their morality. Prison officers conveniently forgot to lock some cell doors; developed selective blindness. Adam felt St George rising: it was with a fine relish, a conscious and surely allowable sense of drama, that he spoke the words he had been looking forward to saying throughout the long journey up to this moorland bastille.

'Well, Howard,' he said, 'I think I have some good news for you.'

'Oh, ah?' Howard Gandy's eyebrows rose a little. 'That'll make a nice change.' The scepticism was not that of the convict but of the countryman, mild and downright.

'Yes.' Adam glanced around, regretting the lack of privacy; but the other prisoners and their visitors seemed mutually absorbed. The elderly couple were still locked in their strange vintage kiss. 'One of the key witnesses at your trial, Philip Springthorpe. I've been chasing him up for a long time. And now he's signalled his willingness to co-operate. In fact, he actually wants to change his testimony.'

There was no emotion on the big bland face of Howard Gandy, except a certain puzzlement. 'So he must have lied, then. At the trial.'

'Yes, in a sense—'

'Why would he lie?'

'That's what we're going to establish, hopefully. I mean, I really think I've got this guy's trust now, I think we've got him on side, though there's always a chance that he won't go through with it. It does bring up the question of perjury, though that's not our problem, that's for the courts to decide. I dare say the Criminal Cases Review Commission will deal with that when we make our presentation. Myself, I'm not bothered about chasing up that aspect of it.'

'It was wrong, though. If he told a lie to the court, that was wrong. He ought to be punished for it.'

'OK, sure.' Adam's own thought processes, darting swiftly ahead, made him a little impatient with this. 'But what you've got to see is the real significance of this. Howard – this is it. This is the breakthrough. And I'm not being overoptimistic when I say that. Doug Jameson feels the same, he's raring to go. And you know solicitors – it takes a lot to make them look on the bright side. Doug's certain that the Commission will have to cave in now. They can recommend your case direct to the Appeal Court – the Home Secretary doesn't have to have a hand in it. Which is good news again. And lucky – but of course in these cases you have to take what luck comes your way, and . . .'

He felt he had got a little carried away, and tried to return his attention to the man sitting opposite him rather than the case that the man represented. How was Gandy taking this? In the eighteen months that had passed since Adam had first picked up on the Pied Piper case, there had been no development of this importance. Perhaps he should have prepared Gandy more: perhaps the significance was too much to take in . . .

'How do you mean, luck?'

Adam hesitated. 'Well, what I mean is, things like public policy don't have any bearing on the fact of your guilt or innocence. And yet they can be the things that help you to the Appeal court. And it seems as if the wind is blowing our way at the moment.'

'I am innocent,' Howard Gandy said. 'I always have been. There's nothing can change that.'

'I know.'

'I haven't exactly been lucky these past twelve years. I'd say the wind's been blowing the other way the whole time.'

As so often when talking to Howard Gandy, Adam was put in mind of the Puritans. Certain images irresistibly suggested themselves: Cromwell, the New Englanders of *The Scarlet Letter*, the Amish. Howard wasn't any kind of religious enthusiast, but he had a directness of speech that was almost biblical. Of course, it could also make him seem somewhat less than human, invulnerable, even arrogant. Shades of the Australian dingo baby case, Adam thought, where the defendants had been judged more on their demeanour than on the evidence; and he made a mental note to include the comparison in the book. Here was another cause for satisfaction: if the case did get to the Appeal Court, Angela had privately let slip to him, then his publishers were almost sure to go ahead with the commission, and with a reasonable advance. There had been several articles in the papers about the Pied Piper case lately, especially since he had done that spot on Channel 4's *Law Stories* programme, and that had made his editor look more favourably on a project which at first she wouldn't touch with rubber gloves. But a genuine certified miscarriage of justice, rather than a mere bee in Adam's bonnet, was needed to make it viable.

'Well, look, I'm not making promises,' Adam said. 'You know I've never done that. But this is as good a chance as we'll ever have of getting you to the Appeal Court.'

He kept his voice low, mindful of the other prisoners in the room. Everyone, though, seemed greyly occupied with their own concerns. Hands were held, listlessly or feverishly, across the tables: urgent murmurings went on, while one couple just looked at each other, as if engaged in some endurance-testing party game.

'So what happens now?' Howard said. There was no sign of emotion on his large round face.

'Doug Jameson's negotiating with Mr Springthorpe's solicitor. We need to get a full statement from him to present to the Commission. I think we're going to have to handle him gently. His wife died not long ago and he's in a bit of a fragile state emotionally – which I think is what's made him crack at last.'

As Adam spoke the words there came, unwanted, most definitely unwanted, a clear memory of the photographs showing little Lee Brudenell's cracked skull. He had forced himself to become acquainted with these when he first took up the Pied Piper case: insurance against forgetting the victim. As with Howard's fresh scar, he had been able to handle it after the first shudder. But sometimes the memory caught him napping.

'Well, I'm sorry to hear about his wife,' Howard Gandy said. 'I remember her. Poor lady. It makes me laugh a bit, though.' He did not laugh, only frowned. 'When you say about handling him gently. I haven't been handled very gently in here. Still. It's a rum old world, isn't it?'

There was no self-pity about him when he said these things: his tone was assertive rather than plaintive.

'I think Mr Springthorpe's testimony will turn the balance, though it's not a question of this whole thing coming down to him. It's always been my view that you should never have been convicted on the evidence at your trial, the whole proceedings were a travesty, and there was already enough to overturn the conviction. But you know what the law's like. The Appeal Court won't open the door unless there is new evidence that was not available at the trial, or some other "consideration of substance". To stand a chance you need something new. And we've got it. So it's really not a matter of Mr Springthorpe being the one to blame, or anything like that.'

'Isn't it?' Howard's eyes – chocolate-brown, eyes that should have been soft and friendly and genial – searched Adam's face. Then he gave a slight shrug. 'Well. If you say so. I can't pretend I understand it all.'

'Me neither,' Adam said, wanting to move on. 'Doug Jameson knows the legal technicalities. What we—'

'I know the difference between right and wrong, though.'

Howard Gandy spoke these words loudly, and for the first time Adam saw a turn of the head, a twitch of attention amongst the other prisoners.

'Sure. That's – that's the main thing, sure, to keep in mind. You know you're innocent and whatever comes along to help you prove that fact to the Appeal Court is great and we'll use it. Thinking in terms of blame is perhaps not constructive, though I do understand.'

For several moments Howard Gandy said nothing. He seemed to Adam to be presenting his scarred face, without comment, as a reply to that. *Here is an eloquence beyond your command.* And Adam felt obscurely abashed, as if in the presence of great authority.

An authority that then relented and became magnanimous, as Howard said, with a trace of a smile, 'Well, blow me. It's a bit much to take in. It does sound promising . . . Have you spoke to Mum about it?'

'No. I wanted you to be the first to know.'

'Can I tell her?'

'You could mention it. I mean, it's a step – it's not the last step. Don't build her hopes up too much.'

'Or my own?' The faint smile remained, rendering him subtle, sphinx-like.

'Just hold on,' Adam said, smiling in turn. 'Just keep holding out.'

19

'Oh, I can do that. I can do that all right.'

Adam didn't doubt it. And even if they were in the end turned down by the Appeal Court, he didn't fear for the effect on Howard Gandy's mental state of such a disappointment, as he might have with some men in his situation. Gandy's strength of mind was such, he thought, that it would survive even that.

And with that thought, Adam questioned himself. Was he such an enthusiastic partisan of this case because, win or lose, no harm would be done? Because he had picked a tough nut who wouldn't break even if it came to the ultimate letdown?

Again he saw the photographs of little Lee, in obscene colour.

'I know you can,' he said hastily. 'And hopefully you won't have to for much longer.'

'Cross fingers,' Howard said. And unfolding his hands, he did so, holding the crossed fingers up for Adam to see. Adam noticed the odd ridges, almost like an extra knuckle, along the middle of the fingers of Howard's right hand. They had been broken some years ago. Two prisoners had put them into the crack of a door and closed the door, slowly.

'Cross fingers,' Adam agreed. 'Oh, there is one thing I needed to check with you. You mentioned that they'd offered you sexual counselling in here when you first came in. Can you put a date to that? Just for the file.'

'I couldn't tell you the date. But it wasn't just then. They've never stopped. It comes up every year, I'd reckon. They put it in different ways. Someone to talk to about your problems, they say. A way of getting in touch with your feelings. All that. It's all the same rubbish. It gets on my nerves. I dare say there's some people in here who do need that. But that's because they've done something wrong. Which I haven't. I'm not being pig-headed about it on purpose. It just doesn't apply to me.'

Adam nodded. Integrity: the true meaning of the word was wholeness, being all of a piece, and Howard Gandy had it. There were no inconsistencies in his position.

'Anything else you need for that file?'

'I don't think so. You've been very straight with me.'

'There's not much to say about the past twelve years of my life, any road,' Howard said, and he said it with the most

20

phlegmatic air conceivable, so that Adam, who over a score of visits had become used to him, still marvelled a little. 'Just stuck in here.' He breathed out a sigh and gave his aloof, sceptical look around the hall. 'I tell you, it's like a bloody life sentence.'

After a moment Adam found himself breaking into a noisy laugh. He stifled it as best he could, but he still intercepted several baleful glances across the hall.

'Well,' Howard said, beaming bashfully, 'you know what I mean. I shall stick it, though.' He was abruptly solemn again. 'Even if this doesn't turn out the way you're hoping. I shall stick it out just the same. No changes.'

It was true that there was little to say about Howard Gandy's twelve years in Whateley. He had joined no educational programmes, sought no minor ancillary responsibilities like that of the elderly prisoner who was now circulating with the tea-trolley. He had made no friends, and fewer enemies than he might have: hardened troublemakers had targeted him but his own imposing size was a deterrent against casual malice. And though such a loner, he had taken up no time-devouring hobbies. There were no matchstick models of Windsor Castle in Howard Gandy's cell. Of course: those were the strategies of people who had accepted their status as long-term convicts. They were here and they were staying. Figuratively, Howard had never taken his coat off.

'Well, that's probably the best way to think at the moment. Hope, but not too much. And I suppose you don't need me to tell you to keep these things under your hat as far as . . . well, in here.'

'Oh, it'll get out. If it does go to appeal, everybody'll soon know about it. No doubt the authorities'll be the first to hear. Dear me. There's one or two – officers who'd hate me even more if they thought I was getting out. There, beggar me, I nearly said "screws". This place must be getting to me at last.'

The tea-trolley drew up beside them. Adam bought two cups of tea. The elderly prisoner in charge did not look at either of them as he served them. But he contrived to bang Howard's cup down on the table in front of him so that much of the tea slopped into the saucer.

'One thing I did want to mention,' Adam said, watching as

Howard calmly and deftly poured the tea from the saucer back into the cup. 'If we do get the result we're hoping for. You're not under any obligation, of course, but I would like to carry on highlighting your case and the issues it raises, hopefully in print.'

'Like a book?'

'Like a book. And obviously no one can tell your story like you can. So if you would be happy to go on giving me interviews, give an account of yourself in your own words . . .'

'Oh, ah, I'll help you. You don't have to ask that. Somebody helps me, I don't forget. Same as if somebody does me a bad turn. I don't forget that either.' Howard drank his tea as if it were a thimbleful, the off-white institutional cup looking in his fingers like something from a doll's tea set. 'Now, I'm not getting my hopes up, like you say, but suppose it does get to the Appeal Court – do I get a chance to give the judges a piece of my mind?'

With a touch of alarm, Adam said, 'Well, it doesn't really work like that. If there is a hearing at the Court of Appeal, the case is put forward by a barrister working from Doug Jameson's brief. I think I told you Doug's got a contact at the bar who's interested in your case and might be prepared to take it on for costs. So he'll do the talking. You don't have to worry about that.'

'Oh, I'm not worried. I'd just like to tell them a few things. Mind you, I suppose it wouldn't be the judge who did my trial, would it?'

'No, no. Three Appeal Court judges. Different kettle of fish entirely.'

'You'll be there, won't you?'

'Oh, yes. If it happens, I'll be there. As a spectator, of course. A very interested one.'

'You know, I was wondering about that the other day. About you, about me. I mean, why?'

'Why the interest? Well, like I told you. It was those letters you wrote to the *Law Stories* programme. A researcher who's a friend told me about them, and it caught my attention. That's my field as a journalist, for better or worse, and once I read up on your case it seemed such a clear miscarriage of justice that—'

'Oh, aye. Don't get me wrong, I'm glad you did. Because I'll say this for you, you don't let things go. Some people might have thought, oh, beggar that, after a while. The thing is, there must be plenty of other cases. Nicer ones. I'm not a nice one, am I? Even if you get me out, people aren't going to like me. I know that. Mud sticks.'

'Actually, you'd be surprised how much support this campaign's getting, from all sorts of people. There really is quite a strong feeling in your favour, even in the press.'

'Ah. Apart from the people who want to take a gun to me.'

'Closed minds,' Adam said. 'You're always going to get them. But this is the aspect of the case that I really want to draw attention to. This element of public hysteria. I think we've come to a very dangerous and unnatural point in our thinking. Whenever the subject of children comes up in this context we go a little crazy. Of course children have to be protected. Of course there are people around who will harm them unless they're prevented. Everyone accepts that. But we've lost, I think, our sense of proportion. Soon we won't be able to like children, to be natural with them. We will actually be afraid of them. That's a terrible thing. Pleasure in childhood – it's one of the best things in the human heritage. And we're going to stampede ourselves into losing it.'

Steadily regarding him, Howard said, 'Are you going to write this in your book?'

'Yes. Yes, I am.'

Howard Gandy nodded. 'Well, I've never cared what people think. I never have. I never shall. I always knew what they said. They thought I was odd. Because I like kids. That's all it is. I love kids, I love being with them, I love playing with them and talking to them. I prefer 'em to most grown-ups. I would have loved to have had kids of my own, or to work with kids, but that didn't happen for one reason or another. That's me.' For the first time, an emotion stronger than bovine resignation was perceptible in his voice, though his face remained impassive, a great moon shadowed by its scar. 'But that means I don't fit in. People made up their minds that I'm not right and so I ended up in here. Isn't it? I'm in prison because my face doesn't fit.'

Adam nodded sympathetically, but he suffered an inward

23

wince. He was thinking of the weeks and months ahead, when an intense spotlight would almost certainly shine on Howard Gandy. Of course no one had more right to have developed a persecution complex, but that truculence was dismaying. It smacked of the professional prisoner, all tortuous self-justification.

'Five minutes. Five minutes now.' The voice of the prison officer on the dais was a shout, utterly inappropriate to this room of intimate murmurings, a sour trumpet-note.

'OK. I'm going up to Lincolnshire next week,' Adam said. 'I'll be seeing Doug Jameson and hopefully Mr Springthorpe too. Maybe to get a definitive statement from him.'

'Not a lie this time.'

Adam balanced his words. 'The whole truth this time. I can't really talk about it in detail until we've landed him, as it were. But I can tell you that the evidence he gave won't stand up any more. I've found something out that flatly contradicts it. With luck that'll be just the handle we need to get to appeal. I'll be in touch as soon as there are any developments.'

Around the hall there was a general buzz of leave-taking. Chairs scraped back. Adam noticed that prisoners and visitors alike seemed oddly relieved. Again he remembered his school: the curious constraint of parental visits, the anguished half-wish for them to be gone so that he could revert to the protective persona he adopted in that enclosed world. It was impossible to be both people at once.

Howard stood up. His height became once again unignorable, very nearly a challenge. 'Thank you for coming,' he said formally. He held out his hand, and Adam shook it. Adam had a moment of sharp consciousness as he did so of how few people would do this. The large, soft, dry hand of Howard Gandy, the Pied Piper killer.

'Hang in there, Howard,' he said. Prisoners were already filing past on their way to the door.

'Oh, ah. I will do. Hang in there, that's funny in a way, isn't it? In the old days that's what they would have done with me. Hanging. Good job really. You wouldn't have had anything to do then, would you?'

His smile was cryptic. Adam, seeking for a reply, felt

24

something touch his ear. He recoiled, shuddered, as he felt its warmth and wetness.

'Sorry.' Howard was frowning. He stayed Adam's hand, and taking out his own neatly folded and spotless handkerchief wiped the spit away. 'I think that was meant for me. Or, well, both of us, maybe. There.'

Adam glared at the file of prisoners moving off down the aisle between the tables, straight-backed, eyes front, seeing and knowing nothing and everything. He found that he was shaking. The little tribute of malice transfixed him: he seemed to feel the whole tree of nerves tingling throughout his body.

'Ah well,' Howard said, huge and imperturbable in valediction, 'that gives you some idea, anyway.'

# THREE

'There. That's him. Tall guy. There. No, don't look, don't look, don't look . . .' Frantic, Emma got Rebecca's arm in a clawlike grip to keep her turning, seemed almost ready to grab her head.

'Emma! How am I supposed to see him then?'

'Wait. Wait till he walks past. When he does I'll give you a signal.'

'Like what?'

'Well, I'll rattle the collecting tin.'

'You're doing that anyway. Can't you just call out to him?'

'I cannot do that, Rebecca! Yes, I want it to happen, but it's got to be in a different way. I just want you to see him and tell me what you think.'

'Like you'd go off him if I didn't like him.'

'Well, I respect your opinion.'

'Me?' Rebecca said. 'I went out with Michael Rouse, and you respect my opinion on blokes?'

Her own laughter was not forced or defensive. Strange. This time last year, a subject that could not be touched without the sensation of a wound gaping raw. And now, nothing. Time didn't heal, of course: events did. But how little it had been, really. A boy had hurt her and she had seemed to feel herself bleeding within. Yet there was even perhaps an embracing of pain, because it was a life-experience and she was hungry for those.

She stole another look at her watch.

Ten to two. Three o'clock, her father said. She tried once more to picture what he was doing, but still there was a blank. That was how it had been with this business since the beginning, when she had found him haunting Tetby Haven in dead of night three weeks ago. She knew about it, yet she

26

stood at a perplexed remove from it. It was somewhat like being a child again, subject to that apartheid of responsibility: adults getting inexplicably on with things beyond your scope. Rebecca had left childhood behind recently enough not to want anything to do with it. In her recent life she had climbed not just steps but flights. She had finished schooling and secured a place at university, and she had lost her virginity and her innocence – separate developments – to that Michael Rouse who no longer mattered, and last October she had watched her mother die and been left a mourner, an initiate of death and bereavement long before her contemporaries. The adult world was hers.

Yet she could not picture, or grasp, what her father was doing at the solicitor's office less than a mile away, up in the higher town of Lincoln that rose, cathedral-crowned, above them. She only knew that it was important. Since that strange night of decision he seemed to have staked at least some of his emotional health on this thing. Strung up and yet dogged, he waited, as far as she could tell, for a payback.

She was worried about him. She had a bad feeling, an intuition: when her mind turned to her father it moved through shadows of foreboding. There was more to this exhumation of an old court case than met the eye, of that Rebecca was sure.

'There he goes – oh, you missed him. I wonder if he'll come back this way. He is well fit actually. Hello, would you like to wear a red ribbon?' Emma said, as a young woman with a child in a buggy paused – first in an age, it seemed, to give their stall a glance instead of passing by – and cast her eye over their assortment of bumf, weighted down with stones against the fluttering wind that funnelled down the lower-town shopping street. 'For Aids Awareness Week.'

'Yes, OK,' the woman said, dropping coins in the tin. 'Oh, how much are those enamel ones?'

'The badges? Well, it's a suggested donation of two pounds,' Rebecca said. 'We can't actually sell them, because we're a charity, you know. Not licensed to vend in the street.'

'Oh, I see, Well, I'll take one.'

'How about a balloon?' Rebecca said, smiling at the child in the buggy, a little boy who looked elfin and wise beneath a vast woolly hat. 'Yeah?'

'There, that's nice, isn't it? To be honest,' the woman said, indicating the legend *Lincolnshire Aids Action* on the stall tablecloth, 'I never knew there was one.'

'Been going a few years now.' Emma, veteran volunteer of three years, pinner of a thousand lapels, spoke proprietorially. 'Of course it's like all these things, you don't get the publicity you really need because of the funding. A lot of that goes on the helpline, which is Tuesday and Thursday nights, free confidential advice on all aspects of HIV and Aids. So we're, you know . . .' fluency deserted her quite suddenly, 'plugging in there.'

'Well, good luck to you. It's a terrible thing.'

'What are we plugging in?' Rebecca teased when the woman had gone. 'Electrical appliances?'

'Shut up, Rebecca. Don't be confrontational. I'm fragile. God, it's cold.'

'You'll have to toughen up. Nurses are supposed to be beefy.'

'And who says?'

'They are.' Rebecca huffed and puffed and blew up a new balloon. 'You see them. All stocky calves and red hands. It goes with the territory.'

'Like you know about nurses. Like when have you ever . . .?' An unfortunate remark was developing; both realizing it, they let it drop between them, firm friends enough to avoid a big embarrassing deal. 'Cold, that's it. Reminded me, I was going to tell you. When I was on the helpline last week. This guy, he was totally for real, he rang in to say there was a computer virus going round where he worked, and could he get Aids from it. Gospel truth, I'm telling you.'

'At least it was a call. I haven't had a proper call since, I don't know, months.'

'There were several that night actually. One guy saying he'd just done an act, actually just that evening, in his car with a girl. I think he just wanted to ring up and brag. It *is* cold. Matt should be here by now. We need relieving.'

'I need relieving, I'm busting.'

'Don't go in the market toilet, it's disgusting. Go in the pub. We'll get something to eat in there, yeah?'

'Slice of lemon, like. Maybe a cherry.'

'Good for Vitamin C.'

'Fibre, eat the cocktail stick . . .'

They could keep this up for hours, wilful nonsense that did the soul good because it was protective. Today, especially, she valued it, with her father up in the old town settling something, and a cold suspense on her of what would happen, how he would be when she met him at three and they drove home, whether exorcised or newly haunted.

Matt relieved them at the stall at just past two. Probably all provincial cities had a Matt, a supply teacher and would-be councillor, calmly ensconced in an immemorial beard, doyen of every voluntary group and charity event. He took his seat at the stall as if relaxing in his own living room. In the building society across the way Rebecca waited on the grey-carpeted sidelines while Emma cashed a cheque. It was, as a calendar behind the counter announced, the twenty-eighth of February. End of that eccentric month, shortest and longest of all. Rebecca couldn't wait for it to be gone. Her mood sought resolutions and new beginnings.

'Wonder if we'll see your fella in here,' Rebecca said as they went into a pub called the Mitre, long and narrow and dark like an upholstered corridor. 'Would this be the right time and place?'

'No it would not. We've got to meet cute, like in films. They've got these nice rolls, like baguettes. Is a baguette a little bag?'

'Is an omelette a little om? I think I'm going to have a spirit.'

In the pub Emma's near six feet of height became blatant, and she had automatically hunched herself. This way, women just resented her. With shoulders back to show her lissomness, black hair uncovering her profile, she was purely hated. 'So, what time are you meeting your dad?' she said as they sat. She already knew: it was a friend's kind opening of the door.

'Three. Well, he should be finished by then. As far as I know.' Rebecca wasn't much interested in the cheese baguette, strenuous eating even for the hungry. She nibbled, then dedicated herself to the vodka.

'So, what exactly is your dad doing today? Is it legal stuff to, you know, to do with your mum?'

'No. He's seeing his solicitor. And they're meeting with

29

some other solicitor. Plus this journalist guy who's set it all up.
I don't really understand it. It's to do with this court case
years ago.' She sucked in the sharpness of lemon. 'You
remember when that little boy got killed on the coast near us?
He was on a camping holiday with his family. Back in the
eighties. There was a lot of outcry about it. They got the man
who did it. They called him the Pied Piper in the papers
because he had this thing about kids.'

'Oh, I know. Well, I seem to remember these photographs
of him, really creepy. Must have been before we moved up
here, though. God, was that in Holfleet?'

'Just up the coast near us. There's that camp site in the
woods. The man, the one they caught, he was from Holfleet.
His mother still lives there. I'd heard about it. It was before
Mum and Dad adopted me, but I heard the story, you know.
I didn't really know about Dad's involvement, not until this
journalist guy started hassling him. It was last year it started.
He kept writing and then ringing up, saying he wanted to talk
to Dad about the case. Dad said no. Then Mum fell ill, so
everything took second place to that. But this guy didn't let it
drop. After Mum died he kept at it. It made me angry. I
thought Dad should tell him to get lost.'

'I don't blame you. Weird. What's your dad got to do with
it?'

'Well, he was one of the witnesses when they caught this
Pied Piper character. It was Dad's testimony that helped put
him away. I didn't know this, until all this business with the
journalist started. Like I say, it was before my time. I asked
Dad and he said he'd had to give evidence all these years ago
and that was about it. He couldn't understand why it was all
being dug up again. Well, apparently this journalist is running
a campaign. He reckons the guy in prison for killing that little
boy never did it, which is what the guy's always claimed. And
he was wanting Dad to go back and rethink his statement.'

'Why should he do that?'

'I don't know. It started playing on Dad's mind, I know
that. Which I think this journalist counted on. He'd lost Mum
and he was in a state and vulnerable. So he kept at him. That's
how I see it, anyway. But then a few weeks ago Dad agreed to
meet him. They talked about it, I suppose; I can't get much

out of Dad at the moment. All I know is Dad's going to help. He says he thinks he made a mistake and he wants to change his testimony.'

Emma's eyes were wide above the wedge of bread. 'Can he do that?'

'Apparently. He says it might mean trouble. But it's something he's got to do.' Rebecca shrugged, wishing for more vodka, wishing more for understanding. 'So he's got this meeting today. I'm hoping,' she added with difficulty, slowly, 'that this – is going to settle things a bit. But that's selfish.'

'How come? How come selfish?'

'I just want my dad back.' She blurted it. She hunted in her purse for distraction.

'God. I suppose you could do without all this.' Emma was tentative. 'After your poor mum and everything.'

'I don't care, you see. Which is bad. I don't care whether that man should have been sent to prison or whether he shouldn't. Or whether Dad said something wrong all those years ago or whether he's got to clear his conscience. I just want him back to normal and this journalist to leave us alone. We were just trying to . . . manage without Mum. That's enough.'

'What's his name? Would I know him?'

'Adam Dowling. I haven't seen him. Apparently he did a thing on TV. And he's got a book out. He's the crusading sort.'

The sort who normally engaged her sympathetic interest. Rebecca, fetching more drinks, acknowledged it to herself. And Emma approached the point obliquely when she came back.

'I suppose it's possible, isn't it? That this Piper man is innocent. You hear of these things – people locked away for years for things they didn't do. I don't mean, you know, that your dad should get dragged into it, but . . . So the guy's mum still lives in Holfleet? Do you know her?'

'See her around. Pat Gandy. She keeps herself to herself. People used to point a bit around the village, you know. That's the one whose son's in prison for murder. I dare say she must have had it rough at first. But then these things get forgotten.'

'Or not.'

Rebecca nodded. 'I don't know what's going to happen. I

31

don't see what Dad can come up with that can change anything. Not after twelve years.'

'What was he . . .?' Emma grimaced in response to her own curiosity. 'It's morbid, but did he see something? He didn't find that little boy or anything?'

'Not that. But I don't know the details. He won't talk to me. Maybe it won't amount to anything, maybe he'll just have to go over his statements and then that'll be it and the rest will be up to the courts.'

'I'm sure it'll be all right,' Emma said. 'Does make you wonder, though, what on earth's going on. I mean, if there's doubt about this Piper guy in prison . . . somebody killed that little boy, didn't they? God. Do you think they've found something like that? Like someone else has confessed?'

'I don't know. Perhaps somebody in this pub, say, could be a killer. You can walk past them in the street. There's always a time before they did it, when they were just one of us . . . It's funny, I never thought much about that poor little boy getting killed. The baddie was inside and that was it. The whole business was finished. But it's not.' And, she thought, we are in it: Dad and I. It was an unsettling thought.

Obviously it was unsettling for her father too. *Dad*, she had told herself each day of the past month, *is not right*. He was hardly working: he had just made the deadline for a couple of articles for music magazines, but a commission for music for a nature programme, as far as she could tell, had not been executed beyond a few sketched pages.

'Try not to worry about it,' Emma said. 'It'll get sorted. Just think of the future. Come October you'll be at York living it up – I suppose they do still live it up at university. Just spare a thought for me among the bedpans. And then having to marry a copper at the end of it.' Emma was in training at the County Hospital.

'I'd better start saving. Hopefully I can get a job in Ingelow over the season again.' Rebecca had passed her A levels and secured her place at York last year. She had decided then on deferred entry and a year out for no clearer reason than indolence and a vague desire to do other things, real things, before going to university. And so she had been at home when her mother fell ill. You couldn't honour that with the word 'luck', but she knew that her mother, dying and looking for blessings, had counted it as such. *At least it's happened now, not next year when Rebecca starts college.* Her mother's way. She had given Rebecca everything; and if she could not make her own death a gift, she could rejoice that it was not a hindrance.

Parting with Emma in the street outside, Rebecca set out for the High Bridge where she was to meet her father. Her route took her past the Aids Action stall, and she waved a hand to Matt, for a moment not recognizing the tall figure standing at the stall idly turning over the leaflets.

'Dad.'

His expression lifted when he saw her. 'Hello, sweetheart. I was earlier than I expected. Thought I might see you here. Ready to go?'

'Ready when you are.' She tried not to study him. 'Did everything go all right?'

'Well, I've said my piece, and everyone seems satisfied. I feel rather . . . footballers say gutted, don't they?'

'Gutted, or over the moon.'

He took her arm and pressed her to walk.

'I feel gutted like a fish,' he said. 'Let's go home.'

On the way to the car he asked her how Emma was doing. He seemed to hear, if not listen to, her replies. They kept up the small talk until they were free of Lincoln's snarl of traffic and heading east towards the coast. After the huddle of the old city the wolds opened out to receive them like a new continent, giant and liberating beneath a powder-blue winter sky.

She said, her vision pierced by arrows of sunlight, 'So, is that the end of it? I mean, will this Dowling character lay off you now?'

'He's got what he wanted. I think it's pretty certain the case will be reopened now. And that should be the end of my direct involvement.' Each sentence was like the careful, considered laying down of a card in a crucial game. 'So that's a relief. But as for the end of it . . . that's different.'

'Well, if . . .' A sharp stab of impatience altered what she had been going to say. 'And am I ever going to be told exactly what it's all about? Or are you just going to carry on shutting me out?'

'You've every right to feel like that,' he said. 'I'm sorry it's been like this. Let's just get home and . . .' He slowed the car as a pheasant, strange and exotic in the brown landscape, fluttered clumsily across the road ahead.

'Just tell me, Dad, are you going to be in trouble with the law because of this?'

'I don't think so. Don't worry about that.'

He had never been a stern man, but he could be immovable. She remembered how this used to baffle her when she first came, an eight-year-old full of poison, to live with her adopted parents and would hurl tantrums at them: trying to demolish and expose the insincerity that was all she expected from adults. Once they struck her and despised her and thrust her away, she would know where she was. But with these people it didn't happen. And though she could drive her mother, if not to anger, then to bewildered grief in those early stormy days, her father had an emotional cut-off point. There was a place inside him where no one could go; the place also, she suspected, where he composed. He was there now. Impatience, even hostility, were no use.

The forty miles to the sea, on good Lincolnshire roads as straight and empty as when first laid out by the legions, was soon gone. Holfleet was there quite suddenly, it seemed: the straggling, unlovely, comfortable village by the dunes, characteristically prodigal with space, so that the main road was as wide as a boulevard and ran in a great slouching curve. Gardens were sprawling holdings, and even the twin rows of Victorian labourers' cottages seemed opulent in their dimensions, each with fifty yards of brick path to its own front door. Running inland were a couple of roads of rural council housing, laid out with the same scrubby amplitude: Church Lane and Hythe Avenue. Rebecca didn't turn her head as they passed them, but her mind swivelled that way: Hythe Avenue was where Mrs Gandy lived her solitary, unimaginable life.

Rebecca's father parked the car in the drive, turned off the engine and sat for a moment looking at the house. They had left a couple of lights on – a habit of her mother's that they had carried over to their strange reduced life. She always said it made the house welcoming. She would sometimes leave the

radio on, too, for the cats. 'To keep them company.' Rebecca
had a clear image of her mother's face as she said these words,
laughing at herself yet quite serious, too. The image was very
young-looking. Anna Springthorpe had died at forty-four, a
beautiful woman right up until her illness rained its final blows
on her. She was a person who would never be old. The truism
struck Rebecca with peculiar force as she looked at her father's
face, drawn and even haggard in the dashboard light. He was
a tall well-built man and his face had a leonine quality, large
and strong-jawed and full-lipped. As a child, and even till very
recently, Rebecca had seen his solidity as something separate
and even unique. But now she could see the bones in her
father's face, and it was not only that he had lost weight
recently: he was subject to time, and she was seeing it.

'Well, it's nice to be home, at any rate,' he said.

And her mother had been right: though it wasn't full dark
yet, the lights glowing in the windows of Salters Cottage did
give it a welcoming look. The house was of rosy Victorian
brick, with a steep roof of red pantile. There was something
defiant in the way it was so sturdily planted here, within a
stone's throw of the dune bank and in sight of a sea that,
though quiescent enough now, had invaded this land within
living memory, cleaving walls and drowning farmland and
floating caravans like boats.

Years ago, Penny Larkinson had told Rebecca that the house
was haunted. People said that about old houses, of course.
Rebecca had never experienced anything there. Only this
evening, perhaps, did she feel that reluctance to enter, that
chill at the threshold traditionally associated with the haunted
house. She didn't fear anything in there, though: the prevision-
ary shudder was for what they brought with them.

Cats came flowingly to greet them as they went in. The
central heating, on a timer setting, had only just begun to bite
at the cold, but the kitchen was still warm from the Rayburn,
although it wasn't only for that reason they went in there,
Rebecca knew. The kitchen – large and quarry-tiled, with
room both for the long dining table and a love seat – was the
place where things happened. On those rare occasions when
her parents had had a row (though the word was hardly apt
compared with what she had known before her adoption)

they had had it here. The living room was a place of adjournment.

'I thought maybe baked potatoes,' her father said. 'There's some cold chicken . . . What do you think?'

'All right.' She had sat down at the dining table, and her hands began idly spinning the empty wooden bowl that stood there. Empty, because it had always been used for fruit, of which her mother was fond: she and her father did not much care for it. Soon perhaps the bowl would be put away or moved, though not with any consciousness of erasure. Thus the little changes, the creeping alterations, unmeant and inevitable.

'Maybe tea will warm us up,' he said. He set the kettle to boil and then, to Rebecca's surprise, took down the teapot from the cupboard above the drainer. They hardly ever, when her mother was alive or since, had tea from a teapot. And in this simple and trivial and even ridiculous thing Rebecca saw the most definite signal that things were not going to be all right.

Her father came and sat down opposite her at the table. His posture suggested that he was just taking the weight off his feet while he waited for the kettle to boil. Instead he began to tell it to her, there and then.

'I saw three people today. My solicitor, of course. He's rather annoyed with me. He said I don't have to do it, there's absolutely no obligation on me. Even with what they've found out, apparently. Though personally I don't see how . . . how I can avoid it. Well, it doesn't matter. It's what I want to do, so he had to go along with that.' He began running his fingertips along the grooves in the wood of the table, slowly and attentively as if he were reading braille. 'The others were Adam Dowling, the journalist, and a man called Doug Jameson. He's the solicitor for Howard Gandy, whom you've heard of. Or at least, he was the junior partner in the firm when Gandy was tried, and he's taken up the case as . . . oh, a crusade kind of thing. He's quite young, very on the ball. I made a new statement which they're going to use – Jameson and Adam Dowling, I mean – in submitting Howard Gandy's case to the Court of Appeal as a wrongful conviction.'

'I don't know anything about this, Dad. It was before you had me. I don't see—'

'I told a lie.' Her father snatched his hand away from the table as if forgoing some seductive temptation. 'Twelve years ago, when that little boy was killed here. He went missing from the camp site on the north road. It was the nineteenth of August, a Monday. They found his body in Tetby Haven later that night. The police arrested Howard Gandy for it. They charged him with murder. Part of the reason they felt confident of the charge was my testimony – what I witnessed. I was at home all that day, alone; your mother was spending the day in Ingelow. It was when we were first making the rockery in the front garden. We'd had a load of rocks and bricks delivered the day before. And that's what I was doing that day, building the rockery in the front garden, which is how I saw Howard Gandy go by, along the dunes, carrying a blue plastic sack over his shoulder. He was heading towards Tetby Haven. The sack was an exhibit at his trial. The sack he carried the little boy's body in.'

Rebecca's breathing was shallow. Hearing these details from his lips – her own father's lips – was horribly like hearing him mouth obscenities.

'So that was the statement I made to the police. And I repeated it when I was called at Howard Gandy's trial at Lincoln Crown Court. He was found guilty, though he always maintained he was innocent, and the judge sentenced him to life imprisonment. He was sent to Whateley prison, North Yorkshire, I think it is. Everybody was glad. Feeling ran very high, as you can imagine. The little boy was two and a half years old. His body was squashed and the back of his skull was fractured.'

'Oh Jesus, Dad, what is this?'

'I'm sorry. I need you to understand . . .' He looked off into the middle distance, his almost Mediterranean–dark eyes dimming; then seemed to pull himself with a physical jolt from vagueness back to precision. 'The testimony I gave was incorrect. No. The testimony I gave was untrue. I didn't see Howard Gandy go past the house that afternoon with that blue sack. I didn't see him at all. I wasn't there . . . here. For most of the day I was at Swinton-le-Marsh.'

A village a few miles north up the coast; a village much like this one. It had a church with a leaning tower. That was all Rebecca could think, though her father had paused as if the faintly ludicrous name should strike some tremendous chord with her.

'A woman called Carolyn Moyes lived there. She was a vet with a practice in Ingelow. I'm afraid at that time I'd been having an affair with her.'

He frowned and pulled his lips tight, as if someone else had spoken those words and he were deprecating them.

'But you were married to Mum then, so . . .' For a moment it didn't sink in. 'Do you mean to say . . .? Oh, Dad, you – you bastard.' She couldn't help it. 'How could you do that to Mum? I can't believe you'd – she loved you so much, and now I find you were having affairs, oh Christ, how could you?'

'One affair. Look, it was a product of the time. It started about six months before then. Your mother and myself were separate, somehow. We weren't right. It was ever since Thomas had died, the Christmas before. A thing like that doesn't necessarily unite a couple.'

'I never heard of it driving the man to have an affair, though.' Rebecca found that she had folded her arms, to hold in her swelling outrage maybe. 'So, let's work it out. Thomas died at Christmas. This Gandy thing happened in August, you were seeing this woman in August and you had been doing so for six months, so you started seeing her, what, about two months after Thomas died? Yes? Your son died of cot death and two months later you start an affair?'

'I can't explain it,' he said, seeming untouched by her hostility, 'so I certainly can't justify it. It was a bad time. Cot death – it still sounds a bit Victorian. This little wisp of a baby passing away. Hardly there in the first place. But the thing is, it doesn't just happen with newborns. Thomas was sixteen months old when he died. He'd started to walk. He could say words. He had a favourite colour. And he died. And we – me and your mother, as a unit – we fell apart. Maybe there's some high-falutin psychological term for it. We just weren't together. And I began seeing this woman. It happened.'

'You made it happen,' Rebecca said with real venom. His

38

coolness was like a goad to her hurt feelings. 'Things like that don't just happen.'

'All right. But I didn't set out to do it, I mean I didn't wake up one morning and decide to have an affair. I didn't want it to happen, and I hated the deception.'

'Oh, that's a nice bit of guilt there.' She hardly knew what she was saying: the revelation could only be batted at with bitter interjections that were like blind hands held up against an assault.

'Yes, I felt guilty because it was wrong. There was never any doubt about that. I dreaded Anna finding out. I didn't want to hurt her, because I loved her, truly loved her.'

'Why betray her then?' It was the only word, antiquely melodramatic though it was, for the way she felt. 'This is Mum we're talking about. Not by birth but she was Mum to me and she's died. And you're Dad to me, and you're telling me this . . . It just seems so awful, it's like killing her all over again. How could you? Did she know? Did she find out?'

He was gazing at her almost raptly, as if reminded of something distant and exquisitely meaningful. Then he shook his head. 'No. You've got to understand, it wasn't as if she was going about her normal life either. She was like a zombie half the time – I just couldn't reach her. That is not meant as an excuse. None of this is an excuse. I'm telling you what happened because there are going to be consequences. I lied about that day. I was supposed to be at home, working on the rockery. Anna thought I was. All that mattered was . . . Anna. Us. If you can believe me, I wanted to end it with Carolyn, that was what we were thrashing out at the time. Anna believed I was at home that day and that's what I stuck to. And if I was there like I said, I would have seen Howard Gandy go past the house towards Tetby Haven.'

'But you don't know that he did. You – you were miles away, in bed with some other woman—'

'Not in bed,' he said with precision. 'And yes, I don't know that he did because I didn't see it. But he'd been seen earlier with that sack. Obviously the whole village was talking about it; people had helped in the search for the boy. And someone had seen him earlier with that sack, on foot, going in this direction along the coast. The sequence of events seemed pretty clear. If it was Gandy who had done it, he would have passed this house on the way to Tetby Haven that afternoon. Which was the period of time he couldn't account for his movements to the police.'

'You said *if*. *If* he had done it.'

'I believed . . . God, I don't know. These campaigners seem to be making a pretty good case for him, but . . . The thing is, you had to know Howard Gandy, what he was like. Put it this way, if he'd still been around when we had you, I wouldn't have wanted you to go anywhere near him. He was a menace. Maybe not in a threatening way, but . . . he had a thing about children. Everyone round here knew it, and they simply didn't trust him. There had been complaints about him. And that very morning Diane Larkinson came knocking here, saying Gandy had been accosting her kids when they went down to the shop on their bikes. She was quite wild. She kept saying something ought to be done – you know that way she has. Almost as if she expected me to do something about it. I suppose that's ironic. Well, as soon as this little boy went missing, suspicion immediately fell on Howard Gandy. Maybe unfairly, but – no. Not when you knew him. Not when you'd been a parent. I think it was only a matter of time before something happened. So, yes. I lied. I lied to cover up what I'd been doing and I stuck to the lie because of that, because if it had once begun to unravel the whole truth would have come out and I couldn't have that, not for Anna's sake. I loved her and I didn't want to lose her . . . And I stuck to it because I believed it was true in a way. I believed, as everyone did, that Gandy was . . . well, he needed putting away.'

'Sounds like a witch-hunt.'

He gave an unamused smile. 'Maybe. But maybe with a real witch. Mine wasn't the only evidence.'

'You still lied to save your own skin.'

'You don't understand,' he said, though with more resignation than irritation. 'A little child had been taken and killed. Another young life wasted, snuffed out. Just like our Thomas. Except this was different. When Thomas died all I could do was . . . curse God, I suppose. I was helpless. But here was a child who had been killed and this time – well, someone should pay. There was this man whom everyone knew about and I could help put him away. Rebecca, what would you have done?'

She didn't answer, and his eyes showed that he felt this to be an unworthy appeal.

'All right,' he said, 'it was self-preservation mainly, I admit it. But you have to understand the way I got caught up in events, and once I was in, there was no way out, not without endangering everything that mattered to me. First and foremost I wanted to protect Anna.'

'Protect her from knowing you'd been sleeping around?'

'Yes. Yes, certainly.' Dry and bleak. 'She was lost for a long while after Thomas died, right down in the pit. She'd had a difficult time with the birth and the doctors had told her in so many words that she wouldn't be able to carry another child. And yes, before you say it – knowing all this didn't stop me having an affair. OK, well, that's for me to deal with. The point is, I knew Anna could not take any more. She had to be shielded, at whatever cost.'

'You said about the trial, about giving evidence. So you told that story on oath, in a court of law?'

'Of course. Like I said, I had to stick to it. I don't imagine that was the first lie ever told in a court. Obviously this is why my solicitor's nervy now. It raises the question of perjury. But apparently it's possible to put a gloss on it, that you made an honest mistake at the time because you were under stress and so on.'

'Oh well, that's all right then.'

He looked hard at her. 'But I don't particularly care about that. I'll take whatever's coming. I admit that I may have done wrong, but I'm trying to explain that at the time it wasn't so easy to see what was wrong and what was right. There was Carolyn, too; she was already – very troubled about what we were doing, and—'

'Don't say her name to me. How can you say her name to me like that?' Try as she might, Rebecca couldn't hold in her anger and pain.

'I never, in my life, meant to hurt your mother. I can only ask you to believe that. It was a bad time, the worst time. It ended. We started again, with you. Thank God we were able to.'

'What happened to her?' Glaring at him, Rebecca put a hateful spin on that last word.

'Carolyn? She moved to Ireland not long after. She'd had it in mind for a while. She had family there. That's all I know.'

The kettle had boiled some time since. Now her father got up, filled the teapot, and brought it back to the table. He placed it there, without cups or milk or sugar, and stared at it as if it were some magical artefact.

'In situations of terrible grief, people aren't quite themselves,' he said after a few moments. 'This is something that bereavement counselling can't help with, as far as I can see. You can't help a person who's not there. It took a long time after we lost Thomas for your mother and me to find each other again. Maybe . . .' his glance was assessing yet somehow timid, 'maybe something similar's been happening with you and me. Since Anna died.'

Rebecca didn't want to give him anything – not even an acknowledgement of the truth of this.

'I wouldn't know. How could I? You've said yourself, everything's lies. You were lying to Mum all those years ago. You lied to the police and at this trial. I mean, how am I to know what is the real you? What about since I've been with you – maybe you've been playing around all the time—'

'Never since then. It was an episode. I loved your mother and I loved her till she died. You'll just have to believe me.'

'I suppose I will. I haven't got any choice in this, have I? Just don't expect me to applaud you. It's a bit late for an attack of conscience.'

'Funny. That's just what my solicitor said. Maybe I would never have come out with it if it hadn't been for Adam Dowling. After Anna died I did keep . . . turning things over in my mind. Perhaps there's something about death that makes you – want to be clean. But as it happened, Dowling's forced my hand. When I met him in London the other week, he had some news for me that I really couldn't ignore. The chap's really done his homework.'

'He knows you lied?'

'He knows the evidence I gave doesn't stand up. I stuck by it at the time in reasonable confidence that it wouldn't be exposed. Like I said, everything pointed towards that version of events. And to be honest it wasn't really scrutinized. Now it turns out that Dowling's found a witness who saw me at Carolyn's place that day.'

For a moment Rebecca felt like laughing. Into these grim events were being woven strands of bedroom farce, of wry comeuppance. It was, in fact, unreal, and something of this must have been expressed in her slow shake of the head.

'I know,' her father said. 'I didn't believe it either at first. I thought it must be some kind of con to get me to co-operate. After all, we're talking about a journalist here. Not a tabloid one, maybe, but still . . . It's not their job to be scrupulous. But this is for real. A woman called Jenny Pearce saw me at Carolyn's that day. Saw my car parked there the whole time, saw me go.'

'But how can she be so sure after all this time?'

'She probably couldn't. But she did make a statement to the police that very day. It was what they call an untendered statement. Nobody spotted the relevance of it. The police took it when the little boy was still only missing. This woman had driven past the camp site on her way to the village that morning, so the police wanted every scrap of information – had she seen anything, whatever. Her information incidentally included me being at Carolyn's, just down the road from her place. That was when I had the old white Rover with the personalised numberplate, crazy extravagance that was. And pretty distinctive. She noticed it was there most of the day, and she saw me leave. I dare say I looked rather furtive,' he said, grimacing and lighting a cigar. 'Of course, when the little boy went missing the police must have taken statements galore from everybody in a ten-mile radius. It was a big hunt. It seems there was a mountain of transcripts for the case. Adam Dowling, to do him credit, has gone through the whole lot. And by himself – I don't think he has any staff. And he's unearthed this statement by Jenny Pearce. I don't think there's any question of the police being dodgy and holding it back or anything like that. There was just so much. Well, Dowling's tracked down Jenny Pearce. She lives in Durham now. She's prepared to say that was her statement but she says she can't really remember at this distance and really doesn't want to get involved. Which leaves it up to me, in a way.'

'You've admitted it?' she said. The smell of the cigar was familiar and comforting. It made a confusing crosscurrent with the antagonism she was feeling towards her father.

'Yes. When Dowling came up with this, I really didn't see any other option. In a way it was a relief. Anna couldn't be hurt by it any more. There was nothing to lose. I hold no brief for Howard Gandy one way or another. I personally think he's dangerous and should be locked up. But he's done nearly twelve years and, I don't know, if they really have a case for him then I'll go along with it. As long as the truth's out and Anna can't be hurt.'

Rebecca got up to fetch two cups. She placed them on the table, went to the fridge for the milk. Her father was watching her back – its straight stiffness which she couldn't control.

'When I say nothing to lose,' he said distinctly, 'I'm aware that there is. Of course there is. Your respect. That's why I . . . need to explain it to you. I'm not asking you to tell me I'm doing the right thing, absolve me, anything like that.'

'I wasn't around.' She busied herself making tea, aware as she did so that she could hardly have chosen an action more suitable to prim, finicking, martyred disapproval. 'It was a thing between you and Mum. Or you and Mum and Carol, or whatever her name was. No, I don't like to think of you cheating on Mum. And covering it up with this really dodgy lie. It stinks, Dad. The whole thing stinks. But you knew that, didn't you?'

'Yes. I knew that.'

'But you managed to cope with it for twelve years.' She gave him a full look.

'Sure. Stranger things have happened. It was a lie but it saved me and your mother's marriage. It meant we still had a basis to carry on. We did carry on, and it was good. We found each other again. We adopted you, and we had a – well, I would call it a wonderful family life. All of that came from the lie.'

Stymied, suddenly feeling close to tears for no clearer reason than a surfeit of emotion, Rebecca stared at her tea. She groped for contradictions that had become slippery.

'That night at Tetby Haven,' she said at last, 'you said you'd made a mistake.'

He nodded. 'That was how it appeared to me just then. If it's a question of whether I would do the same again, then . . . maybe I would. In the light of what I've just said. But I'm prepared to call it a mistake for this campaign of Dowling's. I still wouldn't waste any sympathy on Howard Gandy, but if his conviction was unsound then – then maybe he should be released. I'm still not saying it's ever right to lie, if that makes any sense. I think all lies taint. So I'm prepared to admit the possibility that it was a mistake and to act accordingly. That's all.'

The subtlety, like the cigar smoke, was so utterly and lovably characteristic of her father that again it was strange to feel herself at odds with him.

'Will they let this Gandy guy out of prison? With your new evidence?'

'Oh, well, that's still in the lap of the gods. Gandy's solicitor seems to think they have a very good chance of getting his case to the Appeal Court. Apparently now there's a body called the Criminal Cases Review Commission that deals with these things. They recommend a case for appeal, and then it's up to the judges whether to overturn the conviction or say no and send the guy back to prison.'

'I wonder if his mother knows about this.'

'Probably. I haven't seen her around for a while. I don't think she gets out much.'

'How about if they do let him out, and he comes home?'

Her father shrugged, though she read discomfort in the movement. 'There'll be a lot of hostility towards him, no doubt.'

'And what about you?'

'Like I said, I never trusted him and that wouldn't change even—'

'I mean, what about hostility towards you for this part you've played in the whole thing?'

He tasted his tea. 'Well, if it comes, I'm prepared for it. There are worse things. It really depends on what kind of publicity Adam Dowling gives to it all, if he gets his result. He said something about a book.'

'What?'

'He had quite a successful book out a couple of years ago,

45

apparently, about satanic abuse cases. You know, debunking the whole business. *Devil's Work*, that was it. I haven't read it. But he made it clear he wants to follow this thing up. That's his trade, after all.'

'Can't you stop him?'

'I don't suppose I'm in a position to.'

His apparent unconcern made her blaze. 'Great. So the whole world will know about it. How do you think that would make Mum feel?'

Her father had the capacity for instant stubbornness. 'Mum,' he said, 'will not feel anything, Rebecca. Hard, I know, but true. That's the whole point of me going through with this. She can't be hurt any more.'

'No,' Rebecca said, getting up from the table. 'She can't, can she?'

'Where are you going?'

At the hall door she turned, and was pinned there for a moment by the past. For this was precisely how it used to be, when the tantrums of her early adolescence would send her fuming to the door, her father not seeking to pull her back, not even sitting forward in his chair, but simply allowing his intense reasonableness to reach out to her.

But something had been lost. The reason and sanity and adulthood seemed to belong more to her side now, and it was a horrible transformation. She hated him for what he had destroyed: himself.

'There's something called perverting the course of justice, isn't there?' she said bitterly. 'Surely you've done that. If they find this Gandy's innocent, then that means you let the real killer go free. Somebody killed a little boy and got away with it.'

'I don't accept that,' he said after a moment.

Rebecca shook her head and went to her room, leaving him sitting there, diminished.

# FOUR

O, yet we trust that somehow good
Will be the final goal of ill.

The lines of Tennyson, set to her father's music, were in
Rebecca's head when she woke up. His setting of parts of *In
Memoriam* for tenor and small ensemble had made his name
as a composer, and it was one of the few pieces of his that she
could readily respond to. She lay for a few minutes dwelling
drowsily on the melody. Then, invaded by memory of last
night, she grew angry. She banished the tune and got quickly
out of bed.

Waking proved she must have slept, but she could only
remember writhing and beating the pillow and watching the
ivy tendrils at her window weakly battering the glass in the
wind off the sea. As she showered the revelations of yesterday
came back to her as fully as a well-learned script. The closing
scene showed her father standing in her bedroom door, his
shoulders slumped, asking without hope that they should talk
some more: his stubbornness against hers.

It was nearly seven o'clock – to Rebecca, an almost shock-
ingly early hour. She was surprised at how light it was, her
mental map fixing seven in the morning as a time of Stygian
darkness. She was glad all the same. Her father was a late riser
and she didn't want, this morning, to have to face him across
the breakfast table. Going through the motions of normality
would be awful. Best to get out.

Maybe she had fallen into the trap of being disappointed
that her father was human, as she had lamented that her
mother was mortal. Also she had probably sounded, last night,
far more morally grim than she was. In fact she didn't object
to the lie as such. She herself would always place loyalty above

truth, and would have condoned a lie to protect a loved one. Nevertheless she still burnt, with outrage and hurt. The hurt might have been on her mother's behalf, but it felt like her own.

Downstairs, moving with deliberate quietness, she made a cup of coffee and drank it standing up, looking at the pinboard in the kitchen. A photograph of herself at eight years old, when she had first come to her mother and father, walking with them on the beach: undersized and wary, a little old-faced creature captured by giants and wondering what its fate would be. This shot was taken perhaps only a year after the events her father had related last night: only a year after he had been in the arms of another woman. Yet the couple in the picture, sheltering her so tenderly with their twin presence, still looked to her as they had been when she was a child – the apogee of devoted union, the inverse of the combat and duplicity that was all she had known of adult relationships before her adoption.

Now she knew there was a deadly flaw in that picture. And that made life hard to bear at the moment.

In this house, at least; and there was no very clear idea of her destination in her mind when she left the house, only a desire for escape. A place must have been forming in the back of her mind, though, because she set out on her bicycle, scarcely used unless she was going some distance. As she rode out of the drive into the lane it occurred to her that she should have left her father a note . . . but the adolescent part of her was still in the mood to punish, and decided against it.

She rode down the High Street of the long strung-out village, herself the only traffic apart from a young woman in riding hat and jodhpurs loftily astride a grey horse coming in the other direction. There was a surprisingly strong country-living element on this austere coast, but in an impure form. Expensive cottage conversions stood next to cheap retirement bungalows with peeling wood trim and sunburst fanlights, and the camp site and caravan park threw its ramshackle outworks right up to their rear gardens. It was a working community too. People went to their jobs in the large seaside town of Ingelow from here, an easy distance along the coast road, and there was even local employment – a vegetable canning factory called Coupland's that stood just outside the village, artfully screened by a double avenue of trees. All in all it was a good place to live, to bring up a family: safe . . . But then there had been Howard Gandy.

She had turned and was cycling down Hythe Avenue before she knew it. For no clear reason she had to look at Mrs Gandy's house.

Mrs Pat Gandy – a lean, small, rather hard-faced woman with short straight grey hair, usually wearing a car coat and trousers or slacks on the rare occasions she was seen about, making a brisk and unspeaking trip to the village shop or the postbox. She used to work at Coupland's, Rebecca remembered: and to her knowledge there was no Mr Gandy and never really had been. That was all she knew of this elusive figure – that and her shadowy notoriety as the mother of a man who was in prison for committing an appalling crime.

The house was the last in the road, a semi-detached council house fronted with pebbledash the colour of porridge, old and weathered, and with small metal-framed windows screened by greyish net curtains. The front garden was fenced by a privet hedge so vastly, chaotically overgrown that it had begun forming fantastical shapes, staggering over the path and shooting great stalks of foliage straight upward. Rebecca rode slowly past, with a tingling consciousness that was entirely new – a sense of linked destinies. Also she felt a little ashamed. She had never before speculated, as she did now, on what Pat Gandy must do and what she must think and feel, living alone in that house, a semi-hermit, joined to the outer world only by the steely fact that her son was a convicted murderer. She hadn't speculated because Pat Gandy had been a person who was nothing to do with her. Now it was different. The lines were open.

A child had been killed. Riding away from Holfleet, away from the doleful porridge-coloured house and northwards along the coast road between bare dewy meadows, Rebecca reflected that she could not even recall the child's name. She must have heard it at some time, but the name that always took precedence when the case was mentioned locally or referred to in the press was the name of the killer, Howard Gandy, the Pied Piper – though that was just a journalistic

49

invention. The name of the little boy had faded. Perhaps it was hard to keep alive the memory of a small child, so tentatively located in the world in the first place. Even Thomas, the lost child of her mother and father, was an abstraction to her – though he had not always been so. When the 'honeymoon period' of her adoption was over and she had begun kicking against her new parents, testing them, sounding their love for the flaw that experience had taught her must surely be there, the thought of Thomas had been a gall to her. A mild reprimand would send her into a jealous rage and she would scream their unfairness at them: they would never be nasty to Thomas like this, they would always love him best . . . Her cheeks burnt with the memory of it.

She remembered too her father's godly patience when in one of those tantrums she had torn and savaged a teddy bear that had belonged to Thomas. Even at the time her raging heart had felt the impress of goodness in the way he reacted to this. And yet it was not long after the death of Thomas that her father had begun an affair with another woman. How did you make sense of that? How did you take it on board without mentally capsizing?

Maybe she had come here looking for an answer. Swinton-le-Marsh: the village had one of those pictorial signs, oddly Art Nouveau-looking, showing the leaning church tower. The miles had passed swiftly: the air was still morning-sharp but a convalescent sun was making mild gold on the seaward marsh. She supposed this had been her secret destination from the moment she left the house. Something, needing to be satisfied, had driven her here: the place where a woman named Carolyn Moyes had lived.

But she didn't live here any more, and Rebecca, dismounting and pushing her cycle, had no way of knowing which had been her house. Dutch-gabled brick cottages, bungalows, a big stone house that looked like a converted rectory . . . Mrs Gandy's house seemed physically to express the years of shame and seclusion: perhaps the house of Carolyn Moyes would exude its past too, ooze its shabby and sordid secret through its very bricks. She could have knocked on doors and asked if anybody remembered, but the question remained of what she would do then. She felt hate and wanted to get close to the

situation became. But this lady's hair just grew in natural soft masses. It was something of a revelation to Rebecca's young mind that nature could be gone along with, rather than fought at every step. Odd that something as simple as a woman's hair should tip the balance for her: ironic that in the last stage of her illness, Anna Springthorpe had lost it and had to resort to the height of artifice, a wig.

They had never, as far as she knew, despaired of her or regretted their choice. Finding her inarticulate, practically illiterate, and chronically prone to pilfering and fibbing, they hadn't rushed to redesign her: they had worked with time rather than against it.

They had brought her up: lifted her up. As she thought of it she found it less and less easy to be severe with her father. Judgement: how everybody loved to pass it. The instinct to blame, it seemed, was as deep as the sex urge and no more controllable. And there was, after all, a good side to what had come out: an innocent man would be released from prison. A settling of accounts.

Except, of course, that someone *was* to blame. You could blow away all the lies and rumours and half-truths, but somebody still took a little boy away from a holiday camp site, in her own village, and killed him.

Who?

All at once Rebecca felt unnerved. Looking about her at the bleak strand, she realized how alone she was. And how protected she had been. There in the house on the salt coast, she had been shielded from evil by her mother and father. Her mother was gone but her father lived, and needed her as much as she needed him.

She rode fast, pedalling furiously, welcoming the wind that stung her cheeks. She wanted to be home, to see her father, to continue with life no matter how compromised and problematical it was.

A couple of miles short of Holfleet, the chain came off her cycle, in the middle of the country road.

Normally she was deft and quick with small practical tasks. But the chain, oily, evil-minded, defeated her chilled fingers.

Swearing in a fluent stream, she noticed that a car had drawn to a stop beside her.

'Trouble?'

Their neighbour Diane Larkinson, at the wheel of her chunky four-wheel drive, countered her sympathetic look with a glance at her watch.

'The chain. I can't fix it. It's—'

'Nuisance. I can give you a lift if it's home you're headed.'

'Oh, thanks.' Rebecca hesitated.

'I dare say it'll go on the roof rack.'

A woman in a hurry, Diane Larkinson got out, helped her lift the cycle on to the roof rack and fixed it with elasticated hooks. She was workout-slim in a white jump suit with pixie boots, and was glowingly made up. She was an inveterate shopper who never passed a month without a new outfit, but curiously she looked perennially caught in a certain style moment, perhaps 1981.

'You must be frozen. Jump in, I'm running late.' Diane Larkinson was ever thus, self-importantly rushed for time as if she were a district nurse with breech births awaiting her all along the coast. But she didn't do anything except a kind of pretend business involving the pyramid selling of herbal remedies. Her trifling stock was on the back seat. Climbing in the front, Rebecca had an uneasy feeling she would get sand on the spotless upholstery and that Diane would notice.

'Thanks ever so much. Don't know what I'd have done.'

'Well, pushed it home, I suppose,' said Diane, always literal-minded. 'Seat belt. You're up and about bright and early.'

'Yes. I went for a bike ride.'

'Unusual. So, how's Philip coping? Your dad, I mean.'

'He's fine. Busy. He's got a commission for TV music.'

'Can't be easy for him. Managing on his own. Without Anna, I mean.'

'Well, he still misses Mum. Same as I do. But we're doing OK.'

Diane Larkinson's frosted lips pouted, withholding comment. The airy talk of Philip and Anna was not mere absent-mindedness. The Larkinsons, who lived in a plush vicarage conversion in Holfleet and nurtured some lord-of-the-manor pretensions, had known the Springthorpes before they adopted Rebecca. Their twins, Penny and Stephen, were Rebecca's age, and they had hung around together as children – but

Rebecca had never felt this was entirely approved. Diane's view, she knew, was that you could take the girl out of the gutter but you couldn't take the gutter out of the girl. That this was not mere chippy paranoia on Rebecca's part was shown by an incident that had happened when she was about ten. She came calling for Penny Larkinson wearing her new roller skates. 'You lucky devil,' was the admiring, unbarbed comment of Penny, an easy-going girl, before running upstairs to fetch her own; but while Rebecca waited, Diane Larkinson had treated her to some acid observations about her good fortune.

'Yes, you're a very lucky girl, aren't you?' she had said, darting about the kitchen in her conspicuously overworked way, though they had a daily cleaner and everything was spotless. 'Very lucky indeed, when you think about it. I'll bet you never thought you'd come to live in a house like your mum and dad's, did you? There must be a lot of children who'd be quite jealous of you. They must think it's not quite fair, really. The way you've ended up. I should think you feel like you've died and gone to heaven, don't you? Hm?'

'No,' Rebecca said: because that wasn't how it felt at all.

'No?' Diane gave her a look of flat dislike leavened with disbelief. 'I should have thought you would. They have done a heck of a lot for you, you know. And they didn't have to. There was no need for them to take you on. Out of the goodness of their hearts.' She took hold of a perfectly unwrinkled tea-towel and shook it out violently, with a crack in the air like a pistol shot. 'You should count yourself lucky. It's not really where you belong, is it? So you should jolly well count your blessings, I think.'

Rebecca had never spoken of it, and never forgotten it.

'Well, of course, it goes on, life,' Diane said now. Her speech was full of these strange inversions, as if literally translated from French. She glanced at herself, tanned and bouffant, in the rearview mirror; and at Rebecca. 'So, where is it you're going to college? Warwick?'

'York.'

Diane made an impatient mouth, as if it were the same thing. 'October, I presume. It'll be an experience for you. Penny's having the time of her life at Bristol. Hard work, though. You can't get away with just lounging through it, not in this day and age. They really sort the sheep from the goats. So, till then you're going to be doing what with yourself?'

'I was going to look for a seasonal job in Ingelow.'

'Oh well, we all have to do it,' Diane lectured, as if Rebecca had complained at the prospect. 'Nothing comes for free in this world. I suppose that'll mean Philip will be on his own, when you've gone off to college. Well, never mind, we're always there for him. What is it you're studying?'

'Sociology.'

'Really.' They had reached the junction at the turning into Holfleet: Diane checked and rubbernecked as urgently as if the empty road were Piccadilly Circus. 'What does that lead on to, I wonder. Or perhaps you haven't thought about that.'

'I'd like to work with children one day.'

'Fancy that,' Diane said – rather as if Rebecca had said she wanted to be a clown or a spaceman. 'Stephen's in Turkey, did you know? He's doing voluntary service. No holidays for him . . .'

Rebecca wasn't listening.

She was transfixed by the sight of Pat Gandy, trudging along the soft verge at the side of the road into the village. Though she had her back to the car, there was no doubt that it was she: her hands were dug into the pockets of an ancient green car coat and her small, grey, birdlike head was lowered.

She was so close to the edge of the road that Diane Larkinson might with reason have edged the car out a little as she passed. But this she did not do, and the slipstream of the powerful car caught Mrs Gandy like a fragment of a gale, ruffling her boyish crop of hair and making her sway a little.

Making her, also, turn her head and look wincing into the car. It was a wince more in weariness than protest. Her lined face had the look of a patient animal. It even seemed to Rebecca that Pat Gandy would not have been shocked, only sorrowfully resigned, if the car had run her down.

Their eyes had met, Rebecca thought, but she couldn't be sure.

'That was Pat Gandy, wasn't it?' she said eagerly.

'Was it? I dare say it was. Not very often you see her crawl out of her hole.'

'I don't really know her.'

'You haven't missed much.'

'Do you?'

'Well, as much as I want to. Look at that, they still haven't repaired that window. It's such an eyesore.'

'What about her son? Howard? What was he like?'

'Good Lord, that's not a very wholesome subject for a nice morning.' Diane gave a cool laugh. 'What's this, getting ready for sociology?'

'I was just wondering. I never saw him. I've only heard about him.'

'Well, you're lucky then.' *A very lucky girl.* 'I don't want anything to do with that business, thank you very much. They put him away and that's all I'm concerned about. We had some person from the press on to us a while back, before Christmas I think it was, wanting to dig the whole thing up. I said no thank you very much, nothing to say.'

Adam Dowling, Rebecca thought. Though she had spoken to him, briefly enough, on the phone, she had never seen him either, and she wondered with a sudden and intense curiosity what he looked like.

'Apparently,' she said, cautious but incautious, 'there's a campaign to get him released.'

'Is there now?' Diane's chin went up. 'Where did you hear that?'

'Oh, I read about it.'

'Well, you can count me out of that campaign.' Diane turned into the lane leading to Salters Cottage. 'I shall have to dash, but you'll give my best to Philip, won't you? Your dad, I mean. No, you don't want to know about that revolting specimen, believe me, Rebecca.'

'That's what everyone says.'

'Then they're right. Actually I have only one regret about that business, personally speaking,' Diane added with a kind of hostessy brightness. 'And that's that they didn't hang him.'

Going into the house, with the engine of Diane Larkinson's car purring away up the lane, Rebecca felt as shocked as if she had seen a bloody brawl in the street. There was real hate there, in Diane's words, vituperative and vicious. Last night she had said, in her hurt indignation, that the feeling against

Howard Gandy sounded like a witch-hunt: perhaps those words were truer than she knew.

And her own father had played a rather sordid part in it – yet she longed to see him now and was crestfallen when she saw the note on the kitchen table: *Rebecca. The Stamford people rang. I've had to go over there to sort things out with the hall. Back this afternoon. Hope you're OK. Let's talk later. Lots of love, Dad.*

He was involved in the setting up of a weekend event for young musicians in the old limestone town of Stamford. It was taking up a lot of time that he gave willingly: that was his way.

The villain of the piece.

Life was just too confusing, she thought, slaking young thirst with half a pint of juice from the fridge. She could hate what her father had done twelve years ago, but she couldn't hate her father, not without tearing up the very roots of her own self. And if she were to label what her father had done as villainous, then what word would suffice for the cold-blooded killing of a little child?

It was that unthinkable act that was reaching out its long shadow to touch them. She wished she could remember the name of that unknown little boy with whom she found her life strangely linked. Howard Gandy had a determined campaigner on his side; but who was there to speak for that little boy?

She lingered again by the photograph on the pinboard, examining her small self protected by her parents: imagined a darker shade than theirs falling across that tiny life, snuffing it out. How easily it could have happened: how infinitely far beyond forgiveness such an act was. To kill a child was not just to stop life: it wiped out possibilities, it subtracted from the world. It was, genuinely, devilish.

Who? Why?

A car engine coughed in the lane outside, and her heart rose at the thought that her father might have come back. But the engine note was unfamiliar, and a few moments later a knock at the front door told her she had a visitor.

# FIVE

'Ah, hello. Sorry to disturb you. Is Mr Springthorpe in?'

'No, he's not . . . He's out.'

'Oh, that's a pity. Any idea when he'll be back? He wasn't actually expecting me but I thought I'd call on the off chance. My name's Adam Dowling.'

'He's gone to Stamford,' Rebecca said. 'I don't know when he'll be back.'

'Well, not to worry. Only I'm going back to London tonight. I've been staying in Lincoln. I was over this way and I just thought I'd call for a chat before—'

'I know you've been in Lincoln. He had to see you yesterday.'

'He didn't have to. It was something we agreed.' Adam Dowling spoke coolly, peaceably. 'You must be Rebecca. I believe we've spoken on the phone.'

'Yes. When I told you to leave us alone.'

He smiled. 'I'm sorry if I've been a nuisance. But it was an important matter.'

'Well, to you, maybe.' After the grey areas, the doubt and confusion, it was some satisfaction to be presented with a target.

'Yes. Others too.' A fractional hesitation. 'I don't know how much your father's told you.'

'Some of it. Well, the stuff that matters.' She gave the young man in the porch a full look. She was conscious that she would never have learnt that disillusioning, destructive thing if it were not for this man . . . but she was conscious too that hostility to him was rather like killing the messenger.

'Look, I do understand. That sounds patronizing, I'm sorry. But I do. I'm not a baddie in a black hat. I'm not trying to hurt anyone. We could talk about it if you like. You can ask me anything you want.'

She shrugged. 'Well, if you want to come in . . .'

'Thanks. My car'll be all right there, will it?' Stepping over the threshold he paused and gave her an oddly subtle look. 'You won't accuse me of foot-in-the-door journalism, then?'

She didn't know how to reply to that.

'Would you like coffee?' she said, leading him into the kitchen.

'Thanks.' He sat down at the table – the very seat she had sat in yesterday while her father unlocked the skeleton closet before her eyes. She felt this ought to be either poetically appropriate or hideously inappropriate. But she couldn't get a fix on any feelings at all, and she didn't know what to make of Adam Dowling. The word journalist called up images that were seedy or slick, but he was neither, more like a fresh-faced undergraduate than anything. He must have been at least ten years her senior but only the slight receding of his short fair hair aged him physically – that and his assurance, which while not cocky or overbearing was marked enough to make her feel how completely she lacked it. His eyes were a noticeable blue, his face lean, square, the nose quite short and the eyebrows arched: a Scandinavian kind of handsomeness. Of course she did not really expect a grey mackintosh and a slouch hat in the B-movie reporter style, but still the black jeans and fisherman's jersey slightly surprised her.

'I don't understand why you have to come bothering him again,' she said: her father's defender now. 'I thought that was what yesterday was all about.'

'I just wanted to say thanks to him, personally. What he's doing takes a lot of guts. And I'm genuinely grateful to him. That goes for everybody connected with the campaign. Again, I don't know how much you're aware of. I mean . . .'

'I know why he's changing his evidence.' Arms folded, she waited on the coffee, trying to be clear-headed, even-handed. 'About what happened that day the little boy was killed. He's told me. It was a shock.' Feeling herself closely watched, she went on hurriedly, 'I mean, I'd heard about this Gandy thing – everyone round here has – but I never thought it

60

would have anything to do with us, not now.'

'Well. I was in Holfleet anyway, so I thought I'd look in. Our meeting yesterday was quite amicable, so I thought it'd be all right.'

'Why in Holfleet?'

'Oh, I'm going to see Mrs Gandy. Pat. You probably know her.'

'Yes, of course,' she said, frowning as she poured the coffee, aware that that was less than the truth. 'How is she?'

'She's well. Trying not to build her hopes up, which is probably wise. Thank you.' He took the coffee from her. 'You know, obviously, that I'm trying to get her son's conviction overturned. Your father's been helping with that. Things are looking good. But it's best not to count our chickens.'

'Looking good for who? I mean, is this a guy who should be out of prison?'

'Yes, it is.'

'Can you be sure? I don't know all the details, but I've heard the story. It's pretty horrible.'

'Well, the details are quite simple. A child was murdered near here twelve years ago. His name was Lee Brudenell.'

She remembered the name faintly now. Hearing it spoken made an abstraction suddenly very real.

'It was Monday, the nineteenth of August. A young couple named Colin and Lorraine Brudenell were on a camping holiday with their son. He was two and a half. They'd got here the day before, from Nottingham. Around one Colin Brudenell went up to the village, to the pub, and Lorraine stayed at the site with Lee. She dozed off in a sun lounger outside the tent. When she woke up there was no sign of Lee. Colin came back soon afterwards. They searched; they were frantic as you can imagine. Eventually the police were called and they set up a huge search – ten-mile radius, volunteers, dogs. They found Lee just before nine that night, in Tetby Haven. He had crushed ribs and a fractured skull. He was clothed and there was no sign of sexual interference. Been dead for four to eight hours.' He made a grimace of apology. 'Horrible, as you said. Well, the next day the police arrested Howard Gandy for that murder. He firmly protested his innocence, then as now. He was found guilty at Lincoln Crown Court and sentenced to life imprisonment with a recommended minimum twenty years. And he's been in Whateley jail ever since.'

'And now you're going to get him out.'

'I've taken up his case, along with a very good solicitor, and we're hoping to get it to the Appeal Court. So as to – yes, get him out.'

'Nobody was sorry he was put away, though, from what I've heard. Even—' She looked away. 'Even my dad.'

Adam Dowling nodded. 'Yes. Howard was made out to be a monster. Even before the murder, he wasn't liked. Well, Howard Gandy can be an awkward man, and he's maybe something of a misfit in our modern society. But in many ways he's a very nice man. I've got to know him well over the past year. He's very sensible and has quite a lot of insight, and he's amazingly well balanced and good-humoured under the circumstances. An example to us all, really.'

'So you want to let him out because he's a nice man. I mean, I'm sorry, I'm not being cynical, but this is just like Myra Hindley or somebody – you know, when they get all saintly in prison and along comes a do-gooder who thinks how nice they are and wants to set them free. Isn't it?'

'Myra Hindley did it,' he said. 'That's the essential difference. She was guilty of those crimes, and for that very reason I personally wouldn't waste any sympathy on her. Howard Gandy is a different case. He's innocent. That's why he should be free. He could be the most unpleasant man in the world but if he was innocent, I would still say he should be freed. And all the evidence I've found shows that he is an innocent man.'

'Well. You've obviously done a lot of . . . digging around.' She put a distasteful accent on those words, though actually her imagination was rather caught by the idea.

'Mostly it's a matter of going over old ground. Though the case is twelve years old, you can get hold of everything to do with it if you've got the patience. That's what I've had to do. Every single witness statement, court transcripts, custody records . . . mountains of stuff. But the Appeal Court will only sit up for something new. That's where you need a break. Your father gave us that break.'

'Only when you blackmailed him,' Rebecca said: she

couldn't resist it, for she felt that he was overstating to butter her up.

'I don't see that. I found that your father's evidence didn't match with other facts not revealed at the time of the trial. I contacted him with this, and he agreed to co-operate. In fact I think he's glad to set things straight. There's a slight risk of a perjury charge but he's aware of it, and he's quite willing to go ahead.'

'What if my mum wasn't dead?' She said it brutally because she found him a little too glib: she wanted to wrong-foot him. 'And you've found out this stuff that would really hurt her if she knew. Would you have still come out with it?'

'I don't know. It's hypothetical. But probably, yes.'

'And doesn't that say it all?'

'But I didn't make that happen. Whatever was going on with your parents back then – I didn't create that. It's just part of the truth, and the truth is all I'm interested in.'

'It doesn't work like that, though. It's not very nice learning these secrets about people you thought you knew. It's not very nice to think – well, *if* this Gandy is innocent, then it's not very nice to think my dad helped put him away.'

'Oh, your father didn't do that. He fell in with the prejudice of the time, maybe: he fell in with a handy fiction. But he's told me what a bad time he and your mother were going through, that he wasn't himself, and I accept that. No, the police and the jury and the judge sent Howard to prison. Driven by hysteria. And so he's had twelve years of hell.'

'Is it that bad where he is? I mean, you hear about that Hindley's fellow, Brady – he seems pretty cosy.'

'Brady's in a psychiatric unit. He's officially nuts. Howard Gandy is in an ordinary prison. And he's not segregated at all. He lives alongside all the other prisoners, and they don't take kindly to child-killers. Howard could be segregated for his own protection, if he chose. But he refuses because that would be like giving in, admitting guilt. His belief in himself has kept him going all this time. Now no one can give those twelve lost years back to him. But we can at least make sure they don't become thirteen and fourteen and so on.'

She had been prepared to tell him not to preach to her. But it didn't strike her as preaching. His tone was cool and reasonable: she envied that fluency, being a person who often stumbled from thought to words like someone rushing into a dark room.

'They don't put people in prison for life for nothing,' she said. 'All right, I know about the Birmingham Six and all that, but that's different. Those were terrorism cases and you've got politics involved. But there can't have been some great conspiracy against Howard Gandy.'

'No. There didn't need to be. I think he was judged guilty even before he was ever tried, simply because of his reputation.'

'And didn't he deserve his reputation? Everybody seems to think he was . . . well, creepy with children.'

'This is exactly the point. He liked children, still does. It's maybe an eccentricity. But I think we've become hysterical about this. Our culture's getting frightened of its own children. I can see a time coming when we'll ban Father Christmas.'

'Oh, come on.'

'I'm serious. Look at the representations of him on Christmas cards and so on. He has children around him and he's smiling down at them. Because he loves children and he's based on St Nicholas, the patron saint of children. Throughout Dickens you have characters who love children, and it's usually a sign of their goodness. Mr Dick in *David Copperfield* – nowadays we'd call him an abuser.'

'You're exaggerating.'

'I am slightly. To make the point. I'm not making light of child abuse. But I think in our obsessive fears about the subject we're on our way to inflicting a new kind of cruelty on children. We're going to make them live in a lonely, fearful world of their own. They'll see fun and affection going on amongst adults, but they'll be a caste apart, moving through a shadowy life of suspicion and guilt. We'll actually be poisoning the innocence we're trying to protect.'

'I see what you're saying,' she said cautiously; it was a contentious argument, and she wasn't sure where she stood on it. 'Sounds as if you could write a book about it, anyway.'

'All being well, I hope to.'

'Yes. Dad said something about that.' She suddenly felt his persuasiveness as a blind, and determined to pin him down. 'Presumably if you're telling the whole story, it'll include my family's private life. In print. Intimate hurtful things. But you're not all moral about that, are you?'

He conceded the point with a wry mouth. 'OK. But I've done nothing, and don't intend doing anything, without your father's consent. And yours.' He hesitated, then added, 'In fact, I'll let you see beforehand, and vet, anything I write.'

'Just vet it? Or veto it?'

'Oh, a journalist could never accept that kind of proscription,' he said with a slight laugh.

It was some satisfaction anyhow: she felt she had stood up for her mother. Then she thought again of the photograph on the pinboard, and said seriously, 'It's got to be worthwhile, though, hasn't it? If people are going to get hurt like this. There's got to be justice at the end. Total justice. Not just your man being let out, if he's innocent. Because if he is, then whoever killed that little boy is walking free right now, aren't they?'

'Yes. Yes, certainly. Someone still has that blood on their hands, right enough.'

'Which is just as – unjust, and wrong, as an innocent man being in prison, surely?'

He inclined his head.

'Do you know who did do it?'

'Well, the aim of the campaign has simply been to overturn Howard Gandy's conviction.'

'But you've really gone into the case, like you said. You've been through every detail. Surely you should be the one to pinpoint the truth – the person who killed him. Lee Brudenell.'

'True,' he said. 'Not that I can promise that. All my work's gone into preparing Howard's case for appeal. It would be the ideal justice, though.'

'I think it would make things better. I mean, I think it's what my mum would want.'

She felt the crude audacity of this: Adam Dowling, though, seemed to admire it.

'You do it very well,' he said.

'What?'

'Needle me. I'd better be going. I'm glad we've met. What you said – I really have taken it on board. If you could tell your father I called . . .'

She watched him go to his car. His words suggested that she had won some kind of victory, but Rebecca wasn't sure which one of them had really been won over.

# SIX

Mrs Pat Gandy wasn't in the habit of praying, but it was an impulse to prayer that filled her after Adam Dowling had left, even if the only outlet she found for the moment was to roam about her house, tasting its loneliness, and daring to imagine that loneliness at an end.

The young man had only stayed a short time, and he had cautioned her not to build her hopes too high. The news he brought was that Mr Springthorpe had formally changed his evidence: the solicitor had it in writing, and Howard's case could now be presented to the Criminal Cases Review Commission. But there was no mistaking the journalist's own glow of optimism, and Pat had felt quite overcome. So much so that Adam Dowling, in his tactful way, had gone on to ask her a few more details about Howard's past – background material for the book he intended to write about the case. Going over that had helped her ignore the turbulent hope swelling her heart, but now she was alone Pat could not help but surrender to it.

She wandered into her dim living room – in the early days after Howard's arrest she had kept the curtains closed because people would linger and stare, and the habit had stuck – and looked at the couch and the big antimacassared armchair. The couch was the place where she sat, and it bore the impress of her shape from the eternity of solitary evenings she had spent here with the radio and the TV. The armchair was where Howard used to sit. She had never once sat in it since the day they had taken him away twelve years ago.

She went upstairs, her slippered feet instinctively feeling for the safer places in the worn stair-carpet. She noticed, neutrally, the dingy brown of the landing ceiling, threaded with filaments of old spider-web as dark as shoelaces. The house of a confirmed smoker. Her only real pleasure, she would say to herself, and not with irony.

Pat went into her son's bedroom. Probably, indeed almost certainly, it would be tempting fate to prepare it for his return; and if prayer did not come naturally to her, Pat Gandy had a firm belief in fate. What went around came around: every season had its reason: your sins would find you out. These laws were as real to her as gravity. She felt that a wrong move now would be disastrous. But looking around at this small, cold-smelling room, into which no one but herself had set foot in the past twelve years, she realized that not much would be needed to make it ready, if and when the time came.

It wasn't as if she had kept the room as a shrine. Howard's own character precluded that. He had rather spartan tastes and when he was here the room had always looked like this – plain, almost uninhabited, the single bed neatly covered with the knitted counterpane, the few books and the portable radio neatly ranged on the solitary shelf. There were no pictures on the walls, no photographs, no mementoes: even the swimming and lifesaving certificates of which he was so proud had always been kept in the drawer of the bedside cabinet. In fact when Pat pictured his cell at Whateley her mind came up with an image not very different from this. (She wished she could see that cell. Even wished she could be there with him. The worst of the painful unfairness of their separation was that she couldn't follow him: if they must put him away, she had long thought, then surely she could be allowed to share his incarceration. She would willingly have volunteered.)

Still, despite the absence of idiosyncrasy in this room, Pat Gandy had a powerful sense of her only son as she stood here. She could imagine him here again, very easily: it took little effort. Howard, home. Just as before.

Would he be just as before? Pat wondered. Would it be different?

She felt an inward twitch, the need for a cigarette. She gave the room a last wistful look and went downstairs.

She lit a cigarette in the kitchen, then noticing the time began mechanically to prepare her lunch. She peeled two potatoes and sliced them and put them on to boil. Two potatoes, her perennial ration: enough for a stringy old woman,

68

she thought, especially with this grinding dyspepsia that was almost always with her nowadays. But soon, perhaps, she would be cooking for two again.

Turning to look at the kitchen table with it single raffia place mat, Pat decided she could tempt fate just a little. She hunted in a cupboard, found a second place mat, cleaned the dust from it, and laid it on the kitchen table opposite her own.

Her heart was beating a little fast as she took the slice of liver from the fridge and dusted it with flour. Dark blood formed crescents around the fingernails of her small tough hands. She laid the liver in a smoking pan, then turned down the heat after a moment, absently sucking her fingertips.

Justice, Adam Dowling had said: finally, God willing, there would be justice. It warmed her to hear that spoken in his young confident voice; also frightened her a little. Things were happening fast, and it was hard to adjust. It was hard, above all, to think of life suddenly being on her side.

But surely it was time. These twelve years of loneliness and ostracism had been a cruel sentence for her too. By any standards she had had her punishment, surely.

And there were signs of this. She was sure she had seen a kind, interested look in the eyes of the young Springthorpe girl when she had passed by in Mrs Larkinson's van this morning. Mr Springthorpe had been part of that general vengefulness twelve years ago, but people's hearts changed, of course – not much hope for the world if they didn't, Pat thought – and his adopted daughter, a dark intense girl and quite a looker, had seemed actually to reach out to Pat with those great eyes of hers as she rode by. Nothing of the sort from snobby Mrs Larkinson, of course, but then she had been against Howard from the start. It was Mrs Larkinson who had made a complaint to the police early on that terrible, unforgettable day of the murder, saying that Howard had been 'pestering' her children outside the village shop. Talking to, Pat thought: that was all. And as Adam Dowling had told her, the police took no notice at the time. Nor had they taken any action over what had happened the day before, when a couple holidaying up at Rodham along the coast had made a complaint about a man helping their little girl make a sandcastle on the beach. Yes, that was Howard – he had freely admitted it when they were questioning him later. There was no harm in it. But it was those reports that made the police concentrate on Howard when the little boy was killed – that and his reputation. A fit-up, Adam Dowling called it. No solicitor present at the interrogations: serious inconsistencies in police record-keeping . . . A good brief would be able to make mincemeat of such evidence, he said, if they got to appeal.

And she had nodded, listening intently, placing complete trust in him. She felt rather useless, in fact, though he said not to worry about that; and she had doubts even about the background information she could give him. Howard as a child? He was just Howard. An ordinary little boy, rather solitary and serious: a bit stubborn when he believed himself to be in the right. She remembered him sticking to his guns over a toy car that he felt had been unfairly taken from him by another boy at Holfleet Primary. Marbles were won and lost and willingly handed over, but car races were for fun: it was different. A rule had been broken and Howard didn't like that. He had strong ideas of right and wrong even then. Pat admired that. And he got his toy car back all right – oh yes.

Swimming, that had been his main accomplishment. He was good at arithmetic and woodwork but at swimming he had outshone everyone and when he had left Ingelow Secondary School at sixteen he had his heart set on being a lifeguard. It wasn't unrealistic where they lived, in a holiday area – there were two public pools in nearby Ingelow, as well as at Butlin's, down the coast. Pat remembered how delighted he had been when, at eighteen, he had landed the job of lifeguard at the Ingelow municipal baths: his dream come true. It was a crying shame that it had all gone so sour.

Adam Dowling was keenly interested in the swimming-pool incident, though there wasn't much she could tell him. Somebody had complained about Howard – the parents of a young boy. Something about inappropriate physical contact and force . . . Howard's version was that the boy had been behaving disruptively, dangerously even, in the beginners' pool, and frightening the other children; and Howard had taken him aside and given him a good telling-off. It seemed to Pat part of the general unfairness of things that he should lose his job because of this. Of course, Howard being Howard he wouldn't make an apology, and the manager said he had no choice but to dismiss him. She remembered how they had tried to bring that up at the trial – more unfairness, because it had nothing to do with anything. The manager of the baths had since died, according to Adam, but he was trying to find out more about the incident.

Pat admired his thoroughness: but all she could think of was the pity of it, the waste, because afterwards Howard never again got the kind of job he had his heart set on. 'Unsuitable,' they said, after giving him a week's trial at a children's amusement park, and so he had ended up working as a packer at Coupland's canning factory in Holfleet. Yes, she had got him the job – she was a floor supervisor by then – and she only wished she could have done more for him. He was a bit sad and bitter about the way things had turned out. Not that he ever complained, not Howard: but mothers knew.

And that was their life together – quiet, ordinary – until the day he was taken away. Howard wasn't a drinker and he didn't go after girls – he just wasn't the Romeo sort, as he used to say – and he liked the simple pleasures of beachcombing and birdwatching and going to see the odd football game at Lincoln. And he liked children.

Pat turned the liver in the pan. Blood had formed a brown scum on the surface and she poked at it idly with the slotted spoon.

This was the kind of thing she had told Adam. Though he seemed to want more: Howard's *upbringing* was the word he used. He was fishing to know about Howard's father, naturally. But there was nothing to tell, because Jack *was* nothing, when it came down to it. Pat had married him when she knew no better. He worked for Ingelow District Council then – the last job he ever held down. He showed his true colours not long after they moved here, when Howard was born: the colours of the betting shop and the pub and the dog track. An old story, she supposed, but it wasn't funny when you were in it; and when she thought of him her jaws clenched and her face unconsciously settled into a hard old look. Jack had only been good for one thing, in fact; and how smug that had made him, how he had relished his power.

The smell of the liver was making her feel slightly nauseous, and the grinding in her stomach grew sharper. She knew this was going to be another of those meals that she picked at and then scraped into the bin. She lit another cigarette, preferring it.

Well, there was nothing more to say about Jack Gandy except that he left when Howard was five or six and that was the last she ever heard of him. He had family up north and might have gone there: he had enjoyed National Service and used to go on about rejoining the Forces, so perhaps he did that; she didn't much care. Useless.

In fact – and she hadn't told Adam this – she had thrown him out. The memory was frightening, exhilarating, a little patchy as memories of crisis moments often are. But there had been a final bodily thrust out of the front door, she knew that, and though Jack too had been a big man she had felt at that moment that she could have hurled him all the way to the sea.

And afterwards, Howard's little hand in hers.

'It's just you and me now.'

And she had done it. She had got the job at Coupland's, and brought her son up herself, without a man.

It had meant a sacrifice, of course, but there it was. You found a way.

'Was Jack ever violent to Howard?' Adam Dowling had wanted to know.

'How do you mean?'

'Well, did he beat him, hit him at any time?'

'Oh, no. Nothing like that.'

Pat tested the potatoes with a fork. She would eat them plain boiled, though Howard liked them mashed. For an intense moment of pleasure she allowed herself to imagine Howard sitting behind her at the kitchen table, waiting for his lunch.

'He was everything to me, you see,' she had found herself saying to Adam – she didn't know why – just before he left. 'He had to be.'

Pat Gandy dished up her lunch and set the plate on the table, opposite the empty place. Sitting down, she stubbed out her cigarette and then discovered that she was folding her hands as if saying grace.

Words came from her.

'Please God. Let everything be all right. Give him back to me.' She faltered, felt this was imprecise. 'Give him back to me – and let everything be all right this time.'

# SEVEN

Adam timed it well, so well that Angela nearly jumped out of her skin. As she opened the door to his flat, Adam pushed the champagne cork out.

'My God, Adam, you bloody idiot!' She aimed a blow at him. 'I thought I'd been shot for a minute.'

He laughed, pouring a glass of champagne and handing it to her.

'What's this in aid of?'

'We got the appeal. We've done it.' He allowed the satisfaction of it to flow through him for a moment, then poured himself a glass and held it up to hers. 'Doug Jameson just rang. The CCRC have considered our submission and have recommended the case of the Crown versus Howard Gandy to the Court of Appeal. Which means we've won. We're there!'

'Well, good golly.' Angela gave him a sceptical look. 'So when will it be?'

'Date's not fixed yet. Could be months. But Doug thinks they won't drag their feet over this one.'

'Appeals can be unsuccessful, though, can't they?'

'They can,' he said. The tartness didn't spoil his mood: it added a relish to it. 'They can, and this one won't be. Because I have prepared a bloody good case.'

'The modesty is underwhelming,' she said, but grinned. 'So, does Mr Creepy know yet?'

'Nope. I've phoned his mother. She cried. Come and sit down. I'm going to get you out of that habit, by the way.'

'Calling him Mr Creepy?' Angela chuckled, ignoring his gesture towards the sofa, and sat at the desk in front of his computer. 'So what's this?' she said, scrolling through the text on the lit VDU. 'You're writing up the book?'

'I've made a start. The rest is a mass of notes.' He sprawled on the sofa. He felt like getting delightfully drunk. This was his triumph, and it would be mere coyness to pretend otherwise.

'So this is the 'orrible murder bit, I suppose,' Angela said, reading. Fascinatingly, her face, delicate and English as a Kate Greenaway figure, was barred and striped with warpaint colour: on one side from the glow of the computer screen, on the other from the flashing neon of Rajah's, the restaurant across the road from his flat. The painted-savage look combined with the demureness of her closed knees faintly stirred him.

'Just a straightforward account of what happened that day,' he said. 'From police reports, and the parents' statements. Or what was *supposed* to have happened, anyway.'

' "At about half-past one Lorraine Brudenell lay down in the sun lounger beneath the awning of the tent whilst little Lee played nearby. Lorraine had had a couple of cans of lager with her lunch and was feeling drowsy with the warmth of the day. She didn't mean to nod off to sleep, though she wasn't worried about doing so. The camp site seemed a safe enough place . . ." ' Angela wrinkled her nose. 'God, she sounds choice. I mean, is this a whitewash or what?'

'Lorraine Brudenell did have a drink problem. She admitted that at the time.'

'And where was the father at this point?'

'He'd gone down to the village pub. Oh, they were far from a squeaky-clean family, though of course the press at the time just showed them as these sorrowing victims. It also turns out from the statements of neighbours at the camp site that Colin Brudenell had got into a temper with Lee that day because the boy wouldn't eat the sausages they'd had for lunch. Seems like he could be a rather demanding father.'

'Charming.' Angela finished her champagne and held the glass out for more as she scrolled down. She liked to drink and had a toper's capacity. 'So we don't really know what happened.'

'Well, Lorraine Brudenell woke up to find Lee missing. Seven hours later the police found him dead in Tetby Haven. Officially, ostensibly, whatever, someone came through the woods behind the tent and took that little boy away and killed him, and that someone was Howard Gandy. But as you say, we don't really know.'

Angela frowned at the screen. 'Ugh. This is grim stuff. "The wound to the back of the skull was severe and had resulted, as post-mortem would later confirm, in severe fracture of the occiput: blood and other matter was present in the hair . . ." ' She turned away from the screen, drinking deeply. 'Can't you write a gardening column instead?'

'The pathology stuff's important.'

'Well, the true-crime fans love it, of course.'

'Not just that. The forensic evidence is typical of this case: it doesn't quite add up. First there was the police surgeon who certified the child dead at the scene at about ten o'clock that night. Then they had a consultant forensic pathologist for an examination at the scene. He noted the wrinkling of the hands, which meant the body had been in the water for several hours. And he noticed petechiae in Lee's eyes – that's burst blood vessels. It's a feature of asphyxia. Suffocation. Then there was the fractured skull. But he didn't take a body temperature reading, which is the surest, or the least unreliable way of determining time of death. He didn't do it because it means inserting a thermometer in the anus, and with a child murder like this they're obviously looking out for signs of sexual interference. Introduction of a thermometer might have disturbed evidence, perhaps made it useless for a court. So that was out. Then you had the effect of immersion – a body cools twice as quickly in water, but that's complicated by how long the victim has been dead before being put in the water. Plus Tetby Haven is a tidal outfall, with fluctuating temperatures. So the time of death, four to eight hours before, was a very rough estimate. Then the next day they had the post-mortem. This is where you determine cause of death. Again, doubts. The pathologist concluded Lee Brudenell died from crush asphyxia – basically, what Burke and Hare used to do: sit on people's chests and stop their breath. But there was the skull fracture too. If an injury is inflicted before death it shows up in these cells called leucocytes. The presence of leucocytes was partial and inconclusive. Did the killer strike Lee's head more than once, the last time after suffocating him? Or when disposing of the body? Unanswered questions. And this was the case that Lincoln Crown Court treated as open and shut. In fact the whole thing was less than thorough. Howard Gandy was arrested and the far-from-watertight case was as good as solved.

'Well, I've got to admit it makes you want to read on. But that's the subject matter, isn't it? God forgive us, we do find these things gripping.' Angela frowned at the window. 'Haven't they fixed that sign yet? That flickering would just about drive me mad. You ought to complain.'

Adam chuckled and went over to the window to pull down the blind. A vastly calm person himself, he rather enjoyed a little petulance in women. 'I wouldn't care to. They give me a discount on takeaways because I'm such a regular. You should try the dosas.'

'So where does it go from here? An account of the trial, I suppose. What do I press, "file save" and "exit"?'

'I'll do it. Yes, pretty much. And I want to recreate the atmosphere of public hysteria at the time. Get the reader to feel what everyone felt at the time, a totally emotional gut reaction. Then later, make the reader aware of how he or she has participated in this response, been part of the same . . . conspiracy of prejudice.'

'Is this a title I see before me?'

'Maybe. I might just stick with *The Pied Piper*. I'm sure the news media are going to use that handle a lot when Howard is released.'

'When, not if?'

'When not if.'

Angela came and sat down on the sofa beside him – beside, though with about twelve inches between them. Though they had been seeing each other for about a year, she retained these curious maidenly mannerisms. If she saw him at the offices of Fairway, the publishers for whom she worked, and where indeed they had first met, she was blushing and awkward even though everyone knew about them. He sometimes wondered if the archness was strategic, a post-feminist aberration – How to Keep Your Man. It worked, anyway.

'Full-blooded stuff. Murder, kids, conspiracy,' she said. 'But I'm not sure how you're going to spin it out.'

'Well, there's the story of Howard himself. He's a remarkable character. On that we build the central thesis about our fear of our own kids and how it's destroying childhood.'

'Ah, the Big Idea. That's the stuff I'm not sure about. I mean, when it comes to markets we're talking true crime, right? But we all know your hardcore true crime addict just wants grue. Is he going to put up with the philosophizing?'

'Well, it concerns us all. Look – I was thinking the other day, if I were in a shopping mall and I came across a little child lost, what would I do? Take him to a security guard, OK. How would I do that? Would I hold his hand? I think I would be afraid to. I think I'd probably look for a lady to help me, preferably an old lady. In fact I'd dread the whole experience, it's a minefield. Maybe the day's coming when I'd just ignore that child . . . But the philosophizing, as you call it, will still come second to the story. And this is a real good-and-evil story.'

'With a happy ending, presumably, when your man walks out of jail?'

Adam hesitated. 'Partly.'

'Well, it's controversial, to say the least. You're sure Fairway are the people to do this book? *The Christmas Book of Aromatherapy* is more their line. Of course, what do I know? I'm only a humble editorial assistant. I suppose Maggie's got her own opinion.'

'She's still not totally sold on the idea. But if we could give it a *real* ending, then—'

'God, what was that?'

The thump and crunch sounded like a drum being thrown through a window. Adam got up and parted the blinds, looking down into the car park.

'It's OK. Someone's just gone smack into the back of that car. Trying to squeeze in. Christ, that's going to cost . . . At least it wasn't mine.' Congestion was one of the disadvantages of living in this block of flats tucked into a pocket-handkerchief of Ladbroke Grove land; but though he sometimes grumbled about such things, he made no pretence that he could ever live anywhere else. His father, a roving journalist of the old school, who had covered post-colonial horrors in Africa and East Asia, had favoured the English rural style for his not very frequent time at home: an old vicarage in a minuscule

Hampshire town of the Jane Austen sort. Adam had loathed it, though he doubted if his father had ever realized this. Alastair Dowling had not been very interested in people individually, though he had greatly endeared himself to a radio audience later in his life, when his world-weary and uniquely gravelly tones brought admiring letters from women of a certain age. 'They don't know him,' Adam's mother would say, filing the letters away. His father had died of throat cancer three years ago, and his mother had retired to her native Scotland. Adam, urban to his fingertips, had followed his father's profession but not his tastes – nor his view of human nature, which was entirely pessimistic. Alastair Dowling would have said that if Howard Gandy appeared like a child-molester then he probably was.

'Happy endings,' Adam said, coming back to the sofa. 'I've been thinking about that. Because when Howard walks free from the Appeal Court, then the murder of Lee Brudenell becomes officially unsolved.'

Angela stared at him. 'Whoa. Now you're moving on to something different entirely, aren't you? Fingering the culprit . . . What's put this in your head? Does Mr Creepy have an idea?'

'Oh, it's not a thing we've really discussed. Maybe you could ask him, when you finally meet him.'

'Meet him? Adam, I don't want to, thanks. I know that sounds awful, but I don't.'

'Can you say why?' Adam was as near to being in love with Angela as he had ever been with anyone; yet he brought a detachment to human relations that manifested itself even here, and he scrutinized her, taking in her beauty as an increment to his intense curiosity: why didn't she want to meet Howard Gandy? 'He's a wrongly convicted man: he isn't a child-killer.'

'I know. I believe that, I think. I can't explain it.'

'Maybe it's because doubt remains. Until we find out who really did it.'

Her look was close, not friendly. 'The great detective again. So who started this particular hare?'

'Well, it was Philip Springthorpe's daughter who really brought it home to me. I met her when I was up in

79

Lincolnshire last month, getting her father's statement. Nineteen-ish, very up front.' Remembering Rebecca, he could not help contrasting her demeanour with that of Angela who, only five years her senior, seemed to inhabit the world so differently. Lean, lambent-eyed, Rebecca doggedly staked her claim to exist in it. In comparison Angela Ferrier was a cosseted Persian. 'She wasn't keen about the publicity touching her family. But she said she could handle it if some good came out of it. Like justice. Which got me thinking. I mean, I know more about this case than anyone. Who better to finish the job?'

'Dear me, this girl must have been very persuasive. Did she ask you to sort out the economy while you're at it?'

Adam laughed, and decided the time had come to close up that distance between them. The physical distance, at any rate.

# EIGHT

Wendy Brudenell watched the waltz of lights up above her house and wondered whether to leave her husband.

From here the cars on the ring road, though you knew they were so many noisy throbbing tons of metal belching out fumes, looked airy and insubstantial, graceful things made of light and whizzing round and round for the sheer joy of it. Wendy wondered what this district of Nottingham had been like before they ploughed the main ring road interchange through it, truncating low-lying streets and leaving back gardens, like her own, directly at the foot of a great upraised mass of traffic. There had been more of a sense of community, probably, but she doubted it was any safer: less so, probably. At least now no one – criminals, she meant, burglars – could get into your house through the back way without great difficulty.

It was a bit like a funfair, the waltz of lights. She couldn't remember the last time she had been to a funfair. Ingelow, the nearest seaside resort to Nottingham, had plenty: but Colin wouldn't go there and she couldn't say she blamed him.

'Banjo! Banjo, come on! Banjo, naughty, come on in!'

If she could just get the cat in, she would feel she had achieved something. One little problem off the list. Wendy was used to thinking in these terms. Her life was, perhaps, a continual exercise in damage limitation: if she refused to see it as such, she could not ignore the physical symptoms. Her back ached, always, from a strained readiness, a tension of intervention. 'What are you doing that for?' Colin would say, when in a pub garden she would begin clearing empty glasses from their table and even from the adjoining one. 'Just leave them.' But she had to do it – in case Jake knocked one off, or in case someone else's kids knocked one off and caused a domino effect of annoyance and trouble. It might not happen, she didn't even expect it to, but to prepare against it was to store something up, add a little credit to the account. Worth the backache.

Then there was the asthma, of course, but she was prey to that in any case. It was the asthma that had brought her out here into the cold spring night, to try the effect of fresh air on her pinched lungs. She had to admit that it was worry and agitation that had brought on the attack: and she was out of refills for her inhaler. Colin was meant to be bringing some back from the chemist, should in fact have been back with them hours ago . . .

'Banjo?'

A movement down at the bottom of the garden, by the shed, caught her attention. Wendy tiptoed across the overgrown lawn, rank damp grass cold and unpleasant through her slippers, peering down at the stack of lumber between the shed and the dustbin. Burning cat-eyes turned briefly to her, establishing the cat-shape, and then turned busily away again.

'Banjo, what have you got there? What – oh, naughty. Oh, Banjo, you are a naughty boy. Put it down . . .'

She made a tentative motion with her hand, but the cat growled at once, low in its throat, and she retreated. Well, the bird was certainly dead anyhow, though how much mauling it had had first she didn't like to think. She couldn't tell in the semi-dark what sort of bird it was, but it looked big. The cat was beginning to eat it with loud crunchings and gulping thrusts of its sleek head.

'Anybody'd think I didn't feed you,' Wendy said softly. She was hurt. 'That poor bird, it must have been roosting. You took it when it was sleeping, naughty cat. Well, I'm going in now. Serve you right if you're sick.'

She turned to go into the house – not wanting to, though, not really, because at least here she could talk to and concentrate on the cat, murderous companion. Indoors, Jake was asleep, or should be, and there was only the TV that seemed tonight more taunting than entertaining. It was full of jollity, and images of a life that was slick and explicable and where even the problems and secrets were negotiable, resolved with a quick whisk like a conjuror's pass.

Crossing the lawn, she stumbled and nearly fell. It was that wretched well. The garden used to be a kind of rough patio until Colin, with typical energy, had taken up the slabs to lay a lawn. In the process he had found this old brick-lined well. For safety he had filled it up with rubble, as near to the top as he could – it only went down a few feet now – and had covered the top with a concrete slab far too heavy for the children to lift. But the slab wasn't quite flush with the opening, and in the dark it was easy to forget and trip, with exactly this bone-jarring pain. Everything was against her today, she thought.

She went indoors, limping, and decided finally to give up on the dinner in the oven. It was on a low light but still the chop was like rubber and the peas pebble-hard. She scraped it into the waste bin and then washed the plate, feeling gloomy at this surrender. She had never expected to be doing this as she so often did with her first husband: Colin liked his food and appreciated her cooking.

Where was Colin? A niggling question that got in the way of the greater one – about their future together. And whether they had one.

Drying her hands, she went through to the living room. It looked quite cosy. The toys were put away in the box behind the settee – Colin, handy like that, had made the box from an old packing-case and stuck pictures of the Muppets on the outside, back in the early days – and the electric fire was on. Their home. That simple fact could still give her a warm glow.

About the sideboard, and the things on it, she could not be happy. The bogeymen of this bad-dream day lurked there. One was a half-bottle of whisky, which she had not thrown away because there was a drop left in it, perhaps one pub measure. Colin had bought two of them, drinking that one, taking the other out with him this afternoon. She had thought it strange at first that he should buy two half-bottles, an expensive way of doing it; then had realized, with sadness more than anything, that he had surely not bought them at all.

'I'm going to drink these,' he had said with miserable defiance, though she had had no intention of challenging him. 'That's all I can do. So I'm bloody going to.'

The other bad thing on the sideboard was the letter from

his solicitor, which she had tucked neatly back into its envelope after he had shown it to her. Wendy had read it, but hadn't felt she really understood it. But she could hear its sound even then, like clangorous bells, and feel its suffocating atmosphere like a poisonous smell in her nostrils.

A quarter to eleven. He had been gone nine hours. Not wholly unknown, she had to admit, not these days: but this was something different. And while she wondered, with a renewal of the pain in her lower back, what his mood would be like if he did come in now, it was not the usual awkwardness she feared.

Something different.

Muffled sounds from upstairs reached her ears. With a sigh Wendy went through to the cold hall and carefully climbed the stairs – narrow and steep in these old postwar council houses, as if even then, she thought, they grudged such things to ordinary people – and cleared her throat loudly as she reached the top.

'Now then.' She switched on the overhead light of Jake's room. Her son lay with the Spiderman quilt pulled up tightly to his nose, panting. But at just four years old he lacked a layer of subterfuge: Action Man and Piglet, strange playmates, were still sprawled on the bed. 'I've told you enough times. Go to sleep.'

'I was.'

Wendy shook her head. 'I'm not going to argue. Now that's the last time.'

'Where's Colin?'

Wendy hesitated, noticing with a queer twist of regret the use of her husband's name. Usually Jake would call him Daddy; but not so much of late.

'He'll be home soon. Now settle down.'

Probably, she thought as she turned out the light, Jake was playing up in the hope that she would give in and have him downstairs with her. Her own fault, perhaps, because she did do that quite often. She enjoyed the company of children, never felt the need to groan and complain as so many mothers did: she liked having Jake around, especially when Colin was working, admittedly a rare thing nowadays. But it wasn't on tonight. The ghosts haunting the house since Colin had opened that letter were not of the sort that child-magic could dispel.

As she stepped down in the draughty hall Wendy noticed something signally familiar about the way the lower backache was spreading outward as if radiating a jagged warmth. She went into the toilet and pulling down her jeans and knickers inspected herself.

Yes: she had known somehow. What horrible tricks this simple thing played on you, she thought, washing and then taking a sanitary towel from the packet in the cabinet. She could remember once as a girl of seventeen making this inspection ten times a day with dread in her heart each time: it was after she had been with that boy – was his name Neil? – following a drunken party at her cousin's house. Then she had felt like leaping for joy when at last the bright blobs had appeared. Now it came as the dealing of another doleful hand in a day that seemed to be going relentlessly against her.

She knew how desperately Colin wanted a child of his own with her. He was good with Jake, as long as his temper held – very good in fact, fiercely protective and watchful; but still, Jake wasn't his. She could understand that longing, given what had happened in the past. But you couldn't will a pregnancy, and though she was only thirty-two she had a feeling of time running out.

Maybe this was the sign. If she had been pregnant, that would have been a signal that fate meant them to stay together and make a go of it. But this, surely, indicated the opposite: that she should listen to her inner fears and get out.

It wasn't that she had stopped loving him. She just wanted a quiet family life: the sort of life she thought she would have when she'd married Colin eighteen months ago. She learned, when they were courting, about the terrible happenings of his past: he had cried as he told her. It was that awful loss, he said, that had contributed to the break-up of his first marriage, and she thought that was understandable.

And he could still be so kind, so heart-lifting . . . yet she was afraid she couldn't cope with him. The drinking, the trouble that he seemed to attract like a magnet, the lurching swings of mood: he made such *demands* as a personality. And sometimes she sensed a darkness about him, a darkness that blinded her . . .

The clunk of the car door and the heavy rap at her front door seemed to come almost simultaneously, and Wendy heard herself let out a started squeak. She went quickly to the door and opened it.

'Oh my God, what's happened . . .?'

'Mrs Brudenell? Wendy, isn't it? I think we've met before. It's all right, nothing to be alarmed about. OK if I come in?'

The tall young policeman in the peaked cap and gloves looked very spruce and brisk, a plume of steam from his breath in the cold air and his fair skin flushed: somehow admirable, shy-making, like sailors or dashing airmen in old films. She saw the patrol car parked outside the house, flaring its orange message along the street, and now the shock was over felt the shame of this publicity.

'Is it Colin? What's happened? He is all right, isn't he?'

'Don't worry.' He stepped in, smelling of outdoors: she gestured him to the living room. 'I'm PC Stanton, in case you don't remember. From Bankside station. Nice and warm in here. Your husband's Colin Brudenell, is that correct?'

'Yes. Where is he?'

'Well, he's at Bankside, I'm afraid. He was arrested this evening in the city centre. Normally of course we would give you a ring to let you know, but I understand you're not on the phone.'

'No. We were, but . . .' Unpaid bills. Wendy suffered a slight reflex of resentment at that *normally*: she hated the idea that they weren't normal.

'Like I say, don't worry. Basically we're going to keep him in the cells overnight and send him home in the morning. There'll be charges, public order stuff. It's not major but he has been pretty stupid, I'm afraid. Lucky he wasn't still on probation.'

'Finished first of this month,' she said faintly.

'Well, it's a pity, like I say. But we had to take him in. I don't know how you're fixed, with the little 'un and everything . . .'

'He's in bed. I've – I've got no one to leave him with.'

'Well, I was going to say, I don't see a whole lot of point in you going down there. He'll be home in the morning and nobody can get much out of him at the moment, to be honest. He's absolutely stinking and I shouldn't be surprised if he's

86

conked out by now. So don't worry, he'll be looked after.'

'What did he do? To get arrested? He didn't hurt anybody, did he?'

'Not really,' the policeman said after giving her a quick searching look. 'He might have if he hadn't been so drunk and incapable. He started picking a fight in the Bell—'

'Oh my God, that's a rough place.'

'Exactly. He was lucky really. They just threw him out. Then he went over to the Princes Hotel, as far as we can gather, and tried to get into the residents' bar there. He made an assault on a porter when he was refused admission. That's when we were called. It was the booze, but of course that's no excuse. Had he been drinking earlier, do you know?'

'He – he had a drink here. He was in a state about something . . . Oh God, Colin . . .'

'I know. Playing silly beggars – there's no need for it. What time did he leave the house today?'

'This afternoon. About two, I think.'

'I see. Apparently there was a report about him earlier. Someone was at the High Park cemetery, who we think was Colin, shouting about and smashing glass. An old girl there got a fright. That ring any bells?'

'Lee,' Wendy said, and she felt an ache for Colin, the ache at the centre of her love that overcame all the pain he caused her. 'His son by his first marriage. He's buried there. Colin goes quite often. Lee – Lee was only little when he got killed.'

Only little. Yet how huge was the effect of that lost waif, how vast the shadow he cast. No matter what trials Colin put her through, she knew in her heart of hearts that what had happened twelve years ago lay at the root of them. He would never have gone off the rails but for that. The vein of self-destructiveness that kept breaking out in him – where else could it come from?

Sometimes she suggested visiting the grave with him. But he preferred to go alone. He would linger there for an hour, even two. 'It's like I can hear him singing, sometimes,' he would say. 'He used to sing to himself, sort of crooning, like little 'uns do, making it up as they go along. I swear I can hear it up there. In the air.'

'That's where he's been,' Wendy said, feeling as if she were being torn apart.

'Dear oh dear. So what happened to the lad?'

'Somebody murdered him.'

'Oh my Christ,' Stanton said softly. 'I didn't know. Actually, the sarge was saying something about some trouble Colin had had years ago, something pretty awful—'

'He got this letter this morning,' Wendy said, suddenly feverish with energy. She fetched it and thrust it at the young policeman. 'See – it was that. I'm sure that started it. It's from his solicitor. When he read it he just went crazy. I think it's to do with Lee and when he got killed, but I don't get it. Go on, read it, please . . .'

The young policeman read swiftly, his eyebrows going up.

'Gandy. I remember that feller. Christ. I didn't realize . . . I can see why Colin was in a bit of a state.'

'What does it mean?'

'The Criminal Cases Review Commission, well, that's a government body that looks into these cases where there's some doubt, you know. Dodgy convictions. It does happen, though not as often as some people make out. What it's saying here is that the Commission has recommended the case of Howard James Gandy to the Court of Appeal.'

'The man who killed Colin's little boy.'

'Well, who was convicted of the killing, as it says here. Notifying you as an interested party, blah blah. Interested party, my God, you can say that again.'

'Are they saying this man didn't do it?'

'Well, if it's going to the Court of Appeal, that means there's a serious chance of overturning the conviction. Somebody's obviously built a strong case for his innocence, for it to get this far. The Court of Appeal can still turn it down, though, and send him back to prison if they're not convinced. Sounds as if this feller's got a bit of a campaign behind him.'

'Colin never talks about it much. It was before I knew him. But I know how it hit him and hurt him. I mean, it's inside of him, what happened, it's always with him . . .'

'I suppose it would be. When was this . . .?' Stanton scanned the letter again. 'Crikey, twelve years. Well, if this feller was sentenced to life, he has actually done a fair stretch now. Life doesn't mean life, as you know. Ten years is about the earliest you can expect to get out if you've been a very good boy inside. With this feller, with the crime that he did, the judge probably made a minimum recommendation to make sure he stayed inside. So Colin probably didn't expect to see this guy walk for years yet. It'd be a blow, I can see that. Bring it all back, reading this.'

'Plus,' she said, 'they're saying that this man didn't do it in the first place. So where does that leave . . .?'

'I'd advise Colin to talk to his solicitor about it,' PC Stanton said, seeming to come abruptly to the end of his ration of time. 'He'll no doubt be seeing him anyway, I'm sorry to say, after this latest trouble. Like I say, you can't excuse that kind of behaviour, though I understand what he's going through. He'll really have to get a grip on himself. Now will you be all right tonight?'

'Yes . . . yes, I should think so. Are you seeing him when you go back? I mean – could you give him my love?'

'If he's in a state to take it.' He was heading for the door.

'I hate to think of him in those cells.'

'Well, not the first time, I'm afraid,' the policeman said, and though his smile was no doubt meant to be rueful, friendly, it gave him a wolfish look and she felt it like a callous poke.

'Not so surprising when he's got something like this on his mind,' she said.

'Look, I know it seems hard, but whatever happens with this Appeal Court thing I reckon Colin's best off putting it all behind him. You can't fight the law: you have to abide by it. And you certainly can't try and take it into your own hands.'

She was silent. She was thinking of what Colin had said earlier – about no one caring for the victims. It was true enough. Picturing Jake asleep upstairs, she tried to imagine how she would feel if someone took him away and . . .

It was unthinkable. And by the same token, it was unthinkable that she could leave Colin now. Colin, who was so hurting, so lost. What sort of woman would that make her?

'Try and get him to think on what I've said, eh? All right, Mrs Brudenell–' PC Stanton had put on formality with his cap, was receding from her world as he stepped out to his car

– 'you try and get a decent night's sleep. We'll send him home in the morning.'

'Thank you.' She watched him get into the patrol car, aware from the corner of her eye of a curtain twitching across the street. She closed the door slowly, not wanting to show the haste of shame.

Going back into the warm living room, she mourned to think of her husband in a bleak police cell. That temper of his. He was sorry after – but that didn't stop him. It was as if he simply lost himself.

Then she thought of someone else who was in a cell, a prison cell, and who might now be released from it. What would happen, if they let that man out?

'I'd kill him. If I could ever get my hands on that bastard, I'd kill him.' That was what Colin had said, long ago, on one of the rare occasions he talked about his son's murder. The words chilled her.

He couldn't bring himself to talk about it much – which Wendy had always thought was understandable. He was plainly very bitter, though, about his first wife, poor little Lee's mother. 'Lorraine? Huh. She was drunk, you know, the day we lost him. Blind drunk. How's that for a mother? She never cared.' Wendy remembered him saying it. And with the memory came a curious echo, she didn't know from where: it said, *Never cared . . . or always scared?*

Wendy shivered and bent to warm her hands at the fire.

If they found that Gandy man innocent after all, and let him out, what would happen? Would they start looking for the person who really killed Lee?

She squatted closer to the fire, till her face and eyes stung: but Wendy Brudenell couldn't get warm.

# NINE

Entering the Royal Courts of Justice, walking with her arm slipped tensely through her father's down the echoing corridor of the Appeal Courts, Rebecca could understand why Adam Dowling, striding ahead of them with his head held high, should have that air of strung-up defiance. This was the place of justice: yet the loftiness, the Gothic grotesquerie of the fittings, the smell of polish and dust and age, all gave the impression not of even-handedness and humane recourse but of awful self-sufficient power, archaic as a battle-axe and no more liable to rationality. Here, it seemed, they could do what they wanted with you.

Yet he looked confident, too, Adam Dowling, as he conferred in a murmur with a small slight copper-haired man whom her father had pointed out as Jameson, Howard Gandy's solicitor. Both were smart, stiffly suited, like everyone she had seen so far, even the reporters and TV cameramen outside. They were here on permanent station, her father said, because there was always news. Only Mrs Pat Gandy, who walked meekly along beside Adam with her eyes lowered to the parquet floor, seemed not to have put on Sunday best. She was carrying a handbag that looked new, not just from its shine but from the unaccustomed way she dangled it like a child with a satchel, but otherwise she was in her familiar garb: she looked, in fact, literally transplanted, a piece of everyday home life moving amongst the strange grandeur, like a kettle in an opera.

But then, Rebecca thought, this world was not new to Pat Gandy: in a way she had inhabited it for the past twelve years.

'Are you all right?' her father said, squeezing her arm.

'Sort of. I still don't see why you have to be here,' she said nervously, not for the first time.

'I don't have to be. It's just in case the judges decide they want to question the witnesses. Which would mean stopping things and summoning me down on another day. It's easier to be on hand. Apparently it's not likely anyway. Adam just told me he'd heard the Crown isn't going to contest the appeal.'

'What does that mean? That they've just said yes?'

'It means they don't put up a lawyer to challenge the one speaking for Gandy. The appeal case stands or falls on its own merits. I think it's a good sign.'

'For who?'

Her father shrugged. 'I just want it to be over with.'

Outside it was warm, blissful June, the countryside viewed from the train that brought them down to London this morning looking both brilliant and soft, even the rugged crops appearing tender as budding flowers. Here in the Law Courts it felt as cool as a cave. The bench on which they sat to wait outside Court Four was a narrow lip of cold stone. There were metal-framed windows here, warped, the panes cracked: in a provincial town hall they would be considered a disgrace. Strange how authority could convey itself most powerfully by a kind of dingy thrift.

Adam Dowling was everywhere, talking to Mrs Gandy and patting her hand, whispering urgently to Doug Jameson, shaking the skeletal hand of a youngish, gaunt and brainy-looking man in a gown who, Rebecca thought, must be the barrister presenting the appeal case. Then suddenly Adam was in front of them, smiling, it seemed at her first and then at her father.

'I have to say thank you again for coming down today. It is a help just in case but I really don't think it'll be needed.'

'You seem very confident,' her father said, neutrally.

'I am and I'm not.' Adam ran a fidgety hand through his cropped hair. 'If we do lose, he goes straight back to Whateley and everyone feels tremendously let down. I'm just starting to feel what a responsibility that is.'

'Well, if you do lose, nothing's changed,' her father said.

'True – but it won't feel like that. There's such a momentum, things can't be the same. You must feel something of that yourself.'

'Yes. I'll be glad to have everything settled and clear-cut. I still can't pretend I entirely trust your man or believe in him. Maybe that's just an old gut feeling, like an old wound. If you do get him out I'm sure a lot of people are going to feel the same.'

'Maybe. There haven't been any threats or anything like that. I've had quite a few messages of support.'

Her father nodded. 'Well, what the hell. Let the judges decide. Hopefully I've done my bit.' A moment followed in which the unfortunateness of this remark seemed to hang in the air, a moment in which Rebecca glanced over at the solitary figure of Pat Gandy, patiently seated on a bench further down the corridor, her eyes lowered.

'Well, I think we all have,' smiled Adam, an instinctive smoother-over. 'Listen, Doug Jameson's booked a suite at his hotel. All being well we'll be going back there afterwards for a glass of something and to receive any media that want to talk to us. I know Midland TV are keen to do quite a big spot. Depending on the result, of course. So if you fancied joining us – you know, I wouldn't see it as at all inappropriate.'

'Well, I think I would,' her father said. 'But thanks anyway.'

'Sure. No problem.'

They were actually rather like each other, Rebecca thought: the same almost dogmatic refusal to get rattled, the subtle flavour of their personalities. But Adam looked, as he darted off to speak to someone else, as if not even a negative result today would dash his spirits more than temporarily, in spite of his cautious words; whilst during these past few months, waiting for the Appeal Court hearing, her father had been subject to depressive moods. Yet he and Rebecca had managed in some degree to reach out to each other since that day he had revealed his dismal secret at the kitchen table – there had been gestures, shifts, the gradually forming pattern of reconciliation. It wasn't possible, she found, to retain her resentment at what she had learned, day after day: the emotions didn't work like that, any more than one could spend every waking moment with the fists clenched.

'I'm sorry,' her father said, turning to her, 'you didn't fancy the celebration do, did you?'

'Oh, no thanks. It'll be nice just to get home.'

'We could always pop and see Uncle Denis if you liked.'

'Maybe another day.' Trips to London, often combined with a stay at the Chiswick home of her father's brother, who worked away a lot and cheerfully encouraged them to consider the house as their own, were a keenly appreciated pleasure in Rebecca's life, and she wanted that kept separate. She gave her father's hand a squeeze, noticing the arrival of a slender dark young woman in a fashionable working suit who tapped Adam Dowling on the shoulder in a proprietary way. Rebecca lip-read his words, 'You made it', as he turned and bent to kiss the woman. At that moment, there was a rattle at the doors of Court Four and they opened with a squeaking that seemed almost stagily sinister.

'Here we go,' her father said, rising with a deep breath. Rebecca noticed that Adam at once went over to Mrs Gandy and gently took her arm, though the young dark woman gave him a lingering, still proprietorial touch.

Inside the court Rebecca and her father took seats on the back row of the hard pew-like benches. The court itself was smaller and less imposing than she had expected, the judges' bench and the witness box seeming hardly separated from them at all: she had imbibed an idea, perhaps from *Alice in Wonderland*, of great spaces and towering platforms. The dowdy sparrow-like head of Mrs Gandy was directly in line with her, a few rows ahead, Adam beside her. Jameson, the fiery-headed solicitor, whispered frantically to the hawkish profile of the barrister at the front.

Suddenly, unceremoniously, there were three old men in sight, weirdly robed and wigged. They shuffled about behind their pulpit-like desk, murmuring, sorting out their seats for all the world like pensioners on an outing. Only when they were settled could she get a good look at their faces, and then at last her preconceptions of courts and trials seemed confirmed: the judges stared truculently around them, red-cheeked, dewlapped chins lifted. They looked as stupid and pedantic and old-fashioned as in any caricature. She could not imagine them letting anyone out of prison, ever.

Did she want them to? Well, if Howard Gandy was innocent, then yes, of course. Adam had already half-convinced her. For the rest, Rebecca found herself falling back on the most primitive of formulas: she would know when she saw him.

She would look into Howard Gandy's eyes, and know.

Away to the right there was heavy rattling at a recessed door. A uniformed prison officer stepped through, followed by a very tall man in a houndstooth jacket and tie: behind them came another prison officer. Rebecca recovered with a start from her moment of misunderstanding: the tall man was Gandy. Somehow she had been expecting a prison uniform, the serge of the old lag, unmistakable as a brand.

But Howard Gandy, except for his size, just looked like anybody else. She studied his large clean-shaven face as he was ushered into the dock, but nothing came to her, neither warmth nor chills. He was part of that vast majority of the world's people – strangers: he was the man in the street, everyday and unknowable.

Then, as he looked quite calmly around, she did meet his eyes for a second or two. And she was shaken by a feeling that could only manifest itself, curiously, in a blush. Seeing him in that dock, it was impossible not to conjure images of hunted and baited animals, gladiators, inquisitorial victims. She had not been prepared for a situation so primal and disturbing . . . Occupied with trying to collect herself, she hardly noticed that the judge in the middle had given a signal and that the thin barrister was on his feet and addressing the bench.

'. . . intention being to establish that this new evidence, not made available at the time of the original trial at Lincoln Crown Court, not only offers a consideration of substance but serves to expose certain glaring inconsistencies in the case originally presented against Mr Gandy. I hope to show that the original defense could not have acted on the strength of these and hence could not make good the strong element of doubt that existed in the case of the Crown versus Gandy to begin with . . .'

He was speaking rapidly and, it seemed to Rebecca, rather combatively: she understood that it was a bad move in these appeals to cast any kind of aspersions on the operations of the courts or the police, and Adam Dowling seemed to wriggle nervously in his seat as the barrister proceeded. The judges sat forward, hunched and peering, as if ready to pounce. The person who showed the least unease, Rebecca thought, was Howard Gandy.

She studied him again. The jacket perhaps did sit a little uncomfortably on him, but probably it was hard to get clothes in his size: he was a very bulky man. *Overgrown* was the word that suggested itself. Rebecca thought about that size, and how it must have appeared at the original trial – a little boy dead, evidence photos perhaps circulating, and there stood this looming giant with his great hands and self-possessed, almost superior gaze.

'. . . The case against Howard James Gandy for the abduction and murder of Lee Brudenell as presented at Lincoln Crown Court in December of that year had been very thoroughly prepared by the prosecution and submitted in good faith on the evidence then existing. What we wish to lay before you, my lords, is a demonstration that the compelling *chain* of evidence which led the jury to return a guilty verdict was actually no such thing: that there are serious flaws and certainly one entirely missing link which result in the whole case against Howard Gandy collapsing when examined in the light of what we now know. I would begin by referring your lordships to the vast quantity of police statements taken on the day of Lee Brudenell's disappearance from the camp site at Holfleet . . .'

It was difficult to believe, looking from Howard Gandy to the barrister to the three judges, that they were in any way involved in the same matter, let alone resolving something of critical importance to one of them. The barrister and the judges, who were regarding him with a quizzical detachment rather as if they were interviewing a candidate for a plum position, seemed to be enacting some entirely private professional procedure; whilst Gandy, who seemed to be expected just to stand there in the dock, had a look of vast unconcerned patience, the look of someone hearing a story known by heart.

'. . . It is these precise details of chronology that fresh scrutiny reveals to be dangerously imprecise. There are two witness sightings, apparent sightings, of Mr Gandy in the vicinity of the camp site that afternoon, which were taken at the original trial as corroborative. Both are from people who were holidaying at the adjoining caravan site at that time. The first from Mr Jessop places Mr Gandy as passing by the entrance of Coupland's canning factory at two fifteen in the afternoon, carrying a plastic bag or sack: the second from Mrs

Youens reports him as making his way south along the coast road at half-past two again with a sack. But as your lordships will have observed, careful investigation of the many witness statements reveals that while Mr Jessop mentioned a bag or sack, his wife, Mrs Hilda Jessop, mentioned, I quote, "carrier bags". It has always been Mr Gandy's contention that early that afternoon he made a shopping trip to Ingelow on his mother's behalf and that he returned to Holfleet at between two and half-past two with two plastic carrier bags. We have now Mr Jessop's assurance that his original witness statement also mentioned 'bags' and that he felt compelled to modify it in accordance with police questions when called upon to make a definitive statement. It has always been the testimony of Mr Gandy's mother that her son returned with the shopping in two bags at about two that afternoon. Seen in this light, the evidence becomes more nonsensical than consecutive: we have to believe that Mr Gandy quickly dumped the shopping at home, immediately ran out again and returned to the camp site with the blue plastic sack, abducted and killed Lee Brudenell, all within the space of perhaps fifteen minutes. It seems far more likely that these accounts corroborate something different – two sightings of a man bringing home two carrier bags of shopping. It is worth noting that the statement given by Mrs Youens was recorded on the day following these events and that she was, as she freely admitted, in a state of intoxication on the day itself when first questioned. But this doubt about the credibility of the witness was not made available to the defence *as statements were tendered.* Only later can we—'

'I must ask you to go back a little,' the middle judge said, 'to your use of this word "compelled" in regard to Mr Jessop giving his statement to the police. Do you use that word advisedly?'

'I do but not in the sense of any physical compulsion. I believe this is a case of a witness adapting certain details, which might not seem to that witness particularly important, out of obligation to the police investigation. This is where we touch on the nub of the matter. It isn't my task to make any overt criticism of the conduct of the police investigation or the trial at Lincoln, beyond pointing out what is easily forgotten in the passage of time, that is the justifiable sense of emotional outrage and anger that was caused by the death of Lee Brudenell. It was this which created a special climate about the case, fostered in part by an attentive media—'

'Are you saying that this was a case of trial by media, or by public opinion, something like that?' put in the right-hand judge. 'Because I don't find that in my reading of the case, not at all.'

'No, my lords, I only suggest that the interpretation of a substantial mass of evidence was affected by human abhorrence of the crime – and police constabularies and courts are made up of human beings. It is this human dimension that has been disregarded in certain key matters of evidence which with your permission I will pursue . . .'

Twelve years: that was how long the man in the dock had been in prison. In his position, Rebecca thought, she would probably be looking wildly around for some means of escape, of capitalizing on this unique chance. But now that his destiny was being discussed Gandy kept his eyes fixed mildly on the agents of the law. Only once did he give any sign of the cataracts of feeling under the placid surface: he put up his hand to straighten his tie and Rebecca clearly saw it shake violently – almost blurring like some electric-driven tool. Somehow she felt she was the only one to notice this and the effect was very much as if he had momentarily opened his breast and showed her his heart.

Suddenly Rebecca felt her father's body stiffen beside her.

'. . . which was apparently the strongest link in the chain of evidence but which is now revealed to be the weakest. The account given by Mr Springthorpe of the defendant's passing by on his way to the site where the body was found, bearing the controversial blue sack, is now shown to have been an impossibility. Again this discrepancy is to be found in the mass of untendered statements; but it categorically establishes that this sighting could not have been made, and this has also been fully and frankly acknowledged by the witness himself. Again I must refer to the neglected human dimension in pointing out that the testimony of the witness was affected by factors not made manifest to the defence at the time – a tragic bereavement and corresponding marital breakdown. It is of course at the court's discretion how to view this, but I would personally place it again in the category of human error rather than deliberate misdirection on anyone's part . . .'

Worse, this, than she had imagined: she wanted to touch her father's hand but it was unreachable, his arms folded tightly across his chest and his chin tucked in almost as if he were trying to squeeze himself to death. She couldn't look at the judges: feared their cold eyes searching her father out. She even had a crazy image of them decreeing some vengeful exchange, her father for Howard Gandy, her father dragged off to Whateley prison and Howard Gandy coming home with her to Salters Cottage.

'My lords, I am not being frivolous when I say that the guilty verdict returned in this case was rather like a points verdict in boxing. There was no "knockout": no definitive piece of evidence linking Howard Gandy to this crime. Rather the accumulation of small pieces was deemed to be enough, in total, to convict him for a crime which he has strenuously denied for twelve years, to the detriment of his own treatment in prison. It is our contention that there are now sufficient considerations of substance to reduce that total of evidence, indeed practically to wipe it out. It was accepted at the original trial that the forensic evidence, chiefly attaching to the matter of the blue plastic sack found at Mr Gandy's home, was inconclusive; this is now hardly surprising inasmuch as there is no firm evidence to suggest that Mr Gandy was abroad with that blue sack on the day in question at all. Two days previously, yes, as he freely admitted: he had used it to bring home some gardening supplies. Much was made at the original trial of the fact that Mr Gandy had no alibi for the period under scrutiny, beyond the assertion of his mother that he had brought back some shopping at around two. Mr Gandy's assertion was and is that after the shopping he spent the afternoon as he commonly did walking and beachcombing the wilder coast north of Holfleet. Quite properly the law pointed out that there was no corroboration for this; but it is quite as proper now to point out that the version advanced by the prosecution – that Mr Gandy went to the camp site, took away and killed Lee Brudenell, and transported his body in a blue plastic sack to dump it at Tetby Haven – has now been shown to lack corroboration also. Indeed it is a conviction that can only stand up if we reverse the very basis of English jurisprudence, and make it the duty of the accused to prove his innocence rather than of the prosecution to prove his guilt . . .'

After what seemed hours of passionless recital of facts and procedure, Rebecca felt that something had kindled in the barrister and in the whole court: the little foxy solicitor beside him was nodding vigorously, one of the judges was writing busily on a notepad, even Howard Gandy had lifted his eyes to the skylight in the centre of the ceiling as if he felt the imminence of something. Adam Dowling was leaning forward eagerly in his seat: Rebecca noticed the pure sweet straight line made by his shoulders. Only Pat Gandy's posture was unchanged. Though in the middle of the pew, she appeared to sit apart. She might have been a cleaner or caterer, waiting with absent mind until the incomprehensible business was over and she could begin clearing away.

' . . . to refer before concluding to factors which were given weight at the original trial and which, it is our contention, constituted a serious misdirection. The complaint made to Ingelow police on the morning of the murder by Mrs Diane Larkinson about Mr Gandy's alleged attentions to her children was presented by the prosecution and rightly challenged by the defence. What has not hitherto been pointed out is a discrepancy in the police records of this complaint. It was initially logged as noted but not referred for action – the reason being, as the constable on the switchboard has since confirmed, that Mrs Larkinson was a frequent caller and, as it were, complainer about numerous matters. Only when police took Mrs Larkinson's statement after the murder was the initial report amended and expanded, to the effect that Mr Gandy had allegedly been, I quote, "bothering Mrs Larkinson's children that morning at or outside the village shop". What is at issue here is not what happened but the retrospective application of importance to what happened, and the degree to which this reflected not only the concentration on Mr Gandy as a sole suspect amongst a large and transient population, but the popular prejudice against him. No one disputes that this feeling existed: what is debatable is how appropriate it was for the court to allow it to be smuggled into the trial under the cloak of evidence . . .'

Rebecca inclined her shoulder against her father's. She couldn't tell whether he welcomed or even was aware of the supporting touch. For her part she now felt a kind of excitement, of the wrong kind perhaps: like watching a fencer strike dashingly home.

Suddenly the barrister was sitting down, and she looked round in surprise. His last remarks had been desultory and there seemed to have been no grand peroration, no oratorical finale followed by a dramatic swish of silk as there was in films. But of course, there was no impressionable jury to sway in this court: it was all down to those red-robed figures, harsh whiskerless Father Christmases, now murmuring amongst themselves. She glanced at the clock on the right-hand wall, and saw to her amazement that two and a quarter hours had passed since they had entered the court.

'In view of the fact that the Crown has submitted no brief for this case,' the middle judge was saying, 'we will not take a lunch adjournment. The court is to remain seated while we retire.'

They shuffled out, talking amongst themselves: Rebecca saw one of them chuckle. People began talking, tentatively at first as when the teacher leaves the classroom, then in an urgent babble.

'What happens now?' she said to her father.

'I don't know. I suppose they give a verdict. Or this might be where they ask to question witnesses.'

'God, I hope not.'

'It doesn't matter.' His face was closed. 'Hope they're not too long, I could do with a smoke.'

'I need a pee. I'll wait though.' Somehow she didn't fancy going in search of a toilet amongst those forbidding corridors. 'He isn't how I'd pictured him somehow.'

'Gandy? Well, he hasn't changed much. Hardly at all really. Still – I hope he *has* changed.'

'Dad, it's hard for me, but . . . hearing it all, I can't believe he did do it. You know?'

He nodded, though it seemed to be more in confirmation of something deep inside himself, some long-held echo, than in assent to her words. 'Well,' he said, 'it was all a long time ago. One forgets quite how long, how different . . . You can't really put the past on trial.'

Ahead of them Adam Dowling was bending to speak to Mrs Gandy. Rebecca couldn't tell what he was saying, but all Pat Gandy was doing was shaking her head. Maybe she was stoically preparing herself, after twelve years, for delays: probably wise even if there was a favourable result. In the films people released after appeals walked free straight from the court, making raised-fist signs, but surely it didn't work like that in real life – did it? What Adam had told them about the celebration party suggested he expected something very clear-cut . . .

At that moment Adam turned and, catching her eye, he gave Rebecca a broad smile. She didn't know what to make of it. It wasn't appropriate to anything, yet it had the effect of lessening her feeling of being trapped and misplaced, like a mourner at a funeral of someone she didn't know. When she had recovered from her confusion, she saw that the judges were back.

One was already seated while the other two had some last whispered conference; and that one rested his chin on his hand and gazed, with singular steadiness, at the figure of Howard Gandy in the dock. It was as if he were falling back on some such magic as Rebecca had tried earlier – seeking to know, just by looking at him, scrying his face like a mystic with a crystal. It was impossible to tell whether Gandy knew of this scrutiny: he still had his eyes fixed on that skylight, where a perfectly vertical ray of sunlight was now falling like a golden pillar.

It happened quickly, by any standards, and by the standards of the law in seemingly indecent haste. The middle judge began to speak in a drone that suggested a long preamble. The other two judges sat back in their chairs as if to wait it out. The court stenographer resumed her mysterious passes.

'. . . There are in fact several aspects of this case that merit our concern. Hearsay should certainly be ruled inadmissible by the bench, and we accept that there was misdirection at the original trial in that regard. The requirement of the Appeal Court for new evidence or another consideration of substance has, we feel, been satisfied, certainly as regards the reliability of witness statements. As counsel has demonstrated, the construction of the sequence of events which placed Howard James Gandy at the scene of the abduction and the scene of the body's discovery is at best flawed and at worst nonsensical. Serious lapses of police procedure, though seemingly without deliberate deceptive intent, contributed to this. And we can only deplore the failure to make the movements, histories and alibis of the large number of transient residents in this holiday spot part of a detailed investigation. It seems practically an impossibility to retrace this vast aspect of the case so many years later, which in itself persuades us to reject the option of a retrial, given that we accept the original verdict as unsafe and unsatisfactory. That is indeed our opinion in the case of the Crown versus Howard James Gandy. Accordingly the appeal is granted –' Rebecca saw Adam Dowling's arms go up – 'and the conviction is quashed.'

There was an outburst of noise. The foxy solicitor was on his feet and pumping the barrister's hand, Adam had Mrs Gandy in a squeeze, Howard Gandy had thrown back his head and closed his eyes like a man transfixed with blessing, and Rebecca was puzzled. This, she thought, was like those symphony concerts where people innocently clapped in between movements, not realizing . . . Surely this couldn't be it?

'They won,' her father said, nodding, as she turned a questioning look to him. 'That's it. He's a free man.'

No hushings or rappings from the judges: they were cupping their pendulous ears to hear something the barrister was saying, and meanwhile all order seemed to have been suspended. People were milling about and talking at the tops of their voices and Rebecca didn't even see Howard Gandy taken down from the dock.

'What happens now?'

'I think there's a place downstairs where he comes out,' her father said. 'Come on. Let's get going now.'

They managed to be the first ones out of the court. In the corridor her father didn't slow down, had soon reached the head of the stairs and had left her behind.

'Dad – hang on . . .'

Turning, he looked as if he had forgotten her.

'Dad, can I just see if I can find a toilet? Only—'

'Sorry. There must be . . .' He looked back irritably the way they had come. 'Look, unless you can't wait, we'll find a café or pub and—'

Behind him a man loomed from the stairwell. Her father jumped, almost yelled, as the man clamped a hand on to his shoulder.

'Court Four!' The man swung her father round to face him and it seemed for a moment they would both go tumbling down the stairs. 'Sorry, chief. I'm in a hurry, I need . . . Where's Court Four?' He sounded desperate.

'It's down there,' Rebecca said. 'There on the right.'

'Have you been in there? Is it finished?' The man, with receding fair hair and a sharp-featured, bleak, intelligent face let go of her father but didn't stand out of his way. He gave them each a look that was half glaring, half beseeching.

'Yes, the appeal hearing, they just finished it,' Rebecca said. 'Is that—'

'Colin! What's happening?' A woman was breathlessly coming up, youngish, dressed in a tight trouser suit and somehow looking both plump and gaunt. 'We were late – it was the car, we had to borrow one, you see,' she began explaining at once to Rebecca and her father, as anxiously as if they had been awaiting her. 'Colin wasn't sure of the gears and London – he's not used to driving in London. It was terrible . . .'

'Is it Mr Brudenell?' Her father spoke with a kind of reluctant recognition.

'That's me. Where do I go? It's the Gandy feller, it's that bloody— You been in there? You seen him?'

Her father looked ashen, shadowed, as if he were standing in some other light source from everyone else. His lips moved.

'Yes,' he got out.

'Help me out here, mate,' Colin Brudenell said. His eyes met Rebecca's, with the ghost of a rueful smile. 'I'm dying.'

'Colin, Wendy, there you are . . .' Rescue came: a bald, besuited man who had been in the courtroom, sitting alone. He approached at a perspiring trot down the corridor and literally took the couple in hand, gripping an arm of each and steering them back down the staircase.

'It was the car – we would have been all right if it hadn't been for the car . . .' The woman couldn't leave it, threw a look of appeal up at Rebecca and her father as if begging them to understand.

'Never mind,' the bald man said, tugging like a tag wrestler, 'come on, let's go down, that'd be best.'

'So what happened? Is it over? It must have been quick. That's a good sign. They sent him back, yeah?' Colin Brudenell held his ground, quizzing the bald man with a smile that was like a grin of held-in pain. 'No go, right? He's going back to prison, that's right, isn't it?'

'The appeal was successful, I'm afraid. Gandy's been freed. It's best if you come downstairs—'

'What do you mean, successful?' The fair man's thin face deepened in colour, swiftly and alarmingly. 'I don't get you. How come? What did you do?'

'There was nothing I could do, Colin. It's the judgement of the Appeal Court, you simply have to abide by it. The judges overturned the conviction.'

'You have got to be kidding me. No, wait a minute, there's something not right here.' Colin Brudenell's body sagged, and he made a kind of drained stagger down one step. Again he appealed in turn to Rebecca and her father. 'You were in there, were you? They didn't let him go, did they?'

'Howard Gandy's been freed,' the solicitor said, 'that's the ruling, Colin. There's nothing anybody can do.'

'This man we're talking about,' Colin Brudenell said, ignoring him, blue eyes boring into Rebecca's, 'he killed my little boy, you see. That's what they put him away for. They did him for it and that's the only thing that's kept me going. D'you see?' He spread out his hands in a gesture of terrible reason-ableness. 'Makes sense, right? So they can't let him out. If they let him out then – then the world's gone bloody mad. Bloody mad . . .'

'Shush, Colin,' the woman said, in settled misery, 'Colin, shush.'

'I'm sorry, Colin. They had a good case and they presented it well,' the solicitor said. 'There's absolutely nothing to be done. I did advise you not to come down here and really . . .

Gandy's done twelve years inside. Maybe it's best just to let it lie now.'

Colin looked down, tendons moving in his throat. He shook his head and as he did so Rebecca saw a single tear like a raindrop hit the stone floor.

'So where is he?' he said, quieter now. 'What have they done with him? Is he downstairs?'

'He'll be released through the jailer's gate.'

'Downstairs? All right then. I'm coming . . .'

'Colin . . .'

Colin Brudenell was already plunging down the stairs, the solicitor hurrying to keep up with him.

The woman meekly followed, like a person who never leads. She had bulbous and pained eyes, and when Rebecca met them she thought for a moment the woman was going to mention the car again. Instead she said, 'It's not him.' And then after a sharp breath, 'Not him you're seeing.'

People were coming down the corridor towards the stairs. Her father guided Rebecca to one side and let them pass.

'The little boy's father,' he breathed. 'You gathered. I remember him from the first time. I don't think he knew me. The woman, though, I'm sure that wasn't the mother.'

'God, how awful. Will he – you know, get near him?'

'I imagine there'll be precautions.'

Someone had stopped close by them. Rebecca turned to find Adam, smiling. With him was Pat Gandy, the fashionable young woman from earlier hovering behind them.

'Philip, I've just got to thank you for helping with this. We got the result. It all worked out.'

Her father nodded, but he looked not at Adam but at the little grey lady hovering by his side. 'Pat.'

'Did you put in a word?' she said, with a kind of shy distance. 'Apparently you put in a word.'

'I . . . well . . .'

'Philip helped us to clear things up,' Adam said, with an inclusive gesture.

'Well,' Mrs Gandy said, nodding, her shiny handbag clasped in front of her, 'thank you for that, anyway.'

'Pat, do you want to go on? Angela, would you go with Pat? I won't be a moment.' Adam turned to Rebecca's father, his face perceptibly less public. 'Well, I do mean thank you. I know this is something you're still . . . ambivalent about, but will you come and see Howard walking out? It's going to be a hell of a moment. I think it will give you something to see it.'

'I don't mind,' Rebecca said at her father's enquiring look. She did want to see it; but she didn't know what to feel. The flat terrible echoes of Colin Brudenell's words were still in her head; so was the look in those pale, intense eyes.

Outside they found what the papers themselves usually called a scrum of pressmen gathered around a door in the court precincts, but in fact there was a decorous order about their manoeuvrings, more typical of photographers at a Saturday wedding. Rebecca and her father stood at a distance: her father had put on his sunglasses and seemed wary, but for now all attention was on that vaultlike exit, where Adam was expertly orchestrating the press, exchanging a laughing word here and there in between casting expectant glances over his shoulder.

The wait was not long: a rapid percussion of camera shutters, a swinging of fluffy microphone booms, and Howard Gandy was there, his arm round the tiny figure of his mother. He blinked and smiled shyly as they came forward. In his other hand he was clutching the necks of two plastic sacks on which Rebecca could read quite clearly the stencilled words PROPERTY OF HM PRISON DEPT. Then, with a sudden movement that had the lenses ducking and swinging, he dumped the sacks on the ground and put one great arm out and hugged Adam to his side, squeezing the young man until he laughed and gasped.

For a few moments Rebecca's view was obstructed by a weaving TV camera; when it was clear again she saw to her surprise that it was neither Gandy nor Adam who was stepping forward to speak but Jameson, the solicitor.

'The verdict of the Appeal Court is warmly welcomed by the whole team who have campaigned so hard for the release of Howard Gandy from imprisonment for a crime which it is now established he did not commit.' His voice was high-pitched and pugnacious. 'Mr Gandy wishes to convey his thanks to the legal team who worked on his behalf, to everyone who lent their support to the campaign, and to Mr Adam

Dowling who persevered in researching, preparing and publicizing the case at a time when it seemed that justice would never be served. His thanks and love to his mother, Mrs Pat Gandy, who never gave up on him in twelve long years. Justice has, at last, been served. Now is not the time for bitterness or recrimination; Mr Gandy is looking forward to being reunited with his mother and resuming the normal life of which he was deprived. It remains none the less a sad fact that seldom can an innocent man have been so ill-served by the British justice system, which in the past has rightly prided itself on its protection of the innocent, its even-handedness, its immunity to prejudice and hysteria. It is Mr Gandy's hope, and that of the people who worked for his release, that lessons will be drawn on all sides from the experiences that he has undergone: if so, those twelve lost years of his life will not have been entirely wasted.'

'Do you intend to seek compensation?' a reporter asked.

'The question of compensation is an open one at present,' Jameson piped. 'Mr Gandy's main concern is to get back to living a normal home life.'

'Who do you think is to blame for . . .?' The question was lost in a sudden blare of quarrelling traffic from the Strand. Then one of the booms swung upwards and a woman reporter who had wriggled herself to the front was addressing Howard Gandy directly, literally over Jameson's carroty head.

'Mr Gandy, how do you feel, your first minutes of freedom?'

Howard Gandy flinched a little as at a bright light, then spoke in a Lincolnshire rumble, soft but distinct.

'I feel very pleased to be out,' he said.

There was a massed stuttering of questions, but the woman at the front had the advantage. 'How do you feel you've been treated?'

'Today, I've been treated all right,' he answered, ignoring the solicitor at his shoulder nervously ready to interpose. 'Only today's too late. This should have happened twelve year ago. It's nice, it's terrific, getting out. But it's nothing to crow about because I shouldn't be here doing this in the first place.'

'Do you feel angry at the system?'

'I don't know about the system. It's people that's behind the system, isn't it? They locked me away for no reason. That's not right.' He lifted his round chin, scanning them. 'So like I say, this is nothing to crow about.'

In his dogged refusal to exult, his grey, aloof stubbornness, Rebecca had an inkling of what turned people against this man who even now would not accommodate, would not make his face fit.

'What was it like in prison?'

'It was full of criminals,' he said, deadpan. Beside him Adam smiled, eyes cast down.

'How were you treated by your fellow prisoners?'

'I kept meself to meself. I weren't interested in them. I shouldn't have been in there anyway.'

'Mrs Gandy –' the boom swung downwards and Pat Gandy shrunk as if at a weapon, pressing closer to her son – 'how do you feel about being reunited with your son?'

'It's lovely,' she said in a faint voice. 'What I've always wanted. I've got my son back.'

'Did you ever doubt . . .?'

The question and response were lost in a commotion breaking out on the other side of the precinct. At first the reporters were a little slow in cottoning on to what was happening; then there was a confused shuffling and swinging in the direction of Colin Brudenell.

At first sight it appeared as if Brudenell was having a fight: a pure playground scuffle with a lot of shoving and squeaking of shoes on asphalt. Then Rebecca saw that his adversary was in fact his solicitor who, red-faced and distressed, was trying to hold him back by main strength like a man with a skittish horse.

'Should have hanged him! They should have hanged the bastard!' Colin Brudenell was screaming it, his voice shrill and womanish with passion. One arm had come out of his jacket as he wrestled with his solicitor. His wife flapped her hands and circled round them like an ineffectual referee. 'Watch your kids. Watch out for your kids, people . . . They don't know what they've done . . .' As the cameras homed in on him Brudenell pointed his shirtsleeved arm to the sky, a wild bizarre gesture, half football supporter, half prophet. 'This is supposed to be the Courts of Justice! Where's the justice, eh? Show me. Where's the justice for me?' A policeman had appeared and with crooning patience began urging him away. Borne slowly backwards, Colin Brudenell managed a mad dance on his toes and shrieked to the scurrying reporters: 'What about my twelve years, eh? Who cares about me? Who cares . . .?'

Rebecca's father put his hand on her shoulder; for some reason the touch was enormously welcome, reassuring and anchoring her. 'Victim manhandled away by the law,' he said drily, 'while killer walks away smiling. A gift for a certain type of newspaper.'

'He's not a killer, though,' she said, seeking her father's eyes.

'No. It's official. Well, thank God there's nothing more for me to do.'

Over at the jailer's office, Gandy and his mother had disappeared again. Adam remained, fielding questions from the depleted circle of pressmen. Some, she noticed, were already peeling off and heading towards another court entrance. Another story: grist to the mill.

'Home? Unless you fancy the party,' her father said. 'Rebecca? You OK?'

'Yes,' she said. 'Yes, home.'

But it wasn't of home she was thinking, or not the kindly home of Salters Cottage. Watching Colin Brudenell, hearing that cracked note of self-justification in his baying voice, Rebecca was back in the world of her first childhood, before the adoption. The world of Cathy Groom and the embattled, dully violent men who had lurked in it. Men whose very love – for their women, and for their children – was contorted, turned in on itself, like a clenched fist. She shuddered and shook herself free of it; but as she walked away from the courts with her father she took with her the hard seeds of a terrible suspicion.

# TEN

'I thought we'd have a bit of fish today, lovey,' Pat said, switching off the vacuum cleaner. 'Being as it's Tuesday.'

'Does he still come on Tuesdays, then?'

There was surprise in Howard's question, and Pat found a curious, pleasant satisfaction, so much that it almost made her chuckle contentedly, in answering, 'Oh, yes. Still comes every Tuesday morning. Never misses, except at Christmas.'

It was one of the few things that hadn't changed, the arrival of the fish man, as they called him, in the High Street every Tuesday morning at ten. He sold fresh Grimsby fish from a white van that he parked in the car park of the Beacon pub and it was very good fish. There had always been a little knot of women waiting on Tuesday mornings with purses tucked under their arms – a few less nowadays, perhaps, because people had freezers and cars to take them to the big super-markets in Ingelow; but still, you couldn't beat the taste of fresh fish. Pat herself, since the terrible thing happened, had tended to go along to meet the fish van rather later, when people weren't around. Even after the initial hostility had died down – and that took a long time – she had found it awkward, mixing – and doing things separately, half furtively, had become an ingrained habit.

But now there was no need: she had her son back and his name was cleared. Pat's mind staggered a little at the thought of it.

'Yes, a bit of fish would be nice,' Howard said. He had finished his toast and was reading a letter that had come that morning. As he read he held the letter away from him, narrowing his eyes.

'You want your glasses for that,' Pat said.

'It's all right. I've got used to doing without 'em.'

111

'You mustn't strain your eyes. I wasn't surprised when they tested you and said you needed them, in that place. Your dad had to start wearing them. Not that he bothered, except when he was picking his horses. He could sit down and study them all right. Not bills though, never gave them a look. Didn't you wear your glasses in there?'

'No. I never got into the habit.' Howard picked up his tea-mug and drank slowly, draining it, his eyes on the letter. 'It was safer not to wear them, in my position. Somebody might smash them on to your face.'

It was the casual, informative tone in which he said these things that got to her. There had been several instances in the past few days, since that still scarcely believable day when she had brought him home. He hadn't sat down and poured everything out – that wasn't Howard's way – but he had let things slip, things that he hadn't told her while he was in there, either in letters or during her visits to the prison. Probably he had wanted to protect her – didn't want her worrying any more than she already did: that *was* his way. She looked at him sitting there, and remembered him as a baby, and thought about someone smashing his glasses on to his face – someone doing that to her son, her only child! Hurting him . . . and her being unable to stop it, this time.

All at once Pat started crying, there at the breakfast table in a pool of golden June sunshine.

'Mum, what's the matter?'

'Ooh, Howard . . .' She was quite racked by sobs, and for the moment couldn't speak intelligibly. Tears streamed down her face and she could hear her own voice in deep wretchedness going *boo hoo hoo*, the pure classic crying noise that she had never really heard before.

'Now then. It's all right. Whyever are you taking on like this?' Howard had shifted his chair round the table and put his arms round her, cradling her head on his shoulder. She buried her wet eyes in his shirt, ashamed because she wasn't the weepy sort and also because it was he, if anyone, who had the right to cry after all he'd been through: hardly fair that he was the one consoling her. But it was so nice and comforting.

'I – I feel like it's all my fault,' she stammered out at last.

'How do you work that one out?'

'I feel like I should have said something.' She extracted a tissue from the pocket of her slacks. 'That's what I should have done. That day when it happened. I should have said to the police –' she mouthed the word, disliking it even now – 'that you were here with me all day.'

'I wasn't, though, Mum,' he said. 'It wouldn't be the truth. And that was the whole point. I told the truth and stuck to the truth. Through thick and thin.'

'It would have been easier, though,' she said, wiping her eyes. She noticed for the first time, close up, that the stubble on his chin had flecks of grey. The last time she had had him at home with her he had been twenty-eight years old. 'It wouldn't have mattered, so long as it saved you. That's all that mattered, Howard – ever.'

'Nothing good ever comes of lying,' he said. He patted her hand. 'I've always thought that and I still do.'

'You got treated terrible, Howard. I can't get over that. I'm your mother; I should have stopped it somehow.'

'Well, you couldn't. It wasn't your fault. Now stop whittling.'

'I know. I can't though. I've been worrying so long and now you're home I can't quite believe it.'

'Well, I am, Mum. I'm home now, and everything can go back to the way it was before.'

'Can it?'

'I don't see why not. This is what I've been waiting for. Nothing grand. Just going back home and getting back to normal. Haven't you?'

'Well, that's what I'm a bit afraid of. I mean, perhaps it won't feel the same.'

Howard raised his eyebrows and looked around, thinking. 'It does so far,' he said. 'A bit strange, maybe. It strikes me how quiet it is. It was noisy in there. Echoey. I don't know how I shall be going out where there's a lot of people – that'll feel funny I should think. But I shall soon slip back into it.'

She stroked his back, then got up hastily and began clearing the table. 'You're a brave lad.'

'Not really. Stuck to my guns, that's all.'

She felt silly for crying, and was brisk when she came back from the kitchen. 'So, what does your letter say?'

'It's from Mr Jameson. He's confirming that the Appeal

court has agreed to pay costs. That's something, I suppose. But he says there's still no public statement about the case from the court. He's written to the Lord Chief Justice's office about it. But we can't expect any word from the judge at the original trial because he's died since then.' Howard grunted. 'Well, we'll see. He says something about starting to press for compensation, but it's not that I'm bothered about. It's that apology: that's what I want.'

'You deserve some compensation, though. All you've had to go through.'

'Money's not the same as saying they did wrong. People should own up to things, they shouldn't get away with it. If there was money, I'd take it for your sake, that's all.'

'Well, we could do with it.'

'Don't worry about that. I'll get myself a job soon.'

'Where, though, Howard? There's hardly anything nowadays. Couldn't you use that prison service thing, you know, where they help to find you a job?'

Howard's chin rose. 'That's for ex-convicts, Mum. That's when you've paid for your crime and they get you back into society. I'm not like that. I haven't got any criminal record. I don't want nothing to do with any prison services.'

'Well, it seems a shame . . . Perhaps Coupland's might have a job going. I don't know the people there now – it's all changed since I finished – but it might be worth a try. After all, you worked for them before, and it wasn't your fault you were laid off.'

'It's a possibility. It depends, though. Depends what people think of me now.'

Her eyes met his, mutually acknowledging the question neither of them had yet spoken.

'Well,' she said, unplugging the vacuum cleaner and coiling the flex, 'time enough to worry about that.'

'Oh, I'm not worried. Of course, there's Adam Dowling as well. He wants to do a lot of interviews with me, like, for this book he's going to do. Reckons he'll come up here, rent a place for a while to do 'em. He said it would be quite normal to pay me for my trouble. I don't know, I wouldn't ask it, especially from him, but if it's normal I suppose . . .'

'He's a lovely man. I wouldn't refuse him anything,' Pat

114

said. 'It just seems a shame, though – having to go on digging it all up like that.'

'How do you mean?'

'Well . . .' She had forgotten what an emphatic, uncompromising presence Howard had, or had got used to living without it: it seemed she had retreated into woolly and evasive thinking in her years alone. 'Now it's over, I just . . . I just want an ordinary life, Howard.'

'So do I. But what happened to me shouldn't be forgotten about. I want it to be told. It's not something I can do myself, but Adam can. It's needed. Even now folk probably don't know the truth or don't believe it. Look at that Brudenell feller.'

'I don't want to look at him, thank you. He frightened me that day.' Pat lit a cigarette, eager and shaking.

'Well, Mr Jameson mentions him at the end here. He says not to worry about it and that he's been in touch with Colin Brudenell's solicitor and he'll make sure that something's worked out so there'll be no trouble.' He got up and filed the letter carefully away in a cardboard folder he had brought with him from Whateley: obviously a habit he had got into during the long campaign for his release. Seeing another folded paper on the table, she said, 'What about that one, lovey? Do you need that?'

'No.' Howard took it up and tore it neatly across several times. 'That's just one of those nasty ones, I'm afraid.'

'Oh, no. How do they find out where we live? We're not in the book.'

'Don't worry about it. They'll stop eventually. Folk'll find somebody new to pick on. I'll put that vacuum away for you.'

'Ta, duck.' He started to carry it up the stairs – no heavier than a torch it looked in his great hand – and she spoke before she could stop herself. 'Oh, I don't keep it in the spare bedroom now, love. I think there's a bit of damp in there. I keep it . . .' She bit her lip.

'Aye?' He was still. 'Where?'

'In the cupboard.' She bit her lip, pointed to the little door underneath the staircase.

Howard's eyes held hers for a moment in which the bright new world seemed to plunge into an eclipse of ancient fear.

Then he said, 'Aye. More handy there.' Deftly, without expression, he opened the squeaking door of the cupboard, thrust the vacuum inside, and closed it. Breathing a little heavily, he dusted his hands and came towards her.

'I've been thinking.'

'Yes, lovey?' She looked away, a little wildly, for her cigarettes.

'I was thinking perhaps that we could go out. Me and you. I reckon it would do you good. Plus we've got to get used to it. I'm ready if you are.'

Ashamed of her fear, ashamed of her shame, Pat nodded. She walked through to the kitchen, to hide her face from him. 'Where shall we go?'

'I thought maybe Ingelow.' He had appeared noiselessly behind her: he was amazingly light on his feet for his size. 'We could get the bus. I don't know how much it is now.'

'Two pounds return.'

'Is it?' He sucked in scandalized breath. 'I can't believe how things have gone up. Well, never mind. It can be our day out. It's nice weather for it.'

'It'll be very busy. Start of the season. Tourists everywhere.'

'Well, that's good. It's like being thrown in at the deep end, isn't it?'

'I suppose so.' For some reason she had never liked that expression. 'Well, if you're sure . . . Oh, what about the fish man? Our dinner—'

'We'll have fish and chips in Ingelow.'

'All right then.' All at once she felt better about the expedition, fear giving way to excitement. Fish and chips in Ingelow – how long it had been since she had had a simple treat like that! The chip shops of Ingelow were always winning awards – best Grimsby fish and Lincolnshire potatoes. It would be lovely – and to have a day out with her son, too, that would be wonderful: to be able to walk down the street with him, proudly. 'Will I do as I am?' Halter top and slacks: really it was the only summer outfit she had.

'I don't see why not. I suppose I shall have to get myself some clothes some time. What's in fashion nowadays?'

'Oh, they wear things baggy, as far as I can tell, the young 'uns. So it looks like their clothes are too big for them. That's no good for you.' She chuckled, patting and squeezing his great round biceps. 'Can't make clothes look baggy on you, great strapping feller.'

He laughed.

'And this tum. Mind you, that's all muscle there, isn't it? All hard, look . . .'

'Mum.' His smile was watchful. 'Mum.'

'Sorry, duck. Being daft now.' That was her trouble, she got carried away.

But she still felt light-hearted when they went out together and waited at the bus stop in the village High Street. This was precisely the kind of public exposure that she had dreaded, but it seemed that fortune smiled on them. Three people came by as they waited: two were an elderly couple who had moved to Holfleet a couple of years ago and who gave them a cheerful good morning, and the third was a young man in shorts who hesitated and then stepped up and said he was staying at the caravan site and could they direct him to the village post office?

'Just down there to your left.' It was Howard who answered him, pointing carefully. 'Past the phone box there. You can't miss it.'

'Thanks a lot.' The young man smiled and waved a hand as he left them. Good legs for shorts, Pat noticed; and she felt proud again and pleased at this chance that had allowed Howard to take possession, as it were, of his old home.

They sat upstairs on the bus, right at the front. Howard's eye was quick for changes in the old familiar scenes on the short ride into Ingelow: a new carport here, a widening of the road there. The new superstore on the outskirts of the town, with its red and yellow fascia, made his eyes open wide. 'Where on earth did that spring from?'

'Magic.' She felt silly and happy. 'It just came by magic one day.'

'Magic. Honestly, Mum.' He grunted his calm amusement. 'You should take more water with it.'

Ingelow's wide streets were full of people, but they were not crammed as in August, when you were liable to be pushed into the gutter by fat holidaymakers guzzling ice creams; and Howard appeared quite at ease, walking with an unhurried

117

step, her arm through his. They made a leisurely progress along Victoria Road, which ran all the way down to the seafront promenade where the clock tower stood. It was all cafés and the kind of shops Pat called tatty shops, though she didn't mean it in any derogatory way, enjoying investigating their chaotic contents. She tried on funny hats, squeezed water-pistols, peered into kaleidoscopes, all to the patient indulgence of Howard.

Stepping out from a particularly dark Aladdin's cave of a shop, they stood dazzled for a moment by the sunshine. Howard gave a start: a little girl, not looking where she was going, had bumped into his great treelike legs.

'Whoops. Are you all right there?'

The little girl, no more than four, looked up at him and then, desolately, round at her clucking parents: in the collision she had dropped her candy floss on the ground.

'Leave it, Kelly. It's mucky, don't pick it up. It's your own fault, you should have looked where you were going.'

'No,' Howard said, 'I shouldn't have been standing about like a great lump. Never mind, duck. You wait there just a sec.'

He turned and went into the café next door, and came out a few moments later with a big stick of multicoloured candy floss.

'Oh, you didn't have to do that . . .' The mother's protests were feeble.

'My pleasure. There you are, duck. Keep tight hold of it.'

'Thank you.' A nice little girl; and Howard had made her day. For a moment Pat felt almost tearful. Her son liked children so much; and from that one simple fact such misery and destruction had been let loose. How would they ever, really, get over it? They were putting up a show, now, but this was a special day and they were amongst strangers, comfortably anonymous. For the first time the reality of what had happened in that court in London struck home, and she felt afraid of the future. She very nearly wished for the bleak familiarity, the knowable solitude, of the twelve years past.

'Mum. What's the matter? Come on. It all feels funny, I know. We'll get used to it.'

Ever the mind-reader . . . She felt her arm taken, and she smiled. 'You're a good lad, Howard.'

'I must be the oldest lad in the world, then,' he grumped. 'Forty-year-old lad.' But he looked pleased.

Then, in one of the tatty shops, she came across a display of funny toy penguins, all in different outfits. Something about them delighted her and made her giggle out loud. Though they were on the dear side Howard, always indulgent, insisted that she have one as a gift from him. 'Go on,' he said, 'pick one – pick the one that appeals to you.'

It was hard to choose, but her eyes kept going back to the first one she had spotted – a penguin in a sombrero and poncho, with such a comical expression. 'Oh, it's got to be that one,' she said. 'It's like he's been looking at me all the time.'

Just then a youth of about fifteen, spotty and elfin in a big baseball cap, pushed right in front of her and took the penguin.

'Here you are, Kirsty. This one.' He had a girl with him. 'Call it twat in a hat.'

Pat was disappointed, but she wouldn't have made a fuss. She had got accustomed, perhaps, to giving in to slights. But Howard's great arm had shot out, and he had hold of the youth by his skinny shoulder.

'Get off!'

'You hand that over. My mum wanted that – you know she did.'

'Ooh – "me mum".' The youth mocked Howard's accent.

Pat was suddenly alarmed. 'Howard, it doesn't matter—'

'Give.' Howard's deep voice had dropped until it was more like a vibration, a tremor of distant thunder.

'Piss off, why should I?'

'Because it's fair.' Lower and lower the voice dropped. Howard's great body loomed over the boy's, though from a little way away it might have looked simply as if he were having a friendly word. 'And because I'll make you so sorry if you don't.'

The choked thickness of his voice produced a kind of lisp – *so sorry* – and somehow it was that that triggered the fear in Pat. The girl, too, it seemed: she hadn't taken her eyes off Howard's face and now she grabbed at the youth's arm and actually pulled him away.

'Leave it, Paul, leave it.' She sounded almost tearful. She

slapped the penguin back on to the shelf. Pat couldn't look at their scarlet faces as they passed her.

'Here you are, Mum. Now let's go and pay for it.' Howard handed the penguin to her. His face was all smiles, his voice light and cheerful.

'I suppose that was bad-mannered of them,' she said uncertainly at the till, but her heart was thudding audibly. She had almost forgotten such moments in the past twelve years. She calmed her fear with a smile, remembering how, in his childhood, he'd sworn to look after her. Nothing to get worked up about – the kids had gone.

'Dirty little monkeys.' Howard put away his change and then drew out his hand and, head up, snapped his fingers in the air: a loud, crisp, emphatic noise, like a stick being cleanly broken. 'They're not worth that. Come on then, Mum. Let's go and get those fish and chips.'

# ELEVEN

Rebecca had got a summer job skivvying at an old-fashioned guesthouse in Ingelow called the Cowrie House Hotel. It meant an early start and even earlier rising, a rising that to one of Rebecca's inclinations seemed obscene and unheard of, an act of perversity. But it also meant she was home early. She arrived at half-past seven to help with the breakfast – that strange vast meal called a traditional English breakfast, with its fried bread and tinned tomatoes and other things that no one ever ate except when holidaying in seaside guesthouses – and then there was the washing up and the cleaning of rooms and changing of laundry while the guests were shooed out into the town. Her last duty was preparing vegetables and cold sweets for the evening meal. She was usually finished by half-past two and dismounting from the bus in Holfleet before three.

Her father too was throwing himself into work. After eating some humble pie he had renegotiated the deadline for the nature series music and had worked on it in the kind of frantic flurry that, she suspected, was the real stimulation for his creativity. After visits to the studios in Bristol he had brought back videotapes of the rushes and he would crouch before them far into the night, doodling silently on his electronic keyboard plugged into a headphone set. At mealtimes he would still be working on the scoring, manuscript paper spread out across the dining table where, from her eating and mildly interested perspective, the numerous marks of expression, all *fff* and *ppp* and *sfz*, looked like the onomatopoeia of his own fuming impatience.

Broadcasting work was his bread and butter as a composer. The world did not wait with bated breath for the next Philip Springthorpe opus, though he had a solid reputation: new pieces usually found a premiere at British festivals and one or two had their first performance in America. Compared to much contemporary music Rebecca had heard, her father's was blessedly approachable: he had a lyrical gift that coincided with a shift in taste towards warmer and more traditional values in music. A Lincolnshire-born man, he had returned from London to live here after his marriage. The landscape with its breadth and homeliness, bleakness and light, always stimulated him. Rebecca could hear its ancient spaces in the snatches she had heard of a major work that had been in fitful progress for a couple of years, a *Somersby Pastorale* inspired by Tennyson's birthplace ten miles away across the wolds. But that had to take second place to music journalism and commissions like this one for TV, which meant deadlines. When there was a deadline, her father was a decidedly absent presence.

Then one day towards the end of her second week in her job Rebecca came home to find a neat stack of music paper on the kitchen table with atop it a little figure he had given her when she passed her GCSEs, a cheerful gonk with arms upraised and the word HOORAY stamped on his tummy.

She knocked and went into his study. He was lying on the floor with his hands behind his head. It was a theory of his that contact with the earth, or as near as could be managed, revitalized you.

'You're finished?'

'I'm finished and it's finished,' he said grinning. 'Thank God. Richard Strauss said he could describe a teaspoon in music. I wonder how he would have felt about describing the DNA helix. How was your day?'

'Mrs Headley was saying she'll have to get new sheets. Those nylon ones are too hard to iron, she says.'

'They're not nylon? Not really?'

'Nylon. The ones that catch the pubic hairs.'

'Oh, Rebecca!' He laughed himself upright, darted to the piano stool and began playing to the tune of 'Daisy Bell,' humming and then crooning, 'Stephen, Stephen, give me your answer do . . . I'm half crazy, all for the love of you . . .'

'Dad, pack it in. It's not funny.' His roguish look made her laugh all the same. 'Anyway, it doesn't rhyme properly.'

'Stephen, Stephen, diddly doo de doo . . . I'm not leavin', till I get snogged by you . . . Ow, ow.'

She rained mock fists on his head. 'You bugger. I've told you . . . He hasn't been round again, has he?'

'He's managed to keep away today. Living on his memories of last night, probably. No, no, OK, sorry – not on the bald patch, ow . . .'

Last week Stephen Larkinson had returned to the parental home from doing good things in Turkey. Reacquainting himself with Rebecca, whom throughout their teenage years he had either ignored or patronized, he seemed to see something he had not seen before. Or else, Rebecca thought, he wanted to fit in a fling before going up to university in October. He had haunted her with invitations to a drink which she politely refused, but last night proved he hadn't got the message. Emma had had a party for her twenty-first birthday in a hall in Ingelow. Rebecca's first sight on entering had been of Stephen Larkinson weaving his way purposefully across the dance floor towards her.

'I suppose he's quite good-looking,' Emma had said in a cloakroom tête-à-tête. 'I mean, it does count no matter what they say.'

Certainly; and Stephen was good-looking in the way of a younger branch of the royal family, blond, white-teethed, lots of bone. But she simply didn't go for him, and his endless anecdotes about Turkey seemed mere droning, as if he thought he could simply recite her into submission. And though her age, he seemed blindingly young. She tried to say something of this to Emma.

'That's because we mature earlier. They're all very boy-ey, aren't they? When you really look into them. But then they turn into old farts. I mean where's the happy medium . . .?'

'I take it we're a long way from an engagement, then,' her father said now, vamping the Wedding March on the piano.

'About a zillion miles.'

'Thank God for that. Imagine, I'd be related to Diane Larkinson.'

All at once his right hand picked out the poised opening notes of *The Entertainer*. He smiled over his shoulder. She sat down with him on the stool and he began playing Joplin rags.

He stitched them effortlessly together, medley-style, the *Maple Leaf*, the *Peacherene* and the *Weeping Willow*, all her favourites; and as she used to she filled in the left-hand parts he had taught her, short easy figures that yet made her feel as if she were part of a virtuoso duet. She loved the proud, debonair, witty music and she loved this, felt keenly, along with her happiness, how long it was since they had done it and what hard tests life had been setting them of late.

It was joyous – but it wasn't the same, of course. Nothing was, since the Howard Gandy business. She was still haunted by images of that day in the Appeal Court: Gandy with his reined-in docility like a caged animal in the dock; and Colin Brudenell, a distillation of her own infant memories when adults, flawed titans, acted out explosive tragedies while she clung to the banisters and feared coming into their desperate orbit. Beyond that, though, she was haunted by someone she had never seen: the little child called Lee who had met his death in her own village. He had looked his pitiful last on these scenes, scenes where her own childhood had made its strange wonderful twist towards light and hope. And she even seemed to feel him calling to her, as she used to fancy her parents' dead child Thomas called to her from the woods and salt flats: calling, though, not as a spectral brother but a wronged spirit, piping for justice.

'Damn!' The knocking at the door broke through the last bar of the *Gladiolus Rag*. Her father echoed it, hammering out the opening chords of Beethoven's Fifth. 'Fate knocks at the door. Or is it your ever-loving Stephen?'

'Oh, Dad, you answer it.'

'You answer it, I'll come with you. The heavy father. What are your intentions towards my daughter, young man . . .?'

In the hall the phone rang, as it does, simultaneously with the knocking. Her father took it, gesturing Rebecca wryly to the door. 'Fate,' he mouthed.

Had Stephen seen her coming home? she wondered. Was he going to start acting like an obsessive in a bad thriller?

'Oh hi, Justin,' her father was saying. 'Yes, it is. Yep, full score . . .'

She opened the door and found Howard Gandy on the doorstep.

Behind her she sensed her father's attention.

'Hello,' she said, after what seemed a long time. Howard was just standing there, as if they had asked him to call and he were waiting to be told what it was all about.

'Hello. I've come to see Mr Springthorpe.'

Rebecca looked at her father. He nodded slowly: his eyes had gone curiously dead. 'What? Yeah, sure. Will do. Listen, Justin, can I call you back . . .?'

Howard Gandy came in. He smelt of aftershave. He was wearing a crisply ironed shirt with small checks that made her think of graph paper, and jeans that were a glaring inky blue, the sort of blue that you hated your jeans to be. The stitching stood up stiffly and Rebecca thought with a wince that they had the look of prison clothes.

Her father put down the phone. He took a deep breath, searching for a tone perhaps, the right tone for the occasion: it surely didn't exist.

'Well, Howard. What can I do for you?'

'I don't think you can do anything for me, really,' Howard said.

He was a literal-minded person, Rebecca thought, seeing her father's frown: you asked him something and he answered. It was just unfortunate in its truculent effect.

'Well, come through anyway.'

Her father went into the kitchen. Howard waited immovably for her to go first. Going through she found her father taking a bottle of Scotch from the cupboard. She understood the impulse, feeling the tension herself.

'So what's this about?' He poured one glass.

'Well, I'm living here now. We're bound to bump into each other at some point.'

'True.'

'So I thought we should meet.' Howard watched the whisky go down with the mild attentiveness of a quiet dog. 'I've been settling in and doing various things, but now I've got the chance I—'

'I don't know,' her father said. 'I see what you mean. But I don't think this is really appropriate, somehow. Let's just try and get on with our own lives, eh?'

'That's easy for you to say.'

Her father missed the beat. 'No,' he said, pouring again, 'no, it isn't.'

'I'm not mad at you. Don't get me wrong. I haven't come for anything like that. But you did tell lies about me.'

'I made a mistake.'

'Mm.' Howard nodded. He stood in the middle of the kitchen, in a position of awkwardness which anyone else would have mitigated by putting their hands in their pockets: but he seemed to feel no such need. 'That's what Adam says.'

'Is it? Well, it really isn't his business.'

'He's done a lot for me,' Howard said, with a slight hitch of his chin. He seemed oblivious of Rebecca's presence.

'Adam Dowling came to me,' her father said. 'I helped when he wouldn't take no for an answer. That's the end of it, really. I don't see what he's got to do with anything. No doubt he's got other windmills to tilt at.'

'Actually, he's renting a cottage up here. Just for a month or so. He rang me up last night. It's so he can do interviews and things for this book he's writing.'

'Well. He's going ahead with it then.' Her father's gaze brushed hers for a moment. 'I suppose there has to be something in it for him. Big fat cheque, maybe.'

'He's not like that. I don't think he is, anyway.' Howard glanced at Rebecca for the first time, and there was a kind of quizzical honesty in his look. 'I wouldn't have anything to do with him if he was.'

One of the cats had jumped down from the windowsill and began twining itself round Howard's legs. He bent and picked it up, stroking it. The cat purred and winked in pleasure: only the atmosphere made it look like a hostage.

'So where's this cottage?' her father said.

'Ingelow. I shall be going over there to talk to him. I think he'll be making like tapes. It's to get my side of the story.'

'Make sure you get a reasonable rate for that,' her father said. 'Maybe even some sort of clear contract on how your words are going to be used.' At times he seemed to enjoy flexing his capability of detachment, as someone who can juggle will spontaneously demonstrate with whatever comes to hand. 'I'm serious. Dowling might not be the only one – I mean, some newspaper might want your story. It doesn't have to be him.'

'Of course it does. He's the man who got me out. He saved me.' It was no doubt that habitually solemn tone that gave the words a religious tang. 'He's a good man.'

Rebecca picked up on the implication – or the intended opposite. It spurred her to speak. 'Dad helped him,' she said, trying for Howard's own uncompromising way. 'He helped him do it.'

Howard took no notice of her. 'Any road, I'm not doing it for the money. I just want the truth told.'

'The truth,' her father said into his glass, 'the whole truth and nothing but the truth.'

Howard bent to put the cat down gently. 'I still don't understand how you could lie like that.'

'There's a lot of things one doesn't ever understand in this life, Howard,' her father said, and he seemed to relish rather than regret the condescension. 'Look, I appreciate we need to – meet, I suppose. Clear the air. Fair enough. But I don't see it as appropriate, really, I don't see the point, for us to—'

'I understand most things,' Howard said, 'if they're explained to me.'

'I don't.' Her father put down his glass. 'I don't understand where you get off pestering kids and I never have.'

This crudity was so unlike her father that Rebecca couldn't have been more surprised if he had struck Howard Gandy a blow.

'You're against me. I'm used to that,' Howard said, and it was remarkable how he bleached the words of the paranoia and self-pity you expected.

'I'm against what you do. People are protective of their children. It's not hard to figure.'

'You told a lie about me because you were messing about behind your wife's back,' Howard said. 'That's right, isn't it?'

Her father covered the flinch. 'Obviously you know it all. I don't see that it matters now.' There was such a burning consciousness between Rebecca and her father at that moment that Howard seemed to feel it too: he turned to her and spoke with a kind of neutral appeal. 'I just want to get the facts straight. You see, it's not very nice when people are willing to believe any nasty thing about you. I'm back here to live, permanent. I want to know what folk are thinking. Not because I mind, because I never have in that way; just so I know where I stand.'

'You're a hero, Howard,' her father said. 'You're going to have a book written about you.'

'Well, that's up to Adam. All I want is for folk to know the truth.' Again he addressed himself to Rebecca. 'My name's mud,' he said, as casually as if he had said *My name's Howard.* 'You see? It isn't very nice.'

'No,' her father said, and his face became cold as it rarely did, the cheekbones raw, the laughter lines gone. 'No, it isn't. So you want to know what people are thinking? They're thinking they won't let their kids near you. Just the same as they thought before all this.'

It seemed cruel.

'You're still against me,' Howard said. He grunted. 'Dunno why you spoke up at all.'

'Well, he did,' Rebecca put in, wanting perhaps most of all to erase the feeling of her father's cruelty, 'he did, and – you're out, and we're all going to have to get along.'

She felt that Howard saw her, really saw her, for the first time. His eyes were very penetrating.

'I don't remember you,' he said.

'My daughter wasn't around back then,' her father said. 'She came to us after. Fortunately. You'd no doubt have taken a lot of notice if she had been around.'

'I'm Rebecca,' she said.

'Anyhow I think you'd better go,' her father said, with an impatient movement. 'We've – got it over with now.'

'You were at the court, weren't you?' Howard said to her.

'Yes.' She looked at her father, faintly imploring. 'We have got to live in the same village. As neighbours.'

'That's right. It's rum, isn't it?' Howard turned back to her father. 'I just don't get it. You really had it in for me. Like a lot of people, granted. But now you've gone and admitted you lied.'

'I didn't ask you to come here,' her father said, brisk and clipped. 'I don't see the point and I don't appreciate the visit, not really. The past is dead.'

Perhaps only Rebecca heard the bravado in those last words: saying it to make it true.

'It might be for you.' Howard took a step forward: trying to see her father's face. 'I don't know. I need to know what's going on in people's heads, do you see? In case they start telling fibs about me again. I'll nip it in the bud this time.' His tone was blank, but it was a combative thing to say: Rebecca sucked in a sharp breath.

'You're threatening me?'

'I'm telling you what's what.'

'And giving me what for. Goodness. I'm a bit old for you, aren't I?'

For a moment the dignity all seemed to lie on Howard Gandy's side – a weird disorientating moment for Rebecca, as though she had found herself suddenly left-handed.

'Well. I've done my bit. I told Mum I would and I have.'

All at once Howard was gone, quite noiselessly.

'Well, there you are,' her father said at last, seeming to inject himself effortfully into the silence. 'You've met the notorious Pied Piper.' Such hatred and bitterness clung around him that his next words took her completely by surprise. 'Ordinary, isn't he?'

She didn't know, really, whether he was or not; and she felt too pained to consider.

'You didn't treat him as if he was,' she said.

'I didn't grovel to him for ever daring to think he was a dangerous pervert. That's what it amounts to.' All at once there was a visible deflation about her father, and he put the whisky back in the cupboard. 'It's difficult for you, this. I'm sorry. You're just caught in the middle.'

'No, I'm not.' She felt herself dismissed, childlike. 'I'm part of it. I'm family.'

Going into the living room, he touched her shoulder. She followed.

'Howard was just trying to put the wind up me,' her father said. 'And you too. Which is what I don't like.'

She thought about that. Did she find Howard Gandy frightening? She had to admit she had felt uneasy in his presence – somehow *pinned* by it. But she was uneasy too about the hostility she had seen in her father. It wasn't like him – was it? Gandy's release had posed as many questions as it had solved. Today, she felt, she had encountered not just one but two strangers.

# TWELVE

Mrs Headley, the proprietress of the Cowrie House Hotel, said, 'Unusual for us to be booked up nowadays. Must be this beautiful weather. Of course, when we first started we'd be booked solid till the end of September. People naturally took their holidays at the seaside then. Fortnights, very often. We don't get many fortnights. There were a lot more family bookings then – more children. It's more retired people now. To be honest, I don't miss the children.' She investigated the waste bin with a gingerly hand, then, sniffing, tipped its contents into the plastic bin bag. 'Coke or something. All sticky. There's nothing like that on those sheets, is there?'

'Well, there's something a bit nasty,' Rebecca said, stripping the bed: she had learnt a technique of breathing through her ears for times like these.

'I'm afraid that's the old people for you,' said Mrs Headley, seventy if a day. 'Mark that one separate, dear. Of course, we had a different setup back then. A lot of the rooms were family rooms – parents in with the kids. It's not so popular now. I suppose people think it's not quite the thing, unless they're really babies. Such a lot of things you have to be careful about nowadays.' She chuckled. 'I can remember when I was a girl having a paintbox with a colour in it called Nigger Brown. Isn't that terrible? But we didn't think anything of it. Perhaps we've got a bit too sensitive about things generally. Something for you to look into when you go to college there. I've often wondered what makes people tick, you know. But I've never had the time to go into it, I suppose. You'd need to do a lot of reading, I think.'

As usual the mention of college and reading caused a panicky tightening in Rebecca's insides. She had scarcely dipped into the introductory texts she was supposed to read for October. It had become her habit to bring one to work in her bag, with some hazy idea of reading on the journeys; as yet she hadn't so much as opened it. Today the panic lasted until she finished work. When she sat down on the slatted seat by her bus stop at the promenade corner, she took the book out and applied herself to it. Filled with righteousness, she even hoped the bus would be late.

Two pages in, a gleam of chrome lanced her eyes and an engine muttered in front of her.

'Can I give you a lift?' Adam Dowling, one brown, gold-haired arm along the car windowsill.

'Oh, hi. Thanks.' She tried to look merely surprised rather than excited to see him. 'If it's not out of your way.'

'No problem.' He opened the passenger door for her. 'I'm staying up here for a while. Cottage on the Roman Bank.'

'Yes, I heard.' The inside of the car was hot and smelt of him, his denim shirt and cologne and body, and his wristwatch lay on the dashboard: it was a very intimate space to enter.

'Ah? Actually I didn't know there were any Romans around here.'

'Well, they call it that, but it's not that old really. Middle Ages or something.'

He pulled the car out, making a reckless three-point turn on the busy promenade road. Holidaymakers stood at the kerbs, red-skinned and dour, watching the manoeuvre.

'Certainly busy this time of year. I was lucky to get the cottage. Someone dropped out of a booking. I just moved in last night. Been shopping?'

'I've been to work. I've got a summer job in a hotel.'

'You must be done in. So how's your dad? Busy?'

'He's been working hard. He hasn't been able to concentrate on work for a long time.'

'Understandable.'

'Yes.' She had on a summer dress, and she could feel the backs of her knees adhering stickily to the seat; moving them would cause an embarrassing ripping sound. 'I hear you're going ahead with this book about Howard Gandy.'

'Seems I've got advance publicity. Yes, I am. This road, is it? Yes, it needs doing.'

'Your offer still stands, does it? About me being able to see

132

what you write beforehand – the stuff about my family. I haven't forgotten.'

'Neither have I. But I think, by the way, you're over-estimating the power of books. Of mine, anyway. My name's never exactly going to be at the top of the bestseller lists. We're not talking about nationwide publicity – not for anything that ends up in the book.'

'You had a book out before, Dad said. I've heard a lot of people read that. *Devil* something . . .?'

'*Devil's Work*. Slightly old hat now. Actually I've a copy at the cottage, if you'd like to have a look. In fact, why not stop by and have a cold drink? You can ask me anything you want and I'll try to answer. I'll show you what I've been working on. How about that?'

'All right.'

The cottage was part of an expensively refurbished row perched behind the sea bank, with a view over the aerodrome to the rear. The overhaul was so complete that perhaps only the bricks of the original structure remained, but still nothing could disguise the fact that these were fishermen's cottages and thus irredeemably tiny inside.

'Sleeps four, apparently,' Adam said, opening the front door for her. 'As long as they're midgets. Excuse the mess, but I haven't really unpacked yet.'

The downstairs room – the houseplace, it would have been called in the fishermen's days – was almost filled with sheafs of papers, files, books, bulging holdalls spilling their contents, and two items that were incongruously high-tech against the mahogany and chintz décor – a word processor and a portable cassette player, authentically Japanese and fashionably tubby in shape, both set out on the dining table.

'It's nice,' Rebecca said; feeling for the first time that what Adam did, and the way of life it entailed, were outstandingly desirable.

'I could have done a lot worse. The sea doesn't ever breach that bank, I suppose?'

'About once every fifty years.'

He brought a jug of chilled juice from the kitchen, with glasses loaded with ice. 'And what happens then?'

'Then you're screwed.'

Adam laughed and handed her an icy glass. 'Well, listen, I'm glad we can meet on good terms. I'm not in the business of defaming anybody or prying into private lives. Maybe that's an odd thing for an investigative journalist to say, but, well, let's face it, that term itself is just a glamorous title people like me invent for themselves. It sounds all hard-boiled and sexy. That's to cover up the fact that much of your time is spent ruining your eyesight poring over transcripts that have been photocopied ten times and weren't very clear to start with. It's funny, I'm no great fan of the British police, but in this job you do start to realize what a liquorice-and-string outfit they are. Their resources are quite poor for the amount of admin they have to do. I mean, look at this.' He hunted amongst the papers on the table. 'There – that's a photocopy of police custody records. It's all right, you're allowed to look. Now if your average office used materials like that, it would seem pretty shoddy.'

The sheet reminded her of the kind of cyclostyled form you brought home for your parents from junior school. There was a lot of illegible handwriting in the boxes, but what gave her a visceral shock was seeing the printed words 'LINCOLNSHIRE CONSTABULARY' and below, in an almost insolent scrawl, the words 'GANDEY, HOWARD'

'They've spelt his name wrong,' she said, handing it back, feeling in spite of what he said that she should not see it.

'Oh, yes. One error among many. Well, stuff like that, that's what you have to wade through. And bit by bit you build up a case. You want the truth. I personally don't think the truth is ever harmful. The case I've been working on is the wrongful conviction of Howard Gandy for the murder of Lee Brudenell, and your father was part of that case. The change in his evidence didn't prove Howard's innocence: what it did was knock the props away from the prosecution case that convicted him. In the book the change of evidence made by Mr Philip Springthorpe will be there, yes, but it needn't present him as a villain.'

'The woman he was with was named Carolyn Moyes,' Rebecca said. 'Will that go in? Just as an example.'

'That would depend. I've been trying to trace her so as to talk to her direct, but I've had no luck so far.'

'I see.' The thought of Carolyn Moyes being a real person, now, not an abstraction of twelve years ago, gave her a strange sickish feeling.

'But we're talking about a minor detail. It really isn't that big a deal. The book will mostly, overwhelmingly be Howard's story. That's why I'm here – to get the whole picture. There was only so much I could learn when he was in Whateley. We're going to do taped interviews, and—'

'I know. He said.'

'You've met him?'

'He came round to our house.'

'Right . . . Was he OK? Not, er, hostile?'

'Well, no, only to the idea that people don't trust him. He went on about the truth a bit. To be honest I didn't know what to make of him. He's a strange man. And yet he's— Dad called him ordinary.'

Adam nodded. 'It's all very weird for him, of course. He's trying to adapt, trying to make sense of it all. Hopefully the interviews will help a bit. It'd be interesting if you got to know him, he's really – he's remarkable. Of course he's had a fair amount of hostility since coming out of prison. People won't accept him. He's had nasty letters, phone calls—'

'Dad's not like that.'

'No, no. Of course not.' He was genuinely surprised.

'But Dad still doesn't like him.'

'Yes. He made that clear when we first talked. Not much that can be done, I'm afraid. Local people – many local people – made up their minds about Howard well before he went to prison. But he's determined to live back here just as before. That's the way he is.'

'You said about a villain. The book will have a villain, won't it?'

'I hope so. But have I found him yet? No. It's a pretty cold trail.'

'Did the police ever interview anybody else, apart from Howard?'

'As a suspect, you mean? No. Absolutely nobody. They pulled him in straight away and that was it. End of story, supposedly.'

'You must have felt good, that day at the Appeal Court.'

'It felt great. Not completely great, though. There's more to be done. You helped me see that, actually. Yes, you did. It's easy to get smug. But it's like you said – just freeing the innocent man isn't justice.'

'Plus there was that man – the one whose little boy was killed. That made things – awkward that day.'

'Skeleton at the feast. Colin Brudenell. That is a problem, for everyone. It seems pretty certain he's behind some of the phone calls Howard's been getting. And he gave an interview to his local paper saying some very inflammatory stuff about how he knows that Howard did do it, and that if he ever gets his hands on him he'll tear him apart. He seems rather an emotional character, but you can't be too careful. Doug Jameson, Howard's solicitor, has applied for an injunction which would prevent Colin Brudenell having any communication with Howard or coming anywhere near him. That's a civil matter as yet, though if there's any more of it, it could become a question of criminal action – harassment as a statutory offence. Ingelow police are watching things quite carefully: I understand there's a liaison officer detailed to make sure things are OK with Howard.'

'Really? How do they feel about having to do that? I mean, the fact that he's out at all is like an insult to them, isn't it? When they were the ones who charged him.'

'Well, the officer in charge of the original investigation's retired now, and . . . I'd say they'll handle it OK. It does seem hard on Colin Brudenell, I know. It's like suddenly he's the guilty party.'

'Yes.' She held his eyes. 'I thought he was a frightening sort of man. Like the type of dog that you can't read – whether it'll be friendly or snap.'

Adam returned her look thoughtfully, one long finger to his lips. She noted with absent approval that he wore no rings: she disliked jewellery on men.

'I must admit I don't know what to make of him. Of course, he's refused point-blank ever to talk to me, though God knows I've tried everything.'

'That wasn't the mother at the court, was it?'

'No. His second wife. He remarried a year or two ago. He was divorced from Lee's mother not long after the murder.

The mother's refused all communication as well. So really for the events of that day, from their point of view, I have to rely on statements made at the time. It's a pretty grey area.'

With a strong itch of curiosity, Rebecca thought: I wonder if they would talk to me? But she couldn't see how she could ever bring it about.

'Anyhow, I was going to give you that book.'

He got down on his knees and rummaged about in one of the holdalls. Socks and boxer shorts tumbled out. He handed her a paperback. The title, *Devil's Work*, was printed in foil above a picture of the Tarot card of the Devil and a snapshot of a smiling child: the book looked surprisingly airporty.

'They dressed it up like a pulp horror,' he said apologetically. 'Fairway are like that. But the text will give you an idea.'

She glanced at the flyleaf. *Adam Dowling was born in Hampshire in 1965, son of the journalist and broadcaster Alastair Dowling, and educated at Cambridge. He has reported from Strasbourg and Berlin for the* Observer *and has written extensively for the* New Statesman *and the* Spectator, *as well as researching for the Channel 4 TV series* Law Stories . . .

'So why this kind of stuff?' she said. For all his downplaying of the glamour, she was impressed: he was the genuine article. 'I mean the investigating side of journalism. Is that what you always wanted to do?'

'Probably, I knew that I wanted . . . well, to do good.' He waited, grimaced. 'You're supposed to laugh.'

'Why?'

He shrugged and opened the window to let out a frantic blowfly. 'Angela would. Go on, out you go. The world is big enough for thee and me, or whatever that quote is. Angela, that's the woman I'm seeing. In London.'

It was very adult, the way he said it to her. Rebecca felt flattered, in an oddly cross-grained way: perhaps because she felt herself challenged to be as adult in return.

'Serious?'

He had a way, also flattering, of answering your questions with thorough attention. 'Ah, I suppose so, yes.' The last word was more like *yem* than *yes*. 'How about you?'

'Oh, no time, I mean there's work and then I've got to read up for university in October.'

'Where are you headed?'

'York.'

'Congratulations. That's a damn good place.'

'Well, it's not Cambridge, but I am chuffed,' she said, gesturing with the book. 'Thanks for this, by the way.'

'That was my background, pure and simple. Dad was who he was, and I went to public school, so it was a shoo-in. I didn't do well there, but you don't need to: you just go. They say that hasn't changed much, that system – in fact it hasn't changed one jot . . . Actually, doing good is a bit of a silly way of putting it. Everybody thinks that's what they do in life, isn't it? Except out-and-out nutcases. So call it – doing something that would make a difference. But of course there is a thrill, you know, exposing injustice. Puncturing authority. Maybe that's at the root of it. Finding the dirty mag in the boss's drawer and saying, look everybody.'

'Perhaps you can tell me something. You know when those *News of the World* type journalists investigate some sleazy thing, a massage parlour or whatever. Before it gets to the crunch it always says they "make their excuses and leave". I mean, what excuses *do* they make?'

He laughed. 'You've got me there. I suppose something like, "Thank you for showing me your padded leather torture chamber, but I've just remembered I've left the oven on." Now I've got to make my excuses for the loo.'

He went upstairs. Left alone, she couldn't help nosing into the papers on the table. There was a lot of draft-printed copy and more smudgy photostats of incomprehensible documents. Moving some aside, she came across a large colour photograph. The light was on its glossy surface. It took her perhaps two seconds to realize what it was.

After those two seconds she was shaking and dizzy as if she had done cartwheels and the words came involuntarily from her mouth.

'Oh Jesus. Oh God.'

Adam was back. Though she had pushed the photograph back out of sight he heard her, and he saw her expression.

'Sorry, my fault. I shouldn't leave those around.'

'That was the little boy . . .?'

'Lee Brudenell. Those were the pathologist's shots, after

he'd been cleaned up. The scene-of-crime ones were worse. You OK? Well, that's the real obscenity, I suppose, isn't it?'

'Yes,' she said; and feeling she had caught him in an admission, she pressed it. 'They've got to be caught, whoever could do a thing like that. Doesn't Howard have any ideas?'

'He's never come up with one. Just stuck to the fact that he didn't do it. But maybe when I interview him . . . I want to go into it properly, which I couldn't do when he was inside. His is a remarkable story. I'd say unique, though there was one slightly similar case. A man named Stefan Kiszko. His conviction was quashed about six years ago after he'd done sixteen years of a life sentence for a child murder. It was proved he couldn't possibly have done it. They convicted him on sperm samples from the victim, but this man had a physical disorder that meant he was unable to produce sperm. Which the justice system finally got around to acknowledging after locking him up for sixteen years.'

'My God.'

'Uh-huh. If ever I feel I'm getting paranoid about the ways of British justice, I think of that case.'

'The Howard Gandy thing's different though, isn't it? I mean, his innocence wasn't proved like that. It's possible he could have done it.'

'No,' he said readily. 'It wasn't proved. But the point is the Crown didn't prove he did do it, or anywhere near. Plus, he didn't do it.' Adam began hunting amongst the papers on the table. 'I hide my cigarettes from myself, not that it works.' He dislodged a couple of cassette tapes, and Rebecca saw *Das Lied von der Erde*.

'You like Mahler?'

'He's good for working to. Maybe not those three-hour marathons with ten choirs.' He lit a cigarette.

'Dad's a great Mahler fan.' All at once that night with the house swollen with unheeded music and her father roaming the dark beach was vividly present to her. 'Do you know the *Kindertotenlieder*?'

'That's the gloomy stuff about dead children, isn't it? Bit Germanic for me.'

'Dad was telling me Mahler had this terrible fear of his children dying. Like an obsession, he had to keep trying to

139

exorcise it. And then one of them, a girl I think, did die.'

'If you were superstitious I suppose you could say he killed his own child.'

'Yes. Terrible, isn't it?' Rebecca made a point of walking under ladders and wearing green, but she was intensely superstitious all the same. Dark flower of a seed planted, perhaps, in her first childhood with her birth mother. It wasn't a case of seeing the world as ruled by capricious forces, not quite: rather she knew in her bones that your every action was meaningful, that to press upon the world was to invite it to snap back at you like elastic.

'Whoever did that – terrible thing,' she said, unable to erase the image of that photograph from her mind, 'there was *hate* there. Surely. But why would anyone hate a little child?' A lurching sickness and protest filled her. Too small, too small for such treatment.

'I suppose,' he said slowly, 'for the same reason one hates an adult. The motive for most murders is basically removal. Something stands in your way, so you remove it, by one means or another.'

A summer shower had begun. She went to the window and looked out at the tiny paved yard, where fat sizzling raindrops were landing, blooming, merging. A patch of sky the breadth of her hand was smudged with troubled cloud.

'I think I was in my birth mother's way,' she said. 'She sort of loved me, but . . . she wanted to have me without the trouble of having me. It was the same with her boyfriends. They seemed to love the idea of a kid. Children were great, children were fun, everyone should have children. There'd be lollipops and Sindy dolls at first. But then – they'd start to look at you because, my God, you're *always* there. Pubs close and TV programmes end but a kid is just everlasting. Adam, what do you imagine Lee Brudenell's life was like?'

'I don't know. There's no record of abuse. Lorraine Brudenell was a drinker, we know that. They lived in a bit of a run-down area. Colin Brudenell's had trouble with the law in the past few years – though not before the murder. Again, it's a grey area . . . Feels warm enough to storm. I'd better give you that lift.'

Getting into the car with *Devil's Work* in her hand, it occurred

140

to her to wonder what her father would think of her bringing home Adam Dowling's book. After a moment she tucked it away in her bag.

'Thanks for this.'

'Well, thank you for what you've given me.'

'What?'

'Food for thought.'

Massing cloud was making narrow bars of the sunlight, and above the aerodrome a small plane was caught in one as it descended: it made her think of war, Spitfire and Messerschmitts pinned by spotlights.

'Adam – you know that photograph, that wouldn't ever be in a book, would it?'

'Jesus, no. Even if a publisher tried to reproduce it, which no reputable publisher would, I'd stop it.'

'Someone's hands did that to that little kid. And they're around somewhere.'

'Yes. Exactly.'

'Can you live with that?'

'No. And the most frightening thing is, somebody has been able to live with it, for twelve years. Which suggests they could easily do it again.'

# THIRTEEN

When Holfleet Primary School had its annual sports day the village made something of an occasion of it, perhaps as a substitute for a fête; it wasn't the fête type of village, with its contiguity to the town, its social potpourri and bungalow build-up. This was something Diane Larkinson lamented and she returned to the theme when Rebecca and her father bumped into her in the High Street on the way to the school field.

'There isn't the community spirit. I think they allowed too much unregulated building here; it lost its character. We stayed with friends in the Cotswolds last year and the atmosphere was just so different.'

'It isn't very Aga-friendly here, I suppose,' Rebecca's father said. He was presenting the prizes today, and had reluctantly worn a tie. The reluctance showed: her mother used to say that her father in a tie resembled a tomcat with a bow round its neck. 'But then, who does live in those type of villages? What do they do? Unless they're all lady novelists writing wry little novels about lady novelists living in villages . . .'

'Ah, you'd be surprised, Philip,' Diane said with her sudden laugh, though she did not say how or why he would be surprised. Instead she gave Rebecca a look of puzzled accusation. 'You were working, I thought, Rebecca. Day off?'

'I don't work in the afternoons.'

'Oh! Well, that's news to me. If I'd known I'd have recruited you. We sorely need some help with the refreshments.'

'Well, I'll lend a hand, if you like. Just tell me what to do.'

'Oh, it's only pouring tea and so forth. It's nothing grand, don't think that.'

Rebecca's arm brushed her father's as they walked, and they repeated the pressure.

'Well, whatever it is. Just tell me what to do and I'll help.'

'I wonder if they still have the mothers' race? I can remember running in that when the twins were younger. I did actually win.'

'You did. Mum came last,' her father said with a smile at Rebecca. Her mother, a wonderfully unstrenuous person, cheerfully uncompetitive even at board games – buying Old Kent Road and Whitechapel because she didn't want anything too grand. Her mother, who liked to eat dry cream crackers and tried to convert them to this subtle delicacy; who drew little comical cats on anything, – a page of your diary, the newspaper, – so that you found them and grinned; who hated the sight of tights hanging up to dry; who gardened till after dark, blindly pottering; cut Rebecca's hair expertly and showed no hurt when at fifteen Rebecca wanted to go to a salon; after a hot bath looked so darkly rosy that her eyes shone unnaturally blue, like a blacked-up Othello; snored with a little hoot like an oboe; loved her daughter and her husband penetratingly. They came like this sometimes, a raft of memories.

'Never Anna's style, was it?' Diane said. 'She was more of a dreamer, really, Philip, wasn't she? Which is quite a nice thing to be.'

'Maybe you could enter for the mothers' race today. Why not? You're still a mother,' her father said amiably. 'It'll be grandmother soon enough.'

'Oh, please, not yet I hope.' Her laughter was deeply displeased. 'Penny and Stephen have got a lot of living to do before that. To see either of them caught at this stage is not what I would want for them at all.'

'Stephen coming along today?'

'He will be. Just as we were leaving the house the phone rang and it turned out to be this German girl he met in Turkey. Must be costing her a fortune but there we are. People just seem to get on with Stephen. Speaking of phone calls, I'm hoping we've heard the last from that journalist guy.'

'Adam Dowling? Is he bothering you?'

'Not now.' She was grudging. 'But of course, he's got what he wanted. They let that man out and he's back. I have to pinch myself every morning when I think about it. A lot of people around here are feeling the same. I'm amazed there's nothing that can be done.'

'Tar and feathers?' her father said, with his cool look into the distance. 'Or, just live with it.'

'Yes, well, it's different for you, Philip. Isn't it? You actually co-operated with that campaign in the end, which – well, correct me if I'm wrong. It's what one hears.'

'I gave a statement. It was used as part of a successful appeal. I didn't feel I had a choice, as it happened.'

They entered the school gates, which were festooned with balloons and crepe paper. The thunderstorms of the last couple of days had cleared and the scene on the school field was all sun and breeze, flags whipping and cracking.

'Well, I'm amazed, that's all,' Diane Larkinson said. 'Amazed.'

'The final decision was the court's. Gandy is entitled to live here and there's nothing we can do.'

'That's all very well, Philip, if you haven't got young children,' Diane said. 'Well? You've got to admit that. So suppose something else happens? God forbid, but suppose some child gets interfered with—'

'That'll be all my fault, is that what you're saying, Diane?' Her father stopped walking.

But Diane wouldn't face him. She closed her eyes in a shrug and then, turning, saw Stephen running up towards them.

'Hi, sweetheart! So how was Ilse?' The accent was certainly flamboyant, if not German. 'You must have had a proper chinwag.'

'Oh, she's going crazy. Her parents have stopped her money or something. Hi.' This was for Rebecca.

'Shame. I'd love to meet her,' Diane said. 'Now I'd better get busy. Stephen, you're going to give me a hand, are you?'

'Diane, if you've any more views about me, I may as well hear them now,' her father said.

'Don't expect applause, Philip. That's all I'm saying. You do what you want. Just don't expect people around here to approve it.'

'I think you're confusing me with someone who gives a flying fuck what people around here think.'

Diane did a creditable job of not hearing. She directed a serene Lady Bountiful, village-cricket-match gaze across the field.

Then a vicious look pursed her face and she lifted a dramatic hand to point. 'There. That's what we don't want. And that's what we've got.'

There were not many people seated yet in the rows of school chairs lined up alongside the running track, and it was easy to spot the massive figure of Howard Gandy. He was wearing sunglasses and there was an ice-cream cone in his hand. His mother was sitting beside him and he was bending his head to listen to something she was saying.

'That's OK with you then, Philip, is it?' Diane said. 'You're fine with that? That man sitting there – watching the children?'

'There is absolutely nothing we can do about it. This isn't lynching territory.'

'I can't believe you helped. I really can't. God knows what Anna would have thought.'

'Howard Gandy's innocent,' Rebecca put in. 'The law says so. He's every right to be here.'

'It's really not something you know anything about, though, lovey, is it?' Diane said, smiling at her without looking at her.

'This is that Gandy geezer, yeah?' Stephen said. Exertion had heightened his rosy blond-beast colouring: he seemed overpoweringly beefy and apple-cheeked, like some huge boy from an Enid Blyton story. 'You want me to sort him out? There's Rob Cooper over there. He'll help. The two of us can just take him aside. Just discreetly, you know.' He chuckled. 'Or not so discreetly.' He was cranking up the bullishness, perhaps, to impress Rebecca.

'Best not,' his mother said. 'Best just leave it, Stephen. As Philip says, there's nothing we can do. It's been taken out of our hands.'

'Just make it known he's not wanted. That's all. I mean, nobody does want that guy around, do they? It's democracy,' Stephen said.

Laughing, as at a piece of delightful teenage wackiness, Diane said, 'I don't think so, darling. I see your reasoning, but really – leave it.'

'I'd better go and make myself available,' Rebecca's father said, touching her arm and nodding in the direction of the dais in front of the pavilion. 'See you later.'

Diane was wearing sunglasses on top of her head – glamour

unbuttoned – and as he turned to go she snapped them down over her eyes like a visor.

'Well, then, you still up for lending a hand, Rebecca? Or changed your mind?'

'No. I'll help.'

'I think I'll go say hi to Rob,' Stephen said, with a last puppy look for Rebecca.

'All right, darling. But none of that. Don't even think about it. Promise?'

'OK, Mum. Promise,' he said, all filial decency.

There was not much for Rebecca to do at the refreshment stalls – trestle tables under an awning, with tea-urns and school canteen crockery. Presumably deemed unequal to hot beverages, she was placed at one end with the jugs of warm diluted orange squash and paper cups, which hardly anybody wanted. 'Twenty pence,' Diane instructed her, repeating it, 'Got it? Change in this bowl. Can you manage? Give me a shout if not.' The whole thing reminded Rebecca of the volunteers in charity shops, making great play with receipts and tidying the racks of dead men's trousers. She amused herself watching the children issuing from the pavilion and gathering in a fidgety corral by the dais. Small, fizzy, chaotic, they were the most individual and least self-conscious figures to be seen. Watching them, Rebecca thought that children really did live in a world of their own. They squatted bonelessly, quarrelled like chattering squirrels, made faces, giggled in underground collusion with ducked heads that grown-up haircuts could never make less than spiky. They seemed to be in effortless possession of a secret of sincerity that all the adults in view lacked.

Rebecca served a cup of squash, gave the change under Diane's hawkish eye, and wished that she could roam. It looked nice to wander about the field: there were children's paintings and models displayed along one side, and a group of the younger ones were forming up to do country dancing. The sky was dense with its own blueness, nothing marring it but a single vapour trail like a chalk mark slowly inscribing and erasing itself. It was a day to lie in the grass and smell the earth and know yourself favoured.

She would have liked, too, to go over and say hello to Howard Gandy. She had taken his part out of dislike for Diane, and because everyone seemed to be against him; but she still had her own mind to make up. An innocent lover of children, born out of his time, as Adam suggested? Intellectually she grasped it, but there was still resistance in her gut.

On the dais the headmaster exchanged a last word with her father and then stood up to the microphone. He was a fair youngish man of remarkable good looks which were blemished, if not negated, by a thick ragged inexplicable moustache: the effect was like graffiti on a fine painting.

'Good afternoon, everyone. And welcome to our annual sports day. Marvellous to see so many of you here. We've got wonderful weather this year – some of you may remember we had something of a washout this time last year . . . Presenting prizes today I'm happy to welcome local maestro Mr Philip Springthorpe, who has also made a donation of a package of sweets for every pupil which will be handed out at the end of the day. I'm sure we'd all like to show our appreciation . . .'

There was a fair number of spectators around the field now. Some had parked cars along the side behind the dais and were getting out picnic lunches. A few of them Rebecca didn't recognize, including an old couple who had settled themselves with deckchairs and a windbreak and even a camping stove. They must have been holidaymakers from the camp or the caravan site. It was odd to think of them doing this. Usually locals and tourists moved in wholly separate circles, like medieval orders.

'. . . So without further ado we'll start the first event . . . and good luck to everybody.'

Waiflike in baggy vests and sashes, some of the littlest ones were shepherded into place by mumsy Year One teachers for a sack race. Rebecca kept one eye on Howard Gandy and his mother: she wasn't convinced that Stephen Larkinson wouldn't try something, though there was no sign of him.

Scanning the spectators, she saw with a jolt a figure she recognized.

The man, fair-haired and palely scrawny in a white capped-sleeve T-shirt, was leaning against the bonnet of one of the parked cars. A cigarette dangled from his fingers, but he didn't put it to his lips. He was just still: tremendously still. He might have been dozing upright. But there was light on those pale blue eyes. He was gazing right at the dais, where her father was just sitting down.

All at once the man moved. He began walking towards the dais, with a kind of high plod like a moonwalking astronaut. It didn't look like drunkenness: he was quite steady. His gait had an essence of determination.

'I've got to nip off for a minute,' Rebecca told Diane.

'Don't be long, don't be long!'

Rebecca was already running. She had to go a long way round, to avoid cutting across the sack race, and her heart was drumming when she reached the dais. Her father, seeing her, smiled, just before the hand clamped on his shoulder.

'Excuse me. I've been looking for you. You're the one, aren't you?'

'What . . .?' Her father had been given such a start that at first he stared without recognition into the eyes of the man who had climbed up the back of the dais.

'Your name's Springthorpe, right? Do you happen to remember me?'

'It's . . . Colin Brudenell, isn't it?' Now that the shock had passed, her father's face gave nothing away. 'Yes. We saw you in London – the Appeal Court.'

'That's correct.' There was a stiff, almost courtly sobriety about Colin Brudenell, belied only by the hectic flush under his sharp cheekbones. 'Sorry to barge in on you like this, chief. It's not something I want to do. Only I've got to know, you see. Because you are the one, aren't you? The one who changed his story.'

'I don't think this is really the time—'

'Please. Yes or no. I mean, you know me, don't you? You know what – happened.' He got the word out with fierce concentration, eyes shut, like a stammerer.

'Yes, I know. Look, Mr Brudenell, this really isn't the way—'

'Well, now we're getting somewhere, any road.' Colin Brudenell cocked his head at Rebecca; suddenly there was about him a humourless perkiness, a black hilarity. Had he, Rebecca wondered, spotted Howard Gandy? It didn't seem so, and the teachers patrolling the sack race might impede his view of that part of the field. But this whole situation had a tang, an ugliness that she feared.

148

'Is everything all right?' the headmaster said, smiling nervously.

'It's OK,' her father said. 'I shan't be long.' With a nod for Rebecca to follow, her father got down and ushered Brudenell behind the dais.

'You know what you did. My solicitor's put me in the whole picture. You changed your evidence.' Colin Brudenell folded his wiry arms around himself, like a man in interior pain. 'This is what I can't get my head round. They let the bastard out –' he made a sudden appeal to Rebecca – 'and yet he killed my little boy. That's the law for you. *You* work that out.'

'It wasn't him, though,' Rebecca said. 'They got it wrong. Howard Gandy was innocent.'

'No. No.' Brudenell made a sweeping gesture, a universal rejection. 'No, forget it. Listen, I want to know something. Please. I want you to look me in the face . . .' He placed a finger on her father's chest. Her father didn't back off. 'Just look me in the face, chief, and tell me why that animal should be out. Because knowing he was in there, that was the only thing that kept me going. You can understand that. This is your girl, yeah?'

'That's my daughter.'

Colin gave a sort of sideways bow of acknowledgement. 'She's grown up and you're proud of her. That's how it should be. Now I couldn't do that with my Lee. Imagine how you'd feel if that was your daughter. Just picture it a minute.'

'The courts decided it.' Her father's manner was utterly colourless. 'They decided he was innocent, and so he was freed. It must be hard for you. I'm sorry for what's happened. It's a mess. But look –' suddenly there was urgency, even warmth – 'you're not doing yourself any good with this. Please, try and—'

'Not doing myself any good, you're joking,' Brudenell said with a breathy chuckle. 'I'm feeling brilliant, me. I'm doing a few things for myself. The law doesn't do it. Does it? Bloody useless. Isn't it – eh? We're just talking, so you just tell me, honestly. What good is the law? What does it do for someone like me?'

'The law's still powerful,' her father said. 'And if you carry on like this it'll come down on you.'

The baleful gleaming of Brudenell's eyes dimmed for a moment and he looked wry, thoughtful. 'Yeah. I know. Crazy, isn't it? You'd think I was the baddie. But I'm not, you know.' He turned to Rebecca, and it somehow felt as if his face was an inch from hers as he repeated it. 'I'm not.'

'I'm not a baddie either. I was caught up in it. That's all. I'm sorry you feel like this. You've every right to be angry. But there's nothing to be done.'

'You're sorry –' Brudenell sighed deeply – 'but you still helped 'em. So it doesn't make sense, do you see? You shouldn't have helped 'em. Too many do-gooders in this world. They don't understand what it's like. How could they? Nobody understands what I've been through. They . . .' He seemed to run out of words. 'They – don't understand.'

'You'd better go,' Rebecca said, as gently as she could. 'You're not supposed to be here.'

'You're right, love,' Brudenell said with abrupt freshness. 'Dead right. I've got an injunction against me. I'm to stay away from me-laddo or else. Charming, isn't it? I'm being punished. I was the victim and they're still making me the victim twelve years after.' He jabbed his finger in her father's chest and then laid his hand there, firm and intrusive, as if feeling the very beats of her father's heart. Rebecca was surprised at the way he bore this intrusion, making no move. 'You think about it when you go home, mate, just have a good think.'

'Philip.' It was the headmaster. 'Anything I can do?'

Her father shook his head at him.

'You're OK about that bastard being out,' Brudenell said, removing his hand. 'Well, that's up to you. I'm not. As far as I'm concerned, he's got my Lee's blood on his hands. And somebody's going to have to do something about it. Not the law. Forget it. The law doesn't help. Who knows, maybe *I'll* have to do something about it. Do it yourself, that's my motto . . .' He gave a hard cackle, a last burst of that deadly hilarity, and began walking away backwards. 'Always has been. Do it yourself . . .'

At the last moment, before he turned and ran to his car, Rebecca saw him put up a hand to brush his eyes.

Then with a screech of gears he reversed the car at speed,

leaving deep gouges in the turf, and tore towards the gates.

'Christ, Dad . . .'

'It's OK, it's all right. Should have expected something like that.' Her father breathed deeply; he looked almost relieved. 'The guy's half mad with it all. Leave him be.'

'Half mad, right. It's true about that injunction – Adam was telling me.'

'Adam?'

'When he gave me a lift the other day. He . . . mentioned it.'

'I see. Well, he certainly started something, young Adam.' There was hardness in his eyes, if not his voice.

'Dad, we ought to do something. That man – he's dangerous, surely. Just the fact of him being here—'

'He's letting off steam. I don't think there's any real danger. Anyway, the police are looking out for Howard, aren't they? They must be expecting some ruckus like this.'

'It's no good if they don't know what's happening. I think we ought to ring the police, say what happened. Say this Brudenell man's in Holfleet and he's going around making threats.'

'If he's going to do anything he's hardly going to be swanning around in broad daylight bragging about it. He's just sick, he needs help. Anyway, I've been involved enough. I'm bored with it. Let them all get on with it.'

'Get on with what?'

'Whatever. Maybe just natural justice.' His eyes were bleak, absent. 'I don't mean that. God, just forget about it, OK? Brudenell's had a pop at me and I dare say it's done him good, which is fine. No call to go making more trouble. I want to leave all this – this crap behind.'

He turned away from her, climbed up to the dais.

'Where have you been?' Diane was all peevish repetition when Rebecca got back to the refreshments stall. 'Where have you *been*?

Rebecca ignored her. Her mind felt feverish. When Stephen Larkinson appeared, with his friend Rob – another blond yeoman type who tried to evade his inheritance with hair-braids and stubble – she barely registered her own irritation.

'Two firkins of your finest mead, wench!' Stephen said.

'Forty pence.'

'No discount? Don't we get anything off?'

'No.' Disliking him greatly, she still thought it must be awful to be a boy – to have to expose yourself to such easy brushoffs.

'We've got to fork out, mate. She's hard, this one. Got any money? Come on, dig deep . . .'

All at once Stephen abandoned the Laurel and Hardy act. Howard Gandy had come up to the stall and was waiting his turn behind them.

Stephen looked round, raised his eyebrows, then fixed Howard with a cool stare.

'We in your way?'

'No,' Howard said. 'I'm just waiting my turn.'

'Oh. Right. I just wondered. Only if you're in a hurry. You know. You just say.' Stephen's eyes glittered. Rob giggled.

'Forty pence,' Rebecca said.

'Oh, right. Think we'd better move, Rob mate. It's a bit close here, isn't it? A bit close for comfort.'

Rebecca took his money and tossed it ostentatiously in the bowl. She had always thought *callow* was just a literary word, that people in real life didn't look callow: now she knew better.

'Hello,' she said, smiling at Howard, 'what can I get you?'

He looked as placid as ever, but he returned her smile. 'Two oranges, please.'

Pouring, she encountered indecision, then abandoned it.

'Howard, I think I ought to tell you,' she said, handing him the cups, 'that man who was at the court – Colin Brudenell. He's around here today, I've just seen him. I think you should be careful.'

There was a moment of silent surprise.

'He's supposed to keep away. My solicitor arranged it. What's he doing?'

'He was talking to my dad. He seemed – well, in a state and quite threatening.'

'Well.' Absently Howard drank his squash: it was gone in one gulp. 'I'm not scared of him. He shouldn't be here, though. It's not right. He's breaking the law.'

'I think the police really should know about it.'

He nodded slowly. 'Yes. I'll ring them. We'll go home.'

'No.' It seemed unfair. 'I can ring them. I'll run down to the callbox. You take your mum her drink and watch the sports.

You shouldn't have to spoil your day.'

His eyes bored into her. It was natural enough, she thought, for him to be suspicious. For her part, she couldn't say what had tipped the balance in his favour: maybe simply his dignity compared with Stephen Larkinson's lack of it.

'That's very good of you . . . But don't worry, I reckon it'll be all right.'

'No, I want to do it. It'll set my mind at rest.'

'Well, if you're sure . . . It is nice of you, that.' He glanced over to where Pat was sitting. 'I don't want Mum upset. She's having such a nice time.'

Rebecca nodded. 'Hopefully she won't have to know anything about it.'

'Detective Sergeant Hurst, he's the one who came to see us. Perhaps if you mention his name.' Howard sighed and clucked his tongue. 'I don't know. Such a lovely day. Somebody always has to spoil it, don't they?'

It was amazing, she thought: he had been freed from a prison sentence for murder, and threatening shades still dogged him – yet he remained so prosaic, earthbound. Perhaps that was what people couldn't handle about him. He wouldn't play to the gallery.

'What about the squash?' Diane clucked when Rebecca said she was nipping off again. 'It's not on. It's not on.'

She kept a wary eye out for Colin Brudenell's car on the way to the phone box in the High Street. She thought he looked like a man on the brink – never mind her father's dismissals. It was part of his fastidious nature always to reject the worst scenario, perhaps from a distaste for drama. All the same, his attitude mystified her.

'Ingelow police.' A woman's voice.

'Hello, I'm calling from Holfleet?' Nervousness made her give it that American interrogative lift. 'They're having the sports day at Holfleet Primary School this afternoon, I've just come from there and – well, there's a man hanging around, he's behaving a bit alarmingly.'

'Yes? This is at the school, you say?' Instant alertness and tension – of course. What times.

'Yes. I sort of know him. His name's Colin Brudenell. He's – well, there's a Holfleet man named Howard Gandy, he's just been let out of prison after an appeal. Detective Sergeant Hurst knows about it apparently.'

'Gandy, uh-huh. We know about it.'

'Well, this man Brudenell, he was the father of that little boy who was killed, and he's still got a thing against Howard Gandy. Apparently he's not supposed to be here, an injunction or something.'

'He was making threats to Mr Gandy?'

'He didn't actually see him, I think, though Mr Gandy is at the school. It was my dad he approached – Philip Springthorpe, he was one of the witnesses. He seemed really worked up and he was saying things, threatening things about Mr Gandy. Then he went off in his car really fast.'

'Do you happen to know the registration?'

Rebecca cursed herself. 'No, I'm sorry. It was a white estate, fairly old-looking.'

'All right. Thanks for letting us know. DS Hurst is aware of this situation. I'll pass it on to him. Is there any kind of risk at the school, would you say?'

'I don't think so. Like I say, he just took off.'

'Right, and your name is?'

'It's Rebecca Springthorpe,' she said, with the inescapable tremor of giving your name to the police.

'Address?'

She gave it. It occurred to her that her father would not be pleased. But they had taken her quite seriously, after all; and pleasing her father had become, she realized quite suddenly, less important now. Even through the clashes of her adolescence she had acknowledged his as the high moral ground. Recent knowledge had shifted it.

'Thank goodness!' Diane said on her return, her kohl-rimmed eyes widening, suggesting a thousand orange-squash emergencies. 'Now don't run off again.'

Howard and Pat were still in their seats, she noted with satisfaction. In between serving she watched the events. Their charm diminished as the elder children took over. They manifested little tricks, learnt, perhaps, from television. The girls running the hundred metres did a lot of puffing and leg-shaking before the race and the winner threw her arms up in ecstatic triumph. Rebecca could see the lines of her bra, her first probably, and remembered the feel of it, like a fidgety vest.

'Hi.' Stephen Larkinson was back, alone. 'Listen, what do you think of coming to Powers this weekend?'

Powers was a nightclub in Ingelow.

'Oh, I'm very busy, I'm afraid. There's work, plus all that reading to catch up with. Thanks.'

He was not satisfied with this answer. 'It's pretty good at Powers, you know. They play . . . What music are you into? Not your dad's stuff, Brahms and Liszt and all that?'

'Yes, mainly,' she said, untruthfully, to put him off.

'They play some good stuff. I went to see the Verve last year in Nottingham. It was minging. Think you'll get many bands at York? Sheffield Uni's got a really good programme. Can't wait for October, actually. You know. Home.' He rolled his eyes. 'Sheffield's pretty near York. Maybe we could meet up.'

'Oh – there's Dad.'

The events were over and her father was stepping up to the microphone. 'Well, before I have the pleasure of giving out the prizes today, I feel I should say on behalf of everyone what a great afternoon it's been . . .' Rebecca noticed an unsteadiness in his voice.

'That Gandy geezer,' Stephen said. 'Doesn't he give you the creeps?'

'Should he?'

'Well, you wouldn't remember, of course. I can. When I was a kid – before they locked him up. Mum and Dad always told me and Penny to keep away from him.'

'Why?'

Stephen laughed. 'Because he was creepy.'

'In what way?'

'Oh, he used to hang around. You know. Ask what you were doing. Did you want a game of football or whatever. Did you want to come and see crabs or something in this pool. I mean . . .'

'Well, maybe he did want to show you the crabs in the pool. Kids like things like that.'

'That's so naïve.'

She wasn't offended: all her age-group talked in this way, disdaining the timid stepping-stones of conversation. 'But you're just pre-judging him,' she said. 'Did he ever actually do anything?'

'To me? Huh. Not likely.' Stephen clearly felt his manhood impugned.

'To anybody you knew.'

'He didn't need to. He didn't get a chance. Come on, it was obvious what he was like. Just not right. I mean, some little kids would go along with him, play rounders or whatever. That's where he got that Pied Piper name. But even if you gave him a wide berth, he'd still speak to you. Outside the shop or wherever. Like he just didn't get the message. Why did your dad help him get out, anyway? That journalist geezer kept ringing Mum, going on about this campaign. Did he pay your dad, or something? It all seems funny to me.'

'No, he didn't pay him. His name's Adam Dowling. I know him quite well.' She did not so much convince herself this was true as feel that it had some mystic validity, certainly compared with Stephen's secondhand rumours and bogus bonhomie. The cottage with the overflowing holdalls, the word processor, the book she had started reading last night, even the hideous photograph were vividly present to her.

'You should understand, people don't want a perv like that around. He ought to move away somewhere else. Really,' Stephen said, pursing his lips, 'he ought to be damn well told,' and as he said it it was as if a piercing light shone all through him, from the primness at his heart to the space that was waiting for him in the future, citizen-shaped, respectable, deadening.

Detective Sergeant Hurst arrived on their doorstep early that evening, just as her father was grilling peppered steak for supper.

'Something smells good. Sorry to interrupt. A few minutes of your time's all I need.'

Rebecca hadn't told her father about ringing the police this afternoon. She realized now she should have.

'I understand you made a call to us this afternoon,' the policeman said. 'In regard to a Mr Brudenell.'

'Not me,' her father said, with a curt gesture to the kitchen.

'I rang,' Rebecca said; and, trying to catch her father's eye,

'I didn't like the way he was acting. I was worried.'

'You'd be Rebecca, yes? And Mr Springthorpe.'

'Philip.' Her father removed the grill pan with a clatter. 'I didn't know about this. I didn't think it called for any police action.'

'They look tasty. I'll be very quick.' A smallish man, this DS Hurst – didn't you have to be a certain height to join the police? – smooth-haired and dapper in a way that suggested the slick salesman more than the copper, yet with something spry and witty in his look. 'Apparently the gent in question was making a bit of a nuisance of himself at the school.'

Her father shrugged. 'It wasn't anything.'

'Just give me an idea,' Hurst smiled.

'Well, look, it's a long story. I mean, I don't remember you being around when it happened – the Gandy thing, years ago.'

'I wasn't with the Lincolnshire force then. But I've genned up on it. My boss was in charge of the original murder investigation. He's filled me in. Feels a bit close to it himself, you know.'

'It must be strange for the police,' her father said, 'Gandy's conviction being quashed.'

'Stranger things have happened,' Hurst said, his voice amiable, his glance sharp. 'Most of the original team have gone their various ways. Actually, no formal criticism was made of Ingelow police by the Appeal Court. Which is nice. Now about today. Did Mr Brudenell make any direct threats to you, sir?'

'Not really. He approached me at the school. He was angry – in a state. Because I helped with the appeal.'

'So he was blaming you for Mr Gandy being released?'

'Sort of. He was just ranting really. I can't blame him. He's obviously been through hell.'

Hurst had a notebook out. 'And he made threats in regard to Mr Gandy?'

'Yes, I suppose.'

'He said the law wouldn't help him,' Rebecca said, 'so he'd have to do it himself. That's why I rang. He said there was an injunction or something . . .'

'Oh yes, there is. Mr Gandy's solicitor saw to that – very wise in the circumstances. Obviously there are people ready to have a go at Mr Gandy. Nasty phone calls et cetera. Did you take this seriously, what Mr Brudenell was saying?'

'Not totally. As I said, he was in a state. It wasn't wholly surprising. He made a similar show at the Appeal Court. He's obviously not – reconciled to Howard Gandy being innocent.'

'I gather he's not alone in that.' Hurst gave an interested peep through to the sitting room. 'I like that bust – that's Beethoven, is it?'

'Mozart.'

'Ah. Never look very happy, do they, those composers? Like they've got these terrible troubles weighing on them. Of course they did have, didn't they? Tragic lives usually. So did Mr Brudenell use any physical violence against you?'

'No, no. Really, I've got no complaint to make against him, if that's what this is about.'

'Well, it's gone beyond that. As I said, he shouldn't even be in Holfleet in the first place. After we had the call from –' he didn't say Rebecca's name but made a courtly gesture towards her – 'we sent a car over to check things out. Found him parked in Hythe Avenue – watching Mr Gandy's house.'

Rebecca's eyes, widening, sought her father's in vain.

'I'm afraid the car didn't exactly belong to Mr Brudenell – this is between us, of course. So we had to have his name in the little book, obviously. He's being sent home now. He'll be up in court in due time. Not breaking any state secrets if I say it won't be the first time.' Hurst chirruped at one of the cats, which kept a suspicious distance. 'Of course the big question is what he was playing at – hanging around Mr Gandy's house like that.'

'You think he was planning some kind of assault?' her father said slowly.

'Who knows?' the policeman said with tremendous brightness. 'We'll be keeping a careful eye out, anyway. Obviously we can't play nursemaid to any innocent citizen, not twenty-four hours a day. Nice if we could.'

'How are Howard and his mother?' Rebecca said. 'Do they know about this?'

'I've just been to see them. Mr Gandy seems quite cool about the whole thing. I gather he's used to a bit of attitude from people.'

'It'd be better if he moved away,' her father said. 'He's too known here.'

'Well, maybe,' Hurst said cheerily. 'As I say, an injunction isn't some magic shield. Who had one of them? Was it Superman?' He cocked his head at her father, getting a blank look in return. 'Anyway, it isn't that. You have to rely on the other party abiding by it. So, you haven't seen Mr Brudenell hanging around here before? Or anyone else, any suggestion of something suspicious? No? Well, thanks for your help anyway.' He flipped the notebook away. 'Hopefully he'll wise up and that's the last we'll see of him around here.'

'So what's happening with that case?' her father said, his voice muffled as he looked in one of the kitchen cupboards.

'What case is that, sir?'

Her father brought out mustard powder, shut the cupboard door with a startling bang. 'The Lee Brudenell case. Are they going to reopen it? Gandy's officially innocent, so it must count as unsolved.'

'I can't really comment. But in theory, yes. Obviously we can't have anybody taking the law into their own hands.'

'No. But if that man thinks the law's failed him . . .'

'Well, that does happen. The law is fallible, I'm afraid. Because people are.' Hurst watched her father mixing mustard with smiling attention, as if at a fascinating demonstration. 'And I'm afraid that's pretty much Mr Brudenell's quarrel with you. You changed your evidence, didn't you, sir?'

'You know all about it.'

'Just the basics. But this is it, you see. This is the heart of the matter. We can't help people unless we have the right information.' Hurst's smile grew until, like the Cheshire Cat's, it seemed to be the only thing visible about him. 'We try to do our best. But we need people to tell us the truth. Right from the start. Otherwise it can be too late. I don't know.' He shrugged and got up. 'I wouldn't say this job's taught me anything very much, but one thing I do know – people's lies always catch up with them. Of course, if there's any way you can help with that particular matter, sir . . .?'

'Me? Why?'

'I just wondered. You know, whether anything else has popped up in your memory about that time. It's surprising what people can come up with when they put their minds to it.'

'I've said everything I've got to say.'

Hurst watched him for a few intense seconds. 'Well. Thanks for your time. I'll let you get your supper. Anything else happens – *do* let us know.'

When he had gone her father said, with a laugh that could not conceal the sting within, 'I stand reprimanded.'

'I don't think he meant anything by it,' Rebecca said.

Something about this remark seemed to prick his temper. 'I wish to God,' he said, 'you hadn't made that bloody phone call, Rebecca.'

'Why? You heard what he said – they picked that Brudenell man up outside the Gandys' house. That's hardly innocent.'

'Innocent. Guilty. They're just words,' he said with a strange savagery. He abandoned the mustard. 'I need a shower. I'll do this after.' At the door he paused, said coldly, 'Don't try and play detective, Rebecca. Drop it. You don't know what the hell you'll be getting mixed up in.'

He was gone before she could reply; though the only truthful answer she could have given was that it was too late for that.

# FOURTEEN

Groggy, Rebecca bolted from the house for work in an early morning that was rosy and full of warmth which might be a promise or a threat; if the thunderheads shifted from inland the day would surely bake. Whether her body was acting as some kind of barometer she didn't know, but she had had a bad night: that fretfully disturbed sleep in which the mind insists on finding dream correlatives for the discomfort of cramped limbs and stifled breath – frightening vignettes of jeopardy, being trapped, seized, smothered. Crossing the High Street, she didn't even notice the car, and when the horn sounded it came as more of an irritant than a warning.

'Oi! Dreamy.'

The car had slewed to a halt just ahead of her and waited, engine gunning: Stephen Larkinson thrust his head out. His friend Rob was in the passenger seat.

'Sorry. Miles away.'

'Yeah. Want a lift?'

She saw them exchange a glance, and the engine revved again. It was as if they didn't really want to give her a lift, which suited her anyhow.

'No, thanks.'

''K.'

The car bucketed away, swinging round the long curve of the High Street. It seemed ridiculous to be haring about like that early on a summer morning. Little boys, she thought: vroom, vroom.

Rounding the curve, she saw something odd at the bus stop up ahead. Her first thought was of those supernatural showers, hazelnuts or frogs or angelhair descending from the sky on to one spot of earth. This was whitish-grey stuff, spattering a rough circle of pavement around the bus stop. She started to run forward, recognizing the figure there: Howard Gandy.

Whatever the stuff was, it had covered him. He was standing – crouching, rather – in the midst of it, his arms over his eyes, and coughing in great whoops.

'Are you all right? Howard?' Tentatively she reached out a hand to his shoulder. 'What on earth happened?'

'*God* knows. *God* only knows.' He made the word sound like a fierce oath. He scrubbed his hands across his face. 'I was just standing here. This car came past . . . They just chucked it at me.'

An ammoniac smell assaulted her nostrils. The stuff was flecked, and here and there flinty in texture. There were feathers in it. Howard took his hands away from his streaming face and looked at her.

'Oh my God, your poor eyes, they look so sore . . .'

'They're stinging like mad.' He got out a handkerchief and blotted them. 'It's some sort of muck, isn't it? From birds or chickens by the look of it.' He hawked and spat into the gutter. 'Excuse me . . . I've got to get it out.'

'It's OK . . .' He was right. *Chickenshit*. The Coopers were wealthy professionals who dabbled, Marie-Antoinette style, in cultivation: they kept chickens. 'Did you see who it was?' She knew: her outrage only needed confirmation.

'Two lads, young fellers . . . What does it matter?'

'You should go home and clean up, especially your face. It might be dangerous—'

'But I'm due in Ingelow. I've got an appointment. I'm going to Adam's cottage today. We're starting my interviews.'

'You can't go like that. And your eyes . . . Come on – I'll come home with you. We'll get the next bus.'

'Don't do that. You'll be late yourself – don't you have to go to work?'

'Don't worry. I stayed late the other day, they owe me.'

Her tone gave no hint of the anger she was feeling. A trick like this was so . . . Wasn't chicken, she suddenly thought, some paedophile slang term? And was Stephen Larkinson capable of such subtlety? She doubted it. He had probably just done the nastiest thing he could think of.

'This is kind of you. You don't have to do this.' He blew his nose. If he had wept she wouldn't have blamed him, but it was almost certainly just the ammonia affecting him. Somehow she knew he wouldn't shed tears for this.

And there was something more. Outside his house, that grey secretive house with its great jungly privet hedge, she stopped dead.

'Oh, my God. When . . .?'

He followed her gaze with puckered eyes, shrugged and opened the garden gate, which shrieked with rust.

'Don't know really. It wasn't there last night and it was there this morning.'

'Was that them too?'

'Your guess is as good as mine. It's a bit of a coincidence, I suppose.' He paused, and as if he wished to smooth down her horror said in his most matter-of-fact tone, 'Never rains but it pours, eh?'

The drab pebble dash front of the house had broken out in vivid spray-can colour. 'PSYCHO GET OUT' was written in big looping red capitals between the front door and the window. Then there was a squiggle as if the red paint had run out, and the theme was resumed in green on the other side of the window, the letters slightly cramped, sloping down: 'DIE PSYCHO'.

She stared at it. Her eyes were registering something amiss and for a moment she thought she must be starting a migraine. Then she realized that 'PSYCHO' had actually been mis-spelled both times and that her vision had automatically amended it. The word had been written 'PYSCHO' and somehow it was more sinister in that garbled form – more reckless, more frightening.

'That won't come off, will it?'

'I doubt it. Have to get on to the council. Mum was upset about it this morning. I calmed her down a bit. But now this. This puts the tin hat on it, this does.'

'Mind.' He had stumbled on the overgrown path to the front door. It was opened just then by Pat Gandy.

'God, what now? What's happened? What's that muck?' Her eyes, old and hard, expecting no good, fastened on Rebecca, who was at first surprised and then hurt to be included in their wariness.

'Somebody chucked it. I shall have to clean up.'

163

'Chucked it? Chucked it where?'

'At me, Mum. At the bus stop. Some lads or other. You know Rebecca, don't you? She came along and helped me. It got in me eyes.' He gave courteous way to Rebecca. 'Come in, won't you?'

Indoors Pat Gandy fussed around him, dabbing and wiping ineffectually at his spattered shirt, until he said, 'I don't think it's any good, Mum. I shall have to change. I shan't be a minute.'

'It was clean on as well. Clean on this morning.' She stubbed out her cigarette and at once lit another; they were the long superking type but in Pat's fleshless hand they looked even longer, like some enormous joke cigarette.

'Well, never mind. Can't be helped. I shan't be a minute.' He moved towards the stairs. 'Perhaps Rebecca'd like a cup of tea if there's one in the pot.'

'Oh, I'm fine, thanks.'

'What next, Howard? That's what I want to know. Whatever next? Whatever's going to happen next, I ask you?' It was distress, of course; but the thumping, demanding tone Pat gave even to rhetorical questions must surely be wearing.

'Is there any Optrex upstairs?'

'Optrex? I don't know. I can't remember. Maybe best just use warm water. Unless we should get the doctor. Do you think we should get the doctor?'

'It'll be all right. I just need to clean up.'

When he had gone upstairs Mrs Gandy said, 'What next, I ask you?' more softly and began moving things from kitchen table to sink with a wild clatter.

'It was – muck from hens, I think,' Rebecca said. 'They drove past in a car and threw it.' It felt profoundly strange to be inside the Gandy house at last, but down at the bottom of the strangeness was something else, an eerie familiarity. Although she had never been in this cluttered kitchen with its Formica surfaces and chrome trims, survivors of a period when smooth shininess was universally desired, its varnished knick-knacks and pictorial tea-towels that promised italicized good luck from every seaside resort, its cracked floor-tiles and battered twin-tub and grim cacti, she knew its secrets. It might have been Cathy Groom, not Pat Gandy, rattling the crazed plates into the sink; her own frowzy white school socks might have been amongst the damp heap on top of the gas fridge with its Art-Deco curves.

'Who was it, then? You saw 'em, did you?'

Rebecca said after a moment, 'I'm not sure.' She didn't think putting names to the persecution would help.

'Did you see that on the front? How we going to get that off? And if we do, what's to say somebody won't do it again?'

'I know. Just have to hope that people get tired of it.'

'They never did before,' Pat said greyly, wiping her hands on a towel. 'It's not fair. I'd knock their heads together myself if I had the strength. But what can I do?' She scrabbled in an ill-fitting drawer, taking out something white and popping it in her mouth.

'Do you feel all right? You've had a nasty shock.'

Pat shook her head, jaws working. 'I get pains. I bolt my food, I've always done it. It wasn't that man again, was it? The one who was hanging about yesterday. Bundle, Brundle . . .'

'No, I don't think so. I shouldn't worry about that.' Rebecca felt a faint shock that Pat couldn't remember Colin Brudenell's name. Such distance and vagueness seemed inappropriate.

'Chicken muck. What sort of game's that?' Pat began, grunting, to move the twin-tub out from the wall. 'More washing. Just what we need.'

'Let me help you with that.'

'Ta, dear. Ta.' The monstrous machine in place, Pat leant her thin brown arms on it and seemed really to see Rebecca for the first time. 'You're the one who rang the police yesterday, about that man?'

'That's right.'

'Well, there's some people left with a . . . bloody heart, anyway.' She half swallowed the curseword, so that it came out vowelless: *bldy*. 'I don't know. I keep thinking we ought to go. The council'd move us, I'm sure they would.'

'It must be awful.' She was cautious. 'It'd be a shame to have to leave your home, though.'

'That's what Howard says. I don't know. You have a child and you want to look after him, you want the best for him, make sure he's all right. I couldn't do that for twelve years and it seems like I can't do it now.'

Tears stood in her eyes, and Rebecca tried to think of something comforting. But there was no wobbling of lips, no catch in the throat – Pat just looked nakedly at her, and then she brushed the tears away as if that was her crying over.

Howard came down. His face was pinkly scrubbed, his curly hair combed flat with water.

'Sorry about this, Mum. It should come out on a hot wash.'

'It's not your fault, love. How about your eyes? Why don't I ring the doctor anyway?'

'They're better. Just the water did it. It's just a damn nuisance. Adam'll be wondering where I've got to.'

'Is there a phone in his cottage? You could maybe ring him,' Rebecca said.

'Now that's a thought. I have got his number. That's a good idea, that is.'

While he telephoned in the living room Rebecca wondered if Mrs Headley would be as tolerant of her lateness as she had made out in the first flush of her outrage. She didn't want to lose the job, or at least the wage. The same thing must have been on Howard's mind.

'He's coming to pick us up,' he said, returning. 'I told him how you'd helped me and made yourself late. So he'll pick us both up straight away and you'll be in Ingelow in no time.'

'Oh, there's no need for that.'

'No, he insisted. And me and all. We want to see you're OK.'

'That's right. One good turn,' Pat said.

She felt embarrassed; yet also, curiously, at ease. And she realized that this was because lately being with people meant being at odds with them. She disliked the word alienated, with its superior associations, but that was how she had felt yesterday: whereas now her defensive hackles were down. Among friends . . .?

'Christ. Sick minds,' was Adam's comment when he drew up outside and saw the graffiti. 'And they can't even spell.'

'Eh? Well, I'm not bothered about that. They've got their message across all right,' Howard said, and Rebecca felt a gleam of smugness that she hadn't commented on it.

'No, sorry, of course. Have you told the police?'

'Not much they can do.'

166

'It's as well to keep them informed. If an incident's unreported it doesn't exist. Might be an idea to keep a diary of these things. Are you OK, Pat?'

'Whatever next, that's what I want to know.' It was as if she half expected someone finally to tell her. 'I ask you, what next?'

'Shall you be all right on your own, Mum?' Howard said.

'I'm not going to start being frit in broad daylight in my own home, if that's what you mean. Go on.' She reached up to kiss him.

'Right. Better get you to work.' Adam turned to Rebecca. She suspected he was slightly short-sighted: when adjusting his focus he gave a characteristic little upward hitch of his chin that reminded her of the cats when they spotted something moving in the garden.

'Hope you don't mind chauffeuring me again.'

He smiled.

'You mean that, about a diary?' Howard said, getting in the passenger seat.

'Certainly. I know it's a tall order, but I think these characters should be caught if there's any chance of it at all.' His eyes met Rebecca's in the rear-view mirror. 'Any ideas about the culprits?'

'Huh,' Howard said. 'Take your pick.'

Adam drove with swift assurance. Glancing at her watch as they entered the clovered suburbs of Ingelow Rebecca saw she would be five minutes late at most.

'This other incident's certainly worth reporting,' Adam said. 'I just remembered. Down here, Rebecca? I just remembered, a friend of mine once threw a bucket of water over a Tory candidate who came canvassing at her door. The guy had her up for assault and she had to pay a fine. And what was done to you certainly counts as assault.'

'Well. I'd rather it had been a bucket of water in my case,' Howard said phlegmatically. Then he gave a chuckle. 'I suppose really it counts as assault and battery. You know? Muck from hens. Battery.'

He gave another chuckle, short and explosive, and there was something so droll about it that first Rebecca and then Adam began laughing too. Soon the car was filled with laughter. Meeting Adam's eyes again in the rear-view mirror, Rebecca saw there a reflection of her own feeling about the big man who dwarfed the seat he sat in: admiration.

Yes: weirdly, unexpectedly, among friends.

Rebecca saw Howard and Adam every day for the rest of that week. In the mornings she caught the early bus alongside Howard, who was, he said, an habitually early starter; whether Adam could have done with his arrival at the cottage being postponed by an hour or two was a moot point. She suspected so. Howard said once, with mild amusement, 'I should think he'll still be in his dressing gown or his skivvies – he don't seem to mind me seeing him.' But it was typical that Adam should say nothing and it seemed, besides, that the interviews were very full and needed all the time that could be given.

After work she called at Adam's cottage by the Roman Bank and travelled back to Holfleet with Howard. The afternoon weather was so inviting that they walked the couple of miles home by the seaward route, along the beach and then across the pullover at Holfleet Gap – any further would have brought them to Tetby Haven and they avoided that by an unspoken agreement – and on some afternoons Adam walked with them part of the way, strolling through the surf with rolled jeans, talking.

'I could get used to it here,' Adam said once, pausing to gaze out to sea with his hands crossed above his eyes. 'I never thought I'd say that. Always been a city person. No wonder your father finds it inspiring, Rebecca. I suppose Denmark's the next country you'd come to across there, isn't it? I can just imagine the old Viking longboats coming over that horizon . . . God, I bet it's stuffy back in London. I really don't want to go back.'

'Not even to see Angela?' Rebecca said.

'There is that. I did try to persuade her to come up here for the day, but she won't.'

'Why?'

'Seems to think of it as the back of beyond. It's odd, she . . . well, she just won't.'

A snob, Rebecca thought; and wondered if that had been his tacit thought too.

Just then something whisked past her, a few inches from her ear, startling her. Howard gave a cry. The object struck the side of his head and bounced away.

'Sorry!'

A dozen yards away a boy of eight or nine, gap-toothed and urchinlike in baggy Bermuda shorts, grinned his apology. The object was a Frisbee. Howard stooped to pick it up.

'Ooh, you monkey,' he said. He made a comical business of rubbing his head where it had hit him and then balanced the Frisbee, conjurer-style, on one thick finger. 'They're nice, are these. Mm. Reckon I might keep this one.' He smiled sidelong.

'Eh, that's mine. You can't have it,' the boy said, his grin widening, his great delicate ears reddening.

'Oh, you meanie. Go on then.' Howard threw the Frisbee to the boy with a nifty behind-the-back stroke. 'Good catch.'

'You can have another go if you like,' the boy said shyly.

Rebecca watched them throwing the Frisbee back and forth, Howard sometimes lofting it high, but never too high for the boy to catch it, sometimes doing trick throws under his leg and giving his explosive chuckle when they went wrong. This was the moment when she felt there was a solid reality behind Adam's theory about Howard's nature. Watching Howard playing with the little boy, she didn't find him childlike, which would have been creepy indeed. He was still a grown man, with a grown man's mannerisms. What he seemed able to do was, without effort, revisit childhood – its earnestness, its tirelessness, its appetite. Most people couldn't find their way back to it, not without some wilful artifice. For Howard Gandy, she thought, it was simply one step.

The little boy's mother, lying on a lounger further up the beach, was calling him: time to go home. Howard's face, as he threw the Frisbee one last time, was full of regret; but an adult regret, reflective, even meditative, the face of a man listening to Christmas carols and hearing in them the echo of seasons past and lost.

Later, when Adam had left them and they were taking the sandy path inland between the spiky dunes, Howard surprised Rebecca by saying: 'You must have had it tough, I should think. What with being adopted when you were little.'

'Oh – not that bad.'

'Tell me if I'm being nosy . . . did you lose your parents?'

'I didn't know my natural father. My natural mother's still around somewhere, as far as I know. She couldn't cope with me.' She caught herself in the old slip. When in care she had been encouraged to make a scrapbook of her life-story, and her guardians had gently interrogated her about such phrases, though they were literal repetitions of what Cathy Groom used to say to her. *I can't cope with you, Rebecca. You're too much for me, Rebecca.* What it really meant, they urged her to see, was that she couldn't cope with a *child*. Not her, not Rebecca: there was nothing specially bad or difficult about her that had influenced the situation. In other words, it wasn't her fault. Rebecca had learnt the lesson but had quietly absorbed another one: for Cathy Groom to be able to make any kind of stab at life, her daughter had to be off the scene.

'Single parent, eh? Like my mum, to all intents and purposes. Dad cleared off when I was little. I don't know how Mum managed a lot of the time.'

'Do you remember him?'

'Of course,' he said; for a moment faintly snappish. 'Well, some things. He was a bad 'un. Mum was better off without him. Even – whatever happened, she was better off.' His voice tailed off, then strengthened again. 'Only I don't want to see her struggling now. I'd like to get some sort of job where I bring a decent wage home.'

'What would you like to do?'

'Well. Depends if you're talking realistic or airy-fairy. The thing I fancy, don't laugh, is being a lollipop man.'

'Is that airy-fairy?'

'Well, it shouldn't be. I mean, I'm officially an innocent man now. And officially there's no reason why I shouldn't do any job working with kids, like I've always wanted. Of course, it's not going to work out like that because mud sticks, but . . . Any road, lollipop man's not a full-time job. It's the sort they give to retired people really. Mum still knows some people at Coupland's. I might get work there, maybe.'

'It seems a shame. There must be something like that . . .'

'Well, it's not what you know, it's who you know. And the folk *I've* known for the past twelve years haven't been very choice.'

'Unless Adam could help.'

'Dunno – he's not local. It's different with local people. Like your dad, say. He doesn't like me, does he?'

'It's difficult,' she said after a moment. She knew that her father didn't care for her associating with Howard like this: the way he withheld comment was eloquent enough. Yet it seemed strange, ludicrous even, to think of this – this amiable walking in the gentle afternoon – as representing the raising of some kind of rebellious flag.

'I know,' Howard said. 'I mean, he's your dad, isn't he? Doesn't matter about the blood. It's the tie. I wouldn't want to make any trouble.'

'You don't make any trouble.'

She spoke it plainly, with no great force. But it seemed to affect him deeply. His whole great face, even his neck, flushed a delicate terracotta colour. He said, 'Thank you. I'm glad about that.'

He lapsed into silence then, but that in itself was not uncommon. Howard had no fear of silence, that social anathema; refused to acknowledge, in his stolid way, the necessity of constant speech. At first nonplussed by this, Rebecca had soon grown used to it in his company and even found it refreshing. Perhaps if people had by law to be quiet for certain periods each day, as Muslims had prayers, there would be less stress in life.

She attempted to follow it when she did her stint on the Aids Action Helpline in Lincoln that night, with limited success. There were two of them in the little airless office above a double-glazing showroom – more for security than for the likelihood of endlessly ringing phones – and her fellow volunteer, a husky henna-haired woman, who seemed to carry the sixties about her like a cloud of incense, did a lot of sighing and frowning and humming whenever Rebecca tried it.

Soon she gave in, and in the absence of calls they investigated a new box of leaflets that had arrived from the Terrence Higgins Trust. The office was stuffed with literature of all kinds, from copies of *Boyz*, with its flamboyant male nudes, to incomprehensible digests of medical conferences, but Rebecca had never seen anything quite as mind-broadening as these leaflets, which were directed at gay men who practised sadomasochism. The burden of the text was how to do these things safely, meaning without risk of infection: in the general sense, the acts in the photographs looked anything but safe to Rebecca's startled eyes. Men muscled like statuary grimaced together, stretched and pierced. No women's bodies were to be seen and nothing was being done that could give any pleasure to a woman, which made it odd that Rebecca experienced a dark smothered thrill while she murmured facetious amazement. Perhaps it was because one was unused to viewing men as protagonists of desire: she had seen a standard pornographic video at a party, and the men in that were little more than piston-like presences, attendants at the rite of desire.

She took one of the leaflets home with her that night, with thoughts of friends whom she could scandalize, but soon forgot about it. The weather was sultry and enervating and a great tiredness came over her. She went to bed early, falling asleep to the faint sound of her father playing the piano. He had been working on a composition earlier but she recognized the music that accompanied her drift into night as Debussy – *The Sunken Cathedral*, its spectral bells sending their slow tolls into the summer-charged air.

She was not aware of any dreams when she woke, suddenly, in a darkness rouged with the lurid blush of an unbreaking storm, yet she had that sensation of having been elsewhere that indicates dreaming, and she found to her own surprise that her hand was imprisoned between her clenched thighs. She stirred, her body contested by languor and excitement. Then she realized what it was that had woken her and sat stiffly upright: her father was standing in the doorway, saying her name for the second or third time.

'Are you all right?'

'Yes . . .'

'Thought I heard you cry out . . .' He came into the room, and the landing light revealed his face. He looked haggard, dreadful.

'Dad, what's the matter?'

'Had a bad dream. Can't shake it . . . Are you sure you're OK?'

He studied her, anxious and yet distracted. Rebecca felt

172

awkward, and a little irritated with the premonitory boredom of being told a dream.

'No,' he said, 'it wasn't you in the dream. But you know how it is . . . things get blurred. No boundaries.' He sat down on the edge of the bedside chair, cradling his face as if it were tender with toothache. 'I was dreaming about Thomas. Went through it all again. Even things I thought I'd forgotten. Don't know why.'

'It's hot tonight,' she said sitting up, aware of a patch of sweat that stuck her nightdress to her back like the pressure of a warm hand. 'It needs to storm. I've had a funny sleep.'

'Have you? Rotten, isn't it . . .? I couldn't get my head round it, when I woke up – I was convinced that this was that same night somehow. The night we found him. Thomas.' His pale eyes flashed at her. He was wearing pyjama bottoms but no top and the mat of greying hair that covered his bare torso had a bristling look. It suggested to Rebecca the itchy feel of wearing new wool against the skin and even as she thought this he reached up a hand to scratch viciously between his shoulder blades.

'That was December, of course. The twenty-eighth: Innocents' Day, in the church calendar. It wasn't cold, though. I'm sure it wasn't cold. We were up and about in the middle of the night and I don't remember shivering or anything. The Christmas tree was up, that was in the dream and the weird thing is in the dream I noticed we had it in the hall, not the living room like we usually do. Which we did that year, but I'd forgotten. Totally forgotten.'

Neither he nor her mother had ever talked about Thomas's death in any detail. For a moment, as he placed his hands on his knees and drew a deep breath, it seemed that he was going to leave it once more, say good night and go.

'We'd been worried about one of the cats,' he said. Sleep strips off layers and her father's voice, singularly musical in the day, was a little coarse and throaty. 'We had a cat called Max then. A little toughy. He was quite old. But never had a day's illness. Well, that morning he didn't seem himself at all. We wondered if it was something he'd eaten somewhere. But he didn't perk up at all during that day. He wouldn't eat and he went to sleep in the airing cupboard, which he wasn't really allowed to do but we let him. Thomas noticed it – he always took notice of Max – and he kept saying his name before we put him to bed that night. "Mack?" he kept saying. But he was fine – Thomas was absolutely fine, that was what was so . . . Anyway, we went to bed about midnight, thinking Max would probably have to go to the vet tomorrow, and it must have been about, oh, two hours later and Max woke me up, jumping on the bed and patting my face. Completely transformed. He was just better. His old self, bouncing around. We went down to the kitchen and gave him some food. He gobbled it down and then whacked his ping-pong ball around and then went out through the cat-flap happy as anything. It was nice to see. We laughed and felt so relieved. And it was sort of nice being up in the small hours like that, knowing everything was OK, and it was Christmas-time. We put the kettle on for a cup of tea and Anna said maybe we could have a sandwich. Bit of a midnight feast. I came back upstairs to fetch something – this was in the dream and I'd forgotten it – it was Anna's slipper-socks, so it must have been cold, cold on her feet, though I can't remember the cold . . .'

He fell silent. Rebecca made a murmur, encouraging him to go on, though she didn't want him to. Sleep had left her just then a selfish sensual creature, recoiling from the burden of pity.

'I still don't know what made me open the door of Thomas's room and check on him. He'd been sleeping through for ages. Maybe I just felt like I wanted to include him in that night, the togetherness, the nice feel of it. He was sleeping sort of on his front, with his bottom sticking up. As I thought, anyway. There must have been – one second where I was balanced, like on a knife edge, between thinking he was OK and knowing he wasn't.'

At the window a single puff of air, like a ripple from some distant but vast explosion, bellied the net curtain into the room and then let it fall. The stormy tint in the sky had grown more sickly, but still no thunder sounded.

'I shouted for Anna. It was a sort of lowered shout – crazy: part of me still said not to wake him . . . We tried everything, of course, and we rang an ambulance. It seemed to be a long time coming. I remember going downstairs and switching the kettle off and then switching it on again, like I was trying to recreate the moment before it happened, or something. The ambulance took him away. Although he was surely dead, they took him away. It seemed weird. And that was the end of Thomas.'

His voice had become cooler, almost perfunctory. Rebecca felt ashamed of her own relief that her father was not going to weep.

'I used to dream about him a lot at first. Anna too. She . . . she was rather haunted. That was her grief. Thomas haunting her. But the dreams went eventually. I haven't had a dream like that since . . . God knows when. But I've never liked the sight of a closed door at night. It still gives me a bit of that feeling.' Seeming to become suddenly aware of his unclothed state, he folded his arms across his chest and leant forward as if to go. 'Sorry. I've woken you.'

'No, no. I think I woke up anyway. Must have had a dream myself.'

'I couldn't get out of this one. Even when I was up. It sort of clung and I saw your door and I thought, I must check, I must just check . . .'

'It's all right.'

'You'll always be careful, won't you? Silly question. No, Dad, I'm going to run in front of speeding trains.' He got up. 'But you know what I mean.'

'I know. You too. You take care too,' she said fuzzily, feeling that she had been found empty-handed, must find something to give.

'Best let you get some sleep. You've got to go to work in the morning.' Yet it was as if she were going much further from him than that: even as if she had already gone.

Arriving at the cottage by Roman Bank the next day after work, Rebecca found only Adam inside.

'Howard's just gone down to the beach for a swim. Good idea in this heat. You fancy joining him?'

'No, I'm OK.' It was the opportunity she had wanted to air the thoughts that had been fermenting in her these past days. 'Has Howard had any more trouble from Colin Brudenell?'

'Well, there haven't been any more nasty phone calls or

anything like that. Doug Jameson tells me he's been on to Brudenell's solicitor, and the guy says he's getting himself together and will stick by the terms of the injunction. You haven't seen any more of him?'

'No, nothing like that.' She had told Adam about the encounter with Colin Brudenell at the school sports day; but she hadn't yet given voice to her deeper suspicions. 'I just can't get him out of my head. Isn't it true that most murders aren't committed by strangers? That it's usually someone you know – even someone in the family?'

'Those are the statistics.' Adam was occupied with rewinding a stack of cassettes and marking their labels; now he put them down and gazed at her soberly. 'I know what you're saying.'

'It seems a terrible thought . . . But I can remember the violence that went on behind closed doors when I was little, before the adoption. Not actually to me, thank God. But there was a kind of – smell that it had, an atmosphere.'

'And you sense that around Colin Brudenell?'

'Maybe.'

'As far as I can tell from the documents, there wasn't any suspicion at the time that it was a . . .' he grimaced, 'a family job. But then, of course, the whole investigation focused on Howard. I can't say I haven't thought about it. But what about the way he's behaving? He's wild about Howard's release, swears he should never have been let out. Seems totally cut up.'

'Well. Call me cynical, but he would, wouldn't he? He couldn't say, oh well, let bygones be bygones because that really would look strange – and suspicious. He'd *have* to come on strong like this. I know this is just theorizing. But maybe he's a frightened man. Because now Howard's name has been cleared people are going to want to know who did kill Lee.' Her father's stern words came back to her: *Don't play detective.* She shook them off. 'And what's that phrase? "He doth protest too much, methinks." '

'You think all that threatening stuff is bluff?'

'I don't know. Maybe not. There's no telling how far he'd take it. Even if he did something really crazy – well, then that would show he's just crazy with grief, and they surely wouldn't be hard on him.'

Adam placed one last tape in the player, spooled through it. She heard snatches of Howard's voice, deep, seemingly broken with emotion. 'Amazing to hear Howard tell you what he's been through,' he murmured. 'I know I wouldn't have stuck it.' He took the tape out, marked it, and said, 'I'll be going back to London this weekend.'

For a moment she felt she was being dismissed as an over imaginative schoolgirl; and the sting of that blotted out her disappointment at losing him.

'Oh,' she said.

'Yep. I've got what I need here. And when I do go back, I'm going to try my damnedest to get an interview with Lorraine Brudenell. Lives just outside London – place in Essex. I have actually written to her again, with no reply. Maybe it's time to turn up on her doorstep. Because I think you're right. This is the trail to follow.'

She couldn't help her smile.

'Of course,' he said, smiling too, 'I can't guarantee she'll talk to me.'

'Maybe you're too male. Maybe she might open up more to . . . well, someone else.'

He raised an eyebrow. 'You think I need a female researcher, eh?'

'Well, perhaps it might help.' She was excited. 'And there's this second wife of his too. I wonder if she could shed some light on it. Just to someone who – well, doesn't seem like a threat. Nottingham's not far . . .'

'Whoa. Hold on. This is Colin's household we're talking about. No matter what he is or isn't, he is one angry man. I can't condone anything like that. Seriously. Let me lead the way in this.'

'Well. If you say so.' The acquiescence was tactical: she had her own ideas about that.

'OK. But listen, there is something in London that I really must pick up on. I'm chuffed it's turned up. It was something that was really missing from the whole thesis of the book. I've finally managed to trace someone who when he was a child knew Howard quite well. This was when Howard was grown up. Howard likes you, I don't think he'd mind me telling you about it: basically, when he was a young man he had a job as lifeguard at the swimming baths in Ingelow. He was dismissed for some murky incident involving a young boy, the kind of incident that people have been hanging around his neck all his life. Well, I traced the young boy – grown up now, of course. All he remembers is that there was nothing discreditable about it, except on his own part. He kept bullying a younger boy at the baths, and Howard gave him a good telling-off for it. Apparently Howard knew this younger boy well, taught him to swim and everything, and was very protective of him. The younger boy's name was Mark Wapshott. So I've been trying and trying to find this Mark Wapshott and I'm finally in luck. I've got a message from him: he lives in London now, he's got good memories of Howard and he'll be happy to talk about him. So I'm going to set up a meeting. It's really quite important – and I haven't told Howard about it for that reason. This is the other side of the story. If he's no danger to children, as I want to demonstrate finally, then you can't do better than the testimony of children who knew him. *Really* knew him.'

She thought of Stephen Larkinson, parroting old prejudices – and acting on them. It would be nice to see him refuted.

'By the way, have you seen Pat lately?' Adam asked.

'Last week, I think. Why?'

'Howard went to the doctor's with her this morning. Her stomach. He's only just got her to admit she's having pains. I thought she was looking thin last time I saw her.'

'Oh . . .' She couldn't imagine Pat Gandy ill – Pat, agelessly old, wiry, nut-brown in her unchanging halter tops and slacks. Like Howard, she seemed outside mortality. Then she remembered what Pat had confided to her on the day of the chicken-mud attack: *I get pains. I bolt my food* . . . So she'd been privileged to that information. 'God, he's so devoted to her. All that time apart, and then . . .'

She became aware that a shadow had fallen at the door. Turning, she saw Howard in swimming trunks, huge and damp and dripping, looking expressionlessly in at them. He had appeared as noiselessly as ever: she couldn't really tell how long he might have been standing there.

Then a smile slowly dawned on his smooth face. 'Hello, there. Wonderful day for swimming. How about you? Coming in for a dip? It's the only thing – it cools you so. There's nothing like it.'

'No costume.'

'Paddle then. You'll be all right in that, I reckon.' She was wearing a light wrapover skirt. 'Just feel the sea on your legs. It makes you feel tons better.' He ran his hands through his wet hair. His great rotund body, almost hairless, had the look of a sumo wrestler's, heavy yet buoyant. 'How about you, Adam?'

'Go on then. I swim like a stone, but I suppose it'll be cool.'

Down at the beach Rebecca tucked up her skirt and waded into the sea. Howard was already well out, effortlessly treading water. He waved a hand to Adam, loitering beside her. 'Come on, slowcoach! Give it some wellie!'

'Here goes then. If you see me sink call the coastguard,' muttered Adam. He was pale and slender in swimming trunks, with a narrowing bib of surprisingly dark hair running from the hollow of his throat to his navel. He trod on something sharp and briefly put a hand out to hold her shoulder as he wobbled. 'I hope there's no jellyfish. I absolutely hate jellyfish.'

'You big girl's blouse.' Water as so often bringing out silliness, they splashed each other, clowning: she got a clump of weed and mopped it on Adam's shoulders and then, daring, thrust it down the back of his trunks. She felt his lower vertebrae like beads against her knuckles: his skin seemed to burn to her hand and she tried and failed not to think of the Aids Action leaflet.

'Come on!' Howard called again, and he went up vertically and over, porpoise-like, scarcely making a splash. Adam swam towards him with a cautious breaststroke. Howard disappeared for what seemed minutes and then came up like a fountain beside Adam, laughing at the top of his voice.

'Come out further!' Rebecca heard him say, but Adam shook his head and bobbed where he was. His hair had gone spiky and almost black with the wet and he looked like quite a different person. Howard was different too in the water, but there the change was like a transformation of personality. The cumbrous defensiveness, the frugal reserve, the sense of him as an altogether rough-hewn piece of humanity, were gone. He became a creature not only at home in his element but flamboyantly in possession of it. Weightless and swift he dived and surfaced, flipped and corkscrewed. And once when he came rising up out of the sea behind Adam, he looked so huge and dominating that Rebecca, squinting in the sunlight, felt a momentary fear. The unsuspecting Adam looked as slight as a child, whilst this great barrel-bodied man loomed . . . Then she blinked and saw Howard ducking Adam, both of them laughing. Of course it was all right.

When they left the sea and walked up to the cottage to dress she could almost see Howard's reversion to his old self taking place before her eyes, the gestures diminishing, the sparkle leaving his eyes to be replaced by that look of gazing into a suspicious distance. Yet he seemed greatly content and relaxed too. Adam looked a little chilled and tired and in need of a stiff reviving drink: Howard's boisterousness had perhaps been a bit much for him.

The onshore breeze had freshened further: as she and Howard said goodbye and began the walk back to Holfleet she could feel the smooth tautness of her own legs, laved by salt water and sun. All along the beach and up amongst the dunes holidaymakers were stretching out more comfortably in the breezy air, exposing more flesh: they would be burning tomorrow. Howard fell into one of his restful silences and when he spoke she physically jumped.

'That,' he said, 'is what I missed most of all. In prison.'

He hardly ever said the word and it was like a cold touch of metal in this mellow soft day.

'Swimming?'

'Aye. It was best not to think about it. I dare say at some of these open prisons and what have you they have swimming facilities, but the place I was at . . . well, you couldn't even get a bath. Like I say, I tried not to think about it, but I suppose partly that's why I used to do keep fit and weights and that. Some sort of substitute. Course, it didn't give you that lovely free feeling like having a swim. It was no good pretending. That's the last thing you should do in there.'

'I read about someone, I think it was one of the old Nazi leaders they put in prison for years and years, who used to sit in his cell and imagine that he was walking all around the world.'

'Much good it did him,' Howard said with unusual vehemence. 'Typical prison silliness.'

'Is that what it brings out?'

'Silliness is what it's all based on. I don't mean justice or the law or all that. Just the – prison culture, as they call it. It's daft. I was a lifer, supposedly, so I saw a lot of it. Lifers are meant to be hard nuts. And that's how they saw themselves. But the fact is they couldn't last two minutes out in the real world. Just them being in there proved it. They can't manage at all unless they're with their own sort. And that's not real life at all, it's just a big playpen where they get fed and looked after. Oh, it's grim, all right, but a lot of that they make themselves. Because they've got to be hard nuts. You'd see silly things like the bloke serving in the dining hall rolling up his sleeves to show this new tattoo – horrible home-made effort – and the hard nut getting his dinner would reckon this was a challenge to him, so there'd be all this staring and squaring up. And none of it meant anything. It makes me think of this funny greetings card Adam sent me in there. It's a cartoon of all these cows going into an abattoir and one's going, "Oi, stop pushing in." '

He gave a dispassionate chuckle. They began to climb the path between the dunes at Holfleet Gap. Howard was breathing heavily.

'Fantasy worlds. Then there'd be these cells all plastered with pictures of nude ladies. Literally hundreds of them. Now that was never a problem for me as it happens. I suppose I'm just a bit quiet that way, but if these blokes are missing their wives and girlfriends or whatever it's understandable. But are they saying their whole lives are spent surrounded by full-frontal models, or that that's what they think about all the time? What's real about seeing naked ladies every single minute? Nobody lives like that. I suppose it was meant to show how manly they were. All I thought was they must be pretty weird sad people outside prison. But that's what they thought of me, of course.'

'You must have been so miserable,' she said helplessly. 'I don't know how you managed.'

'Sometimes you get people wanting to write to you,' he said. 'I don't mean when the campaign got started, not that sort of letter. I mean people who just want to write to prisoners, a sort of do-gooding thing. I wouldn't ever do it. In the first place, they'd be writing officially to a convicted murderer, so they wouldn't be writing to me. And besides that, they couldn't get to know me in any real way, not when I was in there. I wasn't myself, shut away in there. Did you ever play Monopoly?'

'Yes,' she said, surprised.

'Well, you know on one of the corners of the board there's a square called "In Jail". You have to go there when you get that "Go to Jail" card. If you remember the picture on that square . . . it's this man looking out between the bars. Just his face, and the way they've drawn it it's all dark and shadowy, hardly like a face at all. And that's how I felt, like him looking through those bars. They'd get all these counsellors, what have you, to talk to me and try and get at my feelings, and I'd just say to them, I'm the man on the Monopoly board. That's me. That's all.'

He was breathing more heavily now. She had never known him get physically tired.

She said, 'Do you want to stop a minute?'

'No,' he said. But he did stop, in the middle of the track, and looking straight ahead of him said, 'And now my mum's poorly. She's got trouble with her stomach. The doctor's given her some tablets but she's got to go to the hospital for some tests. That's lovely, isn't it? Lovely, that is. All them years . . . and now I get out and she's not well. It makes you wonder. It honestly makes you wonder . . .'

He turned away from her, and for a moment she thought he was simply going to walk away and leave her. Instead he climbed off the track and went towards a clapboard hut that stood amongst the dunes. It had once been a stall that sold ice creams and teas – a painted sign above the boarded-up hatch still faintly proclaimed it – but for as long as she could remember it had been like this, a peeling ruin on which even the graffiti was old and faded, and it was hard to imagine what hardly soul had set it up in the first place on such a little-used part of the coast. Howard walked behind it. If she hadn't known how modest and even prim his ways were, she would have thought he was going to take a leak. It wasn't that, though. Following him at a little distance, she found him leaning against the back wall of the hut, his face buried in his arm. He was crying, and even in the midst of her alarm her mind registered that he was crying in exactly the way a child did.

'Howard.' She put out a tentative hand, patted his broad back. It was always heart-wrenching to witness someone in tears like this; and here, something like responsibility tugged along with compassion, pulling her all ways. 'Howard, are you OK?'

He sniffed, swallowed, wouldn't show his face.

'I'm sorry about this.'

'Don't be. God, don't be. It's no wonder. You're only human, it's got to come out . . .' Cry it out: let it out – it was what you were supposed to say in these situations, the supportive thing. But as she patted his back she made a feeble plucking motion too, as if to encourage him to move on: it was only human, likewise, to be embarrassed and uncomfortable and wish that the person crying would just stop.

'No, I'm sorry . . . this is not right. I never meant to . . .'

'It's all right. It's natural. You know, with your mum – I'm sure that'll be OK. I know it's worrying, her having to go for tests and everything, but that's to make sure, so they give her the right treatment. It doesn't mean it's something terrible.'

He struggled to keep down his sobs, fighting like an asthmatic. Then she drew back, startled, as Howard lifted his right fist and drove it like a steamhammer against the peeling timber, twice, and then again and again with increasing vehemence.

'Don't . . .'

He stopped. There was a great bowl-shaped dint in the timber, splintered and bloody. Howard's knuckles dripped, staining the sandy ground at his feet.

'Oh God, your hand . . .'

'All gone now.' He straightened, sniffed, whipped a hand-kerchief from his pocket and wrapped it round his hand all in a couple of moments. The recovery of command was as instantaneous as his loss of it. 'Shall we get going?'

He was already stumping off, rapidly blinking his reddened eyes.

'Will that hand be all right? Let me look . . .'

'No. It's nothing.' Suddenly he gave a metallic laugh. 'I've actually had a very nice day.'

It was a cryptic and disturbing side of Howard that she had never really seen. Of course, Adam had always said that he wasn't by any means an easy person . . .

'It'll be strange when Adam's gone back to London, won't it?' he said as he climbed the grassy bank up to the sandy road leading into Holfleet – great strides that left her struggling in his wake.

'Yes, it'll be strange.' The change of subject offered an easy get-out, which she felt she shouldn't take. 'I suppose, though, that might make you feel upset sometimes too – doing those interviews, where you have to relive the things that happened. It must bring it all back.'

'It's always there anyway.' He cradled his hand. The hand-kerchief was red. 'No need to bring it back. There's nowhere else for it to go.'

'No, I suppose . . .' That was his way, of course, but she felt dispirited as she grasped the truth of it. You could draw a line under most experiences in life, she thought, but not that. Maybe there was a limit to how 'normal' you could expect a person like Howard to be.

'We shall keep in touch, anyhow,' Howard said, his face still stubbornly turned from her. 'Adam said he'll still be popping up now and again. And of course there's the book. So it's not as if . . . car coming.'

They were trudging along the side of the narrow road, which shimmered like a trail of oil in the hot afternoon, and she moved in closer to the verge as the growl of the car engine sounded behind them. It was heading into Holfleet and she readied herself for stares, if the occupants were local. Or worse? She hadn't seen Stephen Larkinson since the episode with the chicken droppings: she suspected he was avoiding her. Well, she would have a few words to say when she did see him, and the only problem was selecting from the many that teemed in her head.

'Christ!'

The exclamation was unlike Howard. She glanced at him in puzzlement, felt his arm grasping hers, urging her on to the grass verge. She looked round. The car was actually an old white rustbucket of a van. It was accelerating and it was heading straight for them. Such a thing was so bizarre that she stood stock still, staring at the letters VW on the front thrusting towards her like some enigmatic message.

'Mind – mind . . .' Howard was pulling at her: her arm hurt. She thought the roaring van must be out of control and had an image of a man dead at the wheel – and then she saw the driver.

Colin Brudenell's face glared through the windscreen. He had an expression of extraordinary concentration and also something like pain as his eyes fixed on Rebecca and Howard. His jaws were clenched and the bone structure of his young-old face could hardly have been clearer if it had been stripped of skin. He revved and revved the clapped-out engine. The bodywork of the van rattled like an almighty tin tray.

'Christ . . .!' Howard said again, and her feet scrambled for purchase as he pushed her, propelled her up the verge. Half off her feet, as if in the midst of a dance, Rebecca turned. Brudenell was wrestling with the steering wheel: at the last moment there was a change, he was trying to slew the van away from them back on to the road. Too late though: she saw those letters VW loom at her, the van lurch right up the verge like a monster lunging, and her emotion was still one of overwhelming surprise when the monster got her.

# FIFTEEN

Rebecca had never been in hospital before. She was unprepared for how public it all was: the attention she received made her feel as if she had achieved something noteworthy. Even her pain, which at first was considerable, was like part of the show: professionals interviewed her about it and her loved ones were present at it.

Visitors came in a seemingly endless series. Perhaps it was ungrateful, but she could not control a feeling somewhere between boredom and exasperation when the next one came peering round the entrance to the ward. Really she didn't want them to have to put themselves through it; hospital visiting was so difficult for the visitor, who with the best will in the world could find nothing to do and little to say.

Her bed was at the end of the ward by the window, but there was not much to see from there: just a view of part of the hospital grounds, two floors down, which was being rather ruthlessly cleared by landscape gardeners. They had pruned a bed of shrubs down until they were little more than naked stalks: the nakedness revealed the way they were all bending in the same direction, presumably to the sun, which gave an effect as of some devastating blast. Directly across the ward from her was an oldish man in a neck collar, who kept letting his pyjama top fall open to reveal a sagging belly clad in wiry hair, some of which was surely the pubic frontier. She didn't know whether he was doing this deliberately. It was, admittedly, hot in the ward: the broad window acted like a greenhouse and the nurses perspired patiently, their spongy shoes squeaking like hot tyres on the polished ward floor.

One of her first visitors was Detective Sergeant Hurst, from Ingelow police. His was very much a flying visit, almost a courtesy, to confirm the facts Howard had supplied to him.

Howard had fallen heavily, but had not been hurt and he had had the presence of mind to note the registration number – extra evidence, though they knew the driver was Colin Brudenell, no other. It was pure bad luck the way it happened, Hurst said.

'He'd been hanging around Holfleet again, looking for trouble, obviously.'

'Looking for Howard,' she said.

'Maybe. Certainly breaking the injunction and disregarding every warning we gave him last time. Plus he'd got himself another nicked vehicle. That old van.'

'I'm glad he didn't pinch a fast one.' She was, she knew, lucky. Mounting the verge had slowed the van's momentum. The bonnet had struck her a glancing blow, knocking her aside rather than under the wheels, and then the van had roared off.

Lucky: she had an impressive array of bruises, a cracked rib, a simple fracture of the radius in her left arm, which was encased in plaster of Paris and which after the first few days spent more time itching than hurting, and a sprained ankle from twisting.

'So. Obviously this was no accident. We're holding Mr Brudenell for questioning at the moment, but if there's anything you'd like to add, anything you can think of . . .?' The dapper policeman rattled a pen on his teeth.

Colin Brudenell's intention, it seemed, had been to hit Howard; but far more important to her was the fact that he couldn't do it. At the last moment he had veered away. She had a clear memory of the horror on Brudenell's face as the tremendous force – it had felt more like a hurricane, or an explosion, than the impact of an object – had bowled her away into unconsciousness.

'Well. I don't really want to press charges, if I don't have to. I mean, I don't want anything to happen to him, not for this. I don't think he meant it to happen. So – I just want to let it lie.'

Hurst raised his eyebrows. 'Well, I can't force you. As it happens Mr Gandy is very insistent on pressing charges against him. I mean, the guy's already got so much against him, he's going to get done whatever. Plainly this was an opportunist thing. He was driving around and he got Mr Gandy in his sights. What else he was hoping to do is another question.'

'Yes,' she said as he scrutinized her. 'Of course.'

'He's in rather a state, actually – Mr Brudenell. Hopefully this incident's knocked a bit of sense into him. We'll see. Anything else you want to tell me?'

'I don't think so.'

'No? Only I've got a bit of a feeling I'm not being told what's going on.'

She shook her head.

'Mr Gandy's been in prison. Mr Brudenell's heading that way if he's not careful. Not the sort of people you want to have *too* much to do with, you know. For the good of your health.' When she still gave him nothing he shook his head, smiling a little. 'You really are your father's daughter, aren't you?'

It was pure chance that she had been there and she felt no bitterness about it. Her one initial anxiety, on finding herself confined to a bed in Lincoln County Hospital, was about college, just a couple of months away: would she be fit to go? Once the doctors had reassured her, and told her she could even go home in ten days, she settled into a peculiar state of calm. In a curious way, hospital forced you into a detached composure: there was nothing you could do, no matters clamouring for attention and action. As for abstractions like responsibility, revenge, blame, they just didn't come into it: not with greater things at stake. Like murder, and the identity of a murderer.

It was partly because of this that she came to half dread the visits of her father, dearly though she loved him. He could not share in the philosophical mood that the hospital bed lent her. Most of his later visits were spent desperately trying to make amends for the outburst he had come out with on her second day in hospital.

'So. You're in hospital and it's a wonder, it is an amazing wonder, that you are not dead. And the reason for this is a person called Howard Gandy. Whom I had warned you about, whom you knew I didn't like you getting involved with. That goes for that bloody Dowling character as well – the whole kit and caboodle. But when you don't listen to me, I'm left standing by while you go ahead, getting more and more mixed up with this chap and all his sick business. And this is how it ends up. Now what am I supposed to feel? Am I allowed to get angry, now my fears have come true? Because I feel bloody angry, Rebecca. No triumph: I don't feel like saying I told you so. I just feel so bloody angry, with you, and with Gandy and bloody Adam Dowling and with that – lunatic who was driving—'

'Dad, you felt sorry for him before.' She wasn't being argumentative, rather trying to get him to see, as she was seeing, that the web they were caught in was too tangled for these simple emotions.

'Well, I'm not now. He deserves – oh, I don't know. I don't feel sorry for anybody very much at the moment. When all this could have been avoided, just by . . .' But he did not or could not say how it could have been avoided: he fumed, glared at the man opposite with his exhibitionist belly, and hissed, 'He came to see me, of course. Your friend Howard. I can't pretend I was glad to see him.'

'He'd understand that.'

'Would he? Right. So now he's a bloody saint. I seem to be the only one who finds this whole thing a bloody outrage. As for that bloody Adam Dowling – I do not like the way he's obviously worked on you. Enlisting you for the damn Howard Gandy fan club. Getting you mixed up in—'

'Dad, I'm grown up. I haven't done anything I didn't want to do. I was just walking home with Howard and there was an accident. It's not a big deal.'

'It was not an accident, Rebecca, and it's a very big deal to me.' He answered the smile of a passing nurse with a bleak stare.

Since then, he had been the picture of regret every time he came to see her. While he fussed over her, she lacked the energy to convince him that he didn't need to: that she understood the desperate anxiety that had been behind that outburst and there was nothing to be made up for. He kept bringing magazines, puzzle books, new tapes for her portable cassette player. He brought, too, the course books she was meant to read for college in October, and in the long hours of idleness – the nurses woke her inhumanly early – she made rapid progress through them. He brought chocolates and fruit and a card 'signed' by their cats and effortfully he dredged up every last bit of cheerful small talk he could find, gazing soulfully at her the while. It was a little wearing.

Of course, she understood. Her mother had died in this hospital: his distress was sharpened on a hard stone of memory. It was no good telling him everything was going to be all right – the associations of the place were just too painful. But the question of what would happen when she came out did arise, and in his desperate determination to be upbeat he came up with the idea of Uncle Denis in London.

'How about going down there for a week or two? It's ages since we've been. Maybe it would do both of us good. A nice break. Go to the theatre. And we could do some shopping, for things you'll need in October. Please ourselves. What do you say?'

'It'd be nice. I'd really like that.' She had to appear only casually pleased: he might have been suspicious if she had shown how eager she was to go to London. In fact she would have been desperate to engineer it, if fate had not thus thrown it in her way, but again she couldn't tell him the reasons.

And there was nothing to stop her. Her job at the Cowrie House Hotel, naturally, was over. Mrs Headley had sent a get-well card with a cheque in it for her last wages, underpaying her by ten pounds. She was a free agent.

Though her father probably wouldn't have appreciated the comparison, his reaction to her accident was not unlike that of Adam, who visited her later on the second day. On first coming into the ward he looked unruffled, rather distinguished – you could easily imagine him, given a white coat, as a junior consultant himself – and when he sat down by her bed she felt relieved that here was a visitor who looked as calm as she felt. He asked how she was feeling and said it was a shock and then began to talk to leaving for London tomorrow.

'I can't delay it any longer. Various things to do – plus I'm hoping to interview the chap I was telling you about. Mark Wapshott. I had a note from him confirming an appointment. Which is good news.' He picked up one of her textbooks. 'Weighty tomes.'

'I've got to get through them by October.'

'Don't go overboard. The prelim stuff in your first term is

usually just to ease you in . . . Jesus, it's bloody awful seeing you in here.'

'It's not that bad. I'm as high as a kite on the pills, you know. It's like a sort of quiet rave.'

'I feel responsible.' His expression was solemn. 'I feel I involved you in this business and that I had no right to do that. I never dreamt of anything like this happening – but perhaps I damn well should have.'

'I am involved,' she said. 'And I want to see it through to the end. Perhaps I could see Lee's mother, maybe help you in other ways. After all, I know Holfleet, I know the coast and the people . . . Somebody killed Lee and we still don't know who. But there are pointers, aren't there? Things are happening. Colin Brudenell couldn't go through with this hit-and-run business, and all he's done is bring a lot of police attention to himself. What does that say about him? Just lost his nerve? Or is he overplaying this revengeful father bit because he's got a secret and he's afraid it's going to come out at last? He certainly seems like a man who's about to crack, one way or another. We can find out the truth, I know we can. Look, Dad's saying about going to London when I'm out. Can we meet then?'

Adam frowned. 'Of course I'd like that. But, Christ, I feel responsible enough already . . .'

'Get out of it. What else can happen?'

'Don't say that.' He took her hand, glanced harshly around him. 'God. Howard's story was meant to have a happy ending.'

'It still will. Anyway, I'm in the land of the living . . . Lee Brudenell isn't.'

Quickly, almost brusquely, he got up and kissed her cheek. 'Call me when you get to London.'

Oddly enough her most restful visitor, the one who caused her the least strain, was Howard Gandy himself. It was a long bus trip for him from the coast, but he came several times to sit by the bed and talk in his rumbling tenor of what he had been doing and how his mother was or, if there was nothing to say, simply to sit stolidly there, observing what was passing, the hurried tedium of ward life – in a way sharing her experience far more than if he had asked her a lot of questions about how she was feeling and what they were doing for her. 'Of course, it was meant to be me,' was the only allusion he made; and when on one occasion she did bring up the subject of Colin Brudenell, he was plain and cool.

'My solicitor rang me again yesterday about it. He'll be up in court soon, about the stolen van I think. I want to make sure he faces charges for what he's been up to in Holfleet as well. Everything. I've had enough of that man now. I tried to feel sorry for him. I tried to make allowances. But that's finished now. He's got it in for me and I'm not having it.'

He didn't say any more about it: she was thankful not to have to face another guilt trip. She was convinced, though she couldn't say so to Howard, that legal action against Colin Brudenell for this was really beside the point. The vacuum at the centre of it all, sucking everybody in, was the unsolved murder of Lee Brudenell. An unanswered question. There could be no peace until it was answered. She saw this very clearly as she lay sleepless, listening to the sounds around her, the snores, the little patient moans, the slippered shuffles down the corridor to the toilet, the clunk of sprung doors, and now and then a kind of subdued, contained commotion, like a distant storm, betokening an emergency somewhere in the building.

Though her friend Emma was training there, she only came up to Rebecca's ward to see her a couple of times, seeming curiously abashed by the presence of the ward nurses. 'I don't know any of these,' she confided. 'And they're ever so cliquey. If you're a trainee they're funny with you. So, when can you have it off?'

'That is the last thing on my mind.'

'I mean the plaster.' Emma giggled fearfully. 'Mind you, I suppose the same applies. I mean, you could hardly – you know, with that.'

'Love would find a way.'

'Stephen Larkinson would.'

'Oh, don't. Only with my corpse. Even then I'd rise up and smack him one. It does itch so.'

'How close is it, let's have a look . . . You could probably poke a knitting needle under there to scratch it. Don't let them see you doing it. Here, there's a woman downstairs who was asking after you. Got a little sprog with her. It's weird, they said she could come up but she um-ed and ah-ed and she's just sort of loitering with intent. Ring any bells?'

'Not really. Are you going down that way?'

'Can do. I'll tell her you're happy to receive, shall I? Funny woman. Looks like she's scared to be in here.'

The woman who came at last into the ward, leading a small boy by the hand, wore large-framed sunglasses that effectively covered half her face. She only removed them when she stood nervously by Rebecca's bed.

Black-eye sunglasses, Rebecca thought: Cathy Groom had had a pair just like them. But the eyes the woman revealed were unharmed – just weary and grey and peculiarly starved-looking. Rebecca remembered, from the Appeal Court, that strange mixture of gauntness and flesh.

'I'm sorry to disturb you. It's Rebecca Springthorpe, isn't it?'

'Yes. You're Mrs Brudenell.'

'Wendy.' There was a small wrapped bunch of flowers stuffed into the top of her handbag and she began awkwardly to extricate it. 'Do you mind me being here?'

'Of course not. Thank you for the flowers, that's kind.'

The little boy, his nose level with her pillows, stared with solemn fascination at Rebecca. He had an olive complexion and huge dark eyes. Most children of his age now were barbered like GIs, but his thick black hair had been left to grow unchecked. Rebecca liked it and had an urge to rub her hand across it. She smiled at him. 'Hello there.'

'His name's Jake. He's four,' Wendy Brudenell said, with an air of apology.

'Hello, Jake.' Noticing the direction of his gaze, she said, 'Do you like my funny arm? You can touch it, it's all right.'

The boy put a finger and tapped the plaster, then smiled at her with shy amusement.

'I didn't know whether to come. I rang the hospital and they said you were doing all right. I wasn't sure whether you'd want to see me really. But I wanted to say sorry.'

'You haven't done anything.'

'Well. Colin has.' She half whispered it. 'I've heard all about it. All I can say is – he didn't mean it to happen. He's not himself. There's a lot of problems. I know that's no excuse.'

'I understand.'

'He doesn't know we've come today.' Wendy peered at her wristwatch. 'That's why I can't be long. There's a bus back to Nottingham at half-past. But I thought I'd just come and . . .'

And what, Rebecca wondered. She thought she detected a confessional urge under Wendy Brudenell's awkward formality, but she didn't know how to tap into it.

'It's a long trek for you. Especially with a little one. I do appreciate it.'

'Oh, he enjoys it, this one,' Wendy said, caressing Jake's narrow shoulders. 'He likes getting away.'

A walking patient went by, wheeling his drip on a mobile stand. Jake stared.

'Colin wouldn't like you being here, then?'

Wendy shifted and wouldn't meet Rebecca's eyes. 'He's not himself,' she said again. 'It's since they let that man out of prison. Colin can't get over that.'

'Howard Gandy. He was here yesterday actually. Sitting in that very chair where Jake is.'

Wendy Brudenell's eyes widened. Her hand strayed to Jake's back and stayed there, caressing.

'Well,' she said, 'I don't know anything about it. I married Colin nearly two years ago. Jake's dad and me got divorced when he was one year old. It was a rotten time. Colin was my new start. He told me what had happened in the past, with his little boy.'

'Lee.'

Wendy nodded, frowning as if Rebecca had blasphemed. 'So all I knew was that this man was in prison and – and thank goodness for that, really. I don't know the ins and outs of it. They must have had a reason to do him for it, mustn't they? Colin's so adamant . . . I mean, what do you think of him? This Gandy one?'

'I think he's an innocent man, just like the law says. I don't believe it was him who—' Noticing Jake's fascination with her Walkman, she handed it to him. 'Here you are – have a go. Over your ears, that's it. Now we switch it on here . . . I don't believe he was the one who killed Lee.'

Wendy's eyes were fixed on her now – though not on her eyes, on her mouth, as if she were lipreading.

'Colin's got a few photos of his – of Lee,' she said softly. 'He looked ever so much like Colin. Spitting image.'

Rebecca bit her lip, recalling the one photograph that she had seen of Lee Brudenell.

'It must be hard,' she said. 'Hard for you too.'

'He blames his first wife a lot. Lorraine. That I do know. He's ever so bitter when he talks about her. He reckons she was drunk the day it happened, not looking after him properly, so it was all her fault. It was no wonder they split up after it happened, I suppose. I don't know. Sometimes terrible things bring people together, don't they?'

'So he blames Lorraine.'

'Well, I've heard him say she couldn't bring up a kid right – it was either ignoring or spoiling. And he'd end up having to do the discipline. I think he had a bad childhood himself so he's very serious about that kind of thing.' Her voice was softer still, merely a murmur. 'Of course there's two sides to every story. You'd have to ask Lorraine.'

She had whispered mutiny: her suddenly stricken expression showed it.

'I suppose he must have had some kind of help, counselling or something, after it happened?'

'Colin doesn't believe in that sort of thing.' Wendy took out an inhaler and drew from it. 'I can't say I blame him because how can you come to terms with something like that? I mean, if our Jake . . .' She couldn't finish it. Her eyes misted.

*Who do you think killed Lee?* It was what Rebecca wished to ask: yet how could she come out with such a cool Hercule-Poirot question? Especially to Colin's wife.

She felt she was learning, though.

'Mum, listen. It's loud,' Jake said with approval, offering his mother the headphones. She put them on. Watching her face, he said, 'I can't hear it now,' with an air of delighted scientific discovery.

'Who do you like best in Sesame Street?' Rebecca said, pointing to the print on his T-shirt.

'Bert. Not Ernie, though.' He shook his head as at an important distinction.

'Colin's had a struggle. All his life.' Wendy handed the headphones back to her son. 'Rotten childhood. Rotten first marriage, and then losing his only kid like that. He's struggled to stay in work and look after us. He's had trouble with the law. I'm not excusing that but I'm just saying he's been ground down by things and – yes, he has got a temper and it gets him into trouble. But it all comes from that time, you see, it's a lot for a man to deal with. And he can be so caring and protecting . . .'

Rebecca nodded. She couldn't guess what had prompted this outburst of loyalty. Whistling in the dark?

'It's all right,' she said, 'I don't bear a grudge or anything like that.'

'He's my husband, you see.' Wendy looked distractedly around her. 'Is there a toilet I can use?'

'Just round that corridor.'

'There's Jake . . . Can you wait a minute, Jake?'

'Will you stop with me a minute while Mummy goes to the toilet?' Rebecca said. She got a solemn nod in return. 'Tell you what – here's a pen. You can draw on my arm. See – it's all right, we can draw all over it.'

Jake leant on the side of the bed, his tousled head close to her. The novelty appealed but he was tremulous too. And before he put the tip of the felt pen to the plaster he looked up at her with a wise, adult directness and said quietly, 'Did Colin do that?'

'He didn't mean to.' It was all she could think to say. Jake nodded, and drew a wild smiling face.

'We'd better get moving.' Wendy was brisk when she returned. 'I just wanted to see you and say – well, sorry. And maybe you could try and understand him . . .' Suddenly she looked as if she tasted something sour. 'Not that I can myself. Jake, let's be having you. Say bye-bye.'

'Bye, Jake.' Rebecca gave him the pen. He was a heart-breaking kid and she wanted to give him everything.

'You'll be glad to go home, I should think,' Wendy said. 'Is it nice where you live? By the sea?'

'I like the sea!' Jake said vigorously.

'Yes. It's lovely,' Rebecca said.

'I've always fancied living by the sea. Be nice, wouldn't it, Jake?' Wendy said; and Rebecca felt she hardly needed to say the words *Just the two of us*.

# SIXTEEN

The visit to London became for Rebecca's father a business trip, though this wasn't planned. Shortly before leaving Lincolnshire he had a call from a programme producer at Radio Three. They had scheduled a series of talks for the Schubert bicentenary this year, to be given by an aged and distinguished musicologist. He had sent in his scripts but had fallen ill and couldn't record them. Philip had broadcast for them often before, could he possibly . . .?

He agreed to do the talks only from his own scripts: the producer agreed if he could have them ready within a week. So, much of her father's time in London was spent either at the British Library, at Broadcasting House or hunched over his laptop, and much of the time Rebecca was left to her own devices. Uncle Denis was with them only for the first day before flying to Paris on a long business trip of his own: in fact he seemed to spend very little time in his attractive Edwardian villa tucked in a quiet Chiswick street lined with lime trees. He was a large rugged hirsute man who worked, with disarming inappropriateness, as a cosmetics buyer for one of the big stores. A nasty divorce had turned him into a career martinet and there was a melancholy kind of carelessness in the way he threw the house open to his brother and niece: Rebecca felt that he wouldn't have much minded if they had gutted the place.

Her father was apologetic. 'Once I've got this stuff out of the way,' he said, peering at a Xeroxed score of the *Wanderer* Fantasy, 'we'll do that shopping. And a show.'

Rebecca didn't at all mind being left to herself. It suited her plans. She was nineteen, in a desirable place during the beautiful finale of summer, and had a college place awaiting her in four weeks' time. The nerviness about roads that had afflicted her since leaving hospital had gone, and the plaster had been removed from her arm the day before they left for London. She was fine, and she had important plans of her own.

She rang Adam Dowling's number on her second morning there. She didn't really expect to find him in, and when he answered on the second ring she stammered, nearly addressing him by her own name.

'Oh, hi, Reb – it's Rebecca. Springthorpe.' At each encounter with him she seemed to start off distressingly young. Would she make it to adulthood by the end of this conversation? 'I'm in London. Dad and me are down here for a week or so. Dad's doing this thing for Radio Three. It was meant to be a break, but he's ended up really busy.'

'Speaking of breaks, how's the arm?'

'It's heaps better, thanks. Very stiff and tender, but the plaster's off. Actually, when I was in hospital somebody came to see me. I think you'll be interested. Wendy Brudenell.'

'Really?' Adam's tone perceptibly quickened. 'On her own?'

'She had her little boy with her. She wanted to apologize for Colin.'

'Not the only one. I still feel pretty bad about what happened.'

She had gone through a whole course of feelings about Adam: looking at the stage she had arrived at now, she found the idea of him feeling bad about her quite pleasing.

'So how's the book going?'

'Slowly. Transcribing Howard's tapes is taking longer than I thought. And I've had other work to do as well, which is frustrating. A follow-up piece on a bunch of young people who got work through the Prince's Trust. Quite a few have packed in and started injecting in squats, but the editorial line at the moment is to be nice to the Prince, so I've got to play that down. I must admit my mind's still mainly on the Gandy case. So what did you think of Wendy Brudenell?'

Rebecca tried to speak with caution. 'I think she's frightened of her husband. I think the little boy's frightened of him. And I think there are things she won't say, out of loyalty.'

'This is interesting . . . Listen, we must talk. Are you free this morning?'

'Free as a bird.'

'Good, because I've got a meeting lined up this morning, and I'd like you to be there. You remember me telling you about Mark Wapshott, who knew Howard years ago? I've finally got an interview, he's coming over to my place in about half an hour. Should be very useful. Then afterwards we could compare notes, you know, talk it up over a cup of tea and a wad. Whereabouts are you?'

She told him, glancing down at herself, suddenly unhappy with the hole in the knee of her jeans.

'No problem. If you take the tube to Notting Hill Gate, then turn into Kensington Park Road . . .'

She followed his directions with only half an ear; she was a person who generally got lost and relied for directions on the kindness of strangers, which had never failed yet.

'OK,' she said, 'I'll see you soon. By the way, what on earth is a wad?'

'Eh? Oh, it's something my father used to say. Wartime slang, I think, for a roll or a bun or something. Come to think of it, I haven't got any buns.'

She thought afterwards that she could have said something like, 'It's all right, I'm not after your buns.' But even if she had thought of it at the time, it might have been inappropriate, the kind of schoolgirlish stuff she exchanged with Emma. This was a meeting of adults, and setting out for Ladbroke Grove Rebecca felt sober and somewhat impressed by herself – rather as if the young, messy, unfinished person she had been just a year ago were looking on in wonder.

For some reason she expected Adam's flat to be amongst the crescents of tall villas with their porticoes and cupolas and balconies that she passed on her wanderings from Notting Hill tube station, and she was surprised when she came upon the little modern block of flats, untruthfully calling itself a mews, squeezed in between a clutch of shops and a garage. It was, she supposed, something like neo-Victorian, with its pink brick and economical bits of wrought-iron decoration, resembling the retro shopping arcades springing up everywhere, and it was all very neat and spruce except that on the side wall there was a single splash of spray-can graffiti. Curiously it was about eight or nine feet up, as if the perpetrator had used a stepladder. 'KATRINA = SLAG' and 'JAMIE G = BABY SNATCHA!' were the words, in that stylised graffiti script that always puzzled her. Where did people learn it, practise it? An earnest teacher at her school had spoken of graffiti as a vital popular art form with an ancient history, but she thought it looked just awful.

She pressed the intercom button by Adam's name.

'Rebecca? Hi, come on up.' Before he switched off, she heard him speaking to someone in the background. Mark Wapshott must be already here. It would be interesting to meet someone who could vouch for Howard with children, she thought; but it was the tightening of the net on Lee's real killer that preoccupied her.

The man in Adam's flat got to his feet politely when Adam ushered her in.

'Let me introduce you. This is Mark Wapshott, who's been filling in some memories of Howard's younger years. This is Rebecca Springthorpe, who lives in Holfleet.'

'How are you?' The young man shook her hand. 'I was just saying to Adam, I haven't been back to Lincolnshire for ages. I should think Ingelow's changed a lot, hasn't it?'

'Yes, it has,' she said conversationally, though she couldn't think of any changes offhand.

'So, you're a friend of Howard's, then?'

'Yes, I am,' she said, not conversationally this time: the reply had importance.

'Well, like I was saying to Adam, I hadn't really thought about him for years. I never dreamt he'd got put in jail. We moved down to London when I was ten. I must have missed all the business about the trial. Still, you don't look at newspapers when you're a kid, do you? I never did. Tell the truth, I don't now. All seems to be bad news, so what's the point?'

That explained, she thought, his accent, which was plain south-of-Watford working class with no trace of Lincolnshire. He was a slender, very fair, very good-looking man who just lacked the few inches of height that would have made him stunning, though his manner was open and straightforward, no hint of God's gift about it.

The strangest thing was, Rebecca had a strong feeling she

had seen him before somewhere. Yet it couldn't have been in Holfleet. Where . . .? The question distracted her enough for her partly to miss what Mark Wapshott was saying.

'. . . terrible to think that could happen. But you do hear of these cases all the time, it seems – miscarriages of justice. Luckily there's a few people around who take these things up. I just wish I could have thrown in my threepennorth before, you know, if it could have helped.'

'Well, hopefully there won't be these kind of witch-hunt trials and convictions in future,' Adam said.

'I suppose everybody's at risk really. You only have to be in the wrong place at the wrong time. Frightening.' Mark Wapshott patted the pockets of his velvet waistcoat. 'What did I do with my cigs?'

'Here we are.' Adam took a packet and a box of matches from a small pine dining table where his tape recorder and notes were set out. 'Feels like it's empty, actually.'

'Damn. Knew there was something.'

'Here. Take a couple of mine to see you through.'

'Oh, cheers, are you sure? Last smokers left in the world, we've got to stick together.' Mark smiled at Rebecca. 'Unless there's three of us?'

'I haven't been tempted yet.'

'Very wise. Well, I'd better be making tracks, unless there's anything else I can help you with . . .?'

'I think we've covered it,' Adam said. 'It's just a matter of getting a true account of what Howard was like with kids, instead of all the rumour and gossip. You've really given me what I need.'

'Well, like I say, I remember him at the old swimming pool because he used to look out for me. I must have been a bit of a wimp in those days. Shrinking violet sort of thing.' He grinned at Rebecca, stretching in a feline way: the muscle delineation on his brown forearms suggested he worked out. Rebecca smiled back; and this time the feeling of recognition was so strong she felt almost dizzy. 'So he took me under his wing a bit, taught me to swim properly, not just the old doggy-paddle. Then we'd have a kick-about with a football on the seafront when he was off. Taught me how to do headers. It was a kind of big-brother thing, basically. That was how he was. I never saw anything dodgy in it, still don't. Like I say, quote me, feel free.'

'Well, I'll send you the transcript before I use anything.'

'No need.' Mark Wapshott shook his head emphatically. 'I know what I've said. But anything else I can do, get in touch, yeah? Well, actually I'm going away from October for a while, so it'd have to be before then.'

'No problem. Going away for long?'

'Maybe. It's a sort of a course I'm doing.'

'That makes two of you. Rebecca's going to college in October.'

'Yeah? Good for you. Take your chances, that's what I say. But not what I do, unfortunately.' Mark grinned ruefully. 'I missed out. My own fault. Art, that's what I would have fancied. See, like this here.' He pointed to a framed print on the wall of the kitchen-diner, a Burne-Jones sketch of hollow-eyed androgynes, one of the few decorative items to be seen. 'Now to me, to be able to do that would be just fantastic, you know? If you had that ability, I can't see that you'd ever want to do anything else. You'd be made.'

'Never too late to try,' said Adam.

'D'you think? I don't know.' The young man sighed, digging his hands into the skin-tight pockets of his jeans. 'So what is it you're going to be studying?'

'Sociology.' He was looking right at her, but there wasn't a flicker of recognition in his face. Maybe he just reminded her of someone, maybe she was simply mistaken . . .

'Now there's another thing that would interest me. That's really getting to grips with what it's all about, isn't it? Finding out how everything ticks. But you've got to have the brains to start with, haven't you?' Humorously he rapped on his own head. 'That's where I'm a non-starter. Mind you, you have to work at it, don't you? You must have worked hard to get there.'

'Sort of,' Rebecca said. 'I think I must have had a bit of luck with the exams as well.'

'No, don't you knock yourself. It doesn't work like that, does it?' he said to Adam. 'You'd know.'

'No, you can't fool the examiners,' said Adam, who Rebecca felt was getting very slightly bored with Mark Wapshott.

'You could apply that to life, really. Anyway, best be off.

Good luck with the book and everything. Nice to meet you,' he said to Rebecca.

'I'll say hello to Howard for you when I see him, shall I?' Adam said at the door.

'You could do, mate. I don't know as he'd remember me. I was only a squirt.' Something wry and melancholy came into Mark's eyes. 'Hard to think you were the same person, really, isn't it?'

Adam saw him out to the vestibule downstairs. Rebecca seized the short opportunity to be inquisitive about this place that he lived in. At once she sensed that he didn't much value it himself. The small dimensions might have made for cosiness, but he had firmly rejected that in favour of the kind of severely functional angularity – a couple of steel-framed chairs, polished floorboards with a single iron-grey rug, Venetian blinds, plain walls – usually associated with large airy spaces. As a result it appeared more like a halt than a home. Apart from the Burne-Jones print the only picture was a framed cover of his book, *Devil's Work*, a touch of vanity which first surprised and then tickled her.

'Have a seat. I'll make us some coffee.' Adam was back, carrying letters, the second post presumably. He tore them open at the dining table, threw them down after a cursory glance. 'Post always looks exciting and it's always disappointing. You're looking really well, by the way.'

'Better than last time?'

'Don't remind me.' He busied himself with coffee. 'When I saw you in that hospital ward I felt like going after Colin Brudenell myself.'

'Crikey.' This also was not unpleasant to learn.

'Howard's still pretty furious, I think. Though he doesn't give a lot away about his feelings, as you know. But he really does want to see Brudenell punished.' He shrugged, uneasy. 'Well, anyway, I'm glad you met Mark. He's a bit of a talker, I'm afraid.'

'Lonely maybe . . . Do you know, I had this feeling I'd seen him somewhere before. Something about his face.'

'Yes? He left your neck of the woods a long time ago.'

'I know. Can't be that. Never mind, maybe it'll come to me.'

'Well, you'll have gathered the kind of stuff he was telling me. God, what a sidelight that throws on Howard Gandy, the sinister Pied Piper of Lincolnshire. Reminds me, I came across a press cutting I hadn't seen before, from the time of the trial. "Face of evil" was the headline, over this photograph of Howard. And I swear, they had *retouched* this photo so that his eyebrows met in the middle. Can you believe that? I'm going to ask a photographer friend of mine to check it to make sure. I mean there may be just a chance that it was a flaw in reproduction, but I'd bet my right arm against it . . . Here you go.'

'So does he remember anything about that incident that got Howard the sack?'

'Only what the other guy told me, really. The lad was misbehaving, being a bit of a bully, and Howard ticked him off. He was being protective – like a big brother, as he said. I suspect Howard might have been a bit . . . well, righteous about it. He does tend to see everything in black and white.'

Rebecca had an uncomfortable memory of Howard beating his fist against timber: of blood trickling disregarded on sand.

'Oh – let me just do this before I forget.' He got out his cheque book. Seeing the name he wrote – *M. Wapshott* – Rebecca said in surprise, 'You're paying him?'

'For his time, travelling expenses. It's not something I'd always do, but in this case I feel I should. The guy's out of work, though he didn't say as much.'

'Sherlock Holmes.'

He grinned. 'You learn to spot these things. Anyway, nobody could tan and work out that much without a lot of time on their hands. So, how's your father doing? Sounds like he's busy.'

'He's fine, I think. Because he's busy. I think he missed Mum when we first arrived at Uncle Denis'. There's this great big mirror in the hall when you walk in, straight in front of you, and Mum always used to hate it – well, in a joking way. She'd skulk past it and stuff like that. I saw him looking. Things like that bring it back.'

'For you too, I should think.'

'Yes. It does. But it's worse for Dad.'

'Really?'

'Well.' She was uncomfortable. 'I belong to the MTV generation, you know. Attention span of three minutes.'

He smiled at her. 'I know that isn't true. Anyway, we're not different generations, are we? Twelve years or so – does that count as a generation? I don't think so. Listen, I'm going to have something to eat. Just a cold collation sort of thing. Join me.'

'I like your flat,' she said while he clattered in the kitchen.

'Do you?' Returning with plates on a tray, he looked around him with a touch of perplexity. 'I'm not much of a home-maker. Men aren't, I suppose. Actually, I sort of miss that old cottage. Certainly for working. The traffic's noisy here plus the damn car alarms going off every ten minutes. Funny, this reminds me of the cottage,' he said sitting down at the table. 'You here. Just need old Howard coming in in his swimming costume.'

It was odd bachelor food that he had slapped out, slices of granary bread, hunks of cheese and salami. But her appetite, a skittish beast that sometimes refused to go at all, was lively today and she ate with pleasure.

'I suppose it must cost a bomb to live here.'

'It does. But, I earn more than anyone decently should for what I do, so I can't complain.'

'You're good at it, though, aren't you? You got Howard out. I finished reading *Devil's Work* as well. I thought it was great. Some of that stuff is incredible – like that guy in America who went to prison for satanic abuse of his daughter, just on the evidence of – well, a hypnotist, was it?'

'Hypnotherapist, yep. Who supposedly recovered these twenty-year-old memories from the daughter, all pure delusion. Well, I'm glad you liked it. Don't make me big-headed, though. After all, it was you who got an interview out of Wendy Brudenell.'

'Well, it was more of a kind of awkward chat. But I did try and pump her a bit. She seemed like she half wanted to get things off her chest. She's definitely spooked by the way Colin acts. They haven't been married all that long and I think she's . . . discovering things about him. Her little boy – I can't get over him. A sweet kid, about four. He looked at my arm and just asked if Colin did that – in the oldest, wisest way.'

'Oh boy.'

She nodded. 'Even more reason to pin down what happened that day at that camp site. Wendy said Colin won't talk about it much. But he does blame his first wife, she said. Totally bitter against her.'

Adam was thinking. 'There were inconsistencies when Lee first went missing and the family talked to the police. First off Lorraine Brudenell said she hadn't had a drink at all. Then she changed it and said she'd had a couple of cans. Colin said he went to the village pub, which he certainly did: there are witnesses who saw him. But there are doubts about how long he was actually in there. Not long, apparently; but it was a couple of hours before he got back to the camp site. He said this was because he got lost on the way back and ended up coming the long way round by Coupland's factory. I wonder.'

'There hasn't been any more trouble from Colin, has there?'

'No. I spoke to Doug Jameson on the phone the other day, and it seems Colin's getting help, acting the good boy.'

'Well, that fits, I mean, it proves what I was saying.'

'It fits, but nothing's proven. Did Wendy Brudenell come out with anything else?'

'Well, she said, "You'd have to ask Lorraine." Which we knew. Just depends if Lorraine'll talk. I still think a female presence is what you need.'

'You do, eh . . .?' The grin vanished as he looked at the slice of bread he was holding and then threw it down. 'This bread's mouldy. God, Rebecca, I'm sorry, don't eat it.'

She swallowed, more amused than anything. 'I have been doing. I never noticed. It won't hurt. After all, you eat blue cheese.'

Adam shook his head, punctiliously troubled, which amused her even more. 'Awful. I can't believe I gave you that. I should have kept it in the fridge. Listen, are you free the day after tomorrow?'

'I think so. Well, I know so.'

'All right. First thing in the morning, we'll head for darkest Essex and turn up on Lorraine Brudenell's doorstep.'

'We?'

'We. Me and my persuasive female researcher. And after

that I'm going to treat you to lunch. Maybe that'll make up for feeding you mould.'

'Oh, you don't have to do that.'

'I'd like to. Please.'

He looked so serious that she had to laugh. 'Well, if you say so. But we could just have fish and chips, like in the old cottage.'

'I was thinking about those chips the other day.' He got up to take the tray into the kitchen, holding it at a fastidious arm's length. 'Just can't get chips that taste like that around here. But no, we'll go somewhere nice. And somehow we'll crack Lorraine Brudenell. Somebody must give something away . . . Oh, could you get that?'

The phone was ringing a few feet from her. To her own surprise she picked it up quite coolly.

'Hello.'

'Hello, who's this?' A female voice, briskly puzzled.

'Er, Rebecca . . . Adam's just here, did you want him?'

'Yes please.'

She heard a curt disdain in the reply that made her say, 'Who's calling?'

'What? It's Angela.'

Rebecca held out the phone to Adam. 'Angela.' She felt that she shouldn't eavesdrop, so she pointed at the door she thought must be the bathroom. He nodded.

'Hi, Angela. Yep. I was supposed to be seeing Maggie tomorrow. No, that'll be OK . . .'

In the bathroom, feeling a little hot and grubby, she splashed cold water on her face and then picked up a can of body spray from the top of the mirror cabinet. Unexpectedly she dislodged a packet of condoms, which very nearly fell into the toilet bowl. She put them back shakily, not so much embarrassed as assailed by a dizzy sense of unreality. She had always been susceptible to this and wondered if it was a result of her adoption quite late in her childhood, when the change in her life seemed too good to be true, almost staged, as if she were entering a very vivid and convincing film. She remembered first learning about condoms and feeling not so much scandalized as sceptical: such a crude relation of form and function seemed more like one of those childish conceptions you unlearned, like little people inside the radio set.

Unbidden, the handsome, almost too handsome face of Mark Wapshott appeared before her mind's eye. She was sure she knew that face . . . but she just couldn't put a context to it. It was frustrating.

When she came out Adam was still talking. She tried not to analyse his expression.

'Yes, it went OK, he was very helpful. Well, no . . . no, I can remember lots of things from my childhood quite clearly, so . . . You can't? Well . . .' He laughed briefly. 'Yes, I'm going there this afternoon. Sure, I'll make it, it's not that late. Really. OK, so I'll see you tonight, yeah . . .? You too. Bye.'

Rebecca pretended to be looking at the Burne-Jones print. Her memory of Angela at the Appeal Court wasn't clear, but she seemed to trace a resemblance to these limpid-eyed, oval-faced maidens.

'I'd better get going,' she said.

'Don't rush. But listen, give me your address, I mean your uncle's place – I'll pick you up. Say about nine?'

'Fine . . . That's not a problem, is it?'

'No. It isn't a problem at all.' He shook his head firmly: she glimpsed a stubborn, even grim side to him. 'Pass on my regards to your father, won't you?'

She said she would; but when she emerged into the dusty sunshine of Ladbroke Grove she thought that she almost certainly wouldn't. Her relationship with her father had seemingly settled down after his outburst in the hospital and the period of awkward contrition that had followed it but she wasn't sure of his reaction if he knew she was getting further involved with Adam and the Pied Piper business. The deception didn't trouble her. She was slipping those moorings now, stirred by the fresh breezes of independence: she was older.

And she didn't come away from Adam's flat with any diminution of this new sense of herself, although his world was so remote from hers. For one thing, she had experience that he didn't. She wasn't sure if his suspicions about the Brudenells were as intense as hers; but the fact was he didn't know about such families, couldn't recognize that acrid scent of menace, falsity, and bubbling chaos that she herself had breathed on and off for her first eight years of existence.

Stopping at a florist's to buy herself a bunch of carnations, she had an almost transcendental sense of wellbeing. By its nature it was fleeting, and it was a sad irony that it should be the sight of a child that undermined it. The little boy was peering into a bubble-gum machine outside. He reminded her of Jake Brudenell. He reminded her that someone was at large who could take a child like that and crush the life from him.

She drove the thought from her mind, and niggled instead at a question that seemed more innocent, though it too had its odour of unease: where had she seen the face of Mark Wapshott before?

# SEVENTEEN

'I've told you, it'll be all right. He said so. Well, he as good as said so. Now you're whittling again, aren't you? You'll bring your asthma on. What have I told you, eh? What are you like?'

Colin's voice on the crowded bus seemed to Wendy uncomfortably loud. Though he was smiling, apparently cheerful, she couldn't quite bring herself to trust it.

'But what did he say exactly?' she said, keeping her own voice low: she didn't want people knowing this business.

'I can't remember word for word, love. I didn't take a tape recorder in there with me. You should have come in with me if you wanted to know all of it.'

'Yes, but there's Jake . . .' Hearing his name, Jake turned from his excited bobbing at the front seat of the double-decker to give them an elfin look.

'He could come in and all, if we could count on him behaving himself,' Colin said. 'You see kids littler than him going into the solicitor's office. Sit there good as gold. God knows what's up with him lately. Ants in his pants all the time. Jake, sit still. Now.'

'He's a bit unsettled, that's all.'

'Is he?' Colin was morose, his eyelids lowered. 'Why's that then?'

'With everything that's been happening.' She hardly vocalized the words, her eyes sliding over to a fat woman across the aisle who seemed to be staring at them. Like a free show, she thought.

'Oh, right. Yep. Big bad Colin's fault again.'

'I didn't say that.' Amplifying at the expense of truth, she said, 'It's not your fault at all.'

'Well, I'm glad you think so, love. I reckon you're the only one who does. Everything's my fault, apparently. As far as the law's concerned, I'm like on the Most Wanted list. I'm Ronnie Biggs, me. I'm Jack the Ripper!'

His voice rose again, and the fat woman's lips drew tight.

'But he said it would be all right, didn't he?' Wendy said. 'The solicitor? You said things would be OK.'

'Oh, so you believe me now.' Colin gave his croon of ironic satisfaction, and Wendy, hating it, mentally veered away sharply.

'I'm just worried.'

His smile was almost skull-like: she must get him to eat. 'When aren't you? You'll make yourself ill, love. Really. There's no need. What he reckons is, they'll go through the charges with the van and that, and the bloody injunction, and they'll bring up the counselling I'm getting, and then they'll probably adjourn it for another time. So they can do the rest.' Her eyes widened: he tossed his head irritably. 'Well, there's summat about harassment being a criminal offence now, not just a civil thing. I dunno. I suppose they're going to lump it all together. But it'll be all right. They'll take a lot of things into account, the stress and the drinking and now this counselling lark. I've got extenuating circumstances.' He chuckled mechanically. 'Sounds like a nasty disease, doesn't it?'

The fat woman was definitely eavesdropping now. Wendy felt wretched enough to break the pacific habit of a lifetime and have a go at her, right here on the bus – almost. In her heart she despised that kind of fishwife carry-on.

Jake was pulling faces at the convex mirror above the driver's cab. They were quite funny faces and if she had been alone with him Wendy might have laughed, even joined in. Colin, though, set his fleshless jaw and reaching out his hand, rapped Jake smartly on the head with his knuckles.

'Pack it. In.' He separated the words like that, in a way that seemed to her too alarming. 'You'll put the driver off and we'll end up crashing. Can't you understand that?'

Jake was too young for this stern logic, she thought; Colin was always expecting too much of him.

Grinding its way slowly out of the city centre, the bus offered unflattering views of Nottingham: glaring streets where it seemed to have rained litter; drab old Midland brick interspersed with the drabber plate glass of modern office blocks.

In town Jake had clamoured to go to the castle and see the Robin Hood statue, but it might have taken too long. Wendy didn't like to think of Colin coming out of the solicitor's to find them gone.

'Did he say anything about that girl?' she asked him quietly.

'No. Only that she's not pressing charges. Which is fair enough seeing as it was an accident.'

'Oh, Colin.'

'Yes it was. An accident is something that you don't mean to happen, and I never meant that to happen. And not with him either, before you say it. I just wanted to scare him, that's all – shake him up. Like I told the solicitor. Any road, she's out of hospital now, apparently, and she's all right.'

Breathless, Wendy gave Jake a warning look; but he was a quick learner – for her, at any rate – and said nothing.

'Another thing he said is I'm going to have to show willing to the court. Getting my life together. Said it would help if I could prove I was actively seeking employment.' He looked at her expectantly – a look she was coming to know. It had a kind of hidden pounce in it, daring her to say the wrong thing.

'It's all very well, but there just aren't the jobs nowadays.'

'Too right,' he said, and she let out a breath of relief. 'Just what I told him. Well, he says, you've got to make the applications, that's what they're interested in. Showing willing. I felt like telling him a few things. I've had more jobs than he's had hot dinners.'

*And never kept any of them.* Once, Wendy thought, she would have been able to suppress that sceptical voice inside her.

'I can show willing all right. If it was needed, I could go and join the army. There's always something brewing, Iraq and that. They need men.'

'Well, I don't like that idea,' she said. 'I don't want you going off and leaving me.' And it was true – which made her, she thought, a pretty awful selfish woman because she kept thinking of going off and leaving him – all the time.

'Why, what good am I to you? You'd be better off without me,' he said, though his softened tone showed that he was touched.

'Mum, can we have beefburgers when we get home?' Jake asked.

Wendy suffered a gripe of fear that Colin would snap at the importunate question, but he smiled and said: 'You can have all the beefburgers you want. You can have me and your mum's, because we're going out.'

'Where?' Jake said.

'Big noses get cut off,' Colin said, winking.

'Where *are* we going?' Wendy said in utter surprise.

'I'm taking you out for an Indian tonight,' Colin said with a lordly expansive gesture in which she saw the man she had married. 'And before you say what about little britches here, it's all arranged. Sonia from number five, she's coming to babysit.'

'Sonia's nice,' Jake said.

'She is, matey. So,' Colin said, 'glad rags on tonight, gel. You and me are going for a slap-up. What do you think of that, then?'

Habitual caution held her back for a moment. 'Sonia . . . will she be . . .?'

'I spoke to her this morning. It's all fixed. She's looked after him before, hasn't she? She's a good kid.'

'Yes . . . Can we afford it?'

'Leave it to me.' Colin patted her hand. 'You leave it to me, gel. It's high time we had a night out and that's all there is to it.'

Wendy felt a smile spreading over her face, ahead of her doubtful brain. It wouldn't solve anything, but it *would* be nice. 'Well,' she said, 'I could fancy an Indian.'

'I'll bet you could, but never mind, you leave the waiters alone.'

Laughing felt like exercising an unused limb. 'You know what I mean. A nice curry. Where are we going? Mind you, I like a surprise. Ooh, Colin, are you sure, though? I mean, don't let me loose in a restaurant. I'm fat enough as it is.'

'Get out of it. Put a stone on you and you'd still look better than these supermodels.'

Wendy felt a flush of pleasure in the roots of her hair. Her fatness, as she saw it, was something she carried always with her, inescapable as the shell of a snail, burden and refuge. Her own father used to tease her about her weight and call her Two-Ton Tessie. But Colin had said the right words, and meant them: they secured her acquiescence, even drowned out for the time being the muttering voices of doubt and fear about his recent behaviour.

But her contentment faded once they were in the house and she looked in the fridge and saw how bare it was, while her cat, Banjo, wound himself round her legs mewing for food they did not have.

'Colin.' He was in the garden with Jake. 'This meal tonight, do you think we'd better give it a miss?'

He came frowning to the back door. 'I thought you were keen.'

'I am. I'm thinking of the money. We've got nothing in. I've only got a couple of quid on me, to get—'

'Bloody hell!' he exploded, and in the garden Jake's head turned with an instinct for trouble. 'Do you think I'm totally stupid, Wend? Do you?'

'I'm not saying that. I'm just wondering, it's a lovely idea, but—'

'I wouldn't have bothered if I'd known you were going to be such a bloody killjoy about it. Any road, you do think I'm stupid, obviously, so we might as well forget it. You don't want to go out for a meal with a stupid person, do you?'

'I don't think that, Colin, I don't—'

'Jake! Put that muck down! You want a lump of muck for your tea, do you? Because you can have it, if that's what you want. Do you?'

Jake stopped what he was doing and regarded his stepfather from beneath long, soft eyelashes. Lately, at such times, he seemed to be simply dumbstruck by Colin, gazing as if the man were speaking some outlandish foreign language.

'Answer me. You answer me now, Jake. Don't just gawp. I want an answer when I ask you a question.'

Wendy felt the old tense ache in her back. The more Colin went on, the more likely Jake was to forget the original question.

'Colin,' she said, 'I don't mind what we do—'

'Hang on. I'm waiting for an answer from that lad. I'm not moving till I get one.'

Wendy tried to signal to Jake with her eyes. But then he surprised her. He spoke up clearly, humbly.

214

'No, Daddy. Don't want muck for tea.'

Jake was helping her: she could swear to it. The soft-fringed eyes met hers briefly. He had seen trouble for his mother, and done his very best. She blessed him and felt like crying.

'No. I should think not and all,' Colin said, grimly mollified. He turned to Wendy. 'We're going tonight, Wendy. Look, I'm sorry I snapped, but I've been looking forward to this. Jake'll have burgers and old moggy'll have his tin of horsemeat and there'll be a box of Maltesers for young Sonia. Do you trust me?'

'Yes,' she said. It was so easy to say, only a word.

'Well then. You start getting yourself ready and I'll go out and get the money and I'll fetch the shopping from the Spar shop on my way back. All right?'

'What money?' She had to say it. 'Where's the money coming from?'

'I'm going to rob a bank, of course. Honestly, love. You are a whittler sometimes. I told you, I'm doing a little job for an old mate of mine and he owes me. I shall go and see him and pick the money up and then I'll be back here and I shall expect to see you looking gorgeous, all right?'

*What mate? What job?* She couldn't go on asking the questions. One way or another it would end in regret.

'All right.'

He kissed her and left, whistling.

When he had gone she stood for a while at the back door, watching Jake playing in the garden, her eyes now and then straying to the flyover beyond the fence – the great road in the sky, thrumming with going-home traffic at this mellow end of the late summer day. Streaks of sunlight bouncing off hurtling chrome left fluorescent daubs on her eyesight. Banjo mewed disregarded at her feet.

The seaside. Wendy let the terrible temptation in. Pack a couple of bags, take Jake and go. Not anywhere near at hand, not Ingelow or Cleethorpes: she had an image of a softer, cosier coast, with white clifftops and little sloping streets. She dreamt about this place sometimes, and wondered where it could be. But the destination didn't matter so much as the escape. Leaving Colin; being free of him. She would no longer have to suffer his moods, his exacting temper, his shifts and fibs. She would be out of the shadow of his lowering obsession with the man they had let out of prison and the turgid schemes of revenge that kept pointlessly brewing in his brain. And she would be easier about Jake. She had work now, cash in hand, cleaning at a Sikh garment factory on the other side of the city. It meant leaving Jake at home with Colin – a thing she wouldn't have worried about in the slightest a year ago. But as she worked she thought about the thin crust of her husband's patience.

And she thought about Lee . . .

But then the glow faded as it always did and she asked herself how she could even contemplate it. Her husband was suffering. He was on tablets and in counselling. He would be up in court again next week. Life had dealt him a succession of terrible blows. Before everything else, he was a family man. Surely to take herself and Jake away would be to destroy him, or destroy what was left of him. As an act considered in isolation, it was hard: as a final blow, it was unthinkably cruel.

There was no way forward, except to do what was expected of her. She put on her best skirt and a broderie-anglaise blouse and did her hair and make-up. She called Jake in and stayed his hungry protests with stale bread toasted. Banjo swiped at her, claws out, when she tried to stroke him. At seven o'clock Sonia, a bespectacled fifteen-year-old who had baby-sat for them once or twice before, arrived bearing a tapestry frame. She was rather young for that, Wendy thought. At Sonia's age she was drinking in pubs and going out with boys. It seemed a whole lifetime ago.

She sat down with Sonia and Jake and watched television. In a dull numb way she was quite prepared for Colin not to turn up again till midnight, and she felt a lift of surprise when he breezed in at half-past seven.

'All ready then? All ready to eat at Gunga Din's?' He rubbed his hands together, chaffing Sonia, making comical faces at Jake. He had a high colour and his eyes were bright but Wendy couldn't smell drink. And she was surprised again to find a bag of shopping in the kitchen. She made beefburgers in rolls for Jake, and fed Banjo. There was a bunch of flowers too.

'For you,' Colin said, embracing and kissing her in the kitchen. 'Who says I never bring you flowers, eh?'

'Nobody.' She already felt like a traitor: she must quell the impulse to ask where the money had really come from.

'I'll ring us a taxi in a while.'

A taxi as well. 'He gave you the money he owed you, then? For that job?' This was all pretend – she knew it in her bones. If there was a job then it wasn't of any conventional or even legal sort.

'Yep, that's all sorted. Might be helping him out a bit more from now on. Cash in hand, you know.' He smiled broadly and emptily at her and came out with a curious phrase, a phrase that for some reason deeply chilled her. 'Everything's just falling into place nicely.'

A question rose to her lips and for a moment she was really about to ask it. Then there was the sound of a car engine outside the house, rough and throaty, and Colin was galvanized.

'Ah – that'll be my mate. Shan't be a minute. Just got to finish this bit of business and then we'll get that taxi.'

'What mate? The one with the job?'

'Yep. Well, in a way, yep,' he said distractedly, on his way to the front door.

After a moment Wendy followed. She stood at the open door, watching. Colin was speaking to a man who was leaning against the bonnet of a parked car, a big old estate scabrous with rust. The man was very tall and thin, almost bald, and wore an unseasonal sheepskin coat. His face, revealed in bronzy half-tones and planes by the streetlamp, looked sleek and sculptured, hardly made of flesh at all.

Colin came over to the garage, the tall man following a few steps behind. His hands were in his coat pockets and hooked over his left arm, rather oddly in the manner of an old lady with a shopping bag, there was a leather holdall.

'You go in, love,' Colin said briskly. 'I've just got to have a few words with my mate here.' He unlocked the garage doors and reached inside to switch on the light.

'What about?'

'It's about that old bike. You know the one I used to ride. He's interested in it.' Colin stamped his feet and rubbed his thin hands together, as if the mild evening were wintry cold. 'Does 'em up, you know. I mean, it's no good to me.'

'Oh.' She didn't look at the tall man, and after a moment she didn't look at Colin. 'All right,' she said, and she thought that this was her most spectacular acquiescence yet, for the tale about the bike was the most naked of lies. He had taken it to the dump two or three weeks ago; as he well knew, as she well knew.

They were using the garage to store things – things that people shouldn't have. Illegal or seedy or perhaps dangerous.

And yet Colin had seemed more himself tonight, more the man she had fallen in love with, than for a long time. It shouldn't have counted for anything but it did: it robbed Wendy of a crucial fibre of her will to protest, to challenge, to demand to know what he was up to.

And after all there was nothing easier, or more innocent, than saying yes and going into the house. That wasn't like doing anything.

'That's it. You go on in.' Colin's smile was fixed. 'I'll ring that taxi in a minute and we'll have a proper night out, you and me.' And again he came out with that strange, satisfied, alarming phrase: 'Everything's falling nicely into place.'

# EIGHTEEN

Lorraine Brudenell lived in a dismal estuarine town in Essex that seemed to have, as far as Adam could tell when he drove into it with Rebecca, no reason for existing. He saw no factories, offices, or shops larger than a newsagents'; the place seemed to be one great nightmare estate of flat-roofed houses that looked like abandoned bunkers.

Moving down here, he thought, was taking penance too far. Then he reproved himself. Thinking in such slick smug terms must be a result of his brief meeting the previous afternoon with Maggie, his editor at Fairway Publishing. A different world. Fairway, long established in a clovered Georgian terrace amongst Savile Row tailors, had recently moved to a large brute construction of concrete and girders on a Hammersmith riverside site. He suspected that the staff rather relished the sexy power of their new surroundings. Arriving in the huge vestibule and collecting his visitor's card from the security desk, he noticed a self-important spring in the lissom step of two young employees hurrying to the space-age lifts. This wasn't fusty old books. This was business, and it throbbed. Angela, though she complained about tight schedules and soulless marketing drives, was as prone to it as the rest.

Maggie, at any rate, was a straight talker. He had given her sample chapters and full synopsis of the book provisionally titled *The Pied Piper*. The first thing she had said to him, plumping herself down and grabbing his typescript from a pile on the desk, was: 'Don't like the title.'

'Well, it can be changed . . . Why not?'

'It's not true-crime enough. You need something with blood or killing or evil in it. Gosh, you look cool. I'm baking. The air-conditioning's a buggering joke.' She was a small, spiky, sassy woman who invariably wore cotton trousers and pumps, which, with her straight black pudding-basin hair gave her a Chinese look. 'Also I don't like the ending.'

'What ending?'

'You tell me. You've got this story of a guy who was wrongfully convicted of a ghastly murder because he liked playing with kids. Witch-hunt, conspiracy, mass hysteria, trial by media, de da de da, fine. And this is symptomatic of an obsessional neurosis about child abuse in our society, very provocative, talk it up round the dinner table, fine too. But you've got to have your baddie. True crime's like pop fiction, it's black and white. Also, if we don't at least finger the real sicko, then people aren't going to be totally convinced about your Gandy man. Let's face it, liking children is just creepy.'

'But the whole point—'

'Yeah, innocence lost, I know, I know. Ignore me, I'm cynical. So, Holmes, who done it?'

Adam drew a deep breath. 'I don't know yet for sure. Things are brewing. I've got all the material – boxes full. I know more about the case than anyone. And I'm currently following up a very strong lead. I'd guess that what I need is really right under my nose.'

'So you're going to name him?'

'I'm going to name him. That will be your ending.'

'Glorious. You'll involve the law first, of course. We don't want to get stuffed for libel. So, sounds like you're going to be burning the midnight oil over your research. I suppose there are a lot of transcriptions? Maybe you should think about using an assistant, just on an *ad hoc* basis.'

'Maybe. Have to be for free though, on the kind of advances Fairway pay.'

'Oh, Fleet Street sees you all right, bloody golden boy. Anyway, I know why you're too tight to pay an assistant. You've got Angela.' She smirked.

'Well, she's helped me out odd times with work in progress, but I hope I don't take advantage,' he said with a less-than-radiant smile.

'Oh, we wouldn't let you, don't worry, we work her too hard. We've got this horror author from the US coming tomorrow. He is *very* hard work so we've got Hayley *and* Angela dancing attendance on him.' Maggie stood up, offering him her jabbing handshake. 'So, new title, not too much philosophizing, and finger the bad guy. Obviously the book's already got a hero. Your good self.' She grinned him out.

The last thing Adam would have liked to be accused of was over-solemnity. But he had left Fairway feeling definitely peeved, and he realized that it was because he was being mocked. Or not him precisely: it wasn't that personal. He just felt that there were things that had to be taken seriously, and that he was almost alone in doing so.

Almost. That was why he valued Rebecca's company today. After some initial doubts about enlisting her as an impromptu assistant, he concluded that there was no one more worthy. She was inward with this case as no one else was; there was none of that flip, dismissive attitude he had noticed at Fairway. Thank God, he thought, for the passionate sincerity of youth. Though in fact when he picked her up she looked to him about twenty-five. She was wearing a summer dress and had put her hair up: he was used to seeing her in jeans, student-sloppy. The change was remarkable.

'Well, I think this is it,' he said now, parking outside a concrete block of flats overlooking a playground of churned mud. Street signs were all but obliterated by graffiti. 'Let's hope she lets us in.'

The woman who answered the door to his knock nodded slowly, blankly, at his explanation; and he fully expected the door to close. But with the barest shrug, Lorraine Brudenell stood aside and let them in.

'This is Mrs Ibbotson,' she said, leading them into a living room where, despite the late summer heat, a gas fire was burning. 'She always sits with me in the mornings. She is my friend, so if there's anything you want to say that's private, you know, then it's no good. I can't ask her to leave.'

Adam said that was fine. Mrs Ibbotson was ancient, obviously deaf, a tiny quaking woman who sat by the fire peering at the sports page of a tabloid newspaper. The presence of an old lady made some kind of skewed sense, because though Lorraine Brudenell was scarcely forty, entering the flat was like entering the fusty solitary home of an old person – indeed, a very old-fashioned old person. He saw things like a mantel-piece mirror in the shape of a butterfly, a walnut china cabinet with a huge teak-clad TV on top of it, a canterbury containing copies of the *People's Friend* and other sedate magazines that he hadn't realized were even published any more, and a square black leather handbag with sharp gold clasps of the thumping sort his grandmother used to carry. It wasn't Mrs Ibbotson's, because Lorraine Brudenell took a pack of ten cigarettes from it and lit one, seating herself on a low settee strewn with lace-edged antimacassars.

'I don't know what you want to talk to me about. It's like I told you the first time, I've really got nothing to say.' Her tone wasn't hostile, just drably perplexed. Adam had seen only out-of-date photographs of Lorraine Brudenell, and felt that he would have been hard-pressed to recognize her. Those from the time of the trial showed a vivid backstreet face, lean-jawed and panther-eyed. The woman sitting hunched on the settee with her knees pressed together, in a shapeless cardigan and pleated skirt, her grizzled hair scraped back in a tortoiseshell comb, looked not so much faded as bleached. It was as if some terrible extraction, not perhaps of soul but of life force, had taken place.

'Well, as you probably know, the appeal against Howard Gandy's conviction was successful, and he was released some months ago. This is obviously a good result for all of us who were involved in the campaign, as it shows there was a clear miscarriage of justice. But it also raised some unanswered questions, which we're trying to follow up. Basically I wondered what your thoughts are about the release of Mr Gandy, about where this leaves the case of your son's murder . . . Anything you'd like to make known, really.'

'Why?'

That one word, spoken without a trace of emotion, completely threw him.

'Um, it's for a variety of reasons really. I suppose what we're talking about, now that Mr Gandy's conviction has been quashed, is an unsolved murder case. I just wondered if there's anything you could tell me that might throw light on what happened back then. Any thoughts, feelings, memories . . .'

'Why?' A first faint shade of animation touched her blank face. 'That's what I'm wondering. I mean, what good's it going to do?'

He took a deep breath of the vitiated air; the heat made him feel giddy. 'It might help get justice at last for your son.'

'Well, it won't bring him back, though, will it?'

'No. I'm sorry, of course. Nothing can do that, I'm afraid.'

She sat back a little, inching her skirt over her knees. Only in the hungry drags she took at her cigarette was there a trace of the woman she had been. 'Well, in that case,' she said, 'I really don't see. I'm sorry. I don't see.'

'It was a terrible loss you suffered.' Rebecca spoke up. 'Nothing can ever make up for it. But what we can do is make sure the person who did such a terrible thing is punished for it. Maybe then you could – have peace.'

'For twelve years I thought they had punished the person who did it,' Lorraine said. 'And I didn't get peace. I've never had any peace, except what my Church has given me. That was Mrs Ibbotson helped me towards that. She's taught me a lot.'

Adam gave a respectful glance towards the old lady, though he couldn't imagine her teaching anybody anything.

'Well, it would stop that person ever doing such a thing again. Which they might,' Rebecca said. 'They might do to another little child what they did to Lee.'

She came out with the name forcefully, even brutally, a very direct appeal. Adam thought he wouldn't have done that. But there was a moment of emotion on Lorraine's face, and she looked away.

'All I want,' she said, 'is to go back to the day before Lee died. But I can't. So all I can do is look forward to meeting up with him later.'

The expression struck him as uncomfortably bizarre: a celestial rendezvous with her dead son for drinks . . .

But Rebecca was nodding eagerly, and said with warmth, 'And you will. And when you do, you'll be able to hold him and know that you helped to find the man who hurt him.'

The hand holding the cigarette trembled a little; but Lorraine was silent.

'I wonder,' Adam said, 'do you have any contact with your former husband, Colin?'

'No.'

'Well, you may know that Colin reacted very badly to

Howard Gandy's release, and he openly refuses to believe in his innocence. He has in fact started something of a campaign of persecution against Mr Gandy, which has led to one or two – nasty incidents. Trouble with the police and so on. Does this surprise you at all?'

'I don't see why it should. Me and Colin have been divorced a good while and he's got a different life. What he does is none of my business.'

The levelness of her tone, so utterly without inflection, was beginning to spook him. It must have been learnt at some prayer meeting.

'Yes, I see,' Adam said. 'I just wondered if he was ever a violent man when you did know him. When you were married to him.'

There was a moment's pause, while her eyes looked him over with unmoved thoroughness. 'It's all a long time ago,' she said. 'I can't see what good it's going to do, going over the past. You can't change it.'

'Was he, for example, a patient man with the children?' Adam said. 'Did you ever feel threatened by him yourself, maybe? These things can be hard to admit to. Everyone wants to protect their family—'

'I haven't got a family. I never did have after Lee was killed, it was all finished then. When you lose a child like that, everything goes.'

'It seems awful to bring all this up,' Rebecca said. 'We wouldn't do it if it wasn't for such a terribly important reason. We're not necessarily talking about secrets. Just that as time goes on, people sometimes feel better about letting things out . . .'

'I was a drinker then. I've made no secret of that. I testified it to my Church. I was still a drinker until a couple of years ago. You might scoff but it is actually one of the worst sins there is. I was in drink the day Lee was taken away. That shows you how much of a sin it is. When you think of what happened . . . But I've prayed for forgiveness for that and I hope that with the help of my Church I'll get it.'

*In drink*. It was so archaic. Yet this seemed to be the only line she would follow.

Rebecca picked up on that and said, 'The person who did

kill Lee – could you ever pray for their forgiveness, do you think?'

'Oh, yes,' Lorraine said promptly. 'Oh, yes, you have to do that too.'

'The Appeal Court established that Howard Gandy did not kill Lee,' Adam said. He leaned forward. 'Who do you think did?'

He was trying to jolt her out of that cocoon of self-abasing piety, following Rebecca's lead.

'It's not for me to stand in judgment on anybody. Everyone has to work things out for themselves, with God. It applies to that person and it applies to me and you –' to Rebecca and then, more severely he thought – 'and you.'

Adam felt himself shrinking at that 'you', just as he did when doorstep preachers tried to catch him in the beam of their faith.

Rebecca startled him by being even more direct. 'Colin blames you for what happened that day.'

Lorraine, unflinching, said, 'I dare say. I was in drink. I was punished. None of us is pure. We're all to blame.'

What was she hiding behind all this holy-roller stuff? He could find no way of posing the question, but neither could he be sure she was hiding anything. His instincts, his gut feeling, whatever faculty it was that helped him penetrate people's defences, just didn't seem to function in the fuggy cabbagey atmosphere of this flat.

'Is there anything you can remember about that day that might help?' he said. 'There was a bit of trouble, wasn't there? About the lunch. Lee wouldn't eat the sausages you made and Colin got angry with him. Was that how it was?'

'Something like that. We weren't a perfect family. But nothing is perfect in this world, because we're made that way. There's no point in dwelling on that. You can't question God. There's some things we're not meant to understand.'

Rebecca said, 'Why did you and Colin split up? Wouldn't you have wanted another child with him?'

Suddenly there was great scorn in Lorraine's look. 'I wanted Lee,' she said. 'That should answer your question. Now I can't do any more.' She got up and bent over the little old lady, speaking into her tiny face. 'Do you want your cup of tea now, Mrs Ibbotson?'

They didn't leave quite empty-handed, at least not literally. On their way out Lorraine Brudenell gave them each a tract and with the first real warmth in her tone urged them to read it.

'What shall we do with this?' Rebecca said in the car.

He looked at his. It was printed on lime-green paper and its hectorings struck him as vaguely intimidating: the hand encircling the globe on the crudely drawn cover looked as if it were about to grip and crush. He tore it up and threw it out of the window, doing the same with hers, and it gave him a mild pleasure; though he thought Rebecca looked flushed and uncertain, as if she wouldn't have done it herself.

'So she's got religion in a big way. Obviously it's been a way of helping her to cope, but . . .'

'Depends what she's coping with,' Rebecca said, echoing his thought. 'Maybe more than losing a child. It might be the things she knows, too.'

'I suppose everyone copes in different ways when the unthinkable happens. Maybe our society doesn't help by making it a bit too unthinkable. We sneer at the Victorians for going into those orgies of grief – but at least they faced it.'

'Well, you know my mum and dad lost a child. I don't know how or if they ever faced it. It certainly did something to them – something that would never have happened in their lives normally.'

Rebecca's eyes across the table were sober, penetrating, and rather beautiful. They were back in London, to Adam's relief, and he had brought Rebecca to an Italian restaurant off Kensington High Street, intimate but quite swanky.

'Go hog wild,' Adam said, seeing her looking for the cheapest thing on the menu. 'You'll be an impoverished student soon. You may as well fatten up for it . . . I suppose the classical reason why people get religion of that sort is they're on a guilt trip. I don't know, I'm an atheist so I'm an outsider looking in, but I can't imagine being in Lorraine Brudenell's place and taking a great shine to the Almighty when I'd been cruelly robbed of my child. More likely to shake your fist at the heavens I would have thought. Unless she felt she was being justly punished in some way.'

'For covering up?'

'Maybe. There again I'm wondering – could you cover up for someone knowing they'd done something absolutely terrible? Is it possible? I suppose it is if you really loved them.' He felt detached from this as he spoke, knowing very well that he himself had never loved anyone that much.

'I don't know. I think it's very possible. I can imagine loving someone that much, where you'd do literally anything to protect them . . . Yes. If you were very deep in. And especially if there was fear mixed in with the love.'

Soon tortellini with pistachio pork arrived – for her: Adam had chicken salad. Watching her dig in, he thought that he wouldn't be able to move for the rest of the day after eating that, then realized that of course she would: she was young. It gave him a pang, because he was used to thinking of himself as a young person.

About to speak, he almost choked: he had just seen Angela. The restaurant was on two floors, with a central staircase of iron, and Angela was just coming down it. Impervious to the warmth as ever, she wore a black wool dress and high suede shoes that made a crisp retort on the stairs – 'fuck-me shoes' as she had once called them in an unbuttoned moment. There was no reason, he thought, for him to be bothered about Angela seeing them; no reason to feel relieved when she walked straight towards the ladies'. He tried to attend to what Rebecca was saying, but his ears soon homed in on the sound of the toilet door and then of those clicking shoes, coming up to their table and stopping.

'Fancy seeing you here,' Angela said, and he had a little hard certainty that she had seen him all right, even before she had gone to the ladies': she was full of these meaningless subtleties.

'I was going to say the same. Angela, this is Rebecca Springthorpe. Angela works at Fairway.'

'We meet at last,' Angela said with a cursory smile. 'All right if I pull up a chair for a minute?'

'Of course. What's happened with the American horror-meister?'

'Oh, he's upstairs. Let Hayley suffer him for a while. I need a break. He is *such* a drone. And he's a disgusting eater. Actually his last book was a mess, the bookshops couldn't shift it with a flamethrower, so he needn't be so cocky. Can I have a bit of this.' She did not phrase it as a question. She took the breadstick from his plate and began nibbling it, her chair drawn up close to his.

'Rebecca's been helping me out with a few theories about the Gandy case. Filling in some background. We've been to see Lorraine Brudenell.'

'Oh, the mother. God, Adam, you've got heaps of material as it is. Really, I know research gets fascinating in itself in the end, but you have to stick to the main story, surely.'

'Oh, I am. But the Brudenells are part of it. Maybe a crucial part. Rebecca's helped me see a few things that suggest a whole new angle.'

'Mm?' Angela placed the bitten breadstick back on his plate. 'I think you can get bogged down with all these theories, though. You know what I mean? You have to stay professional.' Her eyes probed his face.

'If I'd done that,' he said, 'we would never have got Howard out.'

'But that's just it. The work's done. I mean, all that ancient anecdotal stuff from that guy, funny name, Wapping or something—'

'Mark Wapshott. I must get to work on that.'

'You don't have to. At least, I transcribed the tape for you. I put it on one of my disks. It should be compatible.'

'When? I didn't know . . .'

'I took the tape home the other morning. You know, when I'd stayed at yours.' She reached out to dab a crumb from the hairs of his wrist. 'I thought I might as well. I have helped you before.'

'You didn't have to do that.'

'No problem. Looks as if you could do with the help, even if you won't admit it. The notes are just piling up. And a lot of it's stuff that I just can't see you using.'

'You didn't by any chance mention this to Maggie, did you?'

'Only in passing. I mean, she was asking me if I knew how the project was going. She is very committed to it, Adam, she's really up about it.' Angela was very much the professional woman today, dry and brisk, full of blasé lingo. Rebecca was excluded. 'I think it's just a question of tightening it. Standing back from the material maybe.'

'Maybe.' he said. He kept his tone and his look blanched of all agreement.

'Anyway. I'll pop the disk over to you some time. I'd better get back to the poor man's Stephen King in a minute. Listen, when am I seeing you? We're on for Sunday, are we? You know the Pritchards invited us. That thing on a boat.'

'Er, there was something Saturday, wasn't there? The NUJ dinner – testimonial to James Vandyke.'

Angela pulled a face. 'Actually that's iffy, I mean I've still got my brother coming that day and I'm not totally sure how long he's going to be around. So it's fifty-fifty really. Do you need a definite?'

'No, it doesn't matter. Don't worry about it. The ticket says "and guest". Maybe you'd like to come, Rebecca? It's a do at the Café Royal, in honour of James Vandyke, who for once really is a very interesting man. He was a correspondent in Nazi Germany in his young days. All sorts of tales to tell. It should be a good evening. What'd you say?'

'The Café Royal?' Rebecca's eyes widened.

'I don't know about that, will they let her in?' Angela said. She looked at Rebecca for the first time. 'Are you eighteen?'

'There'll be no problem,' Adam said, reflecting how strange it was that he sometimes found that vein of bitchiness in Angela a turn-on. 'But that's only if you'd like to come. It depends how long you'll be in London, of course.'

'I think we'll be going back on Sunday, so . . . Well, I'd love it.'

'It'll be a lot of dreary speeches. Amazing how long-winded journalists can be.' Angela smiled sweetly, put a parting finger on the nape of Adam's neck. 'Better get back, they'll be sending out a search party.'

Adam felt no regret as he watched Angela go – or only the regret that civilized adults should end up scoring spiteful points off each other. The other side of him, however, the stern side, was to the fore: he felt quite justified in what he had done. She was out of order – not only as far as any unworthy suspicions about Rebecca went, but in the way she had encroached on his researches. He didn't like this project being taken out of his hands like that.

Besides, he liked Rebecca a lot. She was direct: you didn't have to follow any long tortuous paths to get to her. There weren't so many rules – she would readily talk about bereavement and then about CDs, without any great grinding of conversational gears. Plus she could make him laugh, as she did with her next remark.

'Thank you for asking me. You don't have to do it, you know.'

'Now that,' he said, 'sounds like our dreaded curse, Low Self-Esteem.'

'Maybe.' She coloured. 'I suppose everybody's got that, though, haven't they?'

'I don't think my father had it.' Adam thought about it, shook his head. 'No, he didn't. He genuinely thought he was a wonderful person.' He had a memory of his father at the breakfast table, taking a piece of toast and applying butter to it with fastidious liberality, carefully wiping the knife-blade along each side of the triangle before crunching into it with the smug relish that would have the young Adam gripping the seat of his chair in an effort not to be sick.

'Not my dad,' Rebecca said. She had cleaned her plate. 'He can't even listen to his own music; it's like torture to him.'

'You inherited his gift at all?'

'No. I can pick a tune out on the piano, recognize a seventh chord, that's about it. Plus I couldn't really inherit – not through blood.'

'Of course, of course. I forget. You're so like him . . . I was just thinking about childhood memories. I suppose you must have two different sets.'

'Well, the ones before I was adopted are – well, they were the pits really, and I don't mean that's anyone's fault. But they gave me some sort of insight, the awful setups I saw back then. I mean when I was talking to Wendy in the hospital, I knew exactly where she was coming from. *Am* I like my dad, then?'

It was good to see that the idea pleased her still: having to reveal Philip Springthorpe's feet of clay had left Adam niggled by guilt.

'You've both got a lot of guts,' he said. 'The way he came

out and admitted what he'd done, for the campaign. The way you handled that – accident with the van. Which I still feel bad about.'

'It'll all be worthwhile – once we find out what really did happen twelve years ago.'

'We're going to get there,' he said. He felt quite serious: her effect on him, perhaps. Let Angela sneer all she liked, but the fact was Rebecca had seen the world of the Brudenells from the inside. Behind their façade of worldliness most young people were paper-thin, nothing to them: not this girl.

She reinforced that by saying, quite quietly, 'Yes. I just hope we're not too late.'

# NINETEEN

'So. I thought we'd head for home tomorrow.'

It was Friday. Rebecca and her father had spent a cheerful morning shopping for things she would need going away to college: she always liked going shopping with him, the way he didn't mind hunting for exactly the right item, his coolness when men all around were snappy or seething. They had come back to have lunch in Uncle Denis' delightful little patio garden – the creation of his ex-wife and the one thing he had left untouched, the interior of the house being reduced to an almost shipshape maleness. Everything was so right that Rebecca thought for several moments that her father must be impishly having her on. But then, of course, he didn't know.

'Tomorrow?'

'Yes, is that OK? I've just got to do this bit of re-recording this afternoon. They still want to play out with the finale of Schubert's Ninth. I wish they wouldn't. Shaw was right about it, it's a white elephant. Though I think Schubert was just pointing up the paradox of the fourth movement in symphony writing. If the form demands apotheosis, what else can you do but finish it off with a laboured romp? Or else just smash the form and end with a cantata – Beethoven's solution. Sorry, I'm off again.'

'Does it have to be tomorrow?'

'Well, I'd like some breezes. It's too stuffy in London. And I need a piano. I've got some ideas for that festival piece . . . Is it a problem?'

'No . . . Though if you really need to get home, couldn't I stay here on my own? Come back by train Sunday or Monday?'

'Oh. But I don't suppose Uncle Denis would mind. I'm just surprised. Have you got something on?'

'Yes. Adam's invited me to this thing at the Café Royal

tomorrow night. It's a testimonial for James Vandyke. He's this veteran journalist who's been everywhere. It sounds really interesting. Adam's got a ticket that says bring a guest, so he asked me if I'd like to go.'

'And you said yes.'

'Well, yes.' She tried to laugh. 'I mean, it's not like being invited for pie and chips.'

'So when was this? He phoned here?'

'No, I met him.' Too late, now, to wish she had told instead of pretending that secrecy would save trouble. She explained, as breezily as she could.

His face was stony. 'It's up to you, obviously . . . Clearly you're set on it, because you didn't think it worthwhile to tell me.'

'I would have liked to tell you. I would have gladly said about meeting Adam. But I thought you'd get ratty about it.'

'Maybe. Ratty for a reason. I don't want to go back over this, because you know already that I wasn't happy with you getting mixed up with him and Gandy and the whole thing. I expressed it a bit wildly, which I'm sorry for. And I didn't want to keep harping on it. But now – Christ, you've only just recovered after being in hospital. I mean I thought you'd surely have changed your ideas . . .'

'I like Adam and I've been helping him out a bit. That's all. Dad, he's not some big villain and nothing terrible's going to happen.'

'Something did.' He waved irritably at an amorous wasp. 'He ought to know better, at any rate.'

'Now you really are treating me like a child. I'm grown up, Dad.'

'There are still things I'd prefer you not to do.'

'Like what? It's not as if you don't know where I'll be. Stephen Larkinson bummed around Turkey for months and his parents didn't mind—'

'That's different.'

'Why, because he's a boy?'

'No, because Stephen Larkinson is a complete prat, and he's going to grow into a man with absolutely nothing special about him at all, and so he's going to have to milk that Turkey trip for years, so he might as well have it. You, on the other hand, I do think and hope and want to grow into a special woman. Hence the concern.'

She wouldn't be flannelled. 'Well, I'm not going to grow at all if I'm wrapped in cotton wool.'

'All right. Like I told you, it's up to you. But I'll still say it – watch yourself. Because that's what I feel.'

'Dad, I'm going up to college next month. You can't watch over me there, it just doesn't work like that—'

'Well, make sure you don't go to college pregnant then.'

She was startled. Her father looked, indeed, as if he had startled himself; but he tried to pass it off, continuing: 'Seriously, why not think of these things? OK, Stephen Larkinson did Turkey. But you don't have to take some soul-nourishing experience to college with you – as if you haven't had enough experiences lately. I think it's better to go without a lot of emotional baggage. Life's going to change soon enough.'

'Well, I hear what you're saying,' she said. 'It's pretty rotten to think you don't trust me, though.'

'Give me some grounds, then. I was trusting you to steer clear of Adam Dowling and all his works after what happened, but now look. Never mind. If you want me to trust you again, I'll give it a go. I'll leave you both sets of keys. Make sure it's all locked up when you do decide to come home.'

It was a pity the week had to end so acidly. The next morning it was plain, as he was getting ready to leave, that her father regretted at least one of his remarks – its sheer crudity was unlike him – but he couldn't take it back without an opening from her that she refused to give. The sting of it, like some throbbing insect bite, had worsened overnight. She was only glad that she had kept a relative cool and not hurled back, as she nearly had, the classic teenage remonstrance: 'It's not fair!' She did feel the unfairness, though, and the lack of warmth in her parting kiss and hug seemed to her quite justified. Watching him drive off, waving, she was tossed between emotions: an awful sadness as he went out of sight, and a ruefully admitted pleasure in the tremendous power that withholding love gave you.

The pleasure of being alone in the house was undeniable too. But perhaps staying in denied her the full flavour of her freedom; also walking helped her think. What she thought, after strolling to the Common and back, was that she would go and see Adam, just on the off chance.

It didn't seem such a bad idea, once the first amazed thumps of the heart were over and she was entering the tube station; after all, she would have done it unthinkingly when he was at the cottage in Ingelow, a time she remembered with peculiar affection. If he was busy working, she would just say hi and go away and see him tonight – an occasion, oddly enough, about which she felt no butterflies.

When she got no answer from his intercom after ringing three times, she found the disappointment so mild as scarcely to be perceptible. Her mood unhampered, she turned to go, and found Angela getting out of her car.

'Not in?'

'No. Well, I don't think so.'

'But you've been ringing? Oh, well.' She took a disk from her handbag, holding it up as if for Rebecca's inspection. 'I just wanted to drop this by. There's a sort of communal letterbox thing here. Will it be all right in there, do you suppose?'

'I should think so.' It was a question to which you couldn't give a convincing answer, Rebecca thought.

'It might break,' Angela said, as if she had suggested something reckless. 'I don't suppose you've got an old envelope or something about you, have you? No? Oh, well. Here goes.'

Rebecca refused to feel inadequate for not having an old envelope.

'Is that the Mark Wapshott interview?' she said, staking a claim.

'Yes, and some other stuff I typed up for him.' Angela frowned up at the sky, which was crossed with heavy boughs of cloud. 'Looks like rain. I'll give you a lift.'

'Oh, it's OK.'

'Don't be daft. You've come down here for nothing, no point in getting soaked as well. Sorry, was there something you need to see Adam about? Do you want to leave a note?'

'No, no. It can wait.'

'Come on then.' Angela opened the passenger door of her car, a smart little Renault. Rebecca didn't fancy it, but neither did she fancy sloping off into the distance, a loitering teen. She got in.

'Still going to this bunfight tonight, then?'

'Yes, I'm looking forward to it.'

'I suppose it'll be a change for you. Is it black tie?'

'I don't know. Adam didn't say.'

'It probably is. I wonder if he's remembered to hire. I keep telling him to invest in his own, he has to go to enough of these things. Where are we going?'

Rebecca thought better of saying any nearby destination, and gave the address.

'So how long are you going to be in London?'

'A couple more days, maybe. I don't really know.'

'So what's it like, the Lincolnshire coast? I've been hearing so much about it. I've stayed on the coast at Norfolk, but I've never really thought of Lincolnshire. I suppose one doesn't.'

'It's . . . quite a beautiful place.'

'Is it? You surprise me. It just doesn't sound it, somehow. Well, I suppose it's settling down up there now, after all this scandalous stuff.' As Rebecca presented her with a flatly uncomprehending face she went on, 'Well, you know, I don't imagine a lot happens up there. Not this sort of thing, anyway.'

'It's quiet.'

'That's what I mean. So at least it's all over now. People will have to leave this poor Gandy chap alone sooner or later, and then it can all die down.'

'I wouldn't say it's really over. I don't think Adam sees it like that. Getting Howard out of jail wasn't the whole thing.'

'Well, actually, it's natural he'd want to take credit for that, but basically Gandy had a very good brief and there was pressure from on high.'

'Oh, yes, everyone knows that, but it was still Adam who did the spadework.' Hero worship wasn't what she felt for Adam, so it was no use Angela trying to demolish it.

'And he's still digging. I don't think he can stop. I think it's gone way past the point where it's relevant.'

'A little boy got killed. Surely everything's relevant.'

Angela laughed. 'That's Adam talking.'

'No.' Rebecca smiled. 'Me.'

'Well, you're obviously very into it, but I can't help thinking

236

it's a bit ghoulish. Are you one of these Gothics, going to sleep in a coffin and always wearing black?'

'I'm not wearing black now.'

'Well, you could be on your day off from being Gothic.'

It wasn't so much the insults, Rebecca decided, as the irritating embroidery Angela gave them.

'Mind you, I suppose you must relate quite closely to the Gandy thing, mustn't you?' Angela said, coolly slipping into a momentary slot in the traffic at the Shepherd's Bush junction. 'With your father changing his evidence like that. Must have really brought it home to you. In quite an unpleasant way.'

'Well, it all turned out for the best. And any stuff about my family in the book Adam's going to let me see first to vet it. So no problem.'

'Really? Well, that's wise.' Their eyes met momentarily with an effect so confrontational that Rebecca almost flinched at it. 'I dare say it's delicate stuff. And, as I've told him, not all really relevant. The business about the abortion, stuff like that. I personally think it's too—'

'What abortion?'

'I'm sorry?' Angela gave her a stare, then changed her intonation. 'I'm sorry. Oh – well, I don't know what to say, I just assumed . . .'

'What abortion? I don't know anything about an abortion. Who?'

'Look, I never . . . I mean, it's there in Adam's researches. I just assumed you knew the whole thing, being so involved. I really wouldn't have said anything, if I'd known—'

'Well, say something now, then. I don't know what you're talking about.'

Angela, with a kind of bland frown, shook her head. 'No. Really, I can't. It isn't up to me to do that. I thought you knew, that was the only reason I mentioned it. I certainly don't think it's for me to tell you. It just wouldn't be right.'

'Who then? Adam?'

'Well.' She gave a dainty pip on the horn at a hasty pedestrian. 'If no one else has.' Angela's gasping puzzlement was so well done; she didn't even allow her triumph to peek through.

★ ★ ★

237

Uncle Denis' house was hell to be in that afternoon, as Rebecca haunted the phone, waiting for Adam to be in. She missed the presence of animals, the furry bodies that pressed companionably against your hand, offering unobtrusive consolation. At last she placed her uncle's onyx chess set by the phone and played a nonsensical game against herself, chiefly for the soothing feel of the weighty pieces, in between ringing Adam's number.

Angela didn't like her, of course. That was what she had to remember. Even people who loved each other sometimes said things to taunt and hurt: just look at her and her father. So there was no need, strictly, to have a bad feeling about this. Probably there was nothing to it, and Adam would swiftly put her mind at rest. But Adam wasn't there. At every ring she got his answering machine, and hearing his voice say the same words over and over gave her a paranoid feeling of being mocked, as if he were not what he seemed at all but something inhuman, robotic.

She plugged on with the nonsense chess game, trying to make herself into two people. Somehow it began to work, and she had her first check when the phone was finally answered by Adam himself. The contrast with the robot Adam was so intense she almost sobbed.

'Hi, how're you doing? We're still on for tonight, are we?'

'Yes, I think so . . . It's something else. I just had to ring you . . .'

'Yes? What's wrong?'

'I saw Angela today. She gave me a lift. We were talking about the case, and my dad, and things like that.'

'Uh-huh.' He was alert: she could hear his stillness.

'She was talking about all this material you couldn't use, private stuff. And she said something about an abortion. I didn't know what she meant but she wouldn't say any more and said it should be up to you to tell me. I've never heard anything about any abortion. I mean, is this something to do with my dad?' The moment's silence was unbearable to her.

He sighed. 'She really had no business saying anything to you about that. Bloody hell, that's—'

'She said she assumed I'd know. Being so involved, she said.

God, what am I supposed to think after that?'

'Listen. This isn't something I ever intended telling anyone. It's just personal stuff. I mean I had it in my files and Angela must have found it. It isn't anything I had any intention of using, in the book or anywhere else. Look, maybe we'd better save it till we meet; it seems bad over the phone—'

'Why does it seem bad? It'd be best if you'd just tell me.'

'Well. OK. You know the name Carolyn Moyes, obviously.'

'She was the woman my dad had an affair with.'

'Right. Which I emphasize again is his business. I only followed it up because of its bearing on the case. And as you know, that involved trying to trace Carolyn Moyes, in case her testimony could add something. As it turned out it wasn't needed. Your dad's new statement was enough. But in trying to track her down I did finally make contact with her cousin, a woman in London. She talked to me. I think what Angela was so charmingly refraining from telling you is about that, what I learnt. Basically, Carolyn Moyes had an abortion in early August of that year. The August when it happened. Twelve years back. Her cousin knew because Carolyn came to stay with her when she was having it done. It was at a clinic in London . . . It's in my files and that's all. I've never mentioned it to your father. I certainly didn't bring it up when I asked him to reconsider his evidence—'

'Carolyn Moyes had an abortion.' Rebecca flicked the white king over with her finger, then began systemically flipping over every piece on the board. 'At the time she was having an affair with my dad.'

'Yes. I understand they stopped seeing each other shortly after that, and she moved away.'

'So she got pregnant by my dad.'

Adam drew a deep breath. 'It's the inference. She was a single woman. She didn't tell her cousin much about it, didn't want to talk about it. But—'

'I didn't know.'

'I didn't suppose you did. I know your father had told you about this affair, but . . . It's a private thing and I swear to you it won't go any further. I'm sorry for the way it came out, Rebecca. I apologize for Angela and to be honest I'm pretty pissed off at the way she—'

'That doesn't matter,' she said dully. 'So – you knew this all the time?'

'Yes. It wasn't something I felt I should tell you. I didn't see what good it would do. It was just surplus information and besides, it's Carolyn Moyes' private business—'

'So my dad fathered a child, eh? Bit careless of him, wasn't it?' In the deathly flippancy she recognized a younger self, adolescent and terrified, rising in response to pressure. 'Jesus. The things you find out.'

'Rebecca, it was all a long time ago.' He stopped as if he had heard the patronage in his voice, and struggled on: 'It was a part of what happened. It doesn't change anything now.'

'I suppose not.' All the chess pieces were on their sides now, a disastrous battlefield. 'I was just thinking about my mum. You know – well, of course you know, you know everything about us – she couldn't have children, after Thomas. She had a baby and he died, and she couldn't have any more children. Meanwhile –' she found herself breathless, her mouth dry as if she delivered a long speech – 'meanwhile, back at the ranch . . .'

'Rebecca, I'm sorry you had to find it out this way. I know it brings a lot of things back and that's why I thought it was best kept secret. It can't do anyone any good to air it abroad and it's something that's got to be—'

'Come to terms with?'

'I was going to say left in the past. Maybe that's not on.' He hesitated. 'Would you have preferred it if I'd told you?'

'I don't know. I don't like to think of you knowing all this time. But I suppose that's your trade, knowing things.' She hardly knew what she was saying. She kept thinking of her mother in hospital and the way she used to stick her tongue out at the nurses. Even in extremity she kept it up, as if to demonstrate that she was still in there, pitifully sheltering in that ruined body.

'Is your dad there? Maybe I should speak to him. It concerns him too.'

'He's gone home. But hey, no need to speak to him, he already knows. Presumably. Even Angela knows. And now me. I just wonder, if my mum was alive, would she know? Or would she still be totally out of the picture?'

'This has upset you. I'm really sorry. Maybe I should come over—'

'No, it's all right. I'm just surprised. Maybe it's one revelation too many. You haven't got any more up your sleeve, have you? My dad was a spy, or something?'

'The last thing I want is to make any more trouble. Why don't we talk about this, and then—'

'No. I mean, there's no need.' Adam had become, for the moment, an irrelevance to her, a patch of her life that had slipped out of focus. 'Look, I'm sorry about tonight.'

'What? Look, we can still go.' He sought for more conviction. 'I think we should go, definitely. Talk, and—'

'No, I can't, I'm sorry. I won't be here.' She was already on her feet. 'I've got to go home.'

# TWENTY

Coming to Salters Cottage in the September dusk, with the stained sky making rosy gingerbread of its tiled roof and twin chimneypots, Rebecca felt like an intruder. As she put her hand on the latch of the garden gate, all the warm homely associations of this act, in this pictorial stillness, came vividly to her only to stand away from her. Her knowledge, her feelings were all wrong for this. She came to this peace with a sword.

She found her father in the living room. He had been listening to music with the score open in front of him. He was on his feet in surprise.

'Hello. I didn't expect you. Why didn't you ring? I could have picked you up from the station.'

He turned down the music. She saw from the score that it was Mahler: the Fourth Symphony. The one with the portrayal of a child's heaven at the end. The movement was just beginning now, and all at once Rebecca hated it. Its piping sweetness was wrong, kinky, like dressing up in children's clothes. She hated the music, all music, all composers; they were full of the most awful bullshit.

'Is everything OK? You didn't have to come back. I was only trying—'

'I had to come back. I needed to talk to you.' She sat down on the edge of a chair, her hands in her lap. 'I've learnt about something.'

'Well?' His tone was determinedly neutral: she knew how he hated drama, would always try to draw its teeth.

'Carolyn Moyes got pregnant and had an abortion.'

He studied her a moment, then got up and walked out of the room. For a moment she thought he was simply going to carry on walking and that it seemed an oddly sensible reaction, the only straight way out. But he came back from the kitchen with a bottle of Scotch and two glasses. He turned off the music before pouring. There was no light on and the glow from the dimming sky gave the room a subaqueous luminescence, as if the house were at the bottom of the sea.

'Here you go.'

Her father handed her a glass of Scotch. Though they had wine together and he knew perfectly well she could drink as mightily as any teenager, he had never before invited her to drink spirits. Another rite of passage, she thought.

'It's true, obviously,' she said, and sipped at the burning drink.

'Yes. It is. How did you find out? Did he tell you – Adam?'

'No. I happened on it. It was through him, but he didn't want to tell me.'

'Has he been in touch with her?'

'No. Why, did you want to send love and kisses?'

He lit a cigar, his hand slightly unsteady. 'Well, now you know. What can I tell you? Yes, that happened. No, it wasn't a thing I intended telling you.'

'Why not?'

'Because it isn't . . .' He searched for a word, and the one he chose seemed to set off an explosion in her mind. 'It isn't very nice.'

She gasped, then laughed. 'You should have been a writer, not a composer. Such a way with words.'

'Not funny and not fair. Rebecca, this thing happened. What do you think: that I'm proud of it?' He swallowed his whisky, poured another, practically a tumblerful.

'Early August, apparently. The day of the murder was the nineteenth of August and that was the day you were at her house.'

'Yes. Like I told you, it was over by then. But there were loose ends to tie up. I had to make sure she was all right. It was as messy and complicated as life usually is—'

'Whose idea was the abortion?'

'Hers.' He puffed and drank like someone trying to make himself sick. 'She didn't want a child. Especially in those circumstances. When she fell pregnant we were already – recognizing that it was going nowhere. We talked about it, we agreed on it.'

243

'Very cosy.' She drained her glass.

'It wasn't cosy at all. It was a hellish end to a bad experience.'

'It can't have been that bad.' The whisky seemed to have mounted instantly to her brain. 'You kept coming back for more. What, did she tie you down and make you do it?'

Grimly ignoring her, he said, 'It was agreed, and that was what she did, and that was the end of it. I wish you hadn't known, but now that you do—'

'Don't say forget it. Please, Dad, don't you dare say forget it. I mean, let me get my facts right here, because you're about to remind me that it was before my time, so I need to be straight. Thomas had died the Christmas before. Mum couldn't have any more children. But you went ahead and had an affair, and you actually got the woman up the stick and she had an abortion, and all the time you didn't think how totally devastated Mum would have been if she'd known about that. Just think what Mum would have felt. Didn't that ever occur to you?'

'You don't know everything, Rebecca.' He was reaching for the bottle again.

'I knew Mum. I know how she would have felt. She loved you so much, and yet the things you did were just like – spitting in her face. Were you frightened she'd leave you? Well, I'll bet she would have. If I'd been her—'

'Don't try and speak for your mother, Rebecca. I knew her long before you did. You don't know about this and you can't judge—'

'I knew my mum. I knew her better than you did. Because you can't have known her much. If you could just carry on, with no insight into what she must be feeling, you must have been totally cut off from her, not caring . . .'

'I was not. Never. I've told you, you can't speak for her.'

'Somebody has to. Nobody else gives a toss. She's just left out of everything. Isn't she?' As he did not answer she went on, 'God, you must have been so cold, so clinical, just keeping it all separate—'

'Mum knew.'

He put his glass to his lips, and the whites of his eyes flashed at her in the rich gloom.

'What?'

'You heard me. Mum knew. If you must have it, then OK. I didn't want to tell you this either – very chicken of me, all right. But I'm not what you've just made me out to be, Rebecca. I won't have that. So you listen up. Mum knew. She found out. She cottoned on. I doubt that these things can be hidden. It was around the time Carolyn discovered she was pregnant. Mum tackled me, and I told. I confessed. All of it: the affair, Carolyn's pregnancy. . . I didn't keep any more secrets. She knew, and she knew about the abortion. And in the end me and your mum stayed together, the way people manage to sometimes. This is what you didn't know.' He stabbed out his cigar. 'Now you do.'

At the window one of the cats had appeared, sitting on the outside sill and mewing to be let in: a quixotic tabby called Queenie who sometimes chose to ignore the cat flap. Rebecca stared into the gemstone eyes.

'So all those things.' she said slowly, 'that I imagined her feeling . . . she did feel. It was real. She knew. . . She must have been hurting so much. I can't begin to imagine how that hurt her,' she said weakly, and in fact her head did seem to swim with the effort of trying to enter her mother's soul, feel the weight of its burden.

'It hurt her a great deal. I know that. Yes, I believe I hurt Anna as much as it's possible for one human being to hurt another. I expected no forgiveness for it, from her or myself. I was prepared for whatever she was prepared to do to me. After that, anything, anything she cared to give me that wasn't a blow was like a gift. For her own reasons, she gave those gifts. She gave me forgiveness – not forgetting, forgiveness – and we worked it out. I know I didn't deserve that – you don't have to tell me. But I'm talking about what did happen, instead of what perhaps should have happened if there was any justice. I would have done anything for your mother. Even when I betrayed her, that applied, though probably that doesn't seem to make any sense. We survived it, together. That's all that matters.'

The cat began paddling at the windowpane with slithery paws. Rebecca watched, unseeing.

'And then the year after that you adopted me,' she said.

'Yes.' He held out the bottle, and when she did not

acknowledge it poured himself another glass.

'So I suppose I was pretty necessary, wasn't I? Mum couldn't have any more kids and you'd just brought that home to her in the most awful painful way possible. So what could make it up to her? A child, of course. We'll get one for ourselves, darling, and then you'll feel better and maybe you'll forget what a bastard I am. I was just . . . I was a new puppy.' Her throat tightened, but she didn't want to cry. She got up, snatched at the whisky bottle and filled her glass. 'That's all. To make things better. To make up for your mistake.'

'It wasn't like that.'

'Wasn't it? It looks that way. I don't know how you're going to convince me otherwise. I mean you're always lying so it's going to be hard to get me to believe anything you say. Of course it was that way, Dad. Surely at some time after you brought me home you must have looked at Mum, all happy with a child, and thought: Phew, thank God for that. So now I know where I came from, right, not a stork or a gooseberry bush. I came from guilt.'

'You don't know what you're talking about.' He had sat back now, his eyes half-closed.

'Dad, you're forgetting. I'm in on the secret now. It's all out in the open and it bloody hurts.' Again she fought with her puckering throat. 'It bloody hurts, Dad.'

'Listen to me.' He sat forward and she could hear the rough edge of drink in his voice, like a crackle on a recording. 'That was not how it was. Your mother and I worked out our problems, and then we decided to adopt. Now you hold on to that. I'm sorry for the lies and I'm sorry for your hurting, and you're hating my guts right now and that's OK, do it but you hold on to what I tell you because it is the truth.'

'You couldn't tell the truth if you tried,' she cried, and though she knew the whisky was pushing her to this wildness she couldn't stop. 'You bastard, Dad. I don't want any more to do with you. I wish you'd left me where I was. You didn't do me any favours, not when I was just part of your sleazy game. I'd rather – I'd rather be with my birth mother. She had her faults but she didn't hide them. She's my blood. I want to find her, she's my real parent, I'm better off with my blood—'

'Blood?' He yelled it: the cat at the window stopped pawing, hunched and startled. 'Don't talk crap, Rebecca. Blood means nothing. Absolutely nothing. Love is all that matters. Did your birth mother give you love, or anything even worthy of that name? Look back. I don't think so. Love is what we gave you, the love of a mother and father. She gave you nothing and we gave you everything. So don't start talking to me about your birth mother, please. You can hate my guts but it doesn't change what I am to you.'

'Oh yes it does. How can I look at you in the same way? Our whole family life was just bogus. I just saved your arse.'

He was shaking his head, slowly, almost mournfully. 'Anna and I had already agreed to stay together, before we thought of adopting. We would have stayed together, whatever. We were . . . joined. We were joined more than ever.'

'Oh, I can't believe this. What, you're going to tell me it made you stronger as a couple? There's an encouragement to cheating bastards everywhere. Anyway, you were still lying after, surely. That's what this whole Gandy business was about, wasn't it? The day of the murder, you were at that woman's. But you lied to hide it from Mum. You reckon you weren't actually screwing by that point, but you still had to lie about being there, to hide it from Mum. Well, isn't that it? Unless it wasn't really over then. A couple of weeks after she'd had an abortion – Christ . . .'

'It was over then.' His face was almost completely in shadow. 'I still saw her, to sort things out, like I told you: but the affair was over.'

'So why couldn't you admit you were with her that day? You reckoned Mum knew by then. You told me you'd spilled the beans by then. No more secrets after that, you said.' She was still throwing angry words at him and not thinking about them much: but deeper down a real puzzlement entered her like a barbed hook. 'Why go into this big lie about that day? Or are you just telling me another lie?'

Her father cleared his throat. He sat forward and though there was now no light to speak of he shaded his eyes with his hand, as if at an intolerable glare.

'I've told you the truth,' he said. Perhaps because of the shading hand, his voice came sepulchral, its bass notes seeming almost to touch her with a physical vibration. 'But not the

247

whole truth, and nothing but the truth. That's the reason for that formula in court – it's because you can have different kinds of truth.'

'I only want one kind.'

'Do you? Well, I don't suppose there's any way of not telling it to you now. I don't want to – you'll see why. I know how much you loved your mum. Knowing that, I can – I can tell it. Nobody, absolutely nobody who doesn't love your mum and her memory as we do can ever know it. I'm not going to hold you to any promise about this. I don't think I have to . . . That day, the nineteenth of August, I did spend much of that day at Carolyn's, as Adam Dowling discovered. Your mother had gone to Ingelow shopping for the day. She knew that I had to sort things finally with Carolyn at some point, but she preferred not to know when I was going to do it . . . It was that kind of agreement. We'd had the shouting and the tears when it came out, and now we were staying together . . . trying to find a ground we could stand on. Anna had been hurt, of course, every bit as much as you imagined. Coming after Thomas's death, it was . . . well, I dare say it was like being in shock. She was functioning, but she wasn't all there, really, though I didn't realize quite how much she – wasn't herself.

'Anyhow, I came home about four. On the way, I noticed a lot of people milling about at the camp site – searching for Lee Brudenell, as I found out later. I didn't take a great deal of notice. I parked the car, went in. Anna was already there. I remember thinking she can't have been home long because there were these sandy footprints still damp in the hall . . . so I thought she must have been walking on the beach. She did a lot of that. I went into – well, not my study, it was the dining room then. There was a French window, before we had it bricked in. She was standing in front of it, and she was looking at me with these huge, huge eyes. Sort of pleading, sort of fearful . . . all I can say is like the eyes of a child who's done something and doesn't know what your reactions's going to be. When I saw her eyes – just her eyes, not the other thing – I knew how completely she was shattered, mentally. She was taking these tablets, had been since Thomas had died, and I think sometimes she took more than she should have. But it wasn't just that: you could see she'd . . . lost herself. That look on her face was . . .' He bunched his shoulders, straining for precision. 'Yes, like a child who brings home a stray kitten and wants to know if we can keep it. In her arms, clenched tight, so tight against her chest, was a little child. A toddler. A boy.' He let out a desperate breath, so sharply, like someone trying to blow out a candle. 'That was Lee Brudenell.'

At the window the cat was still. Rebecca swallowed. The noise was loud in her ears.

'I stepped towards her. I said something like, "Whose is that little boy?" . . . I can't remember. She sort of smiled, but she backed away towards the window. She said, "Ours." I remember that so clearly – this terrible smile, and that word. I shook my head, started to say something. I was sure we could get control of this . . . She said, "He's ours. I've found him again. He was all on his own, he was all alone in the woods near the camp, that's where he's been. I picked him up and brought him home." I remember the little boy's hair under her chin. It was just the colour of Thomas's. There was no sound from him, but she was holding him so tight against her, squeezing him, and when I went nearer to her, trying to say he wasn't ours, she squeezed him tighter to her, like no one would ever tear him away from her again . . .

'I asked again where he had come from. She looked at me like she really didn't trust me now and she said again that she had found him in the woods, all on his own, and she'd brought him home. Anna was not in a normal state of mind, not at all. But I thought about the parents of this child, what they must be going through. And I tried to say something about that, how she must have taken somebody else's child and it wasn't fair to them. She wouldn't have it. "He's ours," she kept saying, quite fiercely, and she gripped tighter and tighter on to this tiny little boy, his face quite crushed into her chest. And then she sort of smiled again and said it was all right, everything would be all right because he'd come back to us. It all went wrong from when he went away, she said.'

Her father's voice broke for a moment, and the silhouette of his hand went up to his face.

'I started moving towards her. I really thought she would – come to herself any moment. I kept my eyes fixed on her face, waiting for her expression to change, for her to realize . . . It didn't happen. She stepped back again and there was this utter wariness in her face, a sort of calculating fear. It was just like a mother animal, threatened. I said to her that it had to stop now, that we had to take the little boy back to where he came from. She didn't say no. She just kept staring at me coming towards her, with this animal expression. And then I looked at that little boy – what I could see of him – and I knew there was no life there. No breath, no movement. She had just – smothered the life out of him.

'I felt faint. I said, "My God, what have you done?" I just couldn't help it. And at that she turned and pushed open the French windows and she ran away from me across the garden.

'I ran after her. I was calling her name, begging her to stop. She started zigzagging across the garden. I remember thinking it was bizarre, us running and shouting like that, the – the wildness of it, it just wasn't us. Anna ran down the side passage. I just missed catching her there. She was panting. She still had this little child squeezed against her, so tight. She was tall, you know, big-framed; she just had him folded to her. All the way home from the camp site, it must have been like that. Loving him to death.

'She carried on running, across the front garden, out of the gate, across the lane. She was going full pelt. One of her sandals came off on the other side of the lane. I kept yelling at her to stop. She would have to eventually, I knew that. But it was as if she thought she could run for ever as long as she kept that little child. She started scrambling up the dune bank on the other side of the lane. That slowed her, yet she had this amazing energy: she just ploughed up there, like someone on an assault course or something. I was still a few paces behind. I wasn't shouting any more, I was saving my breath to catch her.

'I saw her figure stand up there against the sky as she reached the top of the bank. She seemed to pause just for a second, taking this great breath. She could see the beach and the sea, I suppose: maybe it looked like freedom. Maybe she was just dizzy, at the end of her strength. Since Thomas had died she hadn't been eating properly, and then there were the drugs; maybe that energy was just like a feverish firework going off inside her . . . Anyhow, she started off down the slope. I saw her take one step and then she just went down in this great plunge. Down.'

The word was a deep growl that seemed to exhaust her father's voice. Rebecca wanted to speak, perhaps to stop him, perhaps because it might wake her, reveal her to be dreaming this in a sweaty bed. But she was helplessly caught in the amber of new knowledge, unable to move or speak.

'I remember seeing seagulls, up in the sky, over the sea somewhere, just doing their thing. Life going on as usual. I staggered up the crest of the bank, shouting for Anna. You know the seaward side of the bank tends to be crumbly, like brown sugar. And we'd had a hot dry summer that year. Anna had just lost her footing completely. She'd tumbled all the way down to the duckboards at the bottom. I heard the noise, though the worst part of the noise wasn't Anna.

'She hadn't put out her hands to stop her fall, even hurtling down like that. She'd kept tight hold of him against her chest. And there she lay at the bottom, on the duckboards, face down with her legs splayed out, one sandal missing. Very much like a rag doll. The little . . . Lee Brudenell was underneath her.'

'No.' Rebecca amazed herself, finding this word. She put her hands over her face, breathed urgently into them as if into an oxygen mask. 'Dad.'

He seemed to give a great writhing shudder. But when he spoke his voice was still deep and distinct.

'I went down and picked her up. She was weeping, or sort of crooning. I think then her mind had sort of – broken free of what was happening. It couldn't take any more. She was still clutching the little boy, but some of that strength must have gone because I managed to take him from her. There were bruises on her hands and her face, but she wasn't hurt. The back of the little boy's head was bloody, it was . . . a – mess.' With a groan her father tried to steady his breathing. 'His face was bluish. I put my ear to his chest and the chest was so narrow, like a puppet's, and now it really was Thomas all over again . . . Of course I knew, I already knew, it was hopeless but it didn't connect yet, not really. I just felt sort of relieved that I'd stopped Anna and now we could . . . do something. She stood there looking. I don't know how much she was seeing.

But she did put her arms out and made this kind of squeak and said could she hold him again. "Just hold him," she kept saying, "just got to hold him," until I said no. No. And that seemed to get through to her. She just stared at me like a naughty child, hugging herself – but that wasn't Anna staring out of those eyes, Anna was somewhere in there but a long way down, a long way from where all this was happening. Do you hear that, Rebecca?'

She could only move her head a little in reply.

'You must hear that and understand it. I'll keep saying it until you do. Anna wasn't there, not the real Anna, not the woman you and I knew. Her spirit wasn't there. Pain and hurt had driven it out, temporarily. So that wasn't your mother, not in any sense that matters. To be legalistic about it, she wasn't responsible for her actions, not in my eyes anyway.

'But my eyes weren't the eyes of the law. From the moment I took that little broken body from her arms, I knew, in my bones, what we were going to do, what we had to do. There was only one way. I hardly had to glance at the alternatives. Own up? Whatever they would do to Anna, no matter how much allowance they made, no matter what consideration they showed for her circumstances and her mental state – it would break her. There was no way of admitting to this that wouldn't be, basically, the end of Anna's life. And the end of Anna and me. Yes, I was thinking about that. I was thinking more about that than anything, really. I don't suppose anything can sound bizarre to you now, so maybe it wasn't bizarre that in amongst everything I felt a kind of joy. Because I could protect Anna, now. I could be to her what I should have been. I could give her everything. And after all, what didn't I owe her? After what I'd done to her, after what she'd been through, what couldn't she ask of me? And she didn't have to ask. There was no bargain I wouldn't have made. If she had come to me and told me she'd strangled that child with her bare hands and enjoyed it, I would still have protected her, gladly. I needed a sacrifice commensurate with my guilt – you could put it that way, but that's too cool, soulless. And it was my soul that fastened to hers then, for ever. Call that airy-fairy, mystical, stupid . . . all I know is it's true. The bargain was struck and I was glad of it. She had given me a great love, always: I'd betrayed it. Now I could try again to deserve it. I was eager.'

'Oh God, Dad,' she moaned.

'I know.' He spoke with great tenderness. 'I know, love. Well, that's almost it. Anna was . . . I suppose catatonic is nearest to it. I took her back into the house. She was like a sleepwalker. I carried Lee. Indoors she lay down on the couch. She was shivering, her eyes were open. I talked to her gently. I said I wouldn't be long, and I asked her just to stay put, not do anything, not answer the door or the phone or speak a word to anyone. I think, finally, she understood: she nodded at me just once and there was a look in her eyes, as if a little light had broken through, just for a moment.

'I had to be quick. I didn't know where the child had come from – I supposed the camp site, and I remembered the people I'd seen milling about there. He was going to be missed, no doubt already was. I thought of water. I thought of the sea at first, but the tide was way out, and I would be so visible far out on the beach . . . He was very small, even for his age. I wrapped him in a plastic sack, one from Coupland's – we used to buy veg from their factory shop, and I carried him along the dune path to Tetby Haven. How do people do these things? They manage if they have a reason. My reason was Anna. I didn't see anyone on the way. If I had, I suppose I would have tried to brazen it out. If there'd been a policeman or something, some challenge, then I don't know . . . I think I was probably prepared to kill also, if it could have been done. Anything. As long as it was sorted.'

'Sorted,' she echoed. 'A little child, dead. Sorted.'

'Yes. Absolutely,' he said with conviction. 'Oh, I know it's wrong. Repugnant, evil, unthinkable. All that. But it's actually easier to do unthinkable things than think them. In a place like that, yes, you do it. The place I was at was unique, or unique to everyone. You'll know it, one day. It's the place where you lay your love down; the reckoning. There's only one law there, only one thing that counts.'

The darkness in the room was almost complete. Only fragmentary gleams showed at the rims of their whisky glasses, broken haloes.

'I put him in the creek at Tetby Haven. I thought the water

would clean him. He'd be found eventually, I knew, but maybe not for a while. I came back home and that was when I remembered Anna's sandal. I fetched it. I thought about the duckboards too, and I went and checked them. There was blood on one plank. A little hair. I pulled that plank up, they came away easily with the salt, and I brought it home and sawed it up and burnt it. I took my clothes off and I washed them. And I persuaded Anna to take hers off and I washed them too. I remember helping her off with her top, pulling it over her head: she was glassy-eyed, like an exhausted child. But she came out of herself again and she said to me, "He's dead, isn't he?" Her voice was quite normal. I said, "Who – Thomas?" We looked at each other: she nodded. I said yes, he was. He was dead after all. She cried a little – not much. I got her to take a bath. I helped to wash her. She kept looking at the bruises on her hands. I don't know what I was thinking really. Part of me expected a knock on the door, some super-intuitive policeman standing there, saying he knew everything. But I wasn't afraid. I was just taking one minute at a time, and concentrating on Anna. I didn't know what she was going to do. She might have suddenly become – normal, might have started saying we had to call the police. Though I didn't think so. She was ill: what had happened was part of her illness. That's what I kept trying to get through to her. When she was drying her hair I went through to put the clothes in the dryer and after a minute she called out for me – "Philip, Philip." She was all lost and afraid, but when I came back she calmed down. "Thought you'd left me," she said, and she sort of laughed. She was shaking. I held her and said I never would. And I know we felt the truth of that, like an electric current going through us. A little bit later I brought her a cup of tea and as she took it she looked at me with a kind of puzzled frown and said, "I didn't mean—" and I put my finger on her lips. I said I knew, knew it all, and understood it all, and we would start life newly, from now, from this basis.

'A while after that Tony Larkinson came knocking, to tell me about this little boy going missing. I remembered then Diane coming that morning and complaining about Howard Gandy hanging around her kids. Pretty soon there were a lot of people on the green, trading gossip. I joined them for a while, listened. Gandy's name kept coming up, of course. Someone said they'd seen him around the camp site, acting suspiciously. I put it all together. I think I knew there and then what I was going to do and say, if it came to it. And that's pretty much what happened, afterwards. The police were very keen to swallow that particular story. I knew Carolyn wouldn't say anything about my being at hers that day. She was already planning to get away, wanted nothing to do with any of it, especially when it meant publicity. I cooked up the story of being home, in the front garden, around two and seeing Gandy go by on his way to Tetby Haven. That was really the time Anna must have brought Lee home by that same coastal route, where no one saw her, thank God. And it was the time when Gandy couldn't account for his movements. They were so keen to do him for it: all I had to do really was fall in with it. And Anna had to stick to the story, of course. Which she did, faithfully. There was this kind of enormous, terrifying trust about her. She looked to me to know what to do, and she did it.

'Did she know what she'd done? For a while I thought she had complete amnesia about it. I thought she knew something terrible had happened, but her mental state was so fragile it couldn't handle it. So it blocked it out. But I think the memory was there, sort of. Maybe like something that you do when you're terribly drunk: it's remote, it's like something that happened to someone else. What happened after I came home, that was clear enough to her, I think: there was the washing and burning and it connected. But how she found him and brought him home seemed to be a blank to her later. I asked her if anyone saw her coming home with him and she couldn't remember. "In the woods, he was in the woods," that's all she could say. Well, I watched her very carefully. I was still afraid of what she might do – maybe to herself. But she chose to go on living. She chose to handle the memory, the knowledge, in the one sure way – by putting it in a compartment. I guided her that way the best I could. I remember a couple of nights after it happened, she woke up in the night and she gripped my hand, so tight it literally stopped the blood. And she said, "That little boy that died. They'll be burying him soon, won't they?" I said yes, though it wasn't for a while because of the post-mortem. She said, "After that, will things be all right?" Again I said yes. And then she said, in the most perfectly normal, down-to-earth, aware voice: "I couldn't help it, Philip." I said I knew that and it wasn't her fault. She said, "What wasn't?" "Anything," I said, and I think I meant that more than anything I've ever said. "Whatever it is or isn't. It's not your fault." In the morning she was a bit trancelike again, and that went on for some months. Her doctor watched her carefully, gave her different medication: it was only to me that he used the word breakdown. But she got better.' He nodded to himself. 'Yes, she got better.'

Rebecca said slowly, 'I can't believe this. I mean literally. Because once I believe this, then – then I just can't carry on.' She meant it entirely: her life seemed to have narrowed all at once to a closed tunnel, with no further to go.

'Oh, you can,' he said, almost neutrally. 'We did. Because – because life is the alternative, and we had to take it. We lived with it – or maybe we didn't, we let it live with us, and it settled down eventually. It didn't turn on us and attack us and destroy us. And after a while we never spoke of it. It was a part of our lives and it was secret – which is how it is with married couples who love each other. As we did, more and more. Rebecca, what happened was a terrible accident. Yes? But like all accidents it had its circumstances. One of those – losing Thomas – was something that couldn't be prevented. Another – what I did with Carolyn – was something that needn't have happened: I created that. So the circumstances had to be taken into account. And I have no regrets.'

He got up and went to the window, opening it to let the cat in. Along with the swift sleek shape came a waft of salt-sharpened air, with an early tang of autumn about it. Her father stayed on his feet by the window.

'You're going to say now that we let Howard Gandy go to prison for what happened. Again, yes. I wish it hadn't been so. I may as well say that we didn't send him to prison, the law did. But even so, it wasn't right. Well, to a degree. When the police arrested him, when that gift came, I took it. Basically, I didn't care who went to prison as long as it wasn't Anna. Howard Gandy was known as at least a potential child-molester. Yes, I know the revised version. But the fact was, back then nobody around here liked or trusted him with kids, your mother and me included. He was seen as a menace, and putting him out of the reach of kids a bloody good thing. The law was determined to have Howard Gandy and I accepted that gratefully. We had to think of the world as – well, as full of potential enemies, and his being convicted for that crime kept the enemies at bay. Yes, it niggled at me, as time went on. Injustice does, doesn't it? Look at the appalling things happening in the Third World. It niggles at you. But you just don't think about it all the time.'

'Was he heavy?' Rebecca said. 'Was he heavy to carry?'

'No, he wasn't,' her father said, and he gave that shudder again, as if hearing his own voice at last appalled him. 'No more than Thomas.'

Whisky in her throat, Rebecca lurched to her feet.

In the bathroom her father stood over her while she was sick. He stroked her hair back gently from her forehead. Her mind wasn't working in any normal way, so perhaps she only fancied that there was something valedictory about the touch, a preparation for loss.

'Well,' she said, sitting down in the living room again, 'I was right about one thing, anyway. You did have me to make up for the past. But no, it wasn't like getting a new puppy. I was to make up for a dead child. You picked a poor little mite out of the gutter and gave her a wonderful life and that was to make up for the one that was gone. I was a – a sin-offering.' She didn't know from what odd corner of her mind she plucked that term, but it felt so right that she almost hissed it. 'A sin-offering. I was your blood money, Dad—'

'No. Stop it, now, because it isn't true. Rebecca—'

'Oh, it doesn't matter.' She pushed away Queenie's enquiring nose. 'That's just a small part of it. At least I'm alive.'

'Yes, you are. And life goes on. You have to think what to do with it. It's up to you. I've told you this, though I never meant to. Even after Mum died, I was determined to keep the secret for ever, to guard her memory just as I guarded her when she was alive. When Adam forced my hand with the Carolyn business, and pressured me to change my evidence for that day, I went along because I didn't think the secret could ever come out. Not the important secret. Having the stuff about

257

Carolyn come out was grim, but it was negotiable. I could admit that my version of that day was a lie without having to reveal the true version. I still don't see that I shall ever have to, unless you choose to tell it. I don't know how you feel about your mother now: hopefully it's got through, what I've been saying – that she wasn't to blame. But I can't make you not tell.'

'No, I won't tell,' Rebecca said. 'Mum would stop me, anyway. The thought of Mum – or the Mum I thought I knew before. That wasn't real, but I don't suppose the memory will go away.'

'Mum was all you remember her,' her father said.

Ignoring him, she said, 'All this time.' There were worlds of sick wonder in those three words. All this time – her teddy-clutching years and her gawky growing and her tortuous adolescence, the Christmases and birthdays, the long summer days, the gloom of school, the little illnesses and the holidays and the stretches of comfortable domestic anonymity: all this time, it was here. It was in the walls, in the air she breathed, it oozed from the pores of her parents' skin, every single moment.

'Rebecca.' He made an irresolute movement towards her. 'None of it was meant to happen.'

'It doesn't matter,' she said, and the hand she lifted stopped him. 'It's none of my business. I'm not your blood. It's like you say, you have to be involved to understand it. It's some family survival thing and nothing to do with me. I was just a pawn. No, I don't blame anybody. Who is there to blame? Everyone's just shadows, people I thought I knew . . . But I can't be part of it any more. It doesn't make any sense for me to be part of it. And otherwise I'll just – pack in,' she said brokenly, and her hands fluttered about her head, trying to describe the sensation of destructive imminence that hung round her, 'honestly, I'll pack in . . . I can't . . .'

She ran from the arms he extended, as if from a death-embrace.

She lay curled up on her bed that night, but did not sleep. Her father didn't go to bed, and as far as she knew he didn't sleep either: from time to time she heard him moving around in the sitting room. Once she thought she heard him weeping, but a

258

strong breeze got up in the night, moaning around the eaves of the cottage, and she couldn't be sure.

At six she showered, dried her hair, put on clean clothes. She had no need to pack, because her suitcases still stood in the hall where she had left them last night.

'Where are you going?' Her father woke from a rumpled doze in his armchair. Typically he was alert at once.

'Back to London. I can't stay here, Dad. Not now. I just can't.'

He rubbed his unshaven face with a rasping noise, seemed to reject what he had been about to say.

'How long?'

'I don't know.' It was the only honest answer. 'For now.'

'Have you got money?'

'There's still some in my savings account.'

He nodded. 'Ring me if you need some . . . I want you to stay, Rebecca.'

'I can't. Not now. Don't ask me, Dad. Just let me go.'

He gazed bleakly at her, and light-headed as she was with shock and lack of sleep she had a vision of herself as something vast and immovable in his sight, a tree, a primeval rock.

'I'll take you to the station.'

She shrugged. 'Will you be able to? The whisky . . .'

'I stopped drinking before midnight.' He got up. As he did so some loose change slipped from his pockets on to the seat of the chair. She scooped it up and handed it to him. Strange clownlike actions they were going through in an unimaginable dawn.

At the station he carried her cases to the platform and asked her to ring him and then, quickly, kissed her cheek before walking back to the car. She tried to think of the kiss as something in passing, to be disregarded, like a peck at a New Year's Eve party, and she managed to get on the train and take her seat before her hand clawed up and rubbed at the kiss-trace on her face.

# TWENTY-ONE

The morning had been spent unprofitably enough for Adam, interviewing one of the Prince's Trust whizkids who had actually made good. There was no doubt that the rather cocky young man with the old simian face had shown enterprise in building up his speciality flowers business, but he had also been helped by an unexpected legacy, which blurred any conclusions that might be drawn. In fact the project was boring Adam and he decided to get on with producing some copy and scrapping the scheduled interviews with two other beneficiaries. At lunchtime, however, he got something out of the way. Angela called him on his mobile. He hadn't after all seen her on Sunday, and now he met her at a bar in a little gully of a side-street in the monolithic shadow of Fairway Publishing.

'Oh, but we've got to talk about this sensibly,' she said. She was no fool: on the phone yesterday he had confined himself to curt nothings and now he was not aware that his look or his words were especially forbidding, but there was panic in Angela's eyes, the panic of realization. 'I keep telling you, I thought she knew all that stuff. I never dreamt for a moment that I was – well, breaking any secrets. Really, Adam.'

'Even if she had known, it was a very hurtful thing to bring up like that,' he said. Because he had such self-control, he was at an almost embarrassing advantage in situations like this. 'So obviously you were trying to hurt. That much is clear. To be honest, it all is. You knew she didn't know. You used that to hurt her.'

'No, Adam, it wasn't like that—'

'Which is leaving aside the fact that you're ferreting stuff out of my researches and blabbing it out whenever some spiteful fancy takes you. That's no good, Angela. What

260

do you expect, that I'm going to be delighted?'

'Oh, I don't care,' she said. She picked up her empty glass, then banged it back down again and turned her face away. Tears filmed her eyes.

'I apologized to Rebecca on your behalf, anyway.'

'Rebecca.' Her lips curled round the word. 'For God's sake. She's just a kid, Adam.'

'She's six years younger than you.' He went ahead and said it: what the hell. 'And about six years older emotionally.'

'Oh, you bastard.' It was all she could say for several moments, and he experienced a sour triumph. Then she reached out for his hand; and when he withdrew it, bent her head and sobbed. He saw a mascara-stained tear drip on to her sleeve like a drop of watery ink. 'Adam, I can't believe we're talking like this. Over something so – I mean, what does it matter?'

'It matters a great deal to her,' he said. 'Her father too. The relations between them. It matters to me. I don't know whether it matters to you – whether *we* matter to you. If so, I'm sorry, because there's bad news in that direction, Angela.'

She resembled a smacked child as she glared at him, taking this in.

'It's not me,' she said, beginning shakily to gather up her jacket and handbag. 'It's you. If I was to tell anyone about this, they'd be on my side. It's you who's gone off your trolley – you with your bloody pet child-molesters and weirdos and stupid little right-on students . . . I mean, how do you know, anyway? Oh, oh, poor Rebecca. How do you know the little tramp isn't whooping it up on alcopops right now? It's all sentimental rubbish, it's—'

'I know because she's with me,' he said, and was surprised at how easily it came out. 'She came to me, and she's staying.'

Angela's mouth was open. He felt like saying: you're catching flies. Instead he said, 'So that's it, really. Don't ring me any more, please.'

'Don't worry. I won't.' She dropped her handkerchief: it fell near his feet, and there was an almost risible symbolism, he thought, in his not picking it up. 'I'll tell you what,' she said, stooping to retrieve it: the action made her face even more red and distressed-looking and he pitied that, in the abstract. 'I think it's hanging around that Gandy that's done it. It's given you peculiar tastes too.'

A parting shot. Alone, ordering another drink, Adam wondered whether it would have deflected the shot, or brought it nearer home, if he had told Angela all: told her that he had, indeed, slept with Rebecca last night.

It had not been planned or intended, if such things ever were. He had gone on to the Café Royal bash alone after Rebecca's phone call – there had seemed little else to do – but she had been on his mind all evening, and through most of a restless night. His anger with Angela didn't much occupy him then: he was thinking of what an awful way it was for Rebecca to learn such a thing, and how it must have set back relations with her father – which Adam already felt bad about complicating. It was, in fact, a horrible mess, and he cursed his inability to change it. He presumed that he himself was in Rebecca's bad books, too. He had uncovered that sordid little piece of information, even if he hadn't passed it on to her; and she surely resented him for secretly possessing it. Every fibre of his temperament longed for some harmonizing solution, but he couldn't see one. And then early on Sunday morning Rebecca had turned up on his doorstep with her suitcases and asked him, straight out, if she could stay. And saying yes, willingly, seemed like the nearest thing to a solution that was to be had.

She had looked terrible that morning: pale, shuffling like a sleepwalker. He presumed she had had the business of Carolyn Moyes and the abortion out with her father, had ended up in a major quarrel, and fled. But he didn't press her too much; and when she said, with the most naked, pathetic, exhausted appeal, 'I can't be with my dad just now, Adam. I can't. Please,' he accepted it. He said she could stay as long as she liked.

'Does he know where you are?'

'Yes. It doesn't matter, but he does.'

Adam wasn't sure it was the truth, and wasn't sure that it didn't matter either. He felt it would matter a great deal to Philip and he had thoughts of ringing him, just to be sure.

But then he thought differently: she was not, after all, a child. Looking at her sitting at his breakfast bar listlessly forking up scrambled eggs, her eyes smoky with fatigue, he had seen that these were not the emotions of an adolescent. Neither were the experiences behind them, come to that. He felt again that authentic respect for her that had surprised him in the restaurant. He would do as she wanted.

Ignoring Angela's phone calls for the time being, he fussed over Rebecca. After she had slept for a good seven hours on his couch he ran her a bath and then as she sat in her dressing gown he opened a bottle of wine and poured her a large glass.

'We haven't talked about it properly,' he said. 'It might have sounded like flannel on the phone yesterday, so let me say it again. That material was in my files and it was never meant to go any further.'

'I know. Adam, we have talked about that properly. As far as I'm concerned, that's dead. You didn't do anything wrong.'

'Well. Knowing, when you didn't, is a kind of deception.'

'I know I got angry on the phone. I didn't really mean it against you. I – well, I suppose I did at the time. I'm sorry. Right now you're about the only person in the world I trust.'

This was forceful: he hesitated while he absorbed it.

'I'm assuming you confronted your dad.'

'Yes – as soon as I got home.'

'And it all turned out pretty nasty. You don't have to tell me if you don't want. I certainly won't take sides. Of course I don't like to think of you and your dad . . . falling out. Which is what's happened, isn't it?'

She seemed to grope towards a reply to this, from some dark enshrouding dream.

'We're . . . well, we're talking. It's just – we're apart now. Completely. It seems a cheek saying this, when you're putting me up, but could you not ask me any more about that? It's just too— It's a mess.'

'All right. Whatever you say.'

'Thanks. And for this – for everything.'

'Not at all. Now when you're dressed we'll go out for a pizza. I'll just go and shave.'

'Oh – Adam – would you help me do something? I suppose London's the best place; I don't know how you go about it . . . I want to trace my birth mother.'

A deep and bitter estrangement, then, he thought; but true to his word he asked no more questions. Privately he had considered, on discovering the information about Carolyn Moyes' abortion, that the whole affair showed Philip Springthorpe to be unlucky as well as insensitive but such things did happen. Adam's own father had been almost routinely unfaithful to his mother. But of course it was different for Rebecca. He had heard the glowing tone, almost adoring, with which she spoke of her dead mother; the pain on her behalf must be profound. He did wonder what she had said to her father, whether she had perhaps ascended to the judgement seat with a readiness slightly galling to a sophisticated fifty-year-old man, and whether he had lashed out in turn because of it. But he could make a fair guess at what the quarrel had been like and he could fully understand her need for severance. He couldn't bear to be around someone when they were at loggerheads; only physical removal was tolerable. There was perhaps something steely about this, which he recognized again when it came to Angela. Severance was needed there too: he had relied on indignation to carry him through it without softening, and now he had no regrets at all.

They had gone to a place a few streets away and eaten pizza. On his he had hot chilies which had given him the hiccoughs, and that had made Rebecca laugh, at first tentatively, then uproariously when the hiccoughs kept coming back. He thought there was probably an element of hysterical relief in the laughter but he was glad to have provoked it all the same. He admired her, and he felt sorry for her – the two were not at all incompatible. And together they intensified his feeling of being beholden to her, of owing her some personal restitution. He had started it all, after all. And it was with this sense of making urgent amends that he took her in his arms last night and made love with her. With, not to: it was something she frankly desired, almost initiated, and he had absolutely no feeling of taking advantage.

He was not so vain as to imagine that having sex with a girl constituted any kind of restitution in itself, some great gift – he hated the chauvinism in that. Where he was making amends was in the sharing of himself, because this was something he rarely did. He was a miser with himself: for all their time together, Angela had had very little of him. It was in sincere tribute to Rebecca that he blew up his own precious defences with such abandon. She was lonely, or feeling terribly alone: she needed someone to give without stint.

They lay together embracing afterwards, and talked. Her fingers and toes soon grew quite cold, and again he felt chivalrous and protective as he drew the quilt over their nakedness.

'It's weird going to sleep in London,' she said. 'I think of all those millions of people round me.'

'A bit claustrophobic, I suppose.' He stroked her arm gently, tracing the delicate flue: a beautifully simple, beautifully complex shape that surely only a sensitive sculptor, not blind nature, could have produced. The religious thought surprised him. 'Mind you, you're used to having hundreds of miles of sea near you. Different feeling entirely. Nicer, maybe.'

'That depends . . . Have you broken it off with Angela?'

'As far as I'm concerned.'

'She's not the baddie really.' Her voice was muffled against his shoulder as she added, 'No one is.'

'I don't like anyone having access to my research. Except you. It's different with you. You're in on it. And now we're together we can really get to work. I've been collating all Colin Brudenell's statements, and working out the discrepancies—'

'No.'

In the after-love drowsiness the sharpness of her reply made him physically jump.

'What?'

'I don't know . . . I think you should forget all that, what I said about the Brudenells. It was just a daft theory, I was . . . I've changed my mind. Really, I don't think it'll be any use to you, chasing up that end. You've got your story – Howard's story. Why not just stick with that?'

He was baffled.

'Well, I thought you agreed that exposing the real killer was the only way of finishing the job. And the Brudenells seem like the best lead we've got. I've been working on that basis—'

'Let's leave them alone, eh?' she said. 'They lost a little boy. We can't bring him back.'

'OK,' he said. It was a peaceable noise; he was sleepy and contented, and it was important for her mind to win just now. But he needed to know what had changed her, just as he needed to know who killed Lee Brudenell.

And as he left the bar where he had drawn a line under quite a fair paragraph of his life, Adam felt acutely the need for clarity. Rebecca at home right now, in his flat, was a thing he accepted of itself, but he had an apprehensive sense that his life was getting too complicated. He must reduce things to their essences. And that included, he decided, his Howard Gandy material. Rebecca had said something this morning about helping him out to earn her keep, and now it seemed like a good idea. Perhaps that vital beady eye of hers was what was needed: she didn't see in half-tones as he did. Transcribing Howard's interview tapes might be a start, if she would like to do it: at least that part of the case shouldn't touch any sore spot.

Adam whistled to himself as he stepped out in search of a taxi. Remembering Rebecca's mouth on his last night, her body a stirred curve on an axis of beautiful tension, he felt a quite amazing surge of adrenalin. He was far from a spontaneous person, but this irruption of spontaneity into his life had brought rewards he would scarcely have believed. Then he remembered Angela, going back to Fairway with her ruined make-up. It was hard on her – the vulnerability beneath that prim self-possession had shown itself, as shocking and pitiable as a facial scar – and he had perhaps been unfair.

But there had to be truth in a relationship. And for that reason, he was determined that he would get the truth from Rebecca – why she had changed her mind about pursuing the real killer.

# TWENTY-TWO

Pat Gandy wasn't squeamish and once, when she was about fourteen, she had wrung the neck of her mother's old canary when it had had some sort of seizure and was fluttering desperately about the cage with only one wing working. But she hated slugs and when one appeared, seemingly from nowhere, clinging to the bare skin of her wrist above her gardening glove, she screamed for Howard.

'By crikey, Mum. I've never known such a fuss.'

'I hate 'em, Howard. Ugh.' She shivered as he plucked it from her skin and held it up for her inspection.

'Only a little 'un. What shall I do with it? You fancy it on toast for tea?' He chuckled.

'Squash it.'

He obeyed her. She couldn't relax until it was dead.

'A great big girl like you frit of a little thing like that,' Howard said.

'Not so much of the big,' she said, playfully slapping at his knees, red and shiny in shorts. 'Now come here. Tell me you can't smell that smell. Down there – near the fence.'

He crouched down, sniffing. He reminded her of a great big dog and for a moment she wanted to laugh.

'Perhaps I can smell it a bit.'

'More than a bit, Howard. It reeks. I tell you, it's that tom again. He comes over from next door.'

'Well, he doesn't belong to next door, does he? I thought Mrs Mackay didn't like 'em.'

'No, it's not hers. It's a stray, I reckon. But that's the way it comes into my garden, over that fence. And sprays everywhere and makes that awful stink. I don't know what to do. It gets on my nerves.' She began sweeping dead-heads into a binbag. 'I remember when we first moved here, there was this wild tom

267

that was the biggest cat you ever saw. More like a dog really. It only had one eye. It used to sleep on top of our shed and I was worried when you came along in case it got in your pram or your cot and smothered you. I used to try and get Jack to do something about it, put a net over the pram or something like that, but oh no, I was flogging a dead horse there. He took no notice whatsoever . . .'

'Apparently these models of cats you can get are very good,' Howard said. 'You see them advertised in the Sunday papers. It's flat, cut out of metal, a bit like a doorstop, with these reflecting eyes. You put it in your garden and when the cats see it they stay away.'

'I bet they're expensive.'

'Well, maybe not. We'll have to see. I've got that interview next week, remember.' Howard lifted the full grass box from the lawnmower as easily as if it were a toy and, one-handed, emptied it into a binbag. 'I'm looking forward to that.'

The interview was for the job of swimming-pool attendant at the new leisure centre in Ingelow, and Pat had mixed feelings about it. It was wonderful to think of Howard doing a job he so obviously loved, but that of course depended on his getting it; and she was afraid that even now his reputation would prejudice his chances. It was very unfair, when the highest court in the land had declared him an innocent man, but that was the way of it. She didn't want to see him disappointed again. Privately she was pinning her hopes on Mr Jameson, who was trying to get Howard compensation for unjust imprisonment and had mentioned some figures that had made her gasp for breath. If that came true, then they wouldn't need to worry about anything ever again . . . But she knew Howard wasn't bothered about that. He had his heart set on this job. 'You know the manageress at Coupland's will give you an interview any time, as well,' she said. 'Just in case, you know, you don't have any luck with this one.'

'I know, Mum. But I'm concentrating on this first. It's what I want to do.' He stretched and looked up at the sky. 'Reckon it might rain later. I'll finish up here, Mum. Don't go tiring yourself. Have you took your tablet?'

'Yes, I have,' she said, making a face. 'Much good they do.' At once she regretted that, because he studied her closely.

'That pain's no better, is it?' he said. 'I think you should tell the doctor if they're not working. You know what he said.'

'I know. It's just the nuisance of taking them all the time. Anyway, they said they can't do anything until I've had another test at the hospital. I can't see what the fuss is about myself. I've suffered from indigestion for years; it's just one of those things—'

'It's not indigestion, Mum.' He had his hands on his hips. 'Now is it?'

She shrugged and clucked her tongue, though she rather liked it when he gently bossed her like this. Of course she wouldn't dream of telling him what the pain was really like – mostly in the night, when she would grip the headboard and swear under her breath, a salty moustache of sweat clammy on her lip.

'Now you go indoors. I'll tidy up. Do you need any ciggies? The shop shuts at seven. I could go and get some now.'

'I've got a few. They'll last me.'

'I'll get you some. And I tell you what, how about one of them big bars of fruit and nut as well? There's that film on tonight. We'll settle ourselves down nice and comfy.'

That sounded lovely to Pat. 'Here, it's not frightening, is it, that film? I shan't be able to sleep if it's too frightening.'

Howard chuckled. 'It's only a thriller. Something about a nutty man who won't leave this pop star alone. It's not real, you know. It's only made up.'

Indoors Pat washed her hands and put the kettle on for tea and then, after a guilty moment, took a tablet from the packet by the sugar-bowl and swallowed it dry. She'd lied to Howard – she hadn't taken her day's dose. In fact she had missed out several times before. It was something about tablets, and medicines of all kinds. Pat had ideas about naturalness. She wasn't fond of bathing for the same reason; and Jack used to say he liked her nice and natural, he preferred her that way . . . Howard, anyhow, would worry if he knew she wasn't taking her tablets, and she didn't want that, not after all he had been through.

Howard tapped on the kitchen window.

'I'm off down the shop then. Shan't be long.'

'All right, duck. See you soon . . . You be careful!' At the last moment she raised her voice urgently. To see him going off always caused a clutch at her heart since that terrible business with Colin Brudenell's van when the poor Springthorpe girl got hurt. Howard was so calm about things. He discounted danger. Probably he was right, now that the trouble seemed to have blown over, but Pat couldn't be quite easy in her mind when he was out and about.

She had felt terrible over what happened to the Springthorpe girl, though that was only part of a strange mixture of emotions, some not very nice. There was relief that it wasn't Howard who got hurt; there was a small twinge of jealousy about his spending so much time with her. Of course, she was too young for him, totally unsuited; but it did raise the question, what if Howard found a woman he wanted to be with?

Pat wanted him to very much: it was, as it were, her public policy statement that nothing would make her happier than to see Howard marry and settle down. But at the thought of it her heart laboured, and the future became dark.

She was putting the cosy over the teapot when there was a knock at the back door. Uncommon, almost unheard of in the years without Howard, when there had only been the official knock of the gasman or the insurance man at the front; but now it was beginning to happen again, people were becoming friendlier, even the two boys from across the road came round asking if they would sponsor them for a charity walk and had come right in and had a glass of lemonade while Howard put their names down . . . Better, so much better. Pat went to the door humming, opened it, and was flung back six feet against the kitchen wall before she had time to scream.

He was in. He slammed the door behind him and came at her where she was half-crouching against the wall with her head clanging like a gong from the impact. As her mouth opened his gloved hand came down and clamped over it.

'Shut it. Not a word.'

His voice was muffled by the balaclava he wore over his face and he was panting as if he had exerted himself to his last breath. He was wearing one of those camouflage jackets and it made her think of terrorists, but of course this wasn't Ireland

and she had nothing to do with Ireland and she knew, in her gut, who it was. Her mind was spinning and draining like water going down a plughole but Pat knew it all.

He twisted her round on the kitchen floor, nudging her in the back with his knees. Her joints were stiff from gardening and she lurched, nearly falling on her face. He yanked her up by the straps of her halter top.

'Kneel. Kneel there.'

She knelt, her breath whistling. She could imagine the scream she could give but couldn't achieve it somehow, it was like something in the house that was out of reach. Something hard and cold bumped the back of her head, then stayed there, pressing. It felt like a metal pipe.

'Oh, no.' Pat began to moan and pray. 'Oh no, please God no . . .'

'Shut it. You just shut it, there's nobody here to help you, it's just me.' His voice sounded hoarse and raspy and hollow, making her think of gas masks, but there was no mistaking the accent, the clipped harsh vowels. She started crying, though there was no identifiable emotion triggering this – it just came, a strange monkeylike gibbering.

'Oh, go on. Yeah, go on.' She felt the toe of his shoe – a trainer, she had glimpsed trainers – prod the small of her back. 'You do what you like. Makes no odds because you've had it.'

'Please,' she cried, though she didn't know quite what she was pleading for. She tried to be plucky and clever the way women were in those thrillers. 'My son will be home any minute, you'll be—'

'I know. I know about that, missus. That's it, you see. All falling into place . . . Don't turn round!'

He yelled that, making her whimper anew. She had just shifted her head a little because it was hurting where she had bumped it, hurting even more with that pipe pressed against her skull. Of course it wasn't a pipe but a gun. An oily smell; she knew. She was going to die in her kitchen, that was another thing she knew and that was an awful, unthinkable thing but perhaps in a way it was meant to happen.

But it would be Howard who found her here, and that was too terrible. That made her wail again.

'Yeah, that's it. Go on. Makes me laugh, that does, hearing that. About time really.'

She heard a scraunch and he shifted, and she realized he had pulled up a kitchen chair. He was sitting behind her, with the gun at the back of her head. And he was shaking: she could feel it.

'He'll know now, any road. He'll know what it's like to suffer and feel pain and cry and hurt – right bloody deep down inside.' His voice was wrenchingly emotional – not so very far from tears himself, she thought. On the edge: that was the feeling he gave off. Even the pitch of his voice, high and lifted, suggested someone shouting in the wind, on the edge of a precipice, hovering above some vast drop. 'That's what I want for him. Years and years of it. Feeling like that. Hurting. I'm not bothered about you. I want him hurting, do you see? Ah? D'you get it?'

'Don't. Oh, don't. It won't help you. I know what it is but it won't help you . . .'

'Oh, you stupid bitch, shut it.' he said, almost pettishly. 'You don't know. You've got no frigging idea, have you?' He gave a kind of spitting, sobbing cough. When he spoke again she could tell he had lifted the balaclava from his face. 'I don't give a toss about you. You had him. God help you, that's all I can say. I don't care, me. I'm past it. I've had it. I don't care, so long as he hurts. That's all I can— Don't look at me!'

'I wasn't, I wasn't.' She sang it out, octaves of despair. 'Oh, please, you don't have to. You could just go – you could – you could just go—'

'Shut it, that's it!' The chair crashed back and he was on his feet. The muzzle of the gun bored into her aching skull. Her head was wobbling and her mouth drooling as if she were senile. 'I'm going to do you, I'm not messing about . . .'

She heard a smooth noise like a ratchet. Her mouth was wide open but she couldn't get any breath through it. She waited.

Suddenly a bright light flooded into the room. Pat looked round in bewilderment. Through the kitchen window she could see the tomcat on the fence, poised to land and staring, caught in the act. It had triggered next door's security light. She glimpsed the man, his balaclava back, looking wildly about

272

him. Then the tomcat flattened its ears and leapt with an impetus that made the fence shake, landing with a scuffle in the flowerbeds.

The man darted to the window. There was something amateurish – it might even have been comic – about the way he suddenly remembered himself, dodging to one side of the window before peeping cautiously out. She could see the gun now. It was dark and shiny and new-looking. It looked no more or less real than any gun.

Another noise from next door, unmistakable: their back door opening.

It was as if panic were not a reaction but a natural state into which he could at last fall. His voice went high as a girl's and he moved on his toes in a kind of anguished dance.

'Jesus Jesus . . .' The whites of his eyes looked like a race-horse's, wild and strained. Then as his head turned Pat did something. If he was going to do it, it would be now, and it was all she could think of to save her life. She flung her hands in front of her eyes, pressed the palms tight against her cheeks.

'I'm not looking! I won't look!' she cried.

She felt him draw near her. She could have sworn she felt the muzzle of the gun lightly touching the ends of her hair on the crown of her scalp, like a fly. And then another noise – she knew it: Mr Mackay shifting the garden chair they used to prop open their back door – made him give a yelp that was exactly like a dog's and then a long, eerie crooning sound, with sadness in it and frustration and most of all an abysmal helplessness.

She kept her eyes covered, but risked speech.

'I'm sorry. I'm sorry,' she said.

Then something hit her with an explosion of pain and she went over on her side. Her face against the cracked lino, Pat experienced a moment of translucent wonder that a person like her should die from being shot. And then the pain localized and clarified and she realized he had kicked her in the ribs, kicked her only with a half-hearted force, and that the noises he was making now were tearful swearwords, like a wretched boy. A squeak of his trainers on the lino, a waft of cool air, the crash of the side gate. No more noises.

She didn't know how long she lay there, her back aching, her eyes closed tight. She knew he was gone: but her deliverance was a startling as the terror had been, and she couldn't yet grasp it.

From her position on the kitchen floor, she could see straight into the hall. Her eyes were level with the door of the little cupboard under the stairs. She stared at it and it seemed to throb back at her, almost as if there were a light pulsing behind its odd rhomboid shape. The light of the past.

She saw another time, and another man raging and wild, flinging open the cupboard door and pushing the squirming little figure inside. *If you're bad you get punished. Simple as that. Simple as that . . .*

The cupboard door closing. No sound from within. He always cried and protested as he was being put in; but once inside, nothing. No noise.

Such patience.

*Now we'll get some peace.* Voice husky from the exertion, panting: excited. And God forgive her, she would respond.

Pat ground her face against the floor and thought that Colin Brudenell should have done this, that he had not been hard enough on her . . . She closed her eyes: the shape of the cupboard door, a distorted lozenge, still pulsed behind her eyelids.

She could bear the pain, if only she could drive that shape away. Opening one eye, sobbing, she saw that the kitchen clock said five to seven. She thought of something: it was nearly time for her radio programme.

She pulled herself up to a kneeling position.

There was the news bulletin at seven and then her programme. It told the story of the Broadway musical, with excerpts from the shows, and old stars telling anecdotes. It was entertaining. Sometimes she missed it, but she wasn't going to miss it this evening. It was her programme.

She shuffled on her knees over to the worktop where her transistor radio stood. She felt rather like a child, reaching up and fumbling at the switches, her chin on the edge of the worktop. The radio wasn't tuned to the right station and she had a moment of panic: it must be quick, she must drive out the awful thoughts, she must have her programme . . . When she found the station she gave a sigh of contentment, though it came out like a moan.

She was kneeling there, listening to the story behind

*Jesus Christ Superstar*, when Howard came in.

'Mum! What's the matter? What are you doing?'

'I'm listening to my programme,' she said, almost with irritation, and it was only when he put his hand on her shoulder that she started crying.

He lifted her to her feet and half-carried her to a chair in the living room. It felt nice to be cared for like that. She felt everything was all right now. Howard was safe, thank God. The man had gone. Let it all lie.

'Is it your stomach? Shall I call a doctor?' Howard's face peered into hers. He had gone pale. 'What's up? Why's the gate open?'

'Don't fret, lovey. It's . . .' Shifting in the chair, Pat winced at the pain in her back.

'It is your stomach? That's it, I'm calling the doctor—'

'No!' She stopped him. 'It's not that, Howard. It isn't anything.'

'You tell me, Mum.' He drew himself up: he looked powerful and authoritative. 'Don't you hide it from me. Has somebody been here?'

For a while she couldn't stop crying, though the tears now were not so much tears of distress as of an almost passionate gratitude for his presence. He waited, watching her, until finally she told.

She didn't lie. But she told it as a thing that didn't greatly matter. And when she came to the end her tears were dry and her hands were grasping the arms of the chair, ready to head for the kitchen as she concluded, 'But any road, I'd better get the tea.'

He didn't glare at her – Howard had never done, would never do that – but his look was compelling. He placed his hands on her shoulders, keeping her down with the gentlest of pressure.

'What man, Mum?' His voice was quite soft. 'Did you see him? Did you know him?'

'Well, yes.' She couldn't lie to Howard – she didn't see how anyone could. She wiped her face. 'But it doesn't matter, because he's gone. He went, ducky, he went away of his own accord. And I don't think he'll come back, not from the way he—'

'It was that Brudenell man, wasn't it?'

Pat nodded.

'Right.' Howard's great chest rose and fell. 'Right.' And then, very slowly, he turned his back to her. It hurt her to see him doing that. And it frightened her. Because she knew he didn't want her to see his face.

Very rare, the occasions when straightforward Howard didn't want his mother to see his face. A new fear entered Pat: new, and as old as the years.

'What are you going to do, Howard?' she said.

'Why do you ask that?' he said, and she hardly recognized his voice.

'Well, because – I don't want any trouble—'

'You have to make trouble about a thing like this, Mum. Because it's wicked.'

'But that's it, Howard, I don't know whether it is really. Not in that way. He doesn't know what he's doing, you see.' She gazed at her son's great broad back. She had never been good with words but she tried, now, tried desperately. 'That's what I keep thinking. If somebody does something bad, but they don't really know what they're doing at the time, then it's different. You can't really call it wicked, because they can't help themselves. That's how I see it, Howard. Do you understand what I mean?'

'I understand.' Still not his voice.

'That man lost his baby, Howard. I know all the other things, I know, but I still have to remember that. He needs help because he's a danger to everybody and a danger to himself, really . . . It's not up to us. You know what Sergeant Hurst said. We were to get on to him straight away if anything else happened and let him deal with it. He'll know what to do – he's looking after things. Let's ring him, and leave it up to him, and try and forget about it. That's what the police are for—'

'The police?' He half turned, and she saw his snub profile. It looked grim, carved, gargoyle-like. 'What do they do? They don't protect you. It's all a lie. You can't rely on the law. It never stopped that man getting in here and hurting you. It's useless. Don't talk to me about the law, Mum. You have to do things yourself in this world.'

'All right. I see what you're saying, love, but – I sort of understand that man. You see, I've got you. Not to have you at all – to lose you like that – I couldn't have stood it, Howard, I know that. I would have gone mad, that's all there is to it. All those years without you – it was so terrible, Howard, and it made me understand a bit – all those years without you . . .'

After a fractional hesitation, he came and put his arms round her and hugged her, stiffly.

'It's all right, Mum,' he said. 'I'm here now.'

'And that's where I want you. Here with me, safe.'

'You've got to protect the people you love, though.' His voice was a profound vibration against her face. 'I've got to do that. Just like you did with me. You did it for me, Mum—'

'Oh, don't talk about that, lovey,' she said quickly; the cupboard door pulsed again in her mind.

'All right. But I can't forget.'

'Howard. I don't want any more trouble, any fuss and nastiness. I just want to carry on as we were.'

'It would be nice.' His tone was metallic. 'Aye, that would be nice.'

'We can carry on, duck. Believe me. He was trying to frighten us, that's all. He's long gone by now – I'd swear to it. He's sick. He needs help. We can't do anything. It's not up to us.'

Howard took a deep breath and released her.

'All right, Mum.' He nodded. 'Whatever you say. I think what I'll do is go into Ingelow first thing in the morning and talk to Sergeant Hurst myself. See if we can get this properly sorted.'

'That's good, lovey.' She hardly dared to let the relief in. 'That's the way. I could come with you.'

'No need, Mum. You let me sort it. You should rest up. After what you've been through – you need to take care of yourself.'

'Oh, I'm a tough old bird, me,' she said with a gurgling burst of laughter. 'I've seen plenty of things in my time. I can manage this, don't you worry.'

'I'll believe you. Thousands wouldn't. You should go the doctor's anyway, I reckon. You're hurt, aren't you? Tell me.'

'Just a bit of a bruise.' She put a tentative hand to her back.

'He didn't mean it though, Howard, he didn't know what he was doing—'

'Let's have a look.'

She peeled up her top and let him see. She heard his sharp intake of breath.

'They always look worse than they are,' she said. 'Any road, there's nothing a doctor can do, is there? Just have to wait for it to go down. Maybe a bit of that spray might help. The one I used when I had that shoulder. It sort of freezes it.'

'I'll get it.'

Pat sat down on the end of the settee. It was awkward holding her top up round her armpits, so she took it off and sat in her bra. She shuddered at the first icy touch of the spray on her bare back, but after a moment the penetrating sensation, like a kind of burning chill, was making her coo with relief.

'What about your shoulders? Is it hurting there?'

'Just a bit sore and stiff. Do a little bit, duck. Ta. Could you rub it in with your fingers? Oh, that's it. That's nice.' Pat closed her eyes. Everything faded and she felt she was being tenderly, nicely devoured and swallowed up. 'That's lovely, duck. Bit lower. Ooh. You've got a nice touch. Nice and patient.' She arched herself against his hands like a purring cat. 'You always take care of me.'

'I always will,' he said; and she was so cocooned in pleasure she hardly noticed his voice still wasn't his own, not really.

'Harder, lovey. Do it a bit harder.'

'I'd better not, Mum.'

'Harder.' The sound of her own voice surprised her. She opened her eyes a moment, swallowed. 'It's so nice, you see . . . so nice, don't stop . . .'

His hands were still. When he spoke she could feel the vibration through them.

'Dad was a bad man, wasn't he, Mum?'

'Oh, he was.' She wriggled against his hands, not really listening. 'He was terrible.'

'You stopped him, though. I remember that. You did it yourself.'

'Oh, don't think about that,' she said absently. So warm: like fire . . .

278

'That's what I thought.' The withdrawal of his hands was like her soul falling away. She suppressed a groan as he patted her bare shoulder. 'There you are, Mum. Don't get cold.'

Pulling on her top, her cheeks flaming, she said in a blurred way, 'It's all right, isn't it, Howard? Everything . . .'

'Everything's all right,' he said. He was just behind her, but curiously he sounded a long way off. 'Don't worry. It'll all be all right.'

# TWENTY-THREE

Rebecca hadn't told her father that she was staying at Adam's rather than at Uncle Denis' house. On the other hand, she hadn't actually said she was staying at Uncle Denis', so the sin was one of omission, if it was a sin. With what she now knew, that hardly seemed to matter. He knew, at any rate, that she was seeing Adam: helping him with secretarial work was how she put it in her brief phone call, and again it was the truth if not the whole truth. She had begun transcribing his taped interviews with Howard Gandy. It occupied her while he was out. Her father accepted it. He could hardly, she thought, do otherwise.

But after a few days she did take a brief trip over to Uncle Denis'. She wanted some earrings she thought she had left there, and while she was so near and had a key it seemed reasonable to check up on the house. Adam had gone down to Berkshire early that morning, chasing something to do with his Prince's Trust piece, which she gathered his commissioning editor was being picky about.

'The original piece followed six of these bright sparks. There isn't a really interesting story amongst them, so he wants to bring in this other guy at Windsor who has made a big splash. Set up a genuine English restaurant or something. Boiled cabbage presumably.'

He kissed her before he left. There was an awkwardness about this that the sex didn't have. They could go to bed together and they could work on his research together, but when they tried to weave everyday affection into their relationship it all came apart in their hands.

But then what did she expect, Rebecca asked herself as the tube train, obliging serpent, spirited her through its tunnels deep below the autumnal morning. She could ask confidently because she could answer confidently: nothing. She had sought refuge, and the refuge Adam had given her included his body. And perhaps, to a certain extent, his mind. She could hardly look to the future when even the past had become for her a void. Since her father's revelation she was outside the stream of time, moored only in moments.

And how admirably suited London was for this, she thought as she came out into the sunlight at Turnham Green. Here you could literally go to ground at any time, descending and surfacing somewhere else entirely. It cut a lot of things out. That was suitable too. She could hardly have cut more out of her life. It was fearfully reduced. No parents, no past; hardly even an identity. Such a curtailing should have felt clean, liberating. She kept trying to feel it.

Again the great clear mirror in the hall of her uncle's house took her by cringing surprise, just as it used to her mother. Rebecca turned to slip past it, then stopped and made herself look.

The face was supposed to give so much away. In books people's faces were always full of exhaustive expression, in films the camera close-up laid their souls bare. But Rebecca saw a mask. There was no suggestion of what had taken place inside her in the past few days. You could say there was a hollow starey look about the eyes, a harsh set to the mouth, but really they were only generic indicators that could mean anything. The body was, it seemed, a very loose-fitting cover for the soul.

There lay part of the reason why she had withdrawn so completely from her father after he had told her. In that blank, monumental rejection that she had turned to him and his story was an element of protest: how had she not known? How had such a poisonous secret not leaked out somewhere – broken out in disfigurements, Dorian Gray-style, on her parents' faces? That such deception was possible was almost as shattering as the news itself.

They had carried that secret with them: her mother to the grave, her father to that desperate whisky-charged evening. And now it was a secret that Rebecca would have to carry too. No personal guilt attached to it in her case, of course, yet still it was a knowledge that affected her very being, and the burden was heavy. No question of telling it, though: even before her father had finished speaking that night, her heart had entered into a contract of everlasting silence.

She knew she would keep it, too. She had no doubts at all of her capability. A lesson, then: what had at first seemed the hardest thing to comprehend was really the easiest. She could do as they had done. There was no alternative.

Rebecca turned away from the mirror; and in the last instant the mask did slip. She looked, simply, furtive.

She found her earrings in the bathroom. She checked quickly over the house, and didn't intend lingering; there was no sun today and the place had a musty bleak feel. But something made her stop in the dining room and pick up a little jade ornament, a carved elephant that she had never noticed before. It was an unlikely thing for Uncle Denis to have and, convinced at once that his ex-wife must have bought it, she began to think about her aunt. She had seldom seen her and all she knew about their divorce was that it had been acrimonious and suggestive of a venomous unhappiness in the marriage. She looked around her. In this house, love had failed, and a couple who were sworn to each other had torn messily apart. Yet in her parents' house, love had not failed, though the most extravagant test had been put on it.

It was beyond her – the whole thing. Telling herself she wouldn't, couldn't think about her mother, she had really thought about nothing else since that evening. She had even pictured the scenario her father described – yet always at some point, approximately when her mother turned from the French window with a child in her arms, her mind shut down. It came up instead with random memories of her mother – taking her to school, kneeling at the flowerbeds in the garden, brushing out her tremendous fall of hair, dying in the hospital.

Beyond her. She could feel her way, perhaps, around the moral dimensions. Her parents were not murderers to her. They had killed; they had been responsible for death; they had been caught up in a web of circumstances that had ended in death. The formula didn't matter. She had already decided that blame in that sense didn't apply. Instead she was frozen and where there had been love and trust and truth, impenetrable ice had descended.

She had told her father she wanted to find her birth mother, and the morning after arriving at Adam's she had written to an address he found for her in Stockport, something called the Adoption Contact Register: there should be no problems in tracing now, he said. And she had written the letter. But she hadn't phoned, surely the quickest way in. She was aware of it and felt Adam must be too. Maybe – though he was too kind to say it – this reaching out was a childish reflex, arms imploringly stretching for a cuddle.

Was he too kind to say something more? That her reaching out for him was the same reflex? But of course he didn't know what the estrangement from her father was really about, and he never would. He thought it was just a quarrel.

Yet perhaps he detected an artificial heat in the glow she gave off. Last night in bed, the aftermath of tumult had made her hold his face and say, 'I love you.'

He had smiled; kissed her. 'You're lovely,' he said.

Almost the same words: not much alteration. A fool might think they were the same.

She expected nothing, anyhow. Just as well: what, after all, could she expect of a man to whom she couldn't tell the truth – the very truth he was in quest of?

She was back at Adam's flat well before eleven – he had given her his spare key – and while she waited for the coffee to brew she slotted the disk into the computer and the second of Howard Gandy's interview tapes into the cassette player. She had learnt to ready herself for his voice, sounding so present in the room he might have been sitting at the desk with her. Its characteristic measured tones brought back to her all the injustice that had been heaped on him. She could only think of him as a literal martyr now, a garlanded sacrifice. Her strange fancy in the Appeal Court, that her father and Howard would be made part of some ruthless eye-for-an-eye exchange, had not been so irrational after all. She didn't know how she would be able to meet him again, look him in the eye. A different kind of ice had descended there.

She poured coffee and switched the tape on.

'I'm not saying I'm any better than anybody else. Just that I felt the same. I mean, I love kids, that's what I'm all about. And when I heard I thought how absolutely dreadful it was. Something like that – it's just not right.'

She paused the tape while her typing caught up. Even in a few days she'd become a proficient two-finger typist, though her lack of absolute skill was frustrating. When she switched on again there were a few seconds of murmurous silence, then the faint sound of Howard stirring in his chair and clearing his throat.

'Terrible for the parents – I suppose everyone was thinking of that. I know Mum kept saying that and I thought so too. Even though I'm not a parent, I could feel what it must be like for the mum and dad, and the lady who found him, and the police and everybody – the whole thing was terrible. You couldn't think about it really. That's why it's so – well, staggering, finding yourself being accused of that thing. You're just like in a state of shock . . .'

The entryphone buzzer sounded. Rebecca paused the tape and got up. She wondered what she would do if this were Angela.

'Hello.'

'Hi. This is Mark Wapshott. I need to see Mr Dowling urgently.'

She had asked him up and pressed the button before the difference in the voice, the oddness of the words struck her. She had a moment of alarm at her cool confidence in herself as Adam's stand-in: had it led her to make some stupid, even dangerous mistake? Opening the flat door cautiously, she found nothing suspicious about the plump, balding, besuited man she saw – except for the fact that he wasn't the man she had seen here before.

She said, 'You're not Mark Wapshott.'

'That's precisely what I am,' the man said, and he sighed. 'I suppose I'll have to do this.' He held out a passport. 'Wait a second, I've got my driving licence as well . . .'

Bewildered, she looked at the documents. They were real enough, and she recognized the address from Adam's files. She met the man's eyes.

'I don't understand,' she said.

'Is Mr Dowling in?'

'No. I'm his assistant. I'm sorry, I really don't understand. I mean, I met Mark Wapshott when he – this man came here to do an interview—'

'Yes, so I've found out. May I come in?'

She offered him coffee but he refused, perching uncomfortably on the edge of a chair. With the suit he might have been some visiting salesman – except for his manner, nervous yet downright. His high forehead glistened with perspiration.

'The name of the man who came here is Carl Nettles. He's a friend of mine.' He frowned at the cassette player, the blinking VDU. 'I've got to clear this up but I've also got to ask whether it's in complete confidence. It is flaming embarrassing, as you've probably guessed.' Awkwardly he folded his short arms across his chest. 'If you can just give me your assurance, on behalf of Mr Dowling. He's a journalist apparently.'

'Oh, certainly – I mean, I can speak for Adam there. He always protects his sources unless it's agreed otherwise.'

He grunted. 'I've been away for the past three months. Sweden, on a business trip. Carl – the man who came here – was living at my flat during that time. Usher Street, North Acton?'

'That's the address Adam wrote to.'

He nodded. 'Well, Carl's been living there. This was something I didn't know about.' His eyes challenged her. 'Anyway, as a result he got hold of my mail, including letters from Mr Dowling. I've seen them now – asking me if I'd talk to him about a man I once knew back in Ingelow when I was young. Gandy. For some book about this character. I wouldn't, by the way, have responded myself. However, Carl did, posing as me, I suppose because he saw something in it for himself. I understand there was a cheque?'

Rebecca nodded. His composed correctness was both awful and impressive to see.

'Well. That would be it. I suppose he thought he'd have a go. He's also a person who likes playing games, harmless ones as he sees them. I must ask you what it was he said at that interview. I've got it out of him, what he said, but it's entirely possible he's lying to me. Obviously, that's a thing he does.' His gaze was steady, and now it was almost as if he took a proud, baleful pleasure in this self-exposure.

'Well, he – Adam had heard about a boy called Mark Wapshott who knew Howard Gandy well, years ago in Ingelow, and he wanted some background. The man – your friend said, basically, he remembered him, Howard was like an older brother to him, helped him learn to swim, things like that . . .'

Mark Wapshott had closed his eyes and was nodding. 'Well, he could do it easily enough. I had told him all about that part of my childhood. I told him practically everything about myself, to be honest,' he said, laughing unhappily. 'We had a relationship. Not a great one. A bit one-sided, if you see what I mean. He was living with me up until shortly before I left for Sweden, when I threw him out. There was – no help for it. And put it this way: I didn't think he'd have any problem finding a bed. You met him – you've seen what he's like. Quite the Adonis.'

'Yes. I – actually I thought he looked familiar, but I still can't think . . .'

'Well, he's done a bit of modelling in his time. But not really the sort you see on billboards.' He frowned. 'More, er, for a particular scene.'

With that word Rebecca remembered. It came instantaneously. That startlingly explicit leaflet from the Aids Action office, with its straining godlike men. That was where she had seen Mark Wapshott: not in the flesh but in photographs that had lingered starkly in her memory.

Except, of course, that wasn't Mark Wapshott. This plain, unhappy, dignified man was.

'Anyway, I expected that to be the end of it. Then last night I got home from my trip, a few days early as it happened. Found Carl in my flat. Very much at home.' He looked sick. 'Not expecting me, of course. When I threw him out I'd taken his key back. But it turns out he'd had another one cut. Oh, he tried to brazen it out, said he was looking after the place for me, said he thought we could try again when I got back . . . Pathetic really. He obviously hadn't lacked for company in there.' He cleared his throat. 'This isn't easy for me, Miss . . .'

'Rebecca. I'm sorry.'

'So. He'd opened my letters. Found the ones from your Mr Dowling. Saw an opportunity. He'd say what your man wanted to hear, of course: he's good at that. There it is. I'm afraid your

Mr Dowling's been made a fool of, as well as me. I won't apologize as it wasn't my fault. But I regret what's happened, as he's wasted his time and money. I dare say he never suspected anything like this. I can give him a forwarding address for Carl if he wants to try and get his money back. Not my address obviously; I've got shut of him for good this time.' His lips were tight as he got up.

'I don't suppose Adam'll worry about that. I know he'd want to apologize for this inconvenience—'

'Not his fault either.' Mark was stumping towards the door. 'He wasn't to know.'

'You said you wouldn't have responded anyway,' Rebecca said, stopping him. 'Is there no chance you would talk to Adam, you know, with the real story?'

He studied her, then shrugged. 'Not a lot of point, I don't think. Not for this book he's doing. I mean, this is some rehabilitation job, isn't it? I gather Gandy got out of prison from some child charge and your Mr Dowling's writing up his case as a miscarriage of justice. This is what Carl said.'

'That's right.'

'Well, I didn't know Gandy had been in prison. We moved away from Lincolnshire when I was ten, and I never heard anything about him in the news, or it didn't click if I did. It was just his first name I thought of, if I thought of it. Howard the swimming-pool man. I preferred not to think about it actually.' His gaze went pensively to the window. 'Pretty smart of your man to trace me. Apparently some other boy who used to go to the pool in Ingelow remembered me.'

'Yes. He said you and Howard were very close.'

'Close? Is that what it seemed like? Hm. Well, as I said, I didn't know he'd been in prison. But it's no big surprise. I loved swimming as a kid. It was the only thing I had, in a way. I don't mean that to be maudlin. I was chubby and not very sure of myself. Kids take the mick, you know. But with swimming I was in my element. Nothing could keep me away from that pool. Well, he did in the end.'

'You mean Howard?'

'Who else? He was the attendant. Fantastic swimmer. A lot of the kids liked him. But he was just friendly with them. Me he wouldn't leave alone. He was always looking at me. He kept coming into the changing room, wanting to know if I was all right, wanting me to play cricket after. He was – well, look, I was only eight or so. But kids pick up on a vibe. It wasn't right. It was like an obsessive lover.' He grimaced. 'He didn't do anything to me, maybe, nothing that he could be done for. You could call it *romping*, at a pinch.' He put a terrible, soft emphasis on the word. 'He'd try and get you to join in these games. Wrestling. And I remember . . . in the changing room once. He got me on my own, and said did I want to know how to play squash. I said yes, trying to please him. So he put me in a corner and squashed me up against the wall with his body. He was laughing. There you are, squash, he said. I don't know.' He shook his head. 'Harmless? Maybe. All I know is I didn't like it. But he would go on at me if I let on I didn't like these things. Spoilsport, not playing, he'd say. Anyway, I stopped going to the pool. My dad asked me why and I came out with it, sort of. My dad said I should join in games and said I was a sissy. This is a word he was rather fond of.'

Rebecca opened her lips, about to say *I can't believe it*. But it wasn't a matter of belief: not these words, not this look. Her mind was shying at an unthinkable fence.

'I wouldn't go back to that pool, anyway. I swam in the sea when it was warm enough. It wasn't the same. He took that from me, Howard the swimming-pool man. I don't feel kindly towards him for that alone. Maybe that's daft.' He opened the door. 'Anyway, I don't think I'd have anything to tell Mr Dowling that he'd want to hear. Not if this Gandy's the good guy. Sorry. Like I said, kids know.' His eyes assessed her. 'I mean, what I hated most about squash was that he liked it so much. Plainly.'

Twelve years alone in this house, mistrusted and ostracized, was enough to turn anyone into an eccentric, Pat thought. And perhaps over those years she had picked up some strange ways. She felt that people often looked askance at the clothes she wore and commented on her habit of walking along grass verges and in the gutter rather than on the pavement. And they very probably suspected her of being one of those ladies who tippled sherry all day behind the net curtains.

Well, this morning she was tippling sherry. But the bottle

had a layer of dust on it and she thought, though she wasn't sure, that it came from last Christmas. Which proved that she didn't make a habit of it. She was only drinking it now because this was an emergency. She needed it to stop herself crying. Unfortunately it didn't seem to be working, and after the fourth glass she was leaning her elbows on the kitchen table and wailing into her cupped hands.

It wasn't because of what had happened yesterday, not directly. In the small hours she had had a nightmare, but it was a silly thing of monsters and goblins and she woke more in confusion than fear.

The fear began when she got up to go to the bathroom and noticed the light in the transom above Howard's door. Peeping in, she had found him not in bed at all, but sitting up in the old wicker nursing chair by his bed, fully clothed.

'Yes, Mum, I'm all right, I'm reading.'

'You sure, lovey? Sure you're all right?'

A nod. 'You go back to bed.'

Chilled, she did so.

But he wasn't reading: he had no book or paper. He was just sitting there with the light on, looking at the wall. And somehow – though she nodded off again towards dawn and woke to hear him in the bath – she knew that he had sat like that all night and it terrified her.

It was a grey clouded morning with little to be said for it, but he was whistling as he washed his breakfast bowl. He turned to her smiling, his big pink hands bristling with suds.

'Well, I'd best get ready. Going to Ingelow today, like I said. Have a proper talk with Sergeant Hurst. I thought after that I'd pop in the Job Centre. Maybe trawl round the cafés and hotels and places like that, see if there's any jobs going.'

She said, short-breathed, 'I'll come with you.'

'Oh, that'd be a lovely day out for you, wouldn't it, I don't think,' he chuckled. 'No, no. You stop here and rest up. I shall be back before tea.'

'Rest up. I'm not that old,' she said, watching him.

'No. You've had a bit of an upset, though.'

'Oh, that. That's over. It's done with. That's the only way to look at it. Life goes on. It's right, isn't it? You still agree about that, lovey, don't you? I'm not being silly. I'm being sensible.'

'Like I say, Mum. It's up to you. You come first with me, always have, always will.'

Pat waved him off to the bus stop. She knew he wasn't telling the truth, even before she looked in the old cake tin and saw that the ten-pound note, saved for this week's electricity meter cards and TV stamps, was gone. And that was when she went to the glass-doored cupboard in the kitchen and reached to the back and pulled out the bottle of sherry.

The stuff about the Job Centre and the cafés and hotels didn't ring true either. Yesterday when she had mentioned Coupland's he had been quite definite that he wanted to wait and see if he got the leisure centre job he'd set his heart on. No, it was a lie: she knew. Mothers knew. She didn't even believe, now, that he would see Sergeant Hurst. She had swallowed that because she wanted to believe it.

A lie. But Howard would only lie to her if it were something he wanted to protect her from knowing. Something dangerous.

Colin Brudenell lived in Nottingham. She didn't know where, but she was sure Howard did. There had been all that correspondence with Mr Jameson about the injunction against him, and Howard was very methodical. He would know.

Pat seldom went on a train and wasn't sure of the prices, but she doubted that ten pounds would be enough for a return ticket to Nottingham, and she knew he had no other money on him beyond small change. But there were regular coaches to Nottingham from Ingelow bus station, for the trippers, and they were cheap.

Suppose he had gone to have it out with Colin Brudenell, then was that necessarily a bad thing? Howard was steady, not hasty, after all, and maybe if they did meet face to face they might talk, sort things out, come to some kind of truce . . .

Pat slopped more sherry into her glass and drove down a sob with her fist. Who was she kidding? Colin Brudenell was a wild man, a man who had a gun . . .

And as for Howard – could she deny any more that look she had seen in his eyes? Not a new look. The old look. She had prayed that she wouldn't ever see it again: that twelve years' punishment was enough and it would be over.

The old look.

She got up from the kitchen table, clattering the chair back.

She couldn't bear this. Perhaps the sherry had been a bad idea, because she had such dreadful thoughts – or rather they had her. They fastened on her like clinging bats, dreadful thoughts from dark hidden places, poison in their bite.

Pat ran from the house. When the hard slap of the garden path beneath her feet alerted her to the fact that she was still wearing her slippers, she only sobbed again and went faster, staggering and almost falling as she swung the gate heavily behind her. She had to do something but she was useless – she gave herself a slap on the behind and she actually meant it, wanted it to hurt – she was quite useless and she had to have help. It was what she had always needed, she thought, some sort of guidance, a strong arm to keep her right and good . . .

Coming out of Hythe Avenue into Holfleet High Street, Pat nearly collided with a bundled-up woman walking a collie dog. The woman drew her face away frowning. The dog barked at Pat, lunging to the end of its lead, dancing two-legged. She stumbled to the kerb, then looked around her with swimming eyes.

'Oh please, God help me,' she said aloud, and then it seemed to her, perhaps for the second time in her life, that he listened. A silver car slowed and then drew up alongside her and Philip Springthorpe wound down his window and spoke with quizzical concern.

'Pat? Are you all right?'

In the young mind of Jake Brudenell, the man he sometimes called Daddy and sometimes Colin was a kind of stupendous force of nature, unpredictable and not to be questioned. The matter of the names typified it. In Jake's small memory there were intimations that there had once been another daddy, and that he himself hadn't always had this second name that was hard to get his tongue round. But Colin, Daddy, insisted he have this name and would make him practise it. It was just one of the many mysterious diktats laid upon the uncomprehending child, who simply obeyed because not obeying made trouble.

The trouble mystified him because sometimes it was big and sometimes it was small. He could never tell. But that was how it was with Daddy. He even felt quite close to Daddy, because Daddy got upset quickly, cried, then got better and laughed, in a way that other grown-ups didn't seem to. In fact Jake had a shadowy idea of his stepfather as a child like himself, except big and powerful.

So it seemed quite natural that Daddy should be at home with him in the day, while Mummy went to work. Quite natural, even though Jake was sometimes scared. If Daddy drank that whisky, for example, he would get red in the face and shout if Jake made too much noise. Today, though, wasn't like that. His daddy hadn't had any whisky – just a long messy cigarette that smelt funny and that had been given him that morning by Big Jimmy. And it hadn't made him shout at all. He was quite quiet and slow and not banging about as he did sometimes. He had even given Jake a kiss on the top of the head as he sat him down in front of the TV and switched the morning cartoons on.

Jake was glad Big Jimmy hadn't stayed long, though. He knew the tall thin man with hardly any hair was his daddy's friend, but he didn't like it when he came round. He felt that Mummy wouldn't like it, either, but Big Jimmy only came when she was at work. He scarcely said anything, he just looked scary. Usually he brought things in his car, things in boxes, and Daddy would put them away in the garage. He had told Jake that he must never, ever look at those things. Which made Jake wonder.

He wondered too about the object wrapped up in a handkerchief that Daddy kept carrying around this morning. He guessed it was a thing given to him by Big Jimmy too, because it was so secret. Daddy had only got it out after Mummy had gone to work, and now he kept wandering around the house with it, murmuring to himself. Jake knew better than to stare, but from little peeps he could see what was going on. First Daddy had put the wrapped-up thing into a drawer in the sideboard that had a lock on it. Then he walked about and shook his head and got it out again. Next he went into the toilet. Craning his neck, peeping, Jake could just see him lifting the top of the cistern and putting the wrapped-up thing in there. But soon Daddy was pacing around and snapping his fingers and in the end he fetched it out of there, too.

It was strange – but not very strange. Jake liked to have

hiding places for things too. It was a secret, no doubt, and Jake understood those. Yesterday, when Mummy was at work, Daddy had taken him to Sonia's and left him there for the day and told him that that was a secret he must never tell Mummy about. He had gone somewhere – that was all Jake knew, and all he expected to know. Jake breathed secrets.

Still, Jake was curious about what that thing could be, so carefully wrapped up like that.

Suddenly the cartoon on the TV screen disappeared into a wobbling fuzz. It was always doing that. Daddy was good, though, at fixing it, like most things.

'Daddy!'

'What's up?' His daddy came out of the kitchen, the wrapped-up thing still in his hand.

'Telly's gone funny.'

His daddy sighed and came over and knelt down by the TV set. He put the wrapped-up thing on the floor near where Jake was sitting. Opening the front panel of the TV set, his daddy began patiently to twiddle the tiny wheel-like knobs.

'It's a nuisance, is this. This telly's out of the ark, you know. Don't even make 'em like this any more. I shall get us a new one some day, Jake. With a great big screen and a video built in and stereo speakers. Would you like that?'

'Yeah!' Jake watched with interest as shadowy pictures appeared and disappeared through the screen of snow. Then his eye strayed to the wrapped-up thing. His hand stole towards it. Daddy was concentrating on the TV.

Jake's fingers grasped a corner of the handkerchief and, very carefully, lifted it.

'Leave it!'

His daddy yelled the words. His big hand slapped Jake's, hard. Jake drew his stinging fingers back, and started crying.

'Serves you right!' His daddy had scooped up the wrapped-up thing and was holding it tightly to his chest. His face was red and his eyes glared. 'You're not to touch that, ever, ever, do you hear me?'

'You hurt me, Daddy . . .' Jake couldn't control his crying; it just gushed out of him.

'Well, that'll teach you, then. When will you be told?' His daddy was trembling all over. Then all at once the frown on his face changed. It almost looked as if he would cry too. 'Here. Give us your fingers.'

Jake did so. His daddy held them gently, looking at them. Then he kissed them.

'There. All better. You're all right . . . You know I wouldn't hurt you, don't you, Jake? Not really?'

Jake nodded, his sobs subsiding.

'I know I lose my rag. I don't mean it. I just get so . . .' His daddy gave a kind of groan. 'But I'd never hurt you. I wouldn't hurt anybody.' He went on softly, looking into the dancing snow of the TV screen: 'I know that for sure. When it comes down to it – it just isn't in me. Couldn't do it . . . I don't know. Maybe it's all for the best . . .'

They both jumped as there was a knock at the door.

'No rest for the wicked,' his daddy said, getting up. 'I'll do that telly in a minute, matey. Hold on.'

Looking round, Jake saw a tall figure through the frosted glass of the hall door. He thought it must be Big Jimmy. He turned away, not wanting to look at that scary man.

But when the stranger came in, Jake just had to look again. It wasn't Big Jimmy. This man was huge, round, *big* in a way he had only seen in cartoons. And while Big Jimmy was his daddy's friend, it was plain to Jake, seated on the carpet and watching with wet open lips, that this man was not. He had just pushed his way in and was continuing to push his daddy now, coming on like a great unstoppable machine, delivering each push with a precise pressure of his broad pink-palmed hands on his daddy's chest. And they were shouting: or rather, his daddy was.

'You can't come in here! What the— You can't come marching in here! What the hell do you think you're doing?'

'I know what you did.' The big man's voice was much quieter, though deep, an inward rumble that made Jake's hairs prickle. Jake thought of the word *giant*, with all its terrible thrill.

'Get off me! Get out of it. I've done nothing—'

'You can have a go at me all you like. But not my mum. That's different.'

'I didn't hurt your mum . . .' His daddy was backed up against the settee, a few feet from Jake. His face was red, as it often was, but it looked somehow different. Jake's stomach wobbled as he realized that his daddy, that powerful figure, was terrified. He still had that wrapped-up thing in his hand, Jake noticed; it was behind his back, slightly digging into the upholstery as he shrank away. 'You mad bastard, you get out of my house right now. You can't do this—'

'You'll never come near my mum again. Do you hear?' The giant's voice got louder, and his fist went up, right above his head, poised like a great hammer above the smaller man. 'Do you hear me?'

The fist was going to come down in a great arc into his daddy's face: Jake's eager young brain sketched the pattern for him, and it paralysed him with terror.

'Now get out!' His daddy's hand came round from the settee, and the wrapping partially fell away from the thing he had there. Jake saw the dull dark muzzle, dimly comprehending. 'You've got three seconds! Yeah? It's loaded, man. I'll do it. I'll shoot you. I'll frigging kill you, like you killed my baby boy . . .! Yeah? I should have done it twelve year ago . . .'

Jake saw what happened next; it was quite slow and clear. The giant wrapped his huge hands right around his daddy's, forcing the muzzle of the half unwrapped gun upward till it pointed at the ceiling. And while his daddy went redder and redder in the face and made noises of exertion, the giant drove him bodily towards the wall of the living room, until his daddy was absolutely *squashed* between the huge round body and the wall. His shoulder struck a picture which fell off and smashed on the floor. In the clutches of the giant he looked small, small like Jake.

'Get off . . .' His daddy's voice was high, sounding like a squealing pig. 'Get off me, oh God please . . .'

The giant hands still encased the smaller ones in a unbreakable grip. Juddering, they bent the gun back and back until it was pointing right under his daddy's nose. His daddy's voice went higher and higher. Then Jake yelped and jumped at the flash and the bang. They hurt his ears and his eyes and made him put his hands over his face as he burst out crying. An exploding hole had appeared in the top of his daddy's head, which had gone back with a bouncing jerk like a kicked football. Jake had seen it, and all he could do was scream the world down.

'He was a bad boy anyway,' the giant said, puffing a little. Jake's hands came away from his face, curled like claws, and he saw the giant too lifting his hands away with a backward step, so that his daddy fell in a red smeared heap, straight down. 'He was a bad boy, he wouldn't play. So he had to take his punishment. Same as anybody else.' The giant looked down at the bundle at his feet, which part of Jake's screaming brain had already reclassified as a thing that was no longer his daddy. 'A bad boy. I didn't like him.' After a long moment the giant drew his shirtsleeve across his brow, sniffed and turned round. He looked at Jake with eyes that seemed to crinkle at the sides, as if in cheerful recognition.

He said, 'Well now. Do *you* want to play?'

After Mark Wapshott had left, Rebecca went back to her seat at the computer. She tasted her coffee and found it cold. On the desk, amongst others, was a cardboard file containing the transcripted interview with the man they had thought was Mark Wapshott. It was hard even now to think that it was completely worthless.

She felt sharply uneasy. After a paralysed moment she picked up the phone and dialled the number of Adam's mobile. No answer: he was probably interviewing in Windsor. With some irritation she hung up. This was something he needed to know. It threw a whole new light on the case – though a light that made no more sense than sunshine at midnight. Mark Wapshott wasn't lying, she was certain of that. Yet the picture he painted of Howard Gandy was nothing like the Howard she knew; or at least, the Howard who was being put together from these files and researches. Of course, memory by its nature was selective. Maybe Mark's was distorted, discoloured by time.

She was staring at her typed words on the VDU but wasn't conscious of reading them. The phrase that kept running through her mind – *the lady who found him* – might have been a snatch from a song or an advertising slogan, a random item from the mind's stockroom. But she read them over again dully.

They didn't make sense either.

She pressed the rewind on the tape recorder. She must have made an error of transcription, that was all. She sat back and listened again to the eerily present voice of Howard Gandy.

'. . . the mum and dad, and the lady who found him, and the police and everybody. . .'

Rebecca snapped the cassette player off. Her heart gave a thump that seemed to jolt it downwards in her body to somewhere about the level of her stomach. On the screen the restless cursor winked at her.

She began to hunt amongst the files for the first chapters of Adam's book, already printed out in draft copy. He had been correcting them just yesterday, but they seemed to have disappeared; and when she found the folder her shaking fingers almost dropped the lot on the floor. The passage she wanted, though, leaped to her eye after only a few moments.

*And it was not long after this – at 8.59 p.m. – that two police officers found what everyone had been dreading to find. The dead body of Lee Brudenell was discovered in shallow water at the outfall known as Tetby Haven.*

Just in case Adam had made a mistake, she checked the file of contemporary press cuttings. They all stated as a matter of record that the child's body had been found by two policemen. She even found a copy of the officers' statements to Ingelow Magistrates' Court, describing how they had found the body.

What, then, did Howard mean by 'the lady who found him'? He couldn't have been unaware of the details of the case, when he had been at the centre of it throughout the investigation, the interrogation, the trial. If it was a slip, it was a very strange one, especially from someone as precise as Howard. She wondered why Adam hadn't noticed it.

But then Adam was a man with a theory, and a mission. And as such, perhaps he only took notice of facts that supported it – rather than blew it apart.

Rebecca felt as if she had swum out into a calm blue sea and looked round to find the beach out of sight and the waves heaving about her. She tried ringing Adam again, and could have screamed when she heard the voice asking her to try again later.

It wasn't Adam she needed to speak to most, though. All her thoughts arrowed towards someone else. But talking to him, on any level but that of their last frozen exchanges, was going to be difficult. Her doubts were tinged with wistfulness. She didn't just need to speak to her father: she wanted to talk to him. Different things.

She switched on the cassette player once more. Howard's gruff tenor spoke into the room again, telling of the horror of being accused. Rebecca found she couldn't bear to listen to it. She turned it off and sat with her eyes closed, not so much thinking as letting down the barriers to thought. What marched in was an invader of appalling aspect. But it stood fast, in all its grotesque panoply, and would not be moved.

'Oh Christ,' she murmured aloud, and an instant later the telephone rang.

'Hello.'

'Hi, is . . . Rebecca?'

'Dad! Hi!' Her limbs felt liquid with relief simply at hearing his voice: she hadn't known how much she'd missed it.

'I was trying to reach Adam. I . . . Is he there?'

'No. He's left me working here,' she said, skimming over it. 'I don't know when he's going to be back. Anyway, it's . . . nice to hear from you.'

'You too. Are you all right, you know, with everything?'

'I'm OK. I was wanting to ring you actually. There's something I really need to— It's to do with what you told me. About Mum.'

'Maybe it's best not to talk about it.' The constriction in his voice was light, unmistakable. 'The thing is, the reason I'm ringing – I've got someone here with me. It's Pat Gandy. She's in quite a state. I bumped into her in the High Street and I asked her in because – well, she's really in a state about Howard and I'll have to do something.'

He lowered his voice at the end, and Rebecca caught in the background a sound of inarticulate sobbing.

'What about Howard?'

'Well, he's gone out for the day and Pat's convinced he's lying about where. She thinks he's gone to Nottingham, to see

Colin Brudenell. To – well, have it out with him. She's frightened. Apparently Brudenell's been hanging around again and gave her a nasty shock. She thinks Howard's flipped out over it and gone to – sort him out, I suppose. She's sure of it. It does sound like trouble . . .'

Pat Gandy's voice suddenly came into focus, slurred with tears but loud and shrill with conviction. 'I don't want any more. I can't stand any more. No more upsets. It's got to stop and he's got to stop. Somebody's going to get hurt and there's been too much of that.'

'OK, I'm really going to have to help with this. Pat wants to go to Nottingham and try to stop him. She reckons Howard must have gone by bus. It's a slow route so we won't be far behind if I drive her over there now. She can't rest and –' Rebecca didn't know whether this was for Pat's benefit – 'I must say I can't blame her. But she doesn't know where the Brudenells live, which is why I was ringing Adam.'

'The address is in these files. Hang on.' New horrors were marching in now, more than she could face. She found the address and gave it to her father, adding quickly, 'If it sounds like trouble, don't you think it'd be best to call the police?'

'I will ring Sergeant Hurst and let him know what's going on. To be on the safe side.' He paused: Pat's muttering voice faded in the background. 'To be honest, Rebecca, I think it's probably nothing to worry about. But it's best to be on the safe side.'

'Yes. Oh, yes, don't be sure of anything . . . Dad.'

'What's wrong?'

'Oh, Dad . . .' She wished she were in the same room as him: this was intolerable. 'What I needed to talk to you about . . . Mum, and that day. I've got to get it right in my mind.'

'No, love.' He was very gentle. 'Don't. It's been said, it's out and there's nothing to do but leave it. Don't do this to yourself—'

'It's important, Dad, really. I'm not – thinking in the way I was before. I've found some things out here and I've got to tell you . . .' She sucked in a sharp breath as if tasting vinegar. 'I don't think Mum killed Lee Brudenell.'

There was a breathing silence.

'Rebecca, you shouldn't do this—'

'Dad, I think he was already dead. I'm serious. You said Mum was vague and said she'd found him alone in the woods. Was she ever more clear about that? She didn't know what she was doing. She was half-crazy with grief.'

'This is—'

'This is what I need to know. Because I've learnt some stuff that makes me think that maybe Lee wasn't alive when Mum brought him home. Maybe what she found was the little boy's body, and brought it home in her arms, and what happened after that . . . well, it couldn't hurt him. Think about the state she was in, Dad. Thinking of Thomas. Her dead little boy. And there, lying there in the woods – what could she do but bring him home . . .?'

From her father there was silence, but from Pat there was a low, crooning groan, a cadence of lament. And when he finally spoke his voice had something of the same quality.

'Oh God, this is . . . I can't talk about this now. It's too much.'

'Think about it, Dad. Just think about it. It's in the tapes, something that doesn't add up—'

'I can't think about it. Not now.' He sounded very far away, almost a spirit voice. 'Rebecca, I can't. Look, Pat's desperate. I'd better get going. We'll have to . . . I don't know when I'll see you.'

'Soon,' she said. 'I'm coming home soon.' She hesitated. 'I was anyway.'

After a charged moment he said, almost harshly, 'God bless. I'm going to have to go now. I'll ring you later.'

He was gone. She listened to the tone for three seconds and then dialled and asked for a taxi to take her to King's Cross immediately.

Pat was feeling very sick from the sherry, and she would have asked Philip to slow down or even stop the car if the sickness had not been overridden by an anxiety so powerful it subjugated her body entirely. Indeed it seemed little short of some psychic force, for out of that same anxiety she had willed a swift chariot to take her to Nottingham and here it was. And she was glad of Philip too. He was a calm man who made no fuss, not like Jack who would have gone to pieces at a time like this . . .

'I don't know where it is,' she said in renewed alarm, as she realized they were in the suburbs of Nottingham. 'I don't know Nottingham at all. I don't know where it would be . . .'

'I know where the Hernmoor estate is,' Philip said. 'I'll find my way there and then we'll ask someone.'

'You shouldn't be doing this for me,' Pat said in a burst of maudlin gratitude.

'Why not?'

'You've done enough for Howard already.' She couldn't say any more.

Her chariot took her expertly round a ring road, across a flyover that gave a view of lowering clouds brutally kissed by a cityscape of towers and factory chimneys. It was fast but not fast enough, for the pressure of loving despair inside her peaked again and she had to gasp out, 'He took his punishment, you see. That was enough, enough for anybody. It's got to stop now. Anyone can see that, surely?'

'It'll be all right, Pat. We don't know for sure that's where Howard's gone. I'm sure it can all be sorted out. Now, this looks like it . . .'

The housing estate was an old-fashioned island in the midst of booming new roads, and they made its low-roofed pebble-dashed semis look slightly out of scale, like a film set. The streets were laid out, postwar style, in crescents and long broad curves; but there seemed to be no one about as there would have been in the old days, Pat thought – no gossiping mothers, little children on trikes. No one to ask for directions. It was too much to hope, of course, that they would see Howard himself, making his dogged way along these endless streets . . .

'Hello,' Philip muttered, as he swung the car round another bend. 'What's this?'

This was the place. Pat didn't need to read the street sign. Three police cars and an ambulance were drawn up outside a house halfway down the street, and here no one was hidden away in their burrows. Everyone was milling about and talking and pointing, pointing at that house. Pat felt her scalp crawl as if someone had laid a malicious hand across it.

'Oh my God, what's happened?' She was out of Philip's car

before it had stopped moving. 'I knew it, I knew it . . .'

He caught her up and took her arm. She needed that because her legs were like soft rubber and when they came up to the ring of goggling people she couldn't get any words out. It was Philip who asked.

'Bloke's gone and killed himself,' a scraggy young woman said, wide-eyed. 'Yeah! I had the vacuum on, I just thought it was a car or something, but my husband heard it, this terrific bang. Shot himself. Course, they won't tell you.' She nodded at the police constable standing foursquare at the garden gate, talking into a radio. 'Brian next door, he peeped in. Shot himself, blood everywhere.'

'Who is it?'

'Whatsisname. Always got the police round here. Colin, Colin and Wendy.' She pointed. 'Look – that's her. Oh, my Christ.'

As she pointed there was a commotion at one of the police cars and Wendy Brudenell broke away screaming from the frantic arms of two WPCs. She ran towards the house, yelling incoherently. Saliva trickled down her chin. She was wearing a pink work overall. The policeman at the gate stopped her deftly, steered her backwards with locked arms.

'No, love, I'm sorry, not yet, you just can't. Now you go with these officers, please, and we'll sort things out here . . .'

'Where is he? Where is he?' Wendy's voice was a ragged screech that seemed to scorch her throat: Pat was reminded, crazily, of the way girls used to scream at the Beatles, especially when the WPCs half-lifted her away with her feet dragging and stumbling. 'Where is he? What's he done with him?'

Philip questioned the policeman. 'Can you tell us what's going on? This is Mrs Gandy. She thinks her son may have been here. Howard. He had an injunction against Colin Brudenell, Colin was making threats against him.'

'I'm sorry, sir, I really can't tell you anything. We've got a fatal shooting inside. I must ask you to make room.'

'Who's dead?' Pat grabbed at the policeman's sleeve. 'My Howard was coming here, I know he was. Please—'

'All I can tell you,' the policeman said frowning, 'is that we have a fatal shooting, and we believe the dead man is the occupant of the house. There's no one else here as far as we can ascertain.'

'Colin Brudenell shot himself?' Philip said.

'This would seem to be the case. Now, please, give us room and let us get on with our job.' The policeman stepped aside to let in two men in green tunics and canvas shoes, then spoke into the radio again. 'Yes, go ahead . . . Yes, can confirm, child's name is Jake, J-A-K-E Brudenell, aged four years. Mother, Mrs Wendy Brudenell, confirms that the child was in the house with her husband when she left for work this morning. Over.' Behind him another office came out of the house and began trying keys in the lock of the garage door. 'No, no sign at present . . .'

'What about Howard?' Pat cried, but the policeman wouldn't take any notice of her, and Philip drew her away.

'We'll just have to wait and see, Pat, that's all. There's only – only Colin in there by the sound of it.'

'He's been here,' Pat said. 'I know he has. You know, you see. When you're a parent you know. Don't you? You know . . .'

Philip gave her a close look. She felt that he understood her – that those kind eyes understood everything. But all he said was, 'We'll just have to wait. Somebody will tell us what's going on.'

'He's had his punishment. That's all I kept thinking. Twelve years, that's enough, isn't it, surely?' Her feet hurt her because she was still wearing her slippers and she felt sick and wanted to sit down, yet most of all she wanted to be understood. 'I just wanted him back. I had my punishment too.'

Philip squeezed her arm as another car drew up across the street. 'There's Sergeant Hurst,' he said.

DS Hurst gave them a look as he hurried past, but didn't speak. He was in the house for what seemed a long time and Pat's legs couldn't stand any more. She sat down on a garden wall, two houses along, and put her head in her hands. She kept thinking of Howard when he was newborn and they had put him in her arms in the hospital: the way his eyes had looked at her. They weren't shallow and doll-like, the way most tiny babies' eyes were. There was such knowledge in them. She remembered that moment so well. Now there was this moment and it seemed so wrong that the one could lead on to the other, that the wandering path of years should come to this awful destination.

'Pat.' Philip touched her shoulder and she looked up to find that Sergeant Hurst was with them. Her heart leapt.

'Where's Howard, do you know? This is where he was coming—'

'I've only just got over here.' Sweating, Hurst wiped his neck with a handkerchief. He looked a little sickly himself. 'Pat, you really should have told us before about getting another visit from Colin. Especially as there was a gun involved. Is that right?'

'Yes, but Howard said he would tell you. Where is he?'

'There's no sign of Howard at the moment. What we've got is Colin dead, I'm afraid. The neighbours heard a shot and called the police around the time you called me. It looks like suicide which is nasty but, er, we've got an even nastier situation I think. The wee stepson was apparently with him at home but he's not around. They're searching the house still but . . . Well, I'm hoping that Colin parked the lad somewhere else before he did this, though Mrs Brudenell can't think of anywhere. There was no doubt Colin was a bit of a time-bomb, you know, but it's the boy.' Hurst grimaced at Philip. 'Colin had some nasty stuff in his garage, it turns out. Kiddie porn. I'm not telling you this, by the way.'

'Oh, Jesus.'

'So naturally our first concern is—'

'You've got to find Howard.' Somehow Pat stood up and faced the sergeant: it felt as if she floated up like a balloon. 'Listen to me. I'm his mum. A mum knows. I know he was coming here.' She ignored the sobs clutching her throat. 'When you're a parent you don't have to be told. That day . . . I mean I was the one who washed his clothes. His pants. But what could I do? I'm his mum and Jack was gone and Howard was all I had, I mean truly all that I had and . . . He had his punishment, didn't he? Twelve years, that's enough. Maybe it was my fault. I asked him to do – too much for me.' Tears blurred the hard male faces that stared at her and she wiped them impatiently away. 'He had to be everything to me after his father went. I threw his dad out, you see – I did it. He was so hard on Howard, he would put him in that cupboard and he would leave him there, just leave him in there for hours in the dark, and in the end I couldn't bear it. I should have done it before I know but I did do it, I threw Jack out and I put a stop to it for my little boy's sake. Maybe I did it too late. I don't know. Maybe I haven't been – good for him. But he's had such punishment already. Don't hurt him. Please, don't hurt him. It might still be all right, if you just find him . . .' The balloon feeling left her and as she began to sink it was Philip who caught her arm; Sergeant Hurst was already darting away. 'He's not a bad boy – he's not a bad boy . . .'

The train journey to Nottingham had seemed both endless and unreal: a fancy had come upon Rebecca that the carriage was really stationary and the landscape unrolling at the window a mere projection, an illusion. It clung to her as she came blinking out at the station concourse and now, as the taxi bore her on a seemingly endless route about the unfamiliar city, she had the same feeling of being the victim of some spectacular trick.

'Excuse me. Are we nearly there? Hernmoor?'

'That's it.' The driver, a taciturn man in a check cap, gestured with his thumb. Below the expressway she could see an expanse of uniform red-tiled roofs. With alarm she noticed the meter: five pounds, which was all the money she had on her.

'Is this near? I've only got a fiver.'

'Well, it's near. But I have to go round the next junction and come back to get into it. D'you see, that's the access—'

'Can you stop here?'

'I shall have to, duck. It's the fare.' He pulled carefully into the side of the road. As she pressed the note into his hand he said with a sigh, 'Go down there and you come to a footbridge, that takes you across to the estate. Be careful.'

Whipped by the slipstream of passing cars, she trotted along the verge until she came to a crossing at a slip road. On the other side a fingerpost pointed to a cyclepath between high verges: *Hernmoor*. The cyclepath twisted round a steep grassed bank and then sloped up to a railed footbridge that spanned the ring road, lifted aloft on great concrete Vs. On the other side it descended into the red-roofed houses.

She was breathing hard after climbing the helter-skelter upward twirl of the footbridge and her head was down as she came to the horizontal span across the ring road. Her legs gratefully registered the absence of slope. She looked up and quickened her pace, and at that moment Howard Gandy appeared on the other end of the footbridge, coming her way.

His head was down too and he was moving quickly, hands jammed in the pockets of his jacket. He was a few yards from her, almost in the middle of the bridge, when he looked up.

'Howard.'

He stopped dead. She thought he could not have looked more thunderstruck if the dead had risen up to accost him. She went on a little towards him.

'Hello, Howard. What are you doing here?'

He said, 'Nothing,' and their eyes pinned each other, waiting, while a buffeting stream of traffic streaked below them. She saw that his trousers were grass-stained and torn.

'Tell me about the lady,' Rebecca said. The wind gusted and she wiped a strand of hair from her mouth. 'The lady who found him. It's on the tapes. The lady who found Lee.' As he did not answer she said, raising her voice, 'Howard, I know. That was my mum, wasn't it? She found Lee and took him home. She found Lee where you'd left him. And you saw her.' She opened her hands by her sides. 'I know, you see.'

'Aye, it was your mum,' he said. His eyes were heavy-lidded and he spoke almost casually. 'Yes, that was the lady.'

'In the woods?'

'Aye. Near the camp. He was— It was under a tree. Just like he was sleeping, really. I thought it was the best place to put him. I hadn't gone far. I heard her sort of crying out. I crept back and I could see her holding him. Up like this.' He held out his great arms: a ghostly bear hug. 'Then she went away with him.'

'She couldn't hurt him then, could she?'

He frowned at her, his look slightly disdainful. 'Well, of course not.'

'Oh, Howard . . .' She put out an unsteady hand to the railing. 'I don't understand it . . .'

'He was a bad boy. He wouldn't play. It was— He should have behaved. So I put him away. He was bad so I put him away. It wasn't my fault. I can't be blamed.'

'You killed Lee. You—'

'I don't give a monkey's about that. I'm just me. All you people, you . . .' He gritted his teeth, seeming to bite on an enduring exasperation. 'There's plenty of bad 'uns about and I'm not one. I've just got my limits same as everybody else, and it's not fair – I won't have it . . .'

As he spoke he stamped his foot and in his bull-like glare Rebecca suddenly felt vastly afraid. He made a movement and it seemed to her certain that he was going to grab her and throw her over the railing down to the thrumming ring road below. Paralysed, she opened her mouth but her voice was lost in another's.

'Howard! Howard, we need to talk to you . . .'

She saw Sergeant Hurst, red-faced, gripping his jacket round his waist, pounding up the curve of the footbridge and on to the span behind Howard. And beyond him, two heads: her heart jumped as she recognized her father. Toiling on his arm, little birdlike Pat Gandy. Howard turned round.

'Howard, please, everything's fine.' Hurst slowed his pace as he approached. Howard stood facing him, quite still. 'We just need to talk. About Colin and what's happened. OK? Could you come along? Your mum's here. It'll be fine.'

'Where's the little boy?' Out of breath, Pat's voice was weakly scolding. She held out her arms to Howard and there was a sacrificial wildness to the gesture, a biblical abnegation. 'No more – Howard, no more. Tell them. The little boy.'

Hurst gently stopped her going any nearer. 'Howard, his name's Jake,' Hurst said. 'Jake Brudenell. He's missing. We need to talk about this. Will you come, please?'

Howard's shoulders twitched. He cleared his throat. All at once it seemed he couldn't look at his mother and he turned his head.

Rebecca met his eyes and held them.

'No,' she said. 'Oh, no.'

'They know, lovey, they know!' Pat cried. 'Now tell them, for God's sake . . .'

Howard wouldn't look round at his mother. Muscles wriggled in his face.

'Howard, please,' Rebecca said. 'Where's that little boy?'

'You're still not much good, are you, you lot?' Howard said, loudly: it was meant for the sergeant, though he kept his face turned to Rebecca. 'Can't find your behind with both hands. How do you think I got out the house? Through the back garden and over the fence.' He pointed down to where the back fences of the red-roofed houses gave on to a rough-earth wasteland, screened by conifers and leading to a steep verge with the ring road above. 'Right struggle that was,' he said, and for a moment Rebecca was not looking at a child-murderer but at the dry, decent, slightly grumpy man with whom she had walked the dune paths in glorious summer.

'Where is he?' Hurst said. 'Tell us, Howard.'

'I put him away. That's all.' Suddenly Howard made a hissing noise like a boiling pot and indeed it was as if that long, deep exasperation had finally boiled over. 'Oh, I'm telling you nothing,' he said, and now he turned and Rebecca saw that the aloof, unfathomable smile was on his face, a secret triumph even as he threw in his hand. 'Bugger it, I'm telling you nothing. That's it.'

*That's it.* With his strange gift for the ordinary, Howard spoke the words much as if he had decided not to wait in a slow queue any longer, and then grasped the railing and climbed deftly over it. Pat screamed. Hurst and Rebecca's father ran towards the railing where Howard crouched apelike on the ledge above the road, his hands firmly gripping the bars, his curly fringe rippling in the wind. For another couple of instants he met Rebecca's eyes, looking at her through the bars of the railing, the man on the Monopoly board scowling at his unlucky fate. Then with that curious neat delicacy he opened his hands, curling the fingers out, and fell backwards through the air.

Hands scrabbled at the edges of the concrete slab that covered the filled-in well, desperate hands and too many, counteracting each other: Hurst ordered two of the officers to step away. Howard Gandy had been able to lift this on his own, after all.

The slab came up, trailing cobwebs and woodlice. Sharp sucked-in breaths, voices gabbling, arms reaching into the tank-like hole. Hurst craned over the shoulders of the para-medics who rushed in, grasping, lifting, with such urgent gentleness, and his breath seemed to stop for at least a minute.

Soon he knew what he needed to know. He asked a WPC to give the news to Wendy Brudenell and went through the house and out to the street, cordoned off now, spectators pressing around the striped tape and gawping: though some had gone off to catch the end of the other show, the gruesome one on the roped-off ring road. A uniform pointed him to the people he sought. The girl had been feeling understandably sick and was sitting down on the back seat of a cruiser: her father was standing by the open car door and holding her hand.

'We've got a live one this time,' Hurst said. 'They're taking him to hospital. He's just conscious, but the paramedics think he must have passed out from shock in there and they can't find any immediate injuries.'

'Oh, thank God.' The man and the girl both said it, seeming to speak with one voice. Their linked hands tightened.

'Of course, he would have suffocated in there,' Hurst said. 'Not much doubt about the intention. Christ. The world is so full of a number of things, eh?'

'How's Pat doing?' Philip Springthorpe said.

'Not good. I'll go and see her now and tell her about this, it might . . . well, it might do something. One life more.' He shrugged.

'Will you be wanting us much longer?' Rebecca said.

Hurst shook his head. 'Shouldn't be.'

'Because we'd like to go home,' Rebecca said – or her father said: for once again, it was as if father and daughter spoke with one voice.

309

# TWENTY-FOUR

The cemetery was as beautiful as such a place could be, Rebecca thought. In fact that needed no qualification – it was, simply, beautiful. The leaves of the chestnut trees seemed to be a deeper, richer green than any she had ever seen; the grass was so lush; the sunlight seemed to fall more brilliantly here, with more sorcery of dapple and colour than it had even on the meadows and wolds during this morning's drive from the coast to Nottingham.

It was as if nature and man attained more harmony here, in the place of death, than anywhere else. A soothing thought, if so: showing that death was no fearful aberration but the most natural thing of all.

She scattered a little earth down into the grave where Colin Brudenell's coffin lay, then stood in silence with her father for a few moments. The hole in the earth looked so narrow and small, as they tended to; though of course not so small as the little plot next to it, with its headstone faintly tinged with moss that was just beginning to creep across the words LEE BRUDENELL.

A little way away, the clergyman was talking in muted tones to Wendy Brudenell, but she didn't seem to be listening. It was hard to tell through her veil, but her eyes seemed to be fixed on some vague middle distance – of memory, perhaps. It was Jake, standing beside her with his hand clasped in hers, who was looking attentively up into the clergyman's face, as if eager to learn.

Rebecca and her father walked slowly away from the grave. Adam, grey-suited, had stood at a distance throughout; and now he raised a hand to them, tentatively.

'I think I'll go and have a word with Adam,' she said. 'Do you mind?'

'Not at all.'

Her father strolled on towards the chestnut trees. Rebecca went over to Adam. He took her hand. She squeezed it very lightly, then let it fall.

'How have you been?' she said.

'All right.'

'You've had a long drive.'

He shook his head. 'I had to come.'

'It's beautiful here, isn't it?' She looked across at the trees, shading her eyes.

'Yes. It shouldn't be, but it is.'

'So. What are your plans?'

'I don't know really.' His face was pale. 'Try and get on with life, I suppose.'

'The book?'

'There may be a book,' he said after a moment. 'I'm not sure yet. It would be – obviously it would be a very different book. But I don't know. . .' He looked wrecked, Rebecca thought. She guessed he would feel responsible. 'How about you?'

'Well, I've got college very soon.'

'Good. It's good. I'm glad you're . . . Perhaps you'll write to me some time. Let me know how you're getting on.'

'Yes. I could do that.'

'Your father'll find it strange without you, I should think.'

'Yes. We won't be apart, though – not really.'

He seemed about to say something, then changed his mind. He drew in a deep breath.

'You're right,' he said. 'It is beautiful here. Peaceful.'

Rebecca nodded. 'I think it's the silence that does it,' she said. 'Listen – can you hear? Not a sound that there shouldn't be.

'A quiet grave.'

Again she nodded. 'As it should be.'

# The Quick and The Dead

## Alison Joseph

Working in a hostel for the homeless, Sister Agnes had, for a while, felt an unaccustomed contentment with her faith. But when Sam, a sixteen-year-old runaway, is forced to return to her family and then goes missing, Agnes's hard-won equilibrium vanishes.

Sam's friends recall her saying she planned to join anti-road protesters in their tree-top encampment at the edge of Epping Forest. Sure enough Agnes finds Sam there, amidst the beggars, travellers and anarchists, revelling in their fireside talk of apocalypse, though contemplating returning to live with the father who deserted her sixteen years earlier and who, suspiciously to Agnes's mind, has suddenly reappeared. For the moment however Sam seems secure at the camp, though its tents and tree houses can only provide a temporary bulwark against destruction.

But even that safety is illusory. Only hours after Agnes's arrival a body is found. Of a brutally murdered young girl . . .

'Enjoyable . . . with a satisfyingly believable conclusion' *Glasgow Herald*

'Nice one that doesn't start with a bang and end with a whimper' *Newcastle-upon-Tyne Journal*

'A refreshingly different character' *Bolton Evening News*

'One helluva nun' *Hampstead and Highgate Express*

0 7472 5263 7

**HEADLINE**

# The Case Has Altered

## Martha Grimes

The Lincolnshire fens are the setting for Super-intendent Richard Jury's latest case. This landscape is one that can easily deceive, volunteering nothing – much like the locals of the only pub for miles around, The Case Has Altered.

There's been a double murder. The body of one woman is found on the Wash; another woman lies floating in a canal in Windy Fen. Both are connected with the manor house, Fengate: Dorcas Reese worked there; Verna Dunn was the louche ex-wife of the owner, Max Owen – a man with a passion for antiques. So when the principal suspect turns out to be Jenny Kennington, a woman Jury has long loved, he decides he needs someone inside Fengate. Some-one who can impersonate an antiques expert. Who better than aristocratic Melrose Plant, detective *manqué*?

'One of the finest voices of our time. Martha Grimes is poetry' Patricia Cornwell

'Entertaining . . . intriguing . . . thoroughly researched' *Sunday Express*

0 7472 5695 0

**HEADLINE**